Terence

THE
RETURN TO
EVERYWHERE
STREET

Hope you enjoy this! Malcolm.

MALCOLM

F.M.A. Dixon

Burton Mayers Books

Book reading organised by the little green bookshop in basement of the Pier Pub.

This is vol 1 genevieve bought vol I

Copyright © 2024 F.M.A Dixon

Content compiled for publication by Richard Mayers of Burton
Mayers Books.

First published by Burton Mayers Books 2024.

A CIP catalogue record for this book is available from the
British Library

ISBN-13: 9781917224062

Typeset in Garamond

www.BurtonMayersBooks.com

Once again, to Donna, Ellie and Maisie.

EX LIBRIS

RUFUS REGINALD REDMAYNE

Also By F.M.A Dixon:

The Little House on Everywhere Street

The Return to Everywhere Street[1]
F.M.A Dixon

---

[1] Bit of a wee spoiler, there. Sorry.

F.M.A Dixon

The Redmaynes: the story so far...

In *The Little House on Everywhere Street* the Redmayne family—Mr Redmayne (Eric), Mrs Redmayne (Gloriana) and their three children, George (16), Felice (15) and Emile (11)—happily enjoy the benefits of the extraordinary lifestyle afforded them by their extraordinary house, namely that of being able to exit through its doors into three different cities: New York (via the front door), Paris (side door) and London (back door). The children regard this geographically privileged state of affairs as a natural if clandestine part of their everyday lives: it is what they are used to, after all. No more, no less. Until, that is, the unfortunate incident with the New York Water Meter Reader (MIA: Paris) prompts their parents to reset time by 24 hours, and the three Redmayne youngsters come to realise that the house they have been living in all their lives is in effect a Time-Machine.

Experimentation follows. Without their parents' knowledge, George and Felice undertake a brief foray into the past. Not to be outdone, Emile secretly shows off the Time-Controls to a school friend at the Redmaynes' annual summer party and, due to what appears to be a slight mishap on his part, is lost at some unknown point in history. Recriminations follow, but these are soon revolved. The Redmaynes search for Emile. Mr Redmayne travels to Shakespeare's Bankside in 1603 and by chance meets his time-travelling father, Rufus Reginald Redmayne, in an inn. Rufus, the inventor of time-travel and the builder of the extraordinary Little House, is here younger than his son and is intrigued by the fact that Mr Redmayne believes him to be long-deceased in his own time. He privately sets in motion a plan to make sure that his reported demise does not come to pass. Mr Redmayne also meets William Shakespeare, who, with the aid of a rogue ship's monkey, steals Mrs Redmayne's best red crossing-out pen, thus setting in motion the cult practice of randomly crossing-out words in passages of text that sweeps the world thereafter. This theft alerts the Temporal Displacement Agency ('TDA') to anomalies in the timeline caused by the Redmaynes.

Meanwhile, George and Felice have been scouring history books in New York Public Library for any such anomalies in the timeline that might indicate the impact of Emile on history. Finding nothing, they soon become discouraged. Spying a photograph in a bookshop window of a figure that could be Emile, however, as taken by one 'RRR' at the ceremony for the launch of work on the Manhattan—Brooklyn subway in March, 1900, the pair time-travel to Manhattan in 1900 and recover Emile, who they find in the company of their now quite elderly grandfather, Rufus. These events turn out to be part of the old man's covert plan to cheat his long-foretold demise, in further pursuit of which he makes off alone in the time-travelling house and so strands all three of his grandchildren in the past.

All this time Mrs Redmayne has been investigating the exhibits in the Museum of London for any clues about Emile's potential whenabouts. Instead, she comes across a display from the early 1600s featuring what looks very much like a very old version of her husband's best

herringbone jacket. Shockingly, it appears that the owner was lynched by mob on old London Bridge in 1603 for the double crime of insulting a man's pig and quite probably being a Dutch stationer. Dismayed, Mrs Redmayne rescues her husband from the mob by crashing the time-travelling house on to the old bridge. Safe again, the pair travel to Manhattan in 1900, where, to their great joy, they are reunited with all three of their children. Happiness abounds.

The Redmaynes, as one, return in the house to the present. Mr and Mrs Redmayne are shocked to hear of the part played in recent events by his father, whose apparent death some years earlier now appears to have been faked. They are not given much time to process this surprising turn of events, however, as three bowler-hatted agents of the TDA arrive at the house and set about arresting Mr Redmayne for crimes against the timeline. The house is to be impounded, the doors sealed and Mr Redmayne returned to his own time. (Mr Redmayne learns that he was in fact born in the far future, his father's time of origin.) The family will thus be divided forever.

Rufus, at the last, intervenes. Armed with foreknowledge of this untimely appearance of the TDA, he has been busily preparing for the family's escape. He time-jumps the TDA agents to other places / times and reveals to the other Redmaynes his great plan: namely that, since reclaiming the house in Manhattan, he has created a new secret exit, one that leads to a place of sanctuary. He leads the relieved family out through this new exit, emerging first into concealing chalk caves, and then out into the bright sunshine, where, in the distance, the farm where they are to live for the time-being awaits them, until they can find a way to overcome the TDA and return home.

And so the story continues…

F.M.A Dixon

To C. C. FELTON, 2 JANUARY 1844

Devonshire Terrace, London | Second January 1844

My Very Dear Felton.

You are a Prophet... Now, if instantly on receipt of this, you send a free and independent citizen down to the Cunard Wharf at Boston, you will find that Captain Hewett of the Britannia Steam Ship (*my* ship) has a small parcel for Professor Felton of Cambridge; and in that parcel you will find a Christmas Carol in Prose. Being a ghost story of Christmas by Charles Dickens. Over which Christmas Carol, Charles Dickens wept, and laughed, and wept again, and excited himself in a most extraordinary manner, in the composition; ~~and thinking whereof~~ which came to him all at once, you might say, as he walked about the black streets of London, fifteen and twenty miles, ~~many a~~ one night when all the sober folks had gone to bed, and only the youthful Ghost of Christmas Future was afoot and bearing gifts... Oh there is more to the miracle of the Carol and its composition than I could tell you here, my dear Felton, and still be adjudged a sane man; but yet by its transcendent munificence is Charles Dickens hereby reborn and delivered... ~~And~~ For today, by every post, all manners of strangers write all manner of letters to him about their homes and hearths, and how this same Carol is read there, and kept on a very little shelf by itself. Indeed it is the greatest success I am told, that this Ruffian and Rascal has ever achieved...

Hearty remembrances to Sumner, Longfellow, Prescott, an all whom you know I love to remember. Countless happy years to you & yours, dear Felton, and some instalment of them, however slight, in England, in the loving company of

The ~~Proscribed~~ Chosen One.

Oh ~~breathe not~~ call out his name.

The Return to Everywhere Street

CHAPTER 1

A point comes in every family holiday when, after the novelty fades and the hitherto delightful new arrangements first begin to chafe, the thoughts of all—almost as one—turn secretly to home. Private (furtive, even desperate) calculations are made as to how many 'sleeps' remain before a restful night might be enjoyed in the specially adapted comforts of one's own boudoir, where everything was just as you left it and is just as it should be.

Precisely *so*. Quite.

What? Three? *Three* whole nights—*and* days? As many as that? Surely not? *Three*? Surely some mistake? But no. Your math, for once, is good. The calculation is correct.

You must endure three more days trapped in a pleasant environment with the few people you love most in the world. Your family.

Moods darken, tempers fray, especially (though not exclusively) at mealtimes. Conversational topics (yes, all of them) have long since been thoroughly mined and are declared exhausted. Proposed 'group' activities bore in advance and are met with universal distain, or worse, indifference.

Irritation reigns.

Tantrums, like storm clouds, quiver violently on the horizon.

Hope fails. Tears fall, as inevitably and as regularly as the spring rains back home, those sweet, sweet spring rains of home, where everything in the garden will be turning out just *so* about this time of year. Perfect.

If only you were there to see it for yourself. But you're not. Sadly. No. You're enjoying your hard-earned vacation, which you had so looked forward to for so long. Great.

"All happy families are alike," once remarked the elderly patriarch of this particular family, the Redmaynes, to his former best friend, Count Leo Tolstoy, who at once ran off to grab a pen.

"All unhappy families are on holiday," he added as soon as the famously impetuous Count was out of earshot. And perhaps it's just as well he was.

But that's another story. Entirely.

If the foregoing is at all true of ordinary families (like yours) who live in ordinary houses (very much like yours) and who are only enduring ordinary, everyday holidays (like yours, admit it), mere *temporary* absences from home, how much worse must it be for the extraordinary Redmaynes, not so much vacationing as exiled, indefinitely, and from a home—a house—so far from the ordinary as to be like no other?

Reader, if ever Eden were lost, it were here.

Not that the Redmaynes hadn't been putting a brave face on things. Their loss was extraordinary but that didn't mean they had to feel down about it. Did it? No, not at all.

At least not at first, anyway. After all, they had each other. Didn't they?

Which was the most important thing. Wasn't it?

Yes, it was. But other things mattered, too, as they were all about to learn. Family may be the blossoming flowerbed that nurtures the tenderest of shoots, but a time comes when the garden must be flown, when wings must be spread and nests abandoned.

Life, in all its great variety, beckons—and its call must be answered.

Or else.

On the first night in their new home, somewhere in the welcome obscurity of rural France, the Redmaynes' joy at having survived their various scrapes and being reunited as a family was, as is the case all too rarely in life, unconfined. The occasion called for a meal, they all agreed, a special sort of a meal, one that marked both the safe return of the youngest member of the family, Emile, from his misadventure in nineteenth-century New York, and the seeming resurrection from an exaggeratedly early grave of the eldest family member, grandfather Rufus Redmayne, whose clandestine handiwork the entire escapade had apparently been. There was also the highly related matter of their nervy and all too recent escape from the clutches of the TDA, the Time Police, as Mr Redmayne thought of them, who had planned to deport him back to the period of his birth, some seven-hundred years in the future no less, until his father's timely intervention had foiled them at the last, an outcome that he subsequently claimed had been his objective all along, or one of them. Despite everything, he'd meant well—or so he maintained—and probably this was the truth of it.

Nonetheless, regardless of his father's intentions, Mr Redmayne held several very strong reservations indeed about how the old fellow had gone about the business of preserving them all from an otherwise unfortunate fate, but thought it perhaps best to reserve these for another occasion. Because, despite the unscrupulousness of his methods, Rufus had succeeded in the end in saving them all, had he not? And as a result, happily, here they now were, reunited at last. Together. That was enough, for now.

But later, things that needed to be said—important

things—would be said.

That was both necessary and right, whether his stubborn, old, brilliant (and, evidently, no longer deceased) father listened to him or not. Very likely not.

In the meantime, it was clear to Mr Redmayne that his father had thought of everything, or as near to everything as could possibly be anticipated under the circumstances. They were, he speculated, while looking out over the rolling green fields and the hills beyond the farmhouse, most likely somewhere in the Loire Valley, which would especially please his wife and Felice, his ardently Francophile daughter. In fact, witnessing his wife's and all three of his children's shared delight and excitement in exploring their new home was enough for him to put his reservations temporarily out of his mind and join in with the adventure. And why not? After all, despite a certain stubbornness in terms of remaining at a single fixed point in space and displaying only a normal, ordinary (and one-way, at that) rate of progression though time, the accommodations at the farmhouse were both generous and charming.

Yes, no doubt necessarily somewhat less tri-cosmopolitan than they were accustomed to usually, but no less solid and reassuring for all that.

And that's what they needed right now as a family, he felt. Solid, reassuring, normal, ordinary...not jumping around through time and space like some out of control he-didn't-know-whats. *Time vandals.* That's what. Interfering with the timeline. And being pursued all the while by those rascally Time Policemen fellows from the far future. The disreputable Watkins and Co. Mr Redmayne shivered. All policemen made him nervous but the thought of policemen from the future who might track you down by things you hadn't even done yet, that was quite beyond the pale. Not wanting to think about it anymore, Mr Redmayne picked himself up and began to make his way down the gently sloping field towards the farmhouse.

Still, at least they hadn't turned up *here* at once, the Time Police—the *TDA*, *that* was it—which could only be a good sign. Because surely if that darned Watkins fellow had at any point uncovered where the Redmaynes were hiding, he and his men would doubtless be here already. Right now. This instant. On their doorstep. Which suggested they never would find them, in fact. Not here, anyway.

And reassured by this thought Mr Redmayne took one last long look around at the fields and orchards and the distant low chalky hills before going inside and joining in with the others, where, amid general merriment, preparations for a true Redmayne family feast were underway.

And, of course, nobody but nobody in their right mind would ever want to miss out on one of those.

The cupboards, refrigerator and larder had been unusually well-stocked, even by Redmayne standards. Nothing was wanting. And all fresh produce and ingredients, too. It was as if Rufus had known in advance the exact moment they would arrive. But, as Mr Redmayne reasoned at what was a trifle too long a length to his wife a little later that evening when they were alone in their slightly chilly bedroom, probably the wily old arch-schemer *did* know when they would arrive, given the extent of his foreknowledge of future events.

Or perhaps, even, yes, he went on, very likely his father *had timed their arrival here to always be at a particular moment*, that is, so he further reasoned, none other than the very moment that Rufus had prepared the farmhouse to be ready for them, regardless of the point in time of their departure from Everywhere Street, as they now called it. He wouldn't put it past him. No.

Not at all.

In fact, the more Mr Redmayne thought about it, well,

the more he became convinced that this would be exactly the sort of rather quite devious if ingenious step that his father would take, irrespective of how much it disrupted their own personal journeys through time (which was nothing less than the continuity of their lives, after all) (and not to mention the children's, too!). Wouldn't it be, dear? Don't you think? Just like him? But exactly, yes!

No sense of regard for others and not one iota of concern about how his outrageous behaviour impacted on them and their lives at all. Not one bit. None.

Callous, in the extreme, yes, that's what it was. That was the only word for it, in fact.

Callous, cold and, frankly, controlling...

Even when he was supposedly dead he had still to be in control, the sly old buzzard pulling the strings behind the scenes. Didn't he? Manipulating them all.

From beyond the grave, no less.

That really said it all, didn't it? Didn't it? Dear? *Dear?*

But dear, long-exhausted Mrs Redmayne, he now noticed, was already quite soundly—and most enviably—fast asleep. And, as much as he resolved to join her, at once, without a moment's delay, in that sweet Land of Nod, Mr Redmayne actually found it quite difficult to do so, with the strange events of the past few days, or centuries, depending on how you looked at it, seemingly quite determined to play out over and over in his mind, along with all his new concerns about when and where exactly they now where... Until at the *very* last, while the bold, loud, double-noted morning song of the cuckoo and the brazen chink of pale light at the foot of the curtains were now warning him that his long, long (so *very* long) first night in their new home was almost done, only then finally did Mr Redmayne's heavy, heavy (so *very* heavy) eyes begin, as if of their own volition almost, to tumble shut.

And so, then, to sleep...possibly... — Or not.

What? What was that? The boy was lost in time? Emile. No!

Wait. A lynch mob with a disfigured pig on London Bridge? Gloriana. How?

The Time Police. *TDA*. Eviction? From their house. His father, Rufus...

No, what?! And —Awake!

So, *not*, then. No sleep. Not at all. No. None. As good as. Yawn.

Whatever. We get ahead of ourselves.[2] Poor Mr Redmayne's long and troubled night of restless tossing and turning still lay several hours ahead at the point at which he and his family were first marvelling all but open-mouthed at the unexpected bounty of the stores laid out for them upon their arrival.

It appeared as though there was indeed, somehow, *everything*. Certainly everything they could possibly wish for. Asparagus, by the bushel, no less (Mrs Redmayne adored asparagus) (*so* versatile), and all freshly picked! And just right. Firm to the touch but not too firm. Aubergines, three (shiny, very); artichokes, four (distinctly non-shiny, very); baguette (several); basil; bass; beets; butter; camembert; capers; carrots; chestnuts; chives; coffee; cream (fresh); crème (fraîche); currents; dill; earl grey tea (but, of course); eggs (hens, blue, speckled); fennel; flour (buckwheat, plain, rice, rye, spelt); garlic; haricot blanc; haricot rouge; haricot vert; ham; honey; hummus; ice cream; Inca berries; jam; jasmine rice; jasmine tea; Jerusalem melon; kiwi (fruit, not bird) (happily); lamb; lamb's lettuce; leeks (Welsh, obviously); lemon, *Lentilles de Puy*; lettuce (other); mandarin; mint; monkfish; mustard; niolo; olive oil; onions (French); parmesan (Italian); parsnips (again Welsh, if less obviously); peas; pepper

---

[2] That's my fault, you'll say, I suppose.

(various); peppers (capsicum, less various); persimmon; potatoes (Kentish) (curiously); prosciutto; quiche; Roquefort; rhubarb; salmon (wild); turnips (tame); tofu (in-between); Vieux-Boulogne (phew, strong!); umiboshe; vinegar; walnuts; wine (blanc, rouge, sparkling—mais, d'accord); ugli (non-sparkling); yam; yeast; yogurt; xouba and zucchini—all in all, a veritable, alphabetically-organised primer of the many, many ingredients that typically Mrs Redmayne, who now stood running her eyes with approval and satisfaction over the more than ample provisions before her (and who was in any case particularly susceptible to anything organised alphabetically, almost as a matter of principle, let alone food), preferred to utilise in her cooking.[3]

The list of gourmet treats and meals that she might prepare with the foregoing superabundance of ingredients literally leapt one by one into her mind (yes, alphabetically) as she perused the supplies. The Redmaynes would not, after all, be living like paupers, which was something of a relief, and thankfully no one would very likely be going in the least hungry here—in what was, after all, their new lives, which would have been quite unthinkable. She looked around. The kitchen, too, with its large Aga and its walk-in larder, was more than satisfactory. They were lucky. Very lucky indeed. Blessed. Wait, something was missing—

But what? Mrs Redmayne turned about in the sudden quiet of the kitchen. What?

In fact, so absorbed had she been in her contemplation of her unexpected and most fortunate bounty that it had

---

[3] With one notable and rather green exception, which may have been a deliberate omission on Rufus's behalf, as a pre-emptive act of kindness to the other members of the family.

taken Mrs Redmayne several moments to realise that she was now quite alone in the kitchen and that it was her family that was now missing, the others having quickly moved on to explore the rest of the farmhouse. And so— momentarily unnerved by the silence around her—she resolved to follow the excited voices and join them.

Treat it all as an adventure, a vacation, she told herself by way of self-reassurance, and all would be fine. This wasn't the moment to worry. No.

Let the unknowable future bring what it will. As it surely would.

Despite the Machiavellian interventions of her father-in-law.

Que sera, sera. Yes.

But, in their case, she realised after a second, now exiting the kitchen, not definitely so. Not *absolutely* so. No. It turned out that your Fate could be what you made it. Recent events had taught her that much. And this suddenly felt like such a burden that she could only sigh.

They were, all in all, an unusual family, the Redmaynes. Very much so indeed.

But, whatever. It wasn't worth losing any sleep over.

Later she would make scones. And have a nice cream tea.

That would fix everything.

* * *

"Did you see the view from the hayloft? It's spec*ta*cular. I mean, all those woods and rolling hills. *Magnifique*! It's all, I don't know what, so *rustic*. So very *rustic*. And so French! It's beautiful. I *love* it here. Really, I do."

"Really, Sis? We couldn't tell. Couldn't you effuse just a *little* bit more? Just so we're absolutely clear. I'm just saying, we wouldn't want to misinterpret your feelings at all. Let's leave no room for doubt. None."

Felice made a wry, sardonic, but most of all, *pained* face

at her brother. This, too, in its own way, was so French. George responded in kind. Siblings.

"It's just hills and stuff. I don't see what's so French about it. It could be anywhere."

This was Emile, their younger brother. He looked around at the fourth person at the table, his grandfather, who hadn't yet said a word the whole time they'd been seated here at this long, long, very long (and somehow both rustic and very French) table, waiting for dinner, which his mother had proclaimed in very strident tones to be ready at least twenty minutes ago. Which clearly it wasn't, or they'd be eating it already. Obviously.

The old man appeared to be content just watching and listening to them. Weird.

Also, he was dressed in a very old-fashioned way for someone supposedly from the future. Like someone in an old oil-painting[4], or Charles Dickens[5], or someone like that[6].

Emile realised that he himself was wearing a very old-

---

[4] Specifically, the oil painting of his Grandfather that had hung in his Father's study in their old house for the entirety of Emile's life to date. As Emile would later say to himself upon making this connection: Duh.

[5] Charles Dickens: the only Victorian personage, other than Queen Victoria herself, that Emile could readily summon to mind, by dint of the famous author having spent some of his childhood in the proximity of Emile's school in Southwark, which made huge play of the connection, no matter how tenuous in reality. As a result, they read a lot of Dickens in that school, which is, the way this story goes, just as well.

[6] That is, everyone alive in the period 1837 – 1901.

fashioned item of clothing, too, in the form of the black bowler hat left behind at the house by one of the TDA agents after the struggle they'd had. But that was different. Somehow. A trophy.

"No, it's *very* French," replied his sister. "If you hadn't spent all your time wandering the filthy backstreets of London, which actually is all you *ever* did, Emile, then you'd be able to tell, too. It's something in the colouring, the light, like in a Cezanne, or a Manet. Or a Van Gogh. A certain, I don't know, *je ne sais quoi*. But, whatever—you can definitely tell it's France. Definitely. Just by looking."

"Like how you said, whatever."

Emile didn't really care, either way. He glanced around at his tall, silent, weirdly dressed grandfather again, whom he hadn't quite yet forgiven for abandoning them in New York in 1900, even if it had all only been part of his great master plan for saving them all.

Or so he'd claimed. *Afterwards.*

It hadn't felt good at the time, that was the point.

"I like the chicken coop," he announced decisively, after a moment or so, as if he been thinking it over for some time. "That's nice."

"Good. In which case, Squirt, you can have the job of cleaning it out. Enjoy."

Emile sneered at his older brother, who sneered back. Siblings.

Felice, whose ability to tune out both of her brothers was by now so well-established as to be second-nature, gazed around in undistracted admiration at the definitely rustic, and very definitely *French*, interior décor. She was definitely, *definitely* having a moment.

"I love all the exposed beams. All the old wood everywhere. It's so…"

"Don't say *French*! Whatever you do, don't say French."

"…Au*then*tic. That's exactly what it is. Authentic. Solid. And rustic. I love it. I absolutely do."

George mimed a crude gagging motion to his younger

brother, who nodded, his entire face seemingly laughing at once. Siblings.

Siblings for once united against a common enemy, that is, of course, against another sibling. Mais naturellement.

To the surprise of all three, their grandfather coughed a very loud and deliberate cough, making each of them sit up suddenly in their chairs, as if (George and Felice, at least) only then reminded of his presence.

Almost at once Mrs Redmayne appeared on the scene, carrying more hot serving dishes and assorted oddments of crockery than seemed humanly possible, all of which were set down in turn most adroitly on the table, each of her quiet, simple movements composing the personification of grace, as though the act of waiting on diners were nothing but a flowing adagio for which she had trained all her life (which in some ways, sadly, was true) (if no less impressive to behold).

Then, in her wake, trailed Mr Redmayne, equally laden, but far less adroit. He stumbled upon entering, much to everyone's alarm, as his load consisted of no fewer than four steaming bowls of soup.

But happily he quickly corrected his misstep—and without any appreciable loss.

At the table Mr Redmayne Senior, as his younger grandson noted, arched a single eyebrow—ever so briefly—as his soup was plonked down before him with some (albeit minor) splashes.

Then, Mr Redmayne Junior at once exited (stumbling again on the way out) in order to retrieve the final two soups from the kitchen.

George, Felice and Emile smirked privately at one another—all three siblings united at last. Mrs Redmayne, who had taken up her place at the head of table, quelled this junior insurrection with the most infinitesimal of glances, a quick but distinctly steely glare which, for all its tremendous brevity, managed to convey the following sentiments, namely that:

a) The children should not mock their father, who, even though something of an adorable goose quite a bit of the time, remained their father and deserved undeviating respect for that fact alone;

b) They had *company*, did they not? Yes, unless she was very much mistaken, they did. And in the form, no less, of their until quite recently believed to be long-deceased grandfather, and Heaven-only-knows what opinion he will form of the three of you (Yes, *you!*) if you each sit there smirking behind your poor father's back at his, shall we say, charming idiosyncrasies;

c) Worse, still; your grandfather will think *me* a bad mother for raising his grandchildren to have the table manners of wild barbarians, which will never do;

d) Yes, *barbarians*—you know exactly what I mean.

e) There is to be no repeat of this behaviour throughout the course of this meal, which your father and I have actually worked very hard on preparing these last two hours, with no help from any of you, I may add; *and*

f) I shouldn't *have* to be telling you any of this, should I? —Is that quite clear?

g) I repeat, is that *quite* clear?

h) Good.

i) And by the way, Emile, take off that ridiculous hat this instant. Hats are *not* to be worn at the table. No exceptions. *Ever.*

The chastened expressions on the faces of the three Redmayne children indicated that the message, no matter how subliminally conveyed, had been received very clearly indeed, in full, and that no further repetition would be required.[7]

In addition, Emile removed his hat.

As if almost in no time at all Mr Redmayne returned, bearing the two remaining bowls of soup, his face a picture of concentration.

On this occasion he negotiated the offending step-up/down between rooms without any undue difficulty, much (*very* much) to the great relief of everyone present, it has to be said. Another telling off like the last would have quite destroyed the mood.

"You're all very quiet," he remarked, upon joining them at the table. "Have I missed something?"

"No, dear," replied Mrs Redmayne, patting his hand. "We're all rather tired and hungry now, I think. That's all. So, let's everyone start. Yes, do. Emile, darling, it's cream of asparagus soup, that's all. A little crème d'asperges. It won't kill you. So, there's really no need to stare at it with that ghastly look on your face as if it might. I assure you it won't."

Emile appeared decidedly unconvinced. Felice, on the other hand, wore the blissful expression of someone experiencing divinity via the culinary medium of soup.

"Goodness," she exclaimed. "It even *tastes* French!"

George grimaced, broadcasting an audible groan that he at once regretted.

Not that it was his fault, of course. How could it be with Felice and Emile at the table?

So annoying. Something would have to give if they

---

[7] It should be observed that all of this unspoken communication between parent and child took no more than 0.2 seconds to bring to a successful conclusion, a fact that testifies to the unique nature of the close personal bond between family members, as will no doubt be recognised by many of you, if not all.

were all going to survive their stay at the farm here. Probably his sanity. Siblings!

"Why, you're right," he said, after a second, in a doomed effort to redeem himself. "It really *does*, doesn't it?"

Alas, his failed effort at sincerity fooled nobody, least of all his mother. But she let it pass. In response, George wisely decided to leave it there and thereafter devoted his attention to the contents of the bowl before him, which suddenly were of enormous, almost hypnotic, interest.

Emile, on the other hand, seemingly remained unconvinced by the fare before him. He scanned the table in a manner akin to that of a shipwrecked sailor searching the horizon for sight of land but finding only sea in all directions. Or in his case, soup. *Foreign* soup.

His face reflected his growing awareness of the true horror of his predicament.

"What *else* is there? To eat, I mean? Is it all only, like, French stuff? All of it? *Every*thing?"

"Dearheart, I'm sure I really don't know what you mean. There's nothing here you haven't eaten before." Mrs Redmayne ran her own quick eye over the table. "A little leek and pancetta quiche, perhaps? Or the parsnip rémoulade? You always enjoy both of those. Yes, you *do*, dear. Not to mention the striped bass en papilloute? You *love* that. Always. Every time."

"The *what*?"

"The fish thing, there," translated George, helpfully pointing with his spoon.

"In fact, at home," continued his mother, "you actually eat *French stuff* all the time."

"Do I?" Emile was doubtful, despite the earnest, nodded confirmation of his sister. "Well, even if I do, that doesn't mean I *like* it."

"Unfortunately, my lad, I fear you are going to have to get used to it," said his father. "Those New York street hot dogs that you love so much are likely to prove a great deal more difficult to come by, I'm afraid, and for the foreseeable future. There's no getting away from that. And besides, everything here looks absolutely delicious, even if I say so myself. Just *look*."

Despite acting with the very best of intentions, as always, Mr Redmayne unfortunately only succeeded in making his younger son feel that tiny bit more glum than before. As it was, Emile's eyes might indeed have been looking, but his stomach wasn't buying. Not today.

"What I think," began a deep voice not heard at the family table in the lifetimes of any of the three Redmayne children, "is that this is—without a doubt—the best, the *very* best, cream of asparagus soup that I've tasted in over eight hundred years. Anywhere."

All eyes turned to Rufus, the source of this pronouncement. Some few thick, globular beads of soup were clinging with a viscous determination to the two ends of his moustache, but these were only a minor distraction. Sampling another spoonful, he went on:

"Why, it's even *tastier*, I do believe, than the asparagus soup I used to whip up myself every now and then for the great renaissance artist Leonardo da Vinci. You've heard of him? Good... Great artist indeed, yes, but a very fussy eater. *Very* particular. Still, he loved my asparagus soup. Said he thought it actually made him paint even better. Can you *believe* that? *My* soup."

"Really?" Emile looked from his grandfather down towards his own bowl.

"Do you paint?" asked the deep voice.

Emile nodded. "I draw," he said.

"Ah, yes, of course. Very well, then. Eat up—and be a better artist, like the great Leonardo. Pip-pip."

Tentatively, slowly, Emile dipped his spoon into the soup and then raised the contents towards his lips. He sipped. To his surprise, he did not die at once. Not at all, in fact.

Rufus's bright eyes signalled his encouragement, and

Emile tried a second sip, this time with appreciably less apprehension about the disturbing Frenchness or any other potential toxicity of the contents.

"See, my boy? Yes? Good. You know, I suspect you are a much better artist already. As Leonardo always said, Per la tua arte di vivere, prima si deve vivere.[8] Or something very much like that, if not exactly those words. So, yes, eat up, lad. What? Why are you all looking at me like that?"

Felice voiced the unspoken question on everyone's lips.

"You *knew* Leonardo da Vinci?"

"Knew? Still do, although it might be a while yet before I can get back to see him, the old sausage. You know, what with the way things are just now. But that will pass. Maybe you would like to come with me? How's your Florentine Italian? I should warn you now he's a very bad loser at ping-pong. Terrible temper. But he can usually be brought round with a large bag of tangy cheese Nachos. He has something of a particular weakness for those. Quite spoilt, really."

Rufus seemed to realise—a little too late—that he had strayed into enemy territory.

"With your parents' permission, of course," he added, suddenly aware of the hostile glares emanating from the other two senior Redmaynes at the table. "And none of us will be going anywhere like that for a long time yet, I'm sure. Certainly not. No. Look, that parsnip rémoulade does look good, I have to say. May I?"

An inertia composed largely of embarrassed silence seemed to have gripped the table.

Mr Redmayne intervened. "I met Shakespeare

---

[8] 'Always eat your soup up first, then draw...' Something of a loose translation, I admit.

recently, you know. Nice man."

"Yes, dear," said his wife. "His monkey stole my pen, we know. Caused a lot of trouble, I seem to remember, for *everyone*."

"Nice-ish, anyway," said Mr Redmayne. "Bit silly, actually. Over fond of puns. But they all were, I suppose, those Elizabethan playwrights. Something in the water. Turned them all into play*wrongs*, if you see what I mean?"

Nobody but nobody wanted to see what he meant, which kind of made Mr Redmayne's point, if much to his own momentary embarrassment. But lunch, like life, went on...

Indeed it did. His soup bowl now set aside, Rufus had taken up a plate and was helping himself to the main courses. "Ah, yes, *Iago*, wasn't it? The monkey? Yes, the *worst* thief. Worse than his owner. I used to say to him, look, Will, my boy, if we had an infinite number of Iagoes then we'd certainly have no need for you anymore, would we? He never did get the joke. No sense of humour, for all his punning. None. Very serious. Bit self-obsessed. Prone to moods. That's what I found, anyway."

Mrs Redmayne glared at her father-in-law once again, which he took as his cue to close down this line of discussion—and in double-quick time. *Now*.

George had other ideas, however.

"The future, if you don't mind me asking, but what's it *like* there? Seeing as, you know, that's where—*when*, that is—you're from originally, isn't it? Is it all really different to now? I suppose it must be. But how? I mean, what must *computers* be like in five hundred years' time? All quantum-based, I'm guessing? Yes? And operated by AI, too? They *must* be. I find all of that really fascinating, to be honest, the future, I mean, and I'd love to know more."

Emile joined in. "Yeah, and like, in the future does everyone fly everywhere on jet-packs? *Do* they? That's what I want to know."

"Would you like a jet-pack?" asked his grandfather.

"No!" said Mr and Mrs Redmayne, as one.

"Why would you *choose* to live in the past? That's what interests me." This last contribution was from Felice. "*That's* what *I* want to know. Why *not* live in the future? It must be fabulous, you would think. Isn't it?"

Rufus hesitated. "So, many questions, and all at once. It's only natural that you should be curious. That's true enough. But I'm not sure this is the right time to be answering them all. No doubt there will be plenty of time for that later."

He surveyed the line of young, expectant faces opposite him, and relented.

"Very well, for now, I will say this much: I find living in the past, as it were, to be more of an *authentic* experience than living in the future ever could be. It's an eccentric view in my time, I know. But I prefer things, shall we say, to be real. *Solid*, like you said earlier, Felice. Much like here. Though that probably doesn't make much sense right now... There, I've probably said far too much as it is. And judging by the disapproving expressions on both your parents' faces, yes, indeed, I fear I have. So, there we should leave it. No more."

Mr Redmayne intervened. "Yes, I think that's quite enough of that, everyone, George, Felice, and, yes, Emile, you too. You see, children, the less we know about the future, the better. We're supposed to be, how can I put this, *on the lam*, here, are we not? Hiding out. From the *Time Police*, no less. The TDA or whoever. And for what exactly, if I might remind you? Yes, that's right. Crimes against the timeline. So, as I said, the less talk there is about the future and time-travel and all the rest of it, the better. For all of us. Now, try some of that parsnip thingamabob, because I believe it's very good."

Judging now by the expressions on the children's faces, the choice between parsnip thingamabob and unlimited mastery of time was stark. No contest.

"And there's going to be so much to do here, there

won't be any time to worry about any of that other business," said Mrs Redmayne. "All of those apples out in the orchard aren't going to pick themselves, are they? Think of the fun."

George, in particular, it has to be said, did not appear to be thinking about the fun.

"And everything we try here is going to be a new experience," said Mr Redmayne. "We really didn't do this enough. Travel, I mean, which is strange to say. Whenever we went anywhere, we went *in* the house. We never stayed anywhere else because we didn't need to—the house took us there, didn't it? With hindsight, that was probably a mistake, if terribly convenient. Because, you see, my dears, a great deal of the fun of travelling is staying somewhere *new*. New surroundings, new ways of doing things, you know, that sort of thing. *Living*. And we've denied you that experience, I fear. Until now. Seeing you all scampering about all over the place here today and the excitement of that was quite the eye-opener, I don't mind saying."

"I *do* like it here," said Felice. "I do really. And my room has the most gorgeous view of them all. You can see all the way past the woods to the river."

"Mine has the best *window*," said Emile. "You know, that one up in the ceiling, where it slopes down. Above the bed. George, what did you call it?"

"The Velux window, you mean?"

"Yeah, the *Velux* window. It's like a skylight.

"Shrimp, it *is* a skylight."

"Whatever. The point is I'll be able to lie in bed at night and look up and see all the stars. And because we're not in the city—*any* city—there'll be gazillions of them to see. A whole universe full, you bet. I reckon I could even get out on to the roof." Emile noticed the sharp look his mother gave him. "You know, if there was a fire, or anything like that. If I really had to, I bet I could. That's what I mean."

"Well, let's just hope that you never really have to,"

said his father.

George looked as though he were doing a rudimentary mental calculation, which indeed he was. "Where's Grandfather's room?" he asked. "There's the large bedroom at the back, but that's for the Mater and Pater, I assume? And then mine, Felice's, the Shrimp's, but that's all of them taken." He looked up at his grandfather. "Where are you going to stay?"

Rufus put his fork down on his plate. He looked as though he were considering his words carefully. "Not here, I'm afraid," he said after a second or so. "It's too dangerous. No, that isn't right. It's not that it's *dangerous* here, no. Not at all, or no more so than anywhere else. In fact, it's *less so*, in fact, because of some precautions I've taken. What I mean is that I think it would be sensible for us not to be all together all the time. One of us should be kept in reserve, just in case of any *uninvited guests* dropping in without warning. Believe it or not, I don't actually know what happens next. Not anymore. I'm as much in the dark as you all are, which is strange, for *me* at least. Besides, I'm not very good in company. You'd all soon tire of me, and that's a fact. By the way, you're right—the parsnip thingamabob is most excellent."

For a moment the only sound to be heard was that of Rufus chewing his food. The other Redmaynes stared first at each other and then, as one, at the happily oblivious eater.

Mr Redmayne broke the silence. "Father, where will you go? Or should I ask *when*?"

Rufus looked up, surprised. "When? You mean what period? Why, *now*, of course. The present. And not too far away. Not local, by any means, but in easy travelling distance. I won't tell you where exactly, just in case. I might leave you a clue, though, to be on the safe side. That's an idea. You know, in case you need to come looking for me for any reason. Sorry to be so melodramatic. Bad habit. Elizabethan in origin, I suspect.

34

Will, and others. Or possibly Dickens. Charles was so *Victorian* in his thinking. He absolutely loved a melodrama. Wrote them, lived them. Writers through the ages, *tsch*! Poor souls, one and all. Children, avoid writers at all costs, that's my one piece of free advice to you all. Take their books, yes, but *them*, in company, no. Very much no."

Silence. He looked up from his thingamabob. Profound silence. Gradually it began to dawn on Rufus that, contrary to his expectations, his planned imminent disappearance was not being met with universal approval.

He peered around the table at the upturned faces of his family.

"What? Well, of course, I will be back here, regularly. It's not like I'm going to be dead again. Is it? About once a fortnight or so, I'll be popping up. You can count on that. You see, I want, *need*, to tutor the children in math—and not just any old math, either. No. The mathematics of the *future*, that's what they must learn. That's their birthright, their heritage. Someone has to understand how all of this works. And if I can't pass it on to them, it'll be lost. And it won't be just for them, it'll be for the good of the *world*. That much I am sure about. Eric, Gloriana, forgive me, but I just feel it's important to do this."

George noticed an uncertain glance pass instantly between his parents, but he didn't care.

"You're going to teach me the mathematics of time-travel?" he asked incredulously.

It was as if all of his Christmases had come at once, which, mathematically at least, was possible.

"All of you, in fact," continued his grandfather. "My discoveries belong to you all, as Redmaynes. It's your duty, your responsibility, to own them. And, Eric, you *did* realise they would need to be home-tutored from this point onwards? The children? There'll be no going to any school. Oh, no. Not now, not ever. The TDA will be checking everywhere—and at every point in time. But *school*, where's the value in that anyway? School is for ordinary minds. And we are *not* in any way ordinary, we Redmaynes. Are we?"

Emile's allegedly extraordinary mind was reeling from what appeared to be, if he had understood things correctly, two quite definitely extraordinary and hitherto unthinkable ideas: one, he would never have to go to school again; and two, he would be obliged to spend his valuable free time at home learning impossible maths from the future. He couldn't tell whether he should be delighted or depressed, or some mad mixture of both at the same time.

Felice, on the other hand, was intrigued. "What *else* will we be learning at home? I know Maman can handle the languages, but what about everything else? Who's going to teach us drama, or music—or *history*, for that matter? Or geography? What about those? They're important, too."

"Not Geography. Geography is for chumps," said Emile, authoritatively.

"Everything *is* for chumps, it would seem," said Mr Redmayne. "Everything except your Grandfather's special curriculum, that is. Really, Father, this is something that Gloriana and I need to discuss first. It's not something that you can just announce to everyone over parsnip thingamabob or whatever and move on. There are other considerations, other factors, that must be taken into account."

"I've considered them, believe me. Everything has been taken into account. All possible moves. The position is exactly as I've stated it. Checkmate."

Rufus continued with his meal as if he had announced nothing more controversial than the casual observation that perhaps, on reflection, he felt the parsnip thingamabob was a little overdone. Mr and Mrs Redmayne stared at each other wordlessly, however; much as did the three younger Redmaynes, with no one among them quite sure what would happen next.

At the same time everybody present remained

absolutely sure that the arch-manipulator had no doubt already considered all the possibilities from every angle and played his move accordingly. Checkmate indeed. Home schooling for all.

And only George was far more excited than concerned.

The mathematics of time-travel! You certainly didn't get that in old Mr Kelvin's class.

Not ever. Not even if all your Christmases had come at once.

Time-travel!

* * *

Afterwards, throughout the remainder of the meal, the atmosphere was more than a little strained, which Mr Redmayne felt was unfortunate, given the genuine sense of togetherness and excitement that everyone had brought with them to the table. The first meal in the new house. They had been through such a lot recently, all of the Redmaynes, and their relief at escaping the worst of it had been so great that it had spilled over into all of the fun and wonder and sheer novelty of being somewhere new. And not to mention *safe*. Now it all felt a tiny bit…spoiled. He hoped not. It wasn't like they had anywhere else to go. Still, it was typical of his father to be so calculating—and so brusque about it. Twenty years of death evidently hadn't changed him in the slightest. (Mr Redmayne made a mental note that he should use that line later when talking things over with his wife.)

And it wasn't like he felt he should blame his father, either. Not exactly. Old Rufus was what he was. Even right then, sitting there, it didn't seem as though he was at all aware that his cold behaviour or blunt remarks might impact negatively on those around him, on those whose welfare he supposedly cared most about. No, Mr Redmayne realised, watching his father unselfconsciously chew his food, clearly quite oblivious to any change in the mood at the table, that wasn't right. No. It wasn't that his father didn't care; more that he didn't *understand*. That was it. For all of his great genius, there was a level of basic human interaction that would be forever beyond Rufus's grasp. He had weighed up all of the available options open to them under the circumstances, discarded those that didn't work and presented the one remaining viable choice as the only way forward.

And if that were the case, logically, which it no doubt *was*, why be upset about it?

It was still difficult not to resent him for it, however, even if he couldn't help it. Mr Redmayne was therefore doubly glad and more than readily agreed when, as the meal drew to a close (post the most *heavenly* roasted rhubarb clafouti that anyone could imagine), his father suggested that they both should stay behind to clear up and let the others have the run of the place without them for a time. This would give them the opportunity to talk, to bottom out their unusual predicament and gauge what was really necessary in terms of secrecy and withdrawing from the world at large.

And for how long.

"Eric and I will clear up," Rufus had announced, surveying the long array of emptied plates and bowls scattered before them on the table. "Believe me, it won't take us but a jiffy between us both. No time at all. You all run along and enjoy the evening outside while the light's still good. Don't mind us. We'll join you soon as we're done here."

The three younger Redmaynes, whose expectation had been that they would inevitably be stiffed with the washing up, as usual, didn't need telling twice.

They looked at each other with eyes lit up with the excitement of unexpected freedom—and the prospect of no end of new things to do.

"There's all that cricket stuff I found," said Emile, all in a rush, "in the little shed. We could set that up on the grass by the barn, you know, the *stumps* and the little, er, whatchamacallits—the *bails*. That's them. I could bat, George, and you could bowl. At least to start with. Okay? All the gear's there. I've checked."

"And what will I do?" asked Felice.

"*Field*," said both boys together.

"Cheek. You know I'll win in the end. I always do."

And within an instant the three of them were gone, their high voices calling and bickering in the hallway—and then outside. Louder. Free.

Mrs Redmayne glanced knowingly from her husband to her father-in-law. She folded her napkin and laid it down on her placemat. She stood up.

"I think I might take a turn around the apple orchard," she said. "Who knows? Perhaps I'll find a young girlish version of me wandering around there in the trees? After all, absolutely anything is possible in this family, isn't it? And I always did so love the orchard at home."

"I'll join you soon, dear," said Mr Redmayne, holding out his hand to her. "This shouldn't take too long. Half-an-hour, at the most."

She ran her hand through his as she left.

Looking back over his shoulder Mr Redmayne followed his wife's departure with his eyes, admiring once again how very graceful she was in every step. As she always was, of course—and yet it felt to him as if he were noticing this special quality of hers for the first time. He was truly a lucky man, he reminded himself. Blessed. Infinitely so.

Then, turning back round towards his father, he at once felt considerably less lucky—almost, if not quite, infinitely so. But certainly not blessed. Not in any sense.

Old Rufus's time-worn face—gaunt to the point of extremity—now wore a far more serious and indeed altogether rather quite worrying expression, very different than how it had appeared at any time throughout the long family meal. In fact, if anything, it reminded Mr Redmayne of the disconcertingly earnest expression on the sober face of the far younger Rufus during the course of their fateful conversation at the old Cardinal's Cap Inn in Bankside, when the latter was trying his level best to persuade his son to reveal the approximate time and location of his supposed 'death' at some point in the then far future. It was a disturbing, even haunting, look—a look that one did not readily forget.[9] [10] [11] [12] [13]

"Come, my boy, there is much for us to discuss," said the elder Redmayne, with such a gravity that Mr Redmayne almost immediately got over his surprise as being addressed as 'boy' for the first time in well-nigh thirty-five years, or more. "Much indeed, yes. But, first, we must take care of our allotted task, namely, the clearing up. Wait there, would you, just a moment?"

Mr Redmayne's eyes ran up and down the full length of the table, spying discarded dish after discarded dish. Perhaps he had underestimated the scale of the task? An hour, at least. The random shouts and cries of his three

---

[9] But, then again, the freshness of this particular impression may simply have been because, for Mr Redmayne, that unique historical event had in fact occurred only last week.

[10] Or, alternatively, to be fair, 412 years earlier, depending on your perspective—and/or some 60 years previously for Rufus, the whole episode having actually transpired in 1603.

[11] *Last* week, *in* 1603, to be sort of precise. As precise as you could be, under the circumstances.

[12] Time-travel was such a *desperately* tricky business, very difficult indeed to keep straight in your head, and, all in all, in Mr Redmayne's considered opinion, best avoided, if you possibly could manage it.

[13] But, suffice to say, Mr Redmayne had seen that worrying look on his father's face before, at various points in their relative histories, and it hadn't exactly boded well in any of them. Not at all.

children as heard through the open window made him feel a little wistful that he wasn't out there with them already. Still, it shouldn't take *too* long, the washing up, not with the two of them working together.

His father had pressed the palm of his hand flat against the dining room wall and was fiddling with a small panel, one that Mr Redmayne somehow hadn't noticed until now.

"There," said Rufus. "All done. Now, shall we withdraw to the study? I think, yes. Some of the things I have to tell you are probably best for your ears only at this point, I should imagine. Come."

Mr Redmayne, initially confused, looked back down at the table.

It was entirely clear. Not a dirty dish or plate in sight.

"I don't understand," he said, gesturing vaguely before him. "*What* just happened?"

"The table? I re-set it, of course. Don't worry, I'll show you how it works before I leave. It's actually very simple. Even *you* shouldn't experience too much difficulty, I don't think. Well, at least not if you allow the children to help you. They're fine children, I think, Eric, fine minds. Yes, I think so. And they don't crumble under pressure, I noticed that much in New York, and they're open to new experiences. You and Gloriana have done a good job. Splendid. Although I'm not entirely sure if you can take the all of the credit for that or not—they *are* Redmaynes, after all. ... Now, then, where were we? Oh, yes, about to discuss the overall situation and the immediate future, or our collective lack of one. The Redmaynes, I mean. Potentially, anyway. Come with me."

The older man turned to leave the room. Mr Redmayne followed, hardly listening and running his hand along the empty table as he passed it.

"Yes, yes, yes, fine, Father, whatever...but, really, where *are* all the *plates*, the dishes, the *every*thing?" he called to the retreating figure. "Fa*ther*, explain *this* instant, I insist. I absolutely do. Stop! You *must*!"

Rufus, quite unperturbed, looked back. "They're in the cupboard, or rather, cup*boards*, if we're being exact. Like I just said, I re-set everything. Come along. Don't stand there gaping."

"Yes, but what does that *mean*? How it is possible? Explain yourself."

"Decelerated light. Everything in this structure, the house itself, even, is fashioned out of decelerated light. Don't you see? Light *slowed down*, my boy, and recast into, shall we say, solid structures. *No*? I forget sometimes that you only spent your very early years in the far future. But, even so, you would think at least some of it had stayed with you."

Mr Redmayne was thinking now. "You mean to say it's like some kind of advanced form of holography?"

"No, that's exactly what I didn't say. Holography is nothing but a three-dimensional recording of a light field. An *image*. *These* are *solid* structures…"

"Made of out light?"

"Yes! Precisely. Light decelerated to the point where it can be reconstituted in a solid field of your choosing. Solid light. It's how everything is made in my time—*our* time—which is one reason why I prefer the past. It's why I collect precious objects. Rarities. Authentic originals. I thought you knew this."

Mr Redmayne appeared to be mulling over his father's words.

"But how? Photons have no mass. Normally. Hmm… I guess you would need to find a way to make them interact with each other so strongly that they begin to behave as though they *did* have mass, and so then they bind together to form, well, molecules. So, if you slow them down enough and recombine them—*voila*, a new form of matter. Ingenious!"

"Yes, yes, come along. You know, it really isn't that different to how the old house works, is it? Slowing down light is a lot like slowing down space-time, when you think about it. Or speeding it up, for that matter. Do you see?"

"Via the artificial gravity-well, you mean...?"

"Exactly, yes. Just as the gravity-well of the black hole allows for the dilation to be managed in time travel, the same process allows for combinations of photons to become fixed in space *and* time as condensed matter. *New* matter, if you will. See, yes? Like everything else it's simple once you understand it."

"That's brilliant," said Mr Redmayne.

"Yes, it is. I am indeed the author of my own misfortune. Consequently in my own time nobody wants for anything, but nothing is real. Nothing has genuine *substance*. Hence my quest. I could never be satisfied with mere temporary manipulations of matter. For all their convenience they lack, shall we say, authenticity. Now, my boy, if you're quite satisfied, come along. We really must talk about our position here and what we need do next. That's what's important."

Looking around, Mr Redmayne followed his father out of the room, marvelling at the fact that everything he could see around him was apparently constructed out of light. The walls, the doors, the furniture (but surely not the amateurish artworks dotted here and there around the walls[14]). Accustomed as he was to marvels, indeed more so than any other man alive at that time, Mr Redmayne nonetheless found the concept staggering, beyond anything he could imagine.

---

[14] In fact, these 'artworks'—mostly landscapes featuring a distant lone dog scampering on any one of a number of beaches—were all original pieces by Rufus himself and as such were the only 'real' artefacts to be found anywhere in the entire farmhouse. The artist was most put out to overhear them being described by his son as 'a waste of photons' and chastised him roundly.

The future must indeed be a time of unlimited bounty and leisure for all. And yet his father, the reluctant architect of this utopian paradise, was dissatisfied. That was the measure of the man. He was, in no small way, a difficult man to please. Very.

With all of this running through his mind Mr Redmayne followed his father down the corridor towards the study. When they were both inside, Rufus closed the door behind them and at once everything became very quiet. To Mr Redmayne, the sudden hush felt ominous. Towards the rear of the room stood a solid-looking oak desk. It was almost impossible to imagine that it might not actually be oak but a simulation made out of light. The 'woodiness' of it seemed undeniable. Mr Redmayne found himself wanting to run his hand over the desktop, to see if it felt any differently to how it should, to test its reality. But as his father was there, he fought the impulse. Besides, the older man was now rummaging through one of the desk's drawers. Shortly, he held up a normal-enough-looking piece of paper. On it was printed:

THE FIRE-BIRD HOUSED PRESENTLY IN THE
STRONGHOLD BY THE ALDER GROVE.

"Understand?" said the older man. "It's very important."

"I beg your pardon?" said Mr Redmayne, slightly perplexed—and then at once he grew even more so as the piece of paper spontaneously disintegrated into bright wisps of light, before vanishing altogether—as if it had never existed. Gone.

"What on *Earth* was that!"

"That's where and when you can find me, if you really need to—and only if you *absolutely* must. So, did you catch it? The clue?"

"I think so. Yes."

"Good. Always remember, they can track you

anywhere, the TDA, and in any time period. That's critical. Don't forget that. We don't want them turning up with, well, *personal invitations* in their sweaty, grubby hands again, do we? Which is why I've taken certain necessary precautions."

"Come on, now. I didn't know that Watkins fellow was one of those *TDA* people or whatever they are when I invited him to the open house, did I? How could I, when I didn't even know there *was such a thing as the TDA*? Really, Father, if you had seen fit to let us in on your elaborate fake death plan and all the rest of it, then maybe we wouldn't be in the mess we are today. Ever think of that?"

"Yes," said Rufus. "And we would. I ran all of the possibilities."

The certainty of that last statement hung in the air between them for a moment or two like a storm front.

Another thought occurred to Mr Redmayne, catching up.

"What do you mean? *Precautions*? *What* precautions? What have you done?"

"Everything necessary, my dear boy, to keep us all safe. As I am about to explain to you. You'll need to understand it all, so pay attention. Now, this farmhouse won't be found on any map, not at any point in history. Nor will it be visible to or locatable by anybody but ourselves. And, to be clear, by that I mean all of us here now. The Redmaynes."

"Much like *the* house. On Phoenix Yard, or Everywhere Street, if you must call it that. *Our* house, I mean. Only visible to us. Usually. Unless one of us deliberately relaxes that particular restriction, of course."

An unpleasant idea popped into Mr Redmayne's mind. He examined his father's face with a renewed suspicion. Had the old man meddled as far back as the unfortunate incident with the meter man in New York? *Had* he? Mr Redmayne wouldn't put it past him. But if he had, no twinge of conscience was evident now. Not at all.

He merely went on explaining.

"Yes, yes, similar technology here but altogether far more extreme in its execution. The farmhouse is my own construction, using the advanced light mechanics I've already explained to you." Rufus looked at his son as if he were a grade school teacher checking to see if his pupil was keeping up. "Therefore no record exists of its establishment, its sale or purchase, et cetera, nor of this land ever being used for anything other than grazing for wild boar and deer."

"Wild boar?"

"Yes, *Sus Scrofa*. Now, pay attention. Placed at strategic points at the circumference of the farmland are a series of devices that curve space-time back in on itself, so that anyone else who passes through will emerge seamlessly and instantly on the other side. Do you see?"

"So, they'll have no knowledge of being 'jumped', as it were? I suppose it *is* something of an infinitesimal jump at the most."

"That's right, no knowledge. None. They'll pass through without any sense of the event at all. To them, they will simply have travelled from A to B, all in perfect continuity."

Mr Redmayne marvelled at the ingeniousness of it all.

"Remarkable," he said. "And the TDA, they can't track this phenomenon? It must involve a significant temporal displacement effect, after all?"

"Those halfwits? No, this is one trick I haven't shared with the world, at any point in time. How do you think I've managed to evade them for so long? No, they won't find this place, no fear of that. Just like they couldn't find the house. No, trust me, it's out there in the world you'll need to be careful, on your guard, yes."

The old man peered out though the window, almost as if on the look-out for hidden dangers. Joining his father, Mr Redmayne noted some ominously dark clouds gathering above the tree line of the orchard. Then, something else—a ball, he thought—arced across the foreground, describing a perfect parabola of descent. Loud cries, shouts, accompanied its fall. Fun.

"It'll be hard on the children," he said. "They're used to having more freedom. Oh, they'll love it here for a time, but before too long all of this will begin to feel more like a prison than a holiday. Do you think we will *never* be able to return to our old life? Is that gone forever?"

"I don't know," said the older man. "The immediate future is uncertain. *Something* is afoot. I don't know what it is. Something else, *not* TDA—I'm certain of that much. But I'm investigating, or will be soon, I very much expect. In the meantime, you'll all be far safer here. That, I'm also certain about. You'll just need to keep them busy, Eric, my dear boy, stave off the boredom. And I'll be back regularly, to help. Educating them in all of *this* and how it works is important, I think. The technology, I mean. Without that, they're defenceless."

Mr Redmayne nodded. "Now, on that very point," he began…

* * *

Within the best part of an hour or so, Mr Redmayne was more clued into the detailed workings of advanced light mechanics than he believed was strictly necessary, or desirable, for a gentleman thinker of his era, but he accepted that his father preferred to be thorough in everything that he did. Always. Obsessively so. And, as perhaps this was the very trait that had enabled him to survive for so long a time when being hunted across various epochs by the sinister if thus far ineffective futuristic group that Mr Redmayne now rather whimsically liked to refer to, at least privately (i.e. entirely in his own head), as the 'Time-Plods', he thought it best to pay attention for the full hour. By the end of this somewhat (over-)lengthy tutorial, however, he nonetheless felt confident that he could materialise and dematerialise plates, dishes, knives, forks, spoons, napkins, toothpicks, shoehorns and any other household whatnot whatsoever with all of the dexterity and aplomb of the best stage magicians of this or indeed any other historical period to date—and he looked forward to showing it off in style to the children later.

Of course, since there was no question of advanced light manipulation not being a significant improvement on washing dishes, a chore Mr Redmayne especially detested, unless he happened to have a particularly difficult equation or similarly complex problem to think about at the same time, in which case he hardly noticed it at all, this all struck him as a great technological step forward, as something of a quantum step forward, in fact, his favourite kind.

And, yes, although he did appreciate his father's objections to the insubstantiality of the items created out of light by this process, he also experienced a new sense of detachment, of freedom from the responsibility for owning things, by virtue of the fact that nothing was actually 'real', which on the whole he found rather liberating. Because over the years he'd come around to thinking that all the things that you own, well, in the end they rather come to own you. Indeed, everything in the old house had been so precious that at some point he'd started to worry about them all the time—the fine paintings, the historical artefacts, the rare volumes and all the rest of it. Now he didn't have to worry about practically anything at all, apart, of course, from the fact that he and his family were living in an artificial bubble created from the unnatural curvature of space-time in order to avoid detection by menacing and somewhat unscrupulous policemen from the future.

But at least his hands wouldn't chap anymore from prolonged exposure to dishwater, which was something. And for that small blessing he was grateful.

Besides advanced light manipulation, Mr Redmayne

also learned in this hour the precise location of exactly where in France the farmhouse was situated (a few kilometres' south-west of the small village of XX, which in turn lay some three kilometres east of the larger town of XXX[15]). A farmers' market was held every Wednesday morning in the village square and, in terms of food and other provisions, they could buy everything they needed there. Just about. Care would need to be taken especially with the coming and going in and out of the farm, his father had stressed to him, because if any of them were seen either entering or exiting it would appear to the observer that they had just stepped into or out of nowhere. Given that this was probably just the sort of report that the TDA would be looking out for and investigate, it would be best avoided.

At this point Mr Redmayne, feeling his father's maniacal gaze upon him, nodded by way of affirming his comprehension and assent.

He'd got it. Don't attract attention and don't get caught. Check, and check.

"By the way, what name will you go by now?" asked his father out of the blue, as they were exiting the farmhouse and stepping out for a stroll in the pale evening twilight. "Out there in the world, I mean. What name will you assume?"

"What?" Mr Redmayne looked dumbfounded.

He was very attached to his name. The family name. They all were. The name distinguished, and in some real sense, no doubt through their long, repeated (daily) identification with it, it also defined them. They *were* the Redmaynes.

---

[15] Apologies, but you are not allowed to know this, for your own good (among other reasons).

The fabulous Redmaynes, or so he'd liked to think.

But, alas, it would seem, no more. At least, not out there in the world.

No. His father was right. As ever. It wouldn't do.

But poor Mr Redmayne didn't know how he was going to break it to the others.

They strolled on. "I can make some suggestions, if that would help," said his father, perhaps kindly. Perhaps not. It was so hard to tell. "How about Windibottom? It's Saxon, I believe. And no one will ever suspect it's you."

"I really don't think so," said Mr Redmayne. The fabulous Windibottoms? That would never do. Not at all. No, if they couldn't be Redmaynes anymore, they certainly were not going to adopt a comedy alternative as a moniker, not even in the interests of camouflage.

Not now. Not ever.

"That's okay, Father. Thank you But we'll all get together later, as a family, and decide. That's what we do."

His father nodded, as if now somewhat distracted. Mr Redmayne followed his line of sight and saw that the old man was staring off intently over in the direction of the children, who were very involved in their game of cricket on the square of short-cut grass.

It was Emile's turn to bat, it would seem. Even from this distance all of the ancient cricketing paraphernalia appeared far too large for him—in his little hands the long, flat willow bat looked more like some kind of obscure and oversized medieval farming implement—an apple crusher, perhaps—than a piece of modern sporting equipment.

The pads, too, were much too long for his short legs. All in all, he resembled a cricketer who had shrunk in the wash. It was sweet to see, touching in a way that only one's own children or grandchildren can ever be.

"*This* time, Shrimp, why not at least *try* hitting it? Just *once*. That's all I'm saying."

Needless to say this raucous, hectoring call was from George, in his standard big brother mode.

"Why don't you try bowling it *at the wicket*? That would help, George. *Then* I can hit it."

Rufus appeared uncharacteristically wistful. "You know, I scored an unbeaten century against the Gentlemen at the St Lawrence Ground with that bat," he said. "Eighteen seventy-eight, I think it was. Great game, great day out. Or *not out*, I should say. Old WG and Fred never forgave me. Ever."

"Really? Who?"

Turning around, Mr Redmayne was surprised to see that his father had something of a misty damp look in his eye, one that he had seldom seen in it before. *Once* before, perhaps.

It hadn't occurred until that moment to Mr Redmayne that there had surely been an element of *sacrifice* in his father's actions, in faking his own death and maintaining a policy of no contact with them—his family—these last twenty years.

By doing so, he had missed out on much, on the really important things that no time machine could retrieve for you, on birthdays, holidays, family meals and the like.

On life. Once it was gone, it was gone.

The thought put Mr Redmayne in mind of another matter that often occurred to him.

"Father, do you ever think of visiting Mother, in the past, I mean? To see her again? One more time, knowing that you could, as easily as stepping out of the front door?"

His father turned to him, with the barest hint of a kind smile on his lips (another rarity).

"No, my lad. No. It wouldn't do. Not at all. She would recognise me, I'm sure, even *now*, today, old man that I am, and would understand at once why I was there. It would only unsettle her. And that wouldn't be fair—as you well understand. Which is exactly why you've never done it, either, I'm sure."

Mr Redmayne nodded. The temptation was always there, however, as long as the means existed. It didn't go away. Not completely. Not ever. His mother, old Boudicca, had been a rare cheerful soul, extraordinarily so. He imagined she'd needed to be, to cope.

Their minds elsewhere, neither man was alert just then to the warning cries of the three cricketers (one of whom, who shall remain nameless, had shouted, "*Four!*"), as Emile had at last secured a solid contact of the flat wooden bat on the ball, resulting in the most satisfactory sounding *thwack* of willow on leather.

Consequently, the latter round, red and, above all, *hard* missile was now speeding like a comet through the atmosphere towards its inevitable apex, descent and collision with the world below and its unsuspecting inhabitants.

And when the rapidly descending cricket ball did come to earth finally, it struck the poor, obliviously downwards-looking Rufus with the most resounding crack, smack-bang on the right temple, with the result that the unwary old man collapsed to the ground at once—a fearsome, instantaneous crash akin to that of the sudden fall of a building or of the proverbial sack of potatoes.

Or, indeed, much like the fall of the proverbial sack of anything you might care to think of, so long as it is suitably hard, heavy, loose and quite entirely lifeless.

CHAPTER 2

Despite first appearances, to everyone's great relief (and most especially Emile's, given that he had launched the offending missile), the blow to Rufus's forehead from the cricket ball happily proved to be strictly non-fatal. The instantaneous manner of his collapse had alarmed all of the Redmaynes, of course, not least—but not only—the three children (George, in particular, seemed quite beside himself with concern). Mr Redmayne had leapt into action at once, however, and signalled for his wife to come running from the orchard by waving his arms back and forth in an urgent, crisscross fashion, much as though he might be guiding a stricken airliner to a safer portion of the runway, semaphore-style. Not that he planned to carry out any repairs himself, of course, but he would prepare the scene and facilitate the efforts of those might to the best of his abilities, as he saw his role in such matters as largely supervisory and not hands-on.

Luckily, the pilot (and also the Captain, it must be said, if we're talking rank) was alert to the distress call and was soon upon the scene, doling out rapid-fire instructions and words of reassuring comfort in equal measure. In next to no time at all the injured party had been revived and was sitting upright once again on the grass, sporting something of an overlarge cold compress on top of a small if disturbingly bloody and most decidedly nasty-looking wound in the approximate vicinity of his right temple. The padded compress was held in place by two thin strips of sticking plaster[16], positioned in a rather neat and very precise 'X' formation, for maximum effectiveness.

In the light of her recent achievement of the *certificat de formation aux activités des premiers secours en équipe* Felice had insisted upon applying the final touches to the dressing herself, working with all the expert delicacy of a master toy repairer engaged in the restoration of a fine china doll (vintage, but worn in places and marked on head and torso). Once done, she stood back and surveyed her handiwork with an unmistakable look of pride and satisfaction on her face, one which said (and indeed could only possibly say):

'*Voila!*'

Rufus stared up at his granddaughter with gratitude, at all of the concerned faces surrounding him, in fact—his family, the family he had lost for over twenty years, an eternity of a sort. Too long, however you sliced it, was how he viewed it now. Far, far too long.

He had missed out on much, all of *this*: this was his sacrifice.

Then he raised a hand uncertainly to the compress on

---

[16] Which George had insisted should be referred to as a 'Band-Aid', much to Emile's disgust, who was of the view that the term 'sticking plaster' was far more appropriate. The reason why they should be having such a disagreement, now, for the first time in their lives, did not occur to either of them. But it will. Oh, yes. Oh, yes, indeed...

his forehead—and knew at once that it was time for him to go. He raised himself to his feet, still unsteady, a little dazed.

"Father, what are you doing?" said Mr Redmayne. "You took the most terrific blow to the head. You really should rest longer. There may be a concussion. Gloriana?"

"But of course," agreed Mrs Redmayne, as the old man continued to steady himself on his feet. "Rest is imperative after such a blow. And we should be keeping you under observation for at least twenty-four hours, as a precaution, yes?"

Emile had a firm grip of his grandfather's arm. "Are you *sure* you're okay? I'm really, *really* sorry. I am. It was an accident. I just hit it."

"I did shout 'Four!'," said Anonymous.

Felice threw her anonymised sibling a look.

"No, no, I'm quite all right, I can assure you all," said Rufus, gathering himself. "But your concern is touching, all the same. One thing: I would very much like to view the dressing, if that were possible?"

"The dressing? Well, yes, I suppose," said Mr Redmayne, turning once again towards his wife. "The dressing, dear? He wants to view it. Very much, apparently…"

Mrs Redmayne was already rummaging through her pockets with purpose. Within moments she had produced her compact mirror, a gold, shell-shaped piece, complete with a round watch face poking through the centre of its art deco style outer lid—a courtship gift, no less, now many years ago, from her husband.

Timepact, read the inscription on the watch.

Rufus took it from her and peered hard at his patched up reflection.

"Perfect," he said. "That's it. But exactly."

The others looked at each other, without understanding (although Felice did feel a further pang of pride at what she took to be a compliment to her nursing skills) (incorrectly).

The old man snapped the lid of the compact shut with a definitive click.

"I must be away at once. I've been waiting for this moment for over seventy years."

He handed the compact back to Mrs Redmayne, who took it from him with an expression of concern on her face. She turned to her husband.

"Father," began Mr Redmayne, taking his cue, "are you *quite* sure you're alright? You're not making any sense."

"On the contrary, I'm making perfect sense, my boy. I have a date with destiny."

"*Destiny?*" repeated George, suddenly acutely interested.

"Yes, Georgie, my lad. Destiny. I have a date with *myself* no less. Oh, and that caddish Charles Dickens fellow. The bounder has a rare and most precious volume of mine in his possession, one that he really ought to have returned. Time for him to cough it up! Never trust a writer, believe you me!"

* * *

Rufus's premature departure from the farmhouse followed with a haste that disconcerted everybody in its abruptness and at the same time left them with a (mild) sense of being abandoned—if indeed such a mixed sentiment were possible. Still, whatever you might think, that is but exactly how they felt, the remaining Redmaynes. Disconcerted (*okay, go if you want to, goodbye*)—and ever so slightly abandoned (*that's right, just leave us here, then, fine, good, okay*). As one, the entire family watched the old man trek off towards the chalk hills until he was but a small black figure in the distance—seemingly an inconsequential detail in the landscape. Not that he could ever really be such in their lives, of course.

As might be expected, however, the children lost interest first and went in search of something to do that wasn't cricket (in fact, it was a long time before they played cricket again); shortly afterwards, Mrs Redmayne gave up, too, leaving her husband to maintain his vigil alone. Which he did, watching on until the distant figure of his father grew smaller and smaller against the vast green backdrop of the French countryside, and then seemed to vanish altogether, in an instant; and although he couldn't be certain, Mr Redmayne later reflected that this was probably exactly what *had* happened. His father had always been partial to sudden and dramatic disappearances—and, to be fair, reappearances. And so Mr Redmayne anticipated that the elderly patriarch would no doubt turn up once again, assuredly when least expected, much like the proverbial bad penny, on some otherwise inauspicious day or other. It had ever been thus, after all, throughout their respective lives. (And, in one case, death.)

Consoling himself with this thought, Mr Redmayne tried hard to shake off the feeling of abandonment, however mild, that he was experiencing. He had a lot of explaining to do to everyone now about the new house from the future and how it worked. It was about this time that Mr Redmayne had begun to wish his father had perhaps foreseen the advantages of leaving him with some kind of user's manual: *How to Operate Your New House from the Future Made Entirely Out of Light: An Idiot's Guide*, or some such title. After all, he'd enjoyed the benefit of only the briefest of practices at it himself, virtually but an hour or more earlier, hadn't he?

And so it wasn't as if he exactly knew what he was doing, was it? How could it be?

It couldn't. No. Obviously. That was a fact. Sort of.

But now *he* had to explain it all to everybody else.

If only his father hadn't gotten so darned uncommunicative about everything right before his departure, batting back all of their questions—even about where *and* when he might be going—with increasingly infuriating, gnomic answers. That was typical. *I'm going where I've already been, to do whatever I've already done, whatever that was. Or is. I'll see when I get there.* Master of Time? You'd think he was making it up as he went along. Perhaps no doubt he was!

Mr Redmayne came to an abrupt halt. Darn. He also needed to explain about the importance of everyone taking the utmost care to ensure they were not observed when entering and exiting the land surrounding the farmhouse. Oh yes—and, perhaps most importantly—he needed to convey to everyone how from this point forwards it would be necessary to conduct all of their business with the world under an assumed name. Darn. Double darn, in fact.

Out of everything, he expected that this last stipulation would go down the worst, by far. Redmaynes. They'd always been Redmaynes, of course. It was *who* they were. He couldn't imagine any of them would be happy using an alias, let alone even tolerating the thought of *choosing* one. And such as *what*, for example? Rutter? Rutabaga? Blenk*in*sop? *Smith*? No, unacceptable. Nothing else would do. They were, by definition, indisputably, irrevocably, *Redmaynes.* Accept no substitutes. None. Not at all. No.

A light came on just then in the farmhouse kitchen window, a sudden bright yellow square illuminating the swiftly descending gloom. Gloriana, doing something or other. Tidying up, no doubt. His poor lovely wife. A merry dance he'd led her in the end, having first promised nothing less than all the world and time. Now, here she was, little more than a captive on some virtual French farm from the future that was almost quite literally nowhere. Well done *him*. Good job! Three cheers for Eric, the tolerably clever son of the greatest genius who ever lived.

Was it really only yesterday that they were oblivious of all of this, the TDA, everything, and happy together in their fabulous house? Wait a minute. *Was* it only yesterday? *Was* it?

When *was* yesterday? More to the point, when was *today*?

Great Galileo's Ghost!

It was around about this time that Mr Redmayne began to wish he had remembered to ask his father when *exactly* they were now—it was quite important, knowing that, after all.

And so commenced Mr Redmayne's long, restless night, in which, most unusually for him, his mind raced and sleep would not come, no matter how much he tossed and turned, as though a hitherto unimagined new world of anxiety and worry was now suddenly his—and his alone.

Which, of course, it was.

* * *

As it turned out, to Mr Redmayne's great surprise on the next morning (and no small relief), not only were the rest of the household quite sanguine about the possibility of going about under an assumed name but the three children were, as one, positively enthused.

In fact, they threw themselves into the selection process as if it were some kind of delightful new party game, one involving both subterfuge and dare—'Pin an Alias on the Redmaynes and Make a Stranger Believe It'— and in no time they were each trying their best to outdo each other with their respective suggestions.

"Leopold," George had proposed by way of an opening gambit. "Think about it: The *Leopolds*…"

Felice stifled an exaggerated yawn. "Really? Is that the best you can do?"

"What?"

"Well, it should be something more obviously *French*, for one, Genius. You know, seeing as that's, like, *where we live now.*"

"Okay, *Léo*pold, then. Is zat *Français* enough for Mademoiselle? Possi-*bleu*?"

"Really I think it should start with an 'R', for one thing."

"Reuniclus," suggested Emile, apparently seriously.

No one paid him any attention. Not that he seemed to mind.

"How about *Rousseau*?" offered Felice. "That has a certain, I don't know, *grandness* to it. Don't you think? A *je ne sais quoi.*"

"No," said George, "I don't."

"*Regirock*," countered Emile.

"Shrimp, we *can't* name ourselves after Pokémon, no matter how obscure they might be. Someone, someday, Lord help them, *would* notice. *That's* what we're *trying* to avoid. Understand?"

"*Roggenrola*," responded Emile at once, presumably out of sheer bloody-mindedness.

George rolled his eyes. Felice, ditto.

Mr Redmayne, to be frank, was quite disappointed with the cavalier attitude on display with respect to this important element of their shared heritage. He hadn't called this family meeting just so they could act as if they were taking part in some kind of low TV gameshow challenge. They had several very serious matters to discuss.

He turned towards his wife, who had as yet remained quiet throughout.

"What do you think, dear?"

Mrs Redmayne smiled at them all. "Well, it will be a shame not to be Redmaynes anymore, at least on the outside. But, of course, we will always be Redmaynes, in here, where it really matters." She patted her chest. "And, well, of the *suggestions* heard so far, although they were all interesting, I think perhaps Felice has been the closest to what we actually need. Something French, yes, but also something unobtrusive and yet at the same time, something, *us*. Let me see. Yes. I propose *Roussel*, which was, in fact, as I'm sure you recall, dear, my name before *you* proposed to me, all those years ago, and we were married. *Roussel.* I think it satisfies all of the criteria, no? French, unobtrusive and also part of our heritage. *And* it has pleasing connotations of the colour 'red' and so therefore of our present name, which in my view makes it quite perfect. Don't you agree?"

The Redmaynes appeared to be lost in thought, as if each trying on their potential new identity for size. Mr Redmayne beamed in pride at his wife. Once again, she had saved the day.

"Felice *Roussel,*" said Felice, very carefully. "Pleased to meet you."

"Likewise," said George. "George *Roussel.* We must be related. No matter how improbable that seems."

"Emile *Roggenrola,*" said Emile, equally carefully, "I'm related to Pikachu. No matter how improbable *that* seems."

And, happily, everybody laughed. The family restored.

The *Roussel* family—to the eyes of the outside world, at least.

* * *

With the key matter of the family alias resolved to everybody's apparent satisfaction, Mr Redmayne went on to explain about the unique setting of the farmhouse, how it was shielded from detection by all but themselves, even from the TDA, and that care absolutely must be taken to avoid being seen when entering and exiting the perimeter, because to the onlooker it would appear as though they had stepped into—or indeed out of—nowhere, which would never do, for obvious reasons which should not need to be stated. *And—*

"Wait a minute," said George, interrupting despite himself, "you mean it would look like we'd literally just *vanished* or, like, *appeared,* you know, instantly, as if right out of thin air?"

"Like *ghosts*?" added Felice, clearly quite taken with the idea and its possibilities.

"Well, I suppose so, to the simple superstitious mind, yes," replied their father, as if considering a possibility so outlandish that it would never had occurred to him in a million years. Or more. "I imagine such a conclusion *might* be drawn—by *some*, on the basis of the limited evidence and the lack of a viable alternative scientific hypothesis. *Some* people might be inclined to conclude that so-called supernatural forces were involved, yes, I suppose. *But* that outcome is one—"

"*Cool*," chorused the three children, together.

"—*is one* that we must avoid. The point is that we are *not* to draw attention to ourselves here—and so behaving like we were some kind of, I don't know, *hot spot of haunting* or some such, would be somewhat counterproductive, in the extreme. Do we understand?"

"Yeah, but kind of *way* cool, Pops, don't you think?" said Emile, looking at his elder brother and sister. "Just once or twice couldn't hurt, could it?"

"At Halloween," said Felice. "Imagine!"

"Oh, think of the fun we could all have!" said George. "In *costumes*!"

"Look, everyone, *please*," said Mr Redmayne, more than a little exasperated. "Try, *try* to understand, this is important. If we want to stay safe, we—"

"Dear, I think we *do* all understand that, really. Yes, we do, don't we?" said Mrs Redmayne, looking around the table. "But, at the same time it might be useful if we knew exactly where the perimeter is, don't you think? Do we *have* a map?"

"Well, no, I don't think we do. Actually, no. That *is* a problem."

"It is *rather*, dear, isn't it?"

"*We'll* have to map it!" said George, turning to his brother and sister. "The three of us. Wow! Come on!"

The Redmayne children made to leave the table, as

one.

Then, as if waiting for permission, stopped. Sometimes, however, it's the afterthought that matters.

"Well, yes, I suppose so, if you must, *go*," said Mr Redmayne. "But the thing is, I hadn't quite finished."

This last sentence quite trailed off, as his young audience had already largely voted with their feet, in impressive double-quick time, too.

He watched them go, with a most concerned look on his face.

Mrs Redmayne leaned over and laid her hand on his. "Not to worry, dear," she said, in her best consoling voice, as if her husband had, for example, been struck on the head by a cricket ball, "I expect we can hear the rest of it later. Something tells me we're all going to have lots of time on our hands here, more than we all know what to do with. And probably much sooner than we think. Chéri, you look tired. Didn't you sleep?"

He shook his head.

"Hey, I'm doing the drawing!" they heard Emile shout, probably from up in his room. "I'm the best at that."

"Be happy they have something to keep them occupied," said Mrs Redmayne. "It will be worse when the novelty wears off. At the moment it is like a holiday."

"We need to think about school. Seriously. Maybe not today, or this week, even. But soon."

"Yes, that's true. But it's the summer now. They'll expect a break, for a time."

"*Sum*mer? It was September yesterday! Great Galileo's Ghost!"

"I can tell by the state of the orchard. If I were to hazard a guess, I would say it's early to mid-July."

"Good grief," said Mr Redmayne. "My father!"

"Hey wait, you two!" they heard Emile calling out now. "Wait, already! I've got everything we need here. *Wait!*"

Mrs Redmayne patted the back of her husband's hand. "Never mind, my love. Shall we go and see what they're doing? It's not every day we'll be so lucky as to see three such fine young cartographers in action. Is it, Monsieur *Roussel*?"

"Yes, I expect not, dear. You're right, as ever, Madame *Roussel*," said Mr Redmayne, smiling.

But in his heart lingered many doubts.

After a preliminary drawing exercise, most notable for Emile's (loud) vocal insistence on personally sketching out the farmhouse and the surrounding terrain unaided (albeit, it must be said, not without considerable over-the-shoulder editorial input from his two older siblings), the activity of mapping out the perimeter appeared to Mr and Mrs Redmayne to consist largely of the three children arguing amongst themselves while testing the limits of the farmhouse's observability from specific distances.

It was a sort of scientific method, for siblings.

Plotting a giant circle, every ten meters or so Felice and George took turns to walk backwards away from the farmhouse and call out the point at which the farm and all of its environs suddenly vanished from view. The other sibling would then repeat the walk along the same line in order to verify the result, invariably recording some very slight variation on the original outcome (frequently infinitesimal, but critical) (obviously) and a discussion would ensue.

This discussion might continue at length, in a free and frank way, until Emile grew fed up with the pair of them and called *Time* with an emphatic cry of "*Charted!* *Move on!*" while simultaneously marking the point on the map and moving on approximately ten meters to his right, his entire demeanour a model of scientific detachment.

At which point, with the matter already decided, George and Felice would realise the futility of their ongoing disagreement, puff out their cheeks and, while not exactly conceding the point, whatever it was, move on as directed—only to then repeat the exercise in detail.

"My turn first this time!"

"No, *mine*! You were first last time. Remember?"

While Emile knew that, on occasion, he had to make allowances for his elder brother and sister, his patience was not infinite.

"Really, you two!" he called to them. "How *old* are you both? This is *important*. If you aren't going to behave, I'd be better off doing it on my own! Is that what you want? *Yes*? No, I thought not. So, let's try and get on with it—like grown-ups, if you can possibly manage it. Really, the pair of you, I don't know."

For some reason, Mr and Mrs Redmayne seemed to find this exchange both oddly familiar and yet curiously amusing at the same time. They sat together on a bench on the lawn outside the farmhouse, chuckling to themselves while they looked on. It was a situation that might only have been improved by the introduction of a nice hot cup of tea each, and possibly a fresh scone, and Mr Redmayne kept thinking that any second now he would volunteer to go and put the kettle on, except at the same time he was sure that if he did he would miss something which, although insignificant, he would regret forever not having witnessed for himself.

After all, despite having all of time and space to wander through at his leisure for the best part of his life, Mr Redmayne most cherished these small family moments, as nothing else brought him such joy. No treasure like this treasure.

And so the pair sat together enjoying the early morning show, not really needing anything else, not even tea, which *was* saying something.

"Really, dear, you think your father would have left us a map, seeing how important it is," remarked Mrs Redmayne after a time.

"Yes, but you know Rufus. He doesn't think like

anybody else. How could he? He's from the future, after all. The *distant* future, at that."

"As are *you*, dear. Technically. But that doesn't mean you're temperamentally incapable of ever considering others' needs, does it? No, I'm afraid your father would be an unusual man in any age."

"And frequently *is*. That's part of the problem."

"Well, yes."

Emile was losing patience again. "Come on, you two! We don't have all day. If you put as much energy into this as you do into bickering, we'd be nearly finished by now!"

"They probably *do* have all day, actually," said Mrs Redmayne. "And all of tomorrow for that matter, if they think of it."

Mr Redmayne was silent for a moment.

"You know, father was different around mother," he said shortly. "Always. Somehow she brought out the human in him. That's remarkable, too, I think. Especially given their nine-hundred-year age difference. Technically."

"I sometimes forget what an unusual family I married into, you know? Us Redmaynes, *Roussels*, whatever. I would have liked to have met her, your mother. Boudicca. If only the once. Well, I suppose you never know... Where do you think Rufus is now, hmm, *travelling*?"

"Almost certainly. All that talk about Dickens. Who knows *what* he's up to—or when!"

"I expect we'll hear about it eventually. Once he's changed *history* in some way or other."

"Well, we've all done that, haven't we, darling? Even *you*—and just as well!"

"Only the once," said Mrs Redmayne. "And I'm certainly glad that I did! Otherwise we wouldn't be having this conversation, would we, dear?"

"No, I suppose not. So, just as well. Yes, indeed!"

Mr Redmayne stood up. "Tea?" he said, after a moment.

His wife nodded, smiling in response to what was, with a high degree of probability, her very favourite question of all. Mr Redmayne acknowledged her response with a nod, also—and then, before moving off, paused, as though struck by a surprise thought. Oh yes, *that*.

"By the way, dear, I meant to say, the house, well, the *farmhouse*, it's made entirely out of light. Nothing about it is real, as it were. Well, not *real* as we'd understand it, anyway. That's one of the things I'd wanted to say this morning. Milk?"

Mrs Redmayne looked at him—and then nodded again.

Sometimes it was quite impossible to underestimate just what a remarkable family she had married into, even now, after all of this time.

The map, when complete, was, in the not entirely impartial view of Mr Redmayne, "quite magnificent", and he wanted to hang it in a frame above the fireplace, in the spot where currently could be found a rather quite abysmal depiction of a city-wide inferno entitled "Conflagration Viewed from a Distance"[17] [18] [19], which was, in the very partial view of

---

[17] The painting, as a discerning critic once put it, was mostly a cartoon-like mess of angular red, orange and yellow 'flame-shapes' imposed on top of the crudest, thick-line depictions of dwelling-places and other edifices "ever to emerge from any kindergarten art group anywhere and at any point in history. *Fact.*"

[18] The critic being Wenslaus Hollar, no less, who was at the time jockeying with Rufus for best viewing position at the top of St Saviour's Church tower, Southwark, 3 - 6 September, 1666.

[19] Rufus has not at any point admitted any responsibility for starting the Great Fire, with any surviving evidence to the contrary

Mrs Redmayne, "too hideous and depressing to contemplate on a daily basis" and needed to come down at once, if not sooner. That the artist was none other than her father-in-law made little difference. None, in fact.

"I think perhaps where's he from—*when*, rather—they might not, you know, make art, anymore, at least not in the traditional way," said Mr Redmayne, partially in his father's defence. "In which case we're probably looking at the work of a twenty-eighth century grand master. The genius of his time. A unique piece."

"Down," said Mrs Redmayne, entirely unswayed. "It comes down *today*."

But at least everybody was agreed upon the undoubted artistic merits of the grand map.

Mr Redmayne was reminded by it, he said, thinking aloud (and much to Emile's and the others' bemusement), of the type of map typically drawn up during the Renaissance period, *stylistically* at least, in its *form*, as it were—oh, you know the sort of thing I mean (*yes*, you do, *all* of you): Zaltieri's map of Venice, for example, or one of Braun and Hogenberg's many, many representations of several of the major cities of the period, Istanbul, Jerusalem, Venice (again—and *what* does *that* tell you?). All those famous maps? No? As collected in their *Civitates Orbis Terrarum*? No? Really? You know, I believe we have a copy back in the Library in the house, too. No? Yes, well, *those* maps, anyway. Very much like those. Better, actually. Very much so. Yes."

"I like the way the farmhouse and the barn and all the little buildings stand up from the page, almost as if they're

---

remaining, in his most partial view, "entirely circumstantial." Besides what came afterwards was far better, anyway, he claims.
"Undoubtedly so. Ask anyone. Also, *fact*."

not flat but vertical," said Mrs Redmayne. "At the same time, it's as though they're being viewed from above. A very nice effect. I like that."

"Exactly," said Mr Redmayne. "That's *exactly* what I was just saying!"

"I don't think so, dear. It didn't sound like that, anyway. And these little figures standing at the bottom of the map there, by the orchard, are they us? They must be, I suppose. Who else could they be? Silly me. And did you draw all of it, Emile? By yourself? Well, very clever indeed."

"We had a lot of input, actually," said George. "Felice and I gave a lot of direction, didn't we? We both did. — Yes, Shrimp, I think you'll find we did. But, anyway, whatever, the point is that we've now got a working map of the perimeter, which is what we were trying to do, not create some sort of Renaissance masterpiece."

Mrs Redmayne smiled knowingly at her son. "Do try not to be so jealous, Georgie, dear. It's a very unattractive quality."

"Well, George and Felice *did* help with their ideas," said Emile. "That's true. But I drew it all."

"Yes, we did persuade you *not* to put the cow in," said Felice, as nicely as she could. "You know, seeing how it couldn't possibly be a fixed point on the map. Unless it was dead, of course, which it isn't."

"It was meant to be *representative*," said Emile in his own defence, "not a *precise coordinate*. We did maps at school. I like maps."

"Wait, wait a minute," said Mr Redmayne, catching up. "What, there's a *cow*? *We have a cow*? *Here*, you mean? On the *farm*? And it's *alive*, you say? An actual *cow*?"

"Yes, dear. An actual cow—and, yes, *she's* alive. Yes. Thankfully. In the pasture by the orchard. Surely you must have noticed? No? The children, they named her Genivee, which I think is most appropriate for a French cow and very sweet. Of course, she'll need to be milked every day, which is something I'll be quite happy to do. It will remind me of when I was a girl. I did all of the milking on the farm, you know, when I was growing up."

"Great Galileo's Ghost," said Mr Redmayne, visibly taken aback. "He's done it! He's actually done it. My father's turned me into a darned dairy farmer! He always said he would—and now he has!"

"Did he say that? Really? Why? How strange!"

"And, you know, I always thought he was joking, in his odd, oblique, totally incomprehensible way. Like he did. *Does*, I mean. But, golly, he must have known! He *must have* done, all along! Good grief!"

"Well, never mind that now, dear. Genivee's a *very nice* cow, you'll find. Rather lovely, in fact. You should go and make her acquaintance when we've finished here. I'll come with you, if that would help."

Mr Redmayne sat back in his chair, quite nonplussed.[20]

"Anyway, *anyway*," said George, with more than a hint of impatience, "well, *as I was saying*, the important point in all of this is, actually, that we now have an accurate map of the perimeter, you know, of where the distortion in space-time caused by the gravity well kicks in. That's what's important here. And you'll see, if you look carefully, that it extends all the way around the property, including the two pastures and the orchard, and always at a consistent distance of what we measured out to be precisely fifty metres from the nearest wall or boundary. It's an amazing thing when you think about it, it really is. Like, just the *math* involved in plotting it out must be, well,

---

[20] In the traditional, true sense of that word, not its opposite. Pay attention, America. Do at least try to keep up. Thank you. Now, was that *so* hard, really? No, it wasn't.

it's beyond anything I can imagine. Anything! It's just incredible. A curvature in spacetime. Phew, *wow*! And to think only the few of us right here in this room can see it. You know, I'm not just saying this but I don't think I'll ever hear or see anything more amazing than this. I really don't, and that's the truth. It's staggering."

"Well, yes, quite, indeed, about that," began Mr Redmayne, starting to get up, "there's actually *something else* I need to tell you. You'd better sit down. In fact, it would probably be better if I just showed you. Just give me a moment, here."

He went over and pressed the palm of his hand flat against the dining room wall, just as his father had done several hours earlier. A short, narrow oblong panel appeared beneath it, an unexpected development that piqued everybody's interest. It opened. Mr Redmayne concentrated, as if listening hard for something only he might hear, a master safecracker at work, his hand all the while feeling as though for the right combination.

The other Redmaynes looked on. They waited.

There may indeed be many ways for the skilled prestidigitator to make a large dining table seemingly vanish into thin air as if it were nothing but the most masterly of illusions.

Undoubtedly so.

Alas, in truth, almost certainly none of these will involve first making the chair of a member of the audience disappear out from underneath them without the slightest hint or warning (Emile's, unfortunately[21], who crashed to

---

[21] Or perhaps fortunately. If it had been Mrs Redmayne's chair that whipped away from beneath her into nothingness, well, I'm not sure I would've liked to write about what have happened to the Personage Responsible under those particular set of circumstances. No.

the floor most unceremoniously).

Nor is it much likely that they will feature the random appearance on said table of a series of apparently disconnected objects, such as, in ascending order of randomness:

A ladle.

A cradle.

A tablecloth.

A stapler; and, finally...

A small but quite detailed scale model of Table Mountain (a stunning geographical landmark Mr Redmayne had once very much enjoyed visiting while on holiday in South Africa).

And then, *right then*, no sooner than the audience had managed to register the miraculous popping into existence *right there before their very eyes* of this curious and most mysterious miscellany, the objects vanished, all of them, together, at once, only now somehow taking the dining table along with them, the one effect that had been the hapless, would-be magician's single intention all along.

He stood there before them somewhat sheepishly.

Da-Dah?

The audience, it would be fair to say, was quite stunned by this astonishing display; and, perhaps even fairer to say, more than a bit bewildered; and, whether fair to say it or not, even a little terrified.

George, for one, flung himself backwards off his chair, quickly joining his younger brother on the surprisingly cold (and rather hard) wooden dining room floor. Felice threw her arms wildly into the air and let out, much to her subsequent and lasting regret, a tiny, spontaneous squeal of terror, which was far more cute than anything else.

The map, which had been resting on the table top, fluttered to the floor, bringing down the curtain on Mr Redmayne's short career as a stage magician, even as he looked on in horror at what, despite himself, he had just done.

Only Mrs Redmayne had retained her composure, having the benefit of an element of forewarning. The farmhouse and practically everything in it was made out of light, after all. Anything might happen.

Even so, it took her a long moment of collecting her wits before she could muster a casual sounding:

"Are you absolutely quite *certain* you've got the hang of this yet, dear?"

Her husband's normally rosy face was grey, ashen.

"No, I'm *so* sorry, everybody! I am! It was my first time. And, no, I've no idea what I'm doing! George, Emile, are you both okay? Here, let me help you up."

Emile was on his feet again already, however, and was gathering up the map. His precious map. It appeared unharmed. No thanks to the Amazing Pops, mind you, at least so said the expression on his face as he scrutinised it for damage. Nope, fine. And just as well.

George, still a little dazed, was only now beginning to dust himself off. In truth, he appeared somewhat embarrassed, too, probably as he realised there had been no actual danger. His father, fussing, came over to give him a hand.

"No, no, I'm okay," said George, steadying himself and getting up. "What just happened? No, really, what? What's going on? Was that *you*? *How*?"

"Well, yes, that was me, all of it, I'm ashamed to confess," said a now very red-faced Mr Redmayne. "I *am* sorry everyone, truly, but I thought, you know, rather than just tell you all, it would be best—more *effective*—to give a little practical demonstration instead, to *show* you. Not tell. That was my intention, anyway, but of course nothing quite went as I thought it would. Obviously. Emile, are you *sure* you're okay?"

Emile was looking confused. "What happened to my chair? And where's the table gone? And what were all those...*things*?"

"Yes, dear, could you at least give Emile his chair

back? And while you're at it, might you see if you can restore the dining table? I was rather hoping to serve lunch on it in a little while."

"I'll try my best, darling," said Mr Redmayne. "You know, I think I *was* beginning to get the hang of it at the end there. Better stand back though. I'd hate for anyone to become, as it were, you know, part *them*, part *table*." He chuckled at the thought. "Sorry, no, that would *not* be good, certainly not, no. Although there's probably some kind of safeguard against that sort of thing, I should expect. Must be, you would think, no?"

Shrugging off that unusual concern, Mr Redmayne made as if to assume the same position as before, raising the palm of his right hand towards the dining room wall, a picture-book look of concentration forming on his face.

"Wait, wait, no, stop!" said Felice, her patience clearly exhausted. "Stop! Will one of you *please* tell us what's going on? Papa, what *is it* you're doing—and *how*?"

"I'm sorry, dear. I thought I'd explained everything? No?"

"No!" cried the three Redmayne children as one. "No, you didn't!"

"Oh," said Mr Redmayne looking abashed. "Really? Didn't I?"[22]

Mrs Redmayne decided to intervene. "Look, everyone, it's very simple. The house and just about everything in it is made out of light. As such, its appears to be infinitely adjustable. That's all there is to it. Really, there's no need for such a fuss. Now, everyone, I'm going to make lunch. If we could possibly have the dining table back in the interim, that would be splendid. Thank you."

---

[22] And so, you see, some element of *telling* is necessary in any story. Take it from me.

Altogether quite calm now, she stood up. George and Felice looked at each other incredulously.

"Wait, what?" said George. "Say that again. The house is made out of light? How can that be? I don't get it."

"This chair I'm sitting on, that can't be made out of light, can it?" said Felice. "It *can't* be, because, well, *I'm sitting on it!* It makes no sense!"

"Well, I'm afraid it's true, dear, whether it makes sense or not. Now, I must get on. Contrary to what appears to be everyone's expectation, lunch won't make itself. The future hasn't found a way of doing that for us yet, it would seem. Or else your grandfather hasn't seen fit to share that development with us!" Chuckling to herself, she looked over at her husband. "Anyway, if you must, ask your father. He knows the detail, don't you, dear? Now I must go. Omelettes for all in thirty minutes."

As Mrs Redmayne exited, all remaining eyes turned towards her husband. He shuffled uncomfortably.

"Well, I suppose so," he said. "Yes, well, hmm, let me see. It's like this. The farmhouse, here, and most of its contents would appear to be, well, how shall we say, hmm, derived from a technology common in the far future, from where, *when*, rather, your grandfather—*and my*self, technically—originate, as you know. Well, this technology, as far as I understand it, slows down light much the same way that our own house can slow down time. Yes? Well, it can—and when it does, these *decelerated protons* can become fixed in time and space, in new forms. That's the basic principle of it, at least. Understand? Yes?"

"Not really," said George. "No."

Felice, clearly, was thinking it over. "Photons *are* a by-product of agitated matter, though, aren't they? I mean, all matter emits photons. Even *we* do. Everything *glows*. Just that a lot of it isn't in the visible spectrum. That much is obvious. Maybe the technology reverses that state somehow? That would be clever. Rather neat, in fact, when you think about it."

George stared at his sister as if she had just stabbed him through the heart.

"This is all too weird," said Emile, clutching his map. "I really don't want to know. I'm going to my room, assuming it won't switch off or fade away or something like that."

No one so much as looked at Emile. He waited, shrugged, and left.

"I sup*pose*, Felice, yes," said George, steadfastly ignoring his younger brother's preannounced departure. "Yes, that *would* make a *kind of* sense. I guess. I'd really like to see the math. Then I'd understand it."

Felice shrugged now. "Whatever. Think I'll go and help Maman with the lunch. Oh, Papa, everything here is just so exciting! I love it! It's like, I don't know, living in the future—*and* in the present all at the same time! It's just perfect!"

And Felice, before departing, quite spontaneously leaned up and kissed her father on the cheek in a way that was perfectly sweet, perfectly French, perfectly *her*.

Mr Redmayne, watching her go, couldn't help but smile. His perfect daughter. He hoped, wished, she would find it exciting to live here for a good while longer yet.

But then he caught sight of George's grumpy face, and knew in his heart that his wish was most likely both fond and foolish in equal measure. Even living in the house of the future would no doubt soon become old hat, for all of them, especially if they couldn't get out and about at will.

Worse, if they were living on top of one another all the time, well, he didn't want to think about it. Not at all no.

And so, just for now, not having any solution to hand, he didn't.

Fortunately, Mr Redmayne proved successful in coaxing

the dining table back into existence before omelettes were served. And very fine omelettes they were, too, fluffy and light and yet thick and deliciously filling—the equal of, yes, but not better than, no—the very, *very* fine omelettes that each and every one of the Redmaynes loved to eat at Le Terminus Café, just around the corner from the Musée D'Orsay and the tall, narrow and always crowded, three-storey art shop on the Seine, Le Magasin Sennelier, where Felice, Emile and all of the sensible children of Paris annually restocked their art supplies each September before school recommenced for the year.

Yes, the best omelettes in all of Paris were to be had at Le Terminus, that was commonly agreed; but those served up on the freshly resurrected dining table that lunchtime were so good and therefore so very reminiscent of those to be had in the café that it seemed to Mr Redmayne that everyone grew a little wistful at the prospect of not being free to eat at their favourite Parisian eatery for the foreseeable future. At least, that was certainly the way *he* felt, and he imagined that he detected a similar tiny *tristesse* in the others and speculated to himself at its likely origin. But, once again, no matter how much he thought about it, a ready solution was not to be found.

And perhaps, in truth, they were only each a little down about their own thing, something random and private, it being hard to tell for sure and mind-reading still so very difficult to accomplish successfully, even when living in a house from the future.

Or maybe they were just all a little bit full, having over-stuffed themselves with omelette.

That, too, was possible.

Whatever. The real point here is that Mr Redmayne *thought* that they might all be thinking exactly the same as he was, about missing their favourite café in Paris (and, by extension, therefore, about missing all of Paris), and were feeling a bit sad about that, as *he* was, whether they actually were or not.

Which not only says several things about him, but might become quite important later.

Fortunately (once again), Mrs Redmayne was on hand to cut through the inevitable post-prandial dip in everyone's mood, whatever its cause, by announcing that she had decided to go into the local village first thing in the morning for coffee and some other bits and bobs that she needed (some flax, possibly).

And—oh yes—also to find out precisely *when* they were, their grandfather having neglected to share that critical piece of information with them before he unceremoniously strode off into the sunset with an X-shaped sticking plaster on his forehead while mumbling something perfectly unintelligible and quite possibly slanderous about the great Charles Dickens.

This unexpected announcement provoked a further moment of silence, but it was now an *interested* silence, pregnant with possibility, which was quite different to the deathly lull that had immediately preceded it. Questions were taking shape, forming, coming into being—you could practically see it happening with mothing more than the naked eye (mind-reading, it would seem after all, being more easy to accomplish on some occasions than on others).

"Village?" asked Felice. "What village? How come I don't know about any village? What's it called? How many people live there?"

"How far away is it? Which direction?" (George)

"Do they sell ice cream?" (Emile)

"Is there a market? When?" (Felice)

"I bet they sell ice cream. Everywhere sells ice cream." (Emile)

"I bet there's a market. Can we go now?" (Felice)

"Can *we*?" (Felice, Emile)

"Wait, wait, everyone, *wait*…wind back a second, will you?" said George, taking a breath and thereby encouraging the others to do the same. "What do you mean, *when we are*? Don't we *know* when we are? Isn't it still *September*? It was September two days ago."

Mr and Mrs Redmayne looked at each other as if unsure for a moment quite where to begin. So many questions, so few satisfactory answers. None, in fact.

Their children's bright faces peered back at them much as they used to on Christmas mornings, before the present opening ritual began. So much expectation, so hard to deliver.

Mr Redmayne could see their three darling younger selves before him right now, silent, wide-eyed, waiting patiently in the Great Dining Room for the Christmas festivities to commence in earnest. It was as though no time had passed at all; though, of course, it had passed—and taken much with it. But, still, not everything...no.

Mrs Redmayne spoke up. "Well, firstly, the village, it's called XXX,[23] and I'm given to understand that it can found no more than two kilometres south-west of here, so a brisk fifteen minute walk would prove sufficient, I should think. Emile, George, that's about one and quarter miles by your reckoning, but you really will have to make an effort to get used to metric measures, as 'foreign' as that may seem. We live in France now and France alone. And, Felice, dear, yes, there is indeed a market—a farmers' market, yes, so not bric-a-brac or tat—which takes place, I believe, every Wednesday morning in the town square. But alas, seeing how we as yet remain unclear as to *what day of the week it is today*, let alone the week, the *month*, or indeed *the year*, I cannot guarantee the market will be on in the

---

[23] Not sure I should say. I mean, you'd all go there—and the villagers would hate me quite likely as much as those poor people in that other Phoenix Yard all profess to doing. It's not like I send you to go look at their house, now, is it? No, I do not.

morning. I strongly suspect we are in July now, by the way, judging by the state of things in the orchard."

"July!"

"*Ye-esse*," said Mr Redmayne, drawing out the word at length, rather as if he might be unaccountably impersonating a snake, which, as everybody present knew, was hardly ever a sign of good news. "At least, that's what your mother suspects, and I have every reason to think her no less than one hundred per cent accurate in her suspicions. You see, hard as this might be to hear, your grandfather was never much of one for respecting the personal journeys of others through time, not even yours, I'm afraid. Look at *me* for one: I won't be born for another seven hundred and fifty years and yet here I am, thoroughly displaced in time and in all sorts of bother because of it."

"Seven hundred and fifty-*nine*, darling," said Mrs Redmayne, who felt it was her matrimonial duty and indeed inalienable right to pass up no opportunity for reminding her spouse of every single one of the years that he was her elder.[24] They all counted.[25] "You'll be forty-seven soon, assuming it *is* July now. At least."

"*Ye-esse*," said Mr Redmayne, once again, not liking the implications of that 'at least'.

---

[24] Mr Redmayne being five years and nine months her senior, not six whole years, despite how frequently she claimed the latter to be true.

[25] And technically, he was a full eight hundred years younger than she was, given that his birth wouldn't yet take place for that number of years, a fact Mrs Redmayne dismissed as the worse kind of sophistry. Her husband was an older man, by six years. Fact. Fact-ish, anyway.

"And if it's *July* now," said George, "then, how old am I? My birthday's in June, remember? Am I sixteen still, or seventeen?"

"Well, that's tricky," admitted Mr Redmayne.

"Sixteen," said Felice, who didn't like the idea of her elder brother pulling away from her in years any accelerated way. She wouldn't be sixteen herself until the following February.[26] "See, you haven't been alive for seventeen years, have you? You should count your age in days lived, really. That's what I think. Until you've lived enough days to fill seventeen years, con*secutiv*ely, I mean, you're sixteen. That's only fair."

George shook his head. "*Fair?* What are you talking about? What's that got to do with anything? Anyway, looks like I'll be skipping a birthday. Is that *fair?*"

"Wel-*Ille*, actually," said Mr Redmayne, adding to his range of drawn-out syllables, "as your mother, I think realises, we might *all* have skipped several birthdays. It might indeed be July, but we don't know *which* July, do we? It might be *last* July, or it could be *next* July, you never know. It might even be July in five years' time! I certainly wouldn't put it past him, your grandfather. All we can know for sure is that he had this farmhouse ready and well-stocked at a very specific moment in time, and he brought us right to *that* moment. Think about all of the fresh food and everything else that was here when we arrived. No, dearhearts, I suppose all we can hope for at

---

[26] Although, strictly speaking, they were keeping pace still, it just didn't *feel right* that her brother should suddenly leap ahead into his eighteenth year (count them, go on) while she remained very stubbornly fifteen. *Only* fifteen. It was *wrong*, that's what it was. Like, she didn't know what, *cheat*ing or something. And *so very* George.

best is that when planning ahead he at least had the right year. Just a mere few months out would be a blessing."

This was a very sobering thought, for all.

But Felice looked by far the most concerned, however. "You mean, all of my *friends* from school, *Claudia*, everybody else, they might be out there right now and be *five years older* than I am?"

Mr Redmayne nodded, his face assuming as gentle an expression as he could make it

"Sis, *five years*?" said George, somewhat less gently. "Ha! Why not *ten*? We just don't *know*, do we? That's the point."

Felice blanched, her normally rosy cheeks for once turning quite pale.

"Exhale and relax and breathe," she said, rather too hurriedly for it to be an effective manta for stress relief— in fact, if anything it sounded more like a prayer of the last resort.

At the same time she waved her right hand back and forth in front of her face, as though fanning for air.[27]

Mrs Redmayne leaned over and patted her daughter soothingly on her stationary wrist, by way of consolation. It didn't really help. No, not in the least.

Time-travel, as the Redmayne children were starting to realise, was a complex and perplexing business, and maybe, just maybe, best avoided, where at all possible, that is.[28]

---

[27] Once again, not effective.

[28] Sound advice. Very sound advice indeed.

CHAPTER 3

Mrs Redmayne decided to take only Felice with her into the village the next morning, telling the boys this was because their sister's French was immaculate, unlike their own. Now that they no longer had the house to translate everything for them they needed to master the language for themselves. Passable French would not do, not in their current situation. No, it would not. Not at all. Effort must be made, and soon. If they were to present themselves successfully as an ordinary French family—and to be seen as anything else might attract unwanted attention—it simply would not do for two of the three children to speak the glorious French language like idiots or, worse, British people.[29]

"Please don't pull that face, Emile. It's very unbecoming."

---

[29] The truth hurts, I know.

Mrs Redmayne would help them herself, she said. And perhaps if they asked her nicely, Felice might assist them also. Her French was after all, as mentioned, quite immaculate.

"Don't pull that face either, George. You would both do well to take *une feuille de son livre.*"

"What?" said Emile. "I don't understand."

"Exactly," said Mrs Redmayne, who then went off to finalise her preparations for departure and to jolly along her daughter with her own, which could be extensive.[30]

"Don't worry, Squirt," said George. "There must be a way to make *this* house translate for us, too. There *must* be. It *is* from the future, isn't it? Don't worry, I'll look into it. Yup, that'd be a far better use of our time, I reckon, than, like, you know, parsing the *plus-que-parfait* or the *passé antérieur.*"

"The *what?*"

"Exactly."

Mr Redmayne had slept very poorly once again, and he hoped that what had used to be a rarity was not becoming a habit, or the new way of things. This time, his sleep had been plagued by odd and disturbing dreams, most notably of his father being first old and young at the same time and then both simultaneously dead and alive. Alas, when Mr Redmayne woke up with a shock in the night it was of little consolation to realise that reality was actually little different to the dream. Such was his life now.

After that, sleep was hard to come by.

---

[30] And Felice's preparations were in themselves a much under-researched method for slowing down time, or at least they frequently *felt* as if they were slowing down time from the perspective of everyone waiting for her.

Mrs Redmayne, on the other hand, slept beautifully from the moment her head hit the pillow all the way through to morning and her first 'wake-me-up-gently' cup of tea, much as Mr Redmayne (the blurry-eyed provider of the said early morning cup of tea) had once been able to do himself, night after night, almost without fail, like clockwork.

That was *then*, however, before their lives had been turned upside down.

This was *now*.

In the night he *had* been a little concerned about Gloriana's plans for going into the village alone with Felice. They were safe while on the farm, he felt confident of that. But, once out there, who knew? Still, his wife was quite matter-of-fact about it and had few concerns, and in truth he realised they *had* to leave the farm at some point, if only for supplies.

After all, none of them, especially not the children, could stay cooped up here forever. That would just turn it into a futuristic prison, the very fate they were looking to escape by coming here in the first place! No, Gloriana *was* right, as ever. Village, in the morning. And at least then they would find out the date. That would be something.

Nonetheless, when the moment came for the pair to depart, finally, after Felice had exhausted seemingly every possible combination of the (somehow) many, many items hanging in her wardrobe, Mr Redmayne felt a sickening lurch of anxiety deep in the pit of his stomach, an unpleasant sensation which, bravely, he tried very hard not to show. His daughter was quite excited about her impending 'adventure' out in an entirely new place, that was obvious, and he really didn't want remove any of the gloss from that for her. You *had* to be open to life and not afraid of it, that's what Mr Redmayne believed and frequently preached, especially to his children.

But sometimes it was that much harder to live by your principles and beliefs than not.

And this was one of those times.

Still, regardless of his concerns, off they went, the happy, chatty pair, on their market expedition, seemingly without a care between them in the world. For the longest time Mr Redmayne watched as mother and daughter headed out surprisingly quick-footed across the flat green fields towards the little dark ribbon of winding lane that they anticipated should take them all the way into the village. Another day, another departure.

When they were all but out of sight and there really wasn't anything more to be done about it, Mr Redmayne gave up his vigil and headed back towards the farmhouse. Funny. It already seemed that much quieter here without the pair of them. The two boys were nowhere to be seen or heard and were presumably doing anything other than practice their French quietly. He shouldn't blame them if that were the case. He didn't much fancy brushing up on *his* darned French, either. *Non. Pas du tout.*

Instead, Mr Redmayne rather thought he might have a go at making things out of light for a time, while nobody was around. He quite fancied having one of those antique Oberon armchairs to sit and think in whenever he felt the need, just like he had at home in his study.[31]

After all, what could possibly go wrong with that?

Several failed attempts later, he knew exactly what. Instead of now being the proud owner of your classic Oberon-style Parker Knoll armchair in a London Saddle Brown Leather finish, as he had quite rather hoped and intended, Mr Redmayne had, in the last thirty minutes, regrettably, been the less than proud temporary owner of a succession

---

[31] Or perhaps just to sit and worry in, which may as well be done comfortably as not.

of objects that were entirely unsuitable for the purpose of sitting in at length while thinking, even if some were indeed a good deal more 'chair-ish' than others. But none of these could ever be mistaken for your classic Oberon-style Parker Knoll. None.[32]

It was all rather disappointing. Mr Redmayne had thought he would be good at this, once he'd gotten the hang of it, because he tended in general to be quite good at things. Opening the panel itself was easy enough. You just placed the palm of your hand flat on the wall, any wall anywhere in the farmhouse it would seem, and the panel would appear beneath it and open up. Then, the interior of the panel would *engage* with you, via your fingertips largely, as if it were *encouraging you* to think about what you wanted—and where. At least, that was how it felt to the user, in any case. It was quite an *unusual-feeling* connection, in truth, much as being connected in a deep neural way to a futuristic artificial intelligence would be to anyone from the twenty-first century. But it seemed—no, it *felt*—intuitive.

He couldn't think where he was going wrong. Chair, chair, chair! The word repeated over and over in his mind until it became quite meaningless, and his efforts at actualising his thoughts grew feebler and feebler, until he was forced to give it up as a bad job.[33] Why wasn't it

---

[32] His best effort simulated, unusually, a Toblerone resting on a short upright wooden dining chair, a creation that possessed an intrigue all of its own. However, the Toblerone in question, while resembling Mrs Redmayne's favourite confectionary with an uncanny accuracy, right down to the inner silver foil in the triangular packaging, tasted nothing like chocolate, or indeed, like anything much at all.

[33] Another resembled a small hill (to scale). His final and most

working for him? It wasn't his impression that it should be this difficult to master. His father had managed it beautifully. Darn. Mr Redmayne, frustrated, stared out of the window at the empty farmyard. Not a leaf was stirring. *Rien*...

Finding himself unexpectedly at a bit of loose end like this, he wondered once again about what the boys might be up to now—it was *so very* quiet, after all, which was seldom a good sign—and so he thought he might as well go and find out.

It didn't take long, and what he found took him quite by surprise. George and Emile were together in the younger boy's bedroom, under the skylight. In the bright white room, which was flooded with sunlight, Emile sat on the bed amongst a minor army of what appeared to be toys, or models, each about a foot tall, all of the sort of outlandish manga-style characters that he liked to draw. Monstrous-looking things, largely.

But he seemed very pleased with himself, all the same.

George, on the other hand, appeared quite the opposite. Very much so.

Palm flat against the wall, he paused awkwardly, as if caught in the act. His face was red, his expression one of frustration.

"George *can't do* it!" said Emile with delight. "He can't make nothing!"

"Anything," corrected Mr Redmayne. "'George can't

---

discouraging effort vaguely suggested a most unconvincingly rendered bust of Chairman Mao, the model for which a young Mr Redmayne had once met at a convention for romantic poets. Though highly improbable sounding, this is in fact true. Would I kid you about such a thing? No, I would not.

make *anything*.' Try to avoid the double negative.[34] And don't worry, George, neither can I, if that's any consolation."

In truth, it didn't appear that it was.

"It's hopeless," said George. "I was trying to make a cricket bat, you know, so we'd have two. Just in case the first one broke, or something."

"And what did you get?"

George looked even more disconsolate. "A wicker mat."

"Interesting. Very interesting. Oh, I see, there, yes, very nice. It has a very arresting pattern to it, the mat, doesn't it? Don't you think?"

Mr Redmayne seemed to realise that his attempt at filial encouragement was entirely misplaced on this occasion, and perhaps, yes, well, somewhat counterproductive.

"I made all of *these*," said Emile. "They're exactly how I imagined they would be, too. I wish I could show them to Steven. He'd freak, unless he's, like, thirty-two years old by now or something, in which case he probably won't care that much anymore, will he? Blimey, we used to spend *hours and hours* drawing these, me and him. Together. Now, I can just whip them up in seconds, all by myself—and they're *real!* This one's called 'Zyclops'. Like him?"

Emile offered his father an extreme close-up view of his creation, which was, in truth, a little bit too close for Mr Redmayne's comfort.

"What's not to like?" said Mr Redmayne. "He has a very *command*ing big eye thing going on, doesn't he? Right

---

[34] Unless you happen to be Chaucer; then it's fine, apparently.

there, in the centre of his forehead. And, well, so *many* arms."

"I *know*," said Emile.

"And you just *imagined* it like this—and there it was? Just like that?"

"I put my hand on the panel, like George was doing when you came in, and just picture in my head what I want. I *see* it, you know, in my mind, and then there it is. It's amazing!"

"You *picture* it, you say? In your mind? I see," said Mr Redmayne, suddenly tempted to ask Emile how well could he picture the nice brown armchair he used to have in his study back at home, but he held off. "I see, yes, thank you, Emile. That's very helpful. Or at least possibly I *think* I see the problem now, at least, anyway. Quite likely it rather pays to have a more visual type of imagination in order to make this darned thing work well. That's what I'm thinking now. That's quite possibly it, George, don't you think? What do you reckon, my lad? Want to give it another try? George?"

George's attention had been drawn to the window, however. He was peering off into the distance, towards the far hills.

"Someone's coming this way," he said without turning around. "See?"

Mr Redmayne came over and peered out of the window. Even after all of these years his vision was still perfect—twenty-twenty—much like hindsight. And from up here you could see such a long way. Forever, it seemed. Everything. All your mistakes.

"It's your grandfather," he said, at last. "He's back from whenever."

Rufus's unexpected return, so soon after his departure, threw the three Redmaynes in the farmhouse into something of a tizzy, it must be said, if each for quite different reasons. Mr Redmayne feared that his father's sudden reappearance could scarcely bode well, that he must be returning right *now* only because he had some sort of bad news to bring them, or a dire warning—that the TDA had discovered where and when they were, or would do shortly—something of that sort. This was unlikely, he knew. If the TDA were to uncover their location at the farmhouse either now or at any future point in time, they would surely have been here already to round them up. So, by extension, logically, the TDA *never do* succeed in finding them at the farmhouse and Mr Redmayne and his family therefore remained quite safe. That's what his head told him, but his heart found it difficult to accept this logic absolutely one hundred percent, no matter how much good sense it made.[35]

By way of contrast to their father, the two boys on the other hand positively skipped down the stairs and out into the farmyard, exhibiting all the anticipation and excitement of two very lucky children unexpectedly encountering Santa on their doorstep on Christmas morning. Mr Redmayne lagged behind, watching them go. How little they knew the man, he thought. Only last week didn't the conniving old so-and-so abandon them to their own devices in early 1900s New York City? Yes, he did. That was a matter of record. Regardless of his intentions, it was a risky and rather calculated thing to do with your own grandchildren. Cold. Very. Mr Redmayne wasn't sure if he would ever forgive him for it, not entirely.

The boys themselves seemed to hold no such reservations, however.

They greeted their grandfather—and he them—as if he were back fresh from the dead.

---

[35] Mr Redmayne's heart was willing to go as high as sixty-two percent on this, on a good day. No higher.

Again.

Mr Redmayne looked on in disbelief. Hugs, and smiles. Gosh, never would you have imagined he'd been absent a mere matter of days. No, more like a million years. And since when did his dear father do *hugs*? Mr Redmayne couldn't recall ever exchanging a hug of any kind with the old goat, though luckily his mother had made up for that. Great Galileo's Ghost!

Aghast, Mr Redmayne checked himself, suddenly staggered.

Was he *jealous*? And *both* ways?

He *was*. Why was that? He wasn't sure but it was most unbecoming—more, most un*worthy* of him—and he must watch out for and guard against it.

Mr Redmayne's father still bore the X-shaped sticking plaster above his right temple, but barely. His face seemed tired—worn out, in fact. All in all, he looked rather dishevelled. Mr Redmayne experienced a surge of guilt for the way he had been feeling just a moment before. The old man was indeed but recently back from the dead, in a way. Why shouldn't he now enjoy his grandchildren and vice versa?

Perhaps his long absence, *Time*, had mellowed him?

The eyes of the two men met.

"Eric, my son," said the elder Redmayne. "We must talk."

The four Redmaynes sat together around the magically reanimated dining table, which itself might have been forgiven for sharing Mr Redmayne's sense of trepidation about whatever might be happening next, given its own recent somewhat haphazard grip on existence. Mr Redmayne also worried about allowing the boys to hear what his father had to say, but then he remembered the rather severe difficulties they had all gotten into lately as a direct result of keeping secrets and he had resolved not to make that mistake again, as far as was parentally practicable. And so, despite his concerns, he thought he might just drink his tea[36] and go with it, this latest worrying development, whatever it was and wherever it took them. They were, irrevocably, all in this together, in any case.

His father had been telling the story of his latest adventure in time and the boys, understandably, were enthralled, as all boys would surely be to hear such a tale, even two who had some experience of adventures in time of their own and who presently lived in a house from the future wrapped inside an undetectable bubble in space-time.

And so it was.

"What you're saying, *then*," said George, trying to make sense of what he had heard from his grandfather so far, "if I understand it right, is that you travelled back in time in order to meet yourself, a younger version of you, that is, to give yourself a warning? What warning?"

"Not a warning, no, not intentionally, anyway," replied his grandfather, sipping his hot tea. "To *observe* only, that was *my* intention. But the fact that my older self appeared, out of the blue, well, out of the fog, actually, because it was a very foggy night, that *acted* as a kind of warning, whether I meant it or not."

"Because you recognised yourself, is that it?" continued George. "The younger you took that as a warning of some kind? Seeing his—I mean, *your*—older self?"

"Well, no, not at first. No, because I *didn't* recognise me, the older me, not at all. It was all very confusing at the

---

[36] *Mariage Frères Earl Grey Impérial*, his favourite tea-blend, if not his wife's, who was more of a *Darjeeling Paragon* sort of person, as you might expect and had no doubt guessed. Good for you.

time. But as the years passed I began to suspect it had indeed been none other than my much older self that I had encountered that night. You see, what you have to realise is that for the younger me it had been my first, what shall we call it, *trip*. I was very young, not much older than you are now, George, in fact; well, perhaps a few years your senior, yes, but still technically a student in the academy, and I made several elementary errors as a result, as one inevitably does as that age. Yes, even me."

George and Emile exchanged a fleeting guilty look at his point.

"But what's all this got to do with Charles Dickens?" asked Emile, still blushing a bit. "You mentioned him before you left. You did, I remember. And, yeah, as well, what made you decide to go back *now*? Why did you wait, like, for*ever*? Virtually your whole life, anyway. You could've gone back at *any* time, couldn't you? Well, you *could*, couldn't you? Right?"

"That's true, I *could* have done, Emile, you're right, yes. But, you see, I was waiting for *this*," said his Grandfather, touching a hand gingerly to his forehead. "The sticking plaster. Yes, *that*. The old man that the younger me saw all those years ago had a large 'X' in sticking plaster on his forehead, just like this one. And so, when I saw that on my forehead the other day, just like I had back then, I knew it was the right time. And, Dickens, well, he'd been my first 'target', as it were, my first contact in the past. And all I wanted was for him to sign my book, an innocent enough wish you would think. Turned out he hadn't even written it yet! I had the wrong date, would you believe? Well, it *was* my first time. But it was very nearly my first and last—and my most fatal—error. The TDA, they were waiting for me. I expect I hadn't covered my tracks that well afterwards, either. Elementary novice errors, you see."

Emile was thinking. "Wait, so me hitting you on the head with the cricket ball had to happen, it was *meant* to happen! That means it wasn't my fault. It was destiny!"

"Oh, I still think you might have been a bit more careful," said Mr Redmayne.

"No, the boy's right, Eric. It had to happen and it's just as well it did. I knew nothing about the TDA at the time. They came later, trying to use my work against me. So, they tracked me to my first excursion back in time and tried to stop me before I got started. Except, they failed, and I didn't at the time understand how or why. I still don't, not really. That's why I went back, to see if I could find out what happened. There were two of them and they appeared out of nowhere and they thought they had me—but after a moment they were gone. Just like that. They were time-jumped, but not by me. After a time I developed a theory that my older self had intervened somehow, but I know now that wasn't the case. It was somebody—or something—else."

"Somebody or *something*?" repeated Mr Redmayne. "What do you mean by that? Some kind of malfunction in their equipment, possibly?"

"I've no idea. Really, I don't. All my recent trip confirmed is that they *were* time-jumped but by some other agency, still to be determined. That's what I believe as based on the evidence currently available. But my investigations continue. Maybe you're right and it was just a malfunction of some kind, after all. Now I need to make sure. I must look back over any other instances in my life where I had a narrow escape—and there have been many of those—and see if there's a pattern of some kind. I don't know. Maybe it's all just an old man's paranoia."

Mr Redmayne looked very grave. It wasn't like his father not to have all the answers.

"If anyone can figure it out, it's you," said Emile.

"My dear boy, thank you for that vote of confidence," said his grandfather. "I'm touched. But I'm not sure I can do it on my own, not any more, not at my age. I'm going to need your help, I expect."

Rufus looked at his son for a second. "Help from *all* of you, in fact."

"Wait a second, go back," said George, "Charles Dickens, did he witness all of this? He must really have freaked out. You know, people appearing and disappearing like that."

"He did, indeed, yes, as you say, 'freak out'. Of course, yes. It was October 1843, in London. I was naïve, sentimental. Don't look at me like that, Eric, I *was*. For my first trip I desired for my long-time idol personally to sign *my* copy of my favourite book, that was all. So I'd have, not just evidence of what I'd achieved or some mere trifling souvenir of my trip, but something special from the past, something that meant a great deal to me, something to keep, so I'd hoped, always. And you see, I'd particularly cherished *A Christmas Carol* ever since *my* father had given me Dicken's famous novel when I was a boy, one Christmas, an antique first edition. I've no idea where he got it from. It wasn't like him at all, or for anyone of that period really, to value old things, old books, old anything, for that matter. Old London. But it planted the seed in my head. I wanted to see old London for myself—and so, all these years *earlier*, as it were, here we are. All of time-travel, you might say, came out of that desire, that boyhood wish."

"Father, you've never told me any of that before," said Mr Redmayne, thoughtfully.

"*But*," said George, with some impatience, as if everybody but him was missing the point, the real, the truly important point, "just *now* you said Dickens *hadn't written it yet*, when you met him, the book, so how did he react to that? What did he do? He must've thought you were mad."

"Quite possibly. He certainly thought I was American," added the old man ruefully. "He said, and I remember this word for word, even now, that although he was used to Americans exploiting the copyright on his books for their own gain, at least usually they had the good manners to wait for him to have written them first! That's what tipped me off I'd landed in the wrong year! I'd been a full two months out in my calculations. Can you believe it? Well, it *was* my first time. Then, the TDA turned up and, in all of the confusion, Dickens ran off with *my* book. I never did get it back, not even on this last trip."

"Well, that's all very interesting," began Mr Redmayne, "but I think, boys, it just goes to show the perils of—"

George looked as if he might explode. "Sorry, but, you're all still missing the point!"

Mr Redmayne regarded his son with surprise. "Which is?"

"Who wrote *A Christmas Carol*! It's a paradox! If you gave Dickens a copy before he's written it, who wrote it in the first place for you to be able to give it to him? Who came up with the story, who thought it up and wrote down all of the words? It makes no sense."

Mr Redmayne and his father's eyes met once more. This *old thing*, again.

"Ah, I see," said Mr Redmayne in a kindly way. "Well, George, as my father once explained to me, it's like this: such things are only paradoxical if you think of time as a straight line, when actually, really, it's an infinite series of *potential* straight lines. Yes, Dickens *always* wrote the book. Always. My father just took it from one straight line and introduced it into another. But he couldn't have done that, it wouldn't have existed *for him* to do that, you know, if Dickens hadn't written it to begin with. Of course, none of this should ever have happened and it's entirely regrettable that it did. And that's about the truth of it."

"Fiddlesticks," said the elder Redmayne. "That's what I always say to that, as well you know. But your father is right, George, on both scores, I'm afraid."

George appeared unconvinced. A living, breathing paradox could indeed be a difficult beast to slay, particularly for a very logically-minded teenage boy.

His grandfather thought he would try another tack.

"Try looking at it like this, George. Imagine that in this series of lines, they all run parallel, every single one, okay? Every line is separate but no less real and complete, yes? Right, so, in *that* case, each line runs its separate course and never crosses another. Normally they never meet, right?"

"That's right," agreed George. "Parallel lines never meet. That's basic geometry."

"Good. *Normally*, yes, that's true. Well, on one of these lines, on *one* timeline, our old friend Charles Dickens writes *A Christmas Carol*, but on another, a parallel but separate timeline, for whatever reason, he doesn't. Are you still with me? Okay, right. Good. And what *we* do is, we create the circumstances in which the parallel lines can meet. And, of course, as we both know, I'm sure, there *are* conditions, naturally occurring conditions, too, under which parallel lines converge. Do you know what they are?"

It took a moment but the black cloud lifted suddenly and George's face brightened.

"On a *sphere*," he said. "Parallel lines converge *on a sphere*. You know, like on a globe. Of *the world*, I mean, that sort of globe. The lines of longitude converge at the poles, even though they were parallel at the equator."

"Excellent, yes! That's right. And what we do, then, *is*, we bend space-time to make the sphere, and the parallel lines touch, in our case, only temporarily, but that's enough. Now, on both of them, even once they've separated…"

The old man paused to allow his grandson to join the dots and complete the puzzle.

He didn't have to wait long. George looked triumphant.

"*A Christmas Carol* exists! The original was *always* written by Charles Dickens, on one timeline, yes, but after the two timelines converge and then go their separate ways, it now exists on both! Am I right?"

"What?" said Emile, genuinely confused. "I'm lost. Say that again. *Slow*ly this time."

"Shrimp, think of it as being like, you know, the difference between the lines of longitude when you see them on a map and then, like, when you see them on a globe. You know, on a map they never meet, do they? The lines just keep going straight up and they keep the same distance apart all the way, don't they? Well, they do. And that's because the map's *flat*, isn't it? It's a flat surface. But on a globe they *meet*, don't they? You ever notice that? The *same lines meet*, they do. Because, see, the surface is *spherical*, you know what I mean by that? Like, you know, *round*. See? They converge at the top and at the bottom, at the poles. Get it?"

Emile's expression didn't suggest that he got it at all. "So what?" he said. "Big deal. What's all *that* got to do with *anything*?"

Unfortunately, or perhaps, contrarily, fortunately, there was no time for any further explication of this subject, by anyone, as all were interrupted by the premature return to the farmhouse of Mrs Redmayne and Felice, with the rather glum face of the latter suggesting that the excursion into the local village had proven something of a non-event, a wash-out, and even, when pressed later, in her own words, a total dead loss.

And, worst of all, the village itself had seemed hardly at all French, at least not in any way that Felice recognised as such, and to be fair, probably never would.

On principle. No. Not at all.

Zut, mais non!

* * *

That the trip to the village had proven a disappointment, particularly for Felice, was something of a major understatement. Not only did the *petit bourgade* lack any of the more picturesque features that she had hoped for and so vividly imagined—no narrow winding streets, no perfectly mediaeval little church, no attractive historic square with ornamental 'bulb' Roman fountain—it also appeared entirely devoid of the more basic amenities that you might expect to find, well, anywhere and everywhere.

Sure, yes, there *was* a pleasant enough-looking baker's shop and a butcher's (both closed) (very) (why?) (*why?*), and a tiny supermarché (open, *yes*, but as noted, *tiny*) (with aisles so narrow that it was quite impossible for two unacquainted people to pass with the remotest decency), and, even worse, for Felice, without the least hint of 'character'[37][38] to any of it. None.

No food or produce market, either (not today, at least), no sign of any marché-aux-puce (ever)—and worst of all, no brocante shop. No delightful tat today!

Oh, how Felice had wanted there to be a tiny little brocante shop packed from top to bottom and back to front with bric-a-brac aplenty for her to root through on, well, not just *this* trip into the village, but on *every* trip, all in the fond hope of next time perhaps finding that one darling little random piece that she couldn't possibly live without and couldn't imagine how she had somehow managed it until now.

An antique-looking corkscrew, say, or a watch that

---

[37] 'Character' what was Felice looked for most in a shop, even more than actual goods.

[38] Though if you were ask Felice to define what she meant by 'character' in a shop, you would get nothing more helpful in response than, 'Oh, I don't know, a certain *je ne sais quoi...*' Trust me on this. I've tried. More than once.

didn't keep time anymore but had the sweetest, roundest face, with extravagantly oversized Roman numerals.

Or one shoe. One *very nice* shoe, not necessarily in her size.

Something of that sort. Was that too much to ask? One shoe? Apparently so.

But at least they *had* recovered the date, the crucial piece of information that Mr Redmayne had once again neglected to retrieve from his father (he was *about* to do that, or so he assured his wife later) (but in his defence, his father *had* been telling them all the most interesting story about his encounter with Charles Dickens in 1843, and the discussion that followed had grown rather intense) (but *important*). *And*—Mr Redmayne came to a halt—

—Oh yes, *what* date did you say it was again, dear?

July 16th, 2020. That was the date. A Thursday. If this information were relayed to her husband with something of a look of supreme self-satisfaction on Mrs Redmayne's behalf, it was not only due to the fact that her prediction of the month had proven quite correct but because she'd made it solely on the basis of her personal assessment of the current state of the orchard. She still had it, that instinct honed in childhood while growing up on a farm (not so different from this one) in les Pays de la Loire, and this despite the rather exotic cosmopolitan life she'd lived since. In truth, the idea of spending her twilight years, when they came, as they would, on a quiet out of the way farm such as this was really quite attractive to her, though Eric would likely be bored silly and she could never imagine him leaving the house (assuming he had a choice, that is).

Never mind. In addition, she was also rather pleased it was July as that meant that the early season apples would be ready for harvesting in only a few weeks' time and everybody's help would be required with that, or so she announced quite happily (but alas not even the prospect of harvesting their own French apples could bring any cheer to Felice, it seemed, and she continued to mope) (in classic mode) (*so* French).

An idea was forming in Emile's mind, as clearly as an apple ripening in time-lapse cinematography. It went from bud to flower to full fat mature fruit in a matter of seconds, right before everyone's eyes. A miracle of modern cognition.

"July? Wait, wait, that means school's good as *over*, doesn't it? For the summer, I mean? I couldn't go now even if I wanted to! It's the holidays!"

"Well, you know, by that reckoning, school's been out for me for at least a month, Shrimp," responded George, perhaps all too predictably (George never wasted *any* opportunity to remind his brother and sister how much longer the summer vacations lasted in American schools than in Europe). "As always, kiddo, I win that one."

"Possibly not," said his grandfather. "Surely, my boy, to the truly enquiring mind, school is *never* out? Yes? Don't you agree?"

"Well, yes, of course," said George, instantly convincing himself that he had actually always felt that to be true, deep-down.[39] [40] "That goes without saying. I was only, you know, like, joking right now. That's all. Honestly. That's the truth."

Emile was obviously left quite unmoved by any of this, however.

"I don't care," he declared. "*I'm* on holiday—and *that's* the truth! Hey, Felice, I can make things out of light,

---

[39] Very deep indeed.

[40] In fact, this seemingly casual exchange proved to be possibly the most influential in George's life, altering his attitude entirely from his point forwards towards, well, everything.

anything I like. I can. Want to come see? George can't do it. Not properly. Can you, George? No, he can't. I win *this* one, I reckon. *Ha!*"

"That's entirely enough gloating over your brother's failures for one day, Emile, thank you very much," said Mrs Redmayne.

But she needn't have intervened, as George didn't seem to be paying Emile any attention, in any case. All of a sudden he seemed rather moodily preoccupied by another matter.

He looked up, as if surprised to see everyone's eyes fixed on him.

"What? Hmm, no thanks, Emile. Sorry. There's something else I need to do. Maybe later. Okay?"

And with that he hurried off at once.

Watching him go, Emile shrugged for dramatic effect, a gesture intended to signal his total failure to comprehend—once again—an elder sibling's erratic behaviour. Like, teens, *huh*?

He turned to his sister. "What about it, Felice? What d'you say?"

In Felice's eyes her freshly extinguished interest in life could be seen rekindling itself Phoenix-like back into existence. She scrutinised her younger brother closely. Any untruth right now would not be tolerated. Exaggeration would be punished. This was clear.

"So, Emile, tell me. What exactly do you mean by, you know, 'make anything you like'? What, like, *anything*?"

"Anything, yup," he said, so chipper as to expel all doubt. "Exactly that. Absolutely. Anything at all—and *everything*. We were practicing in my room while you were out. George and Pops are both, well, really, really bad at it but I'm not. I'm really good. You just need to picture what it is you want, that's all, you know, in your mind—and then there it is. It's like magic."

"Really?" Felice took him by the arm, her interest in life now seemingly miraculously on the way to full restoration. "Show me, child. Lead the way, my fine, wee, comically Cockney fellow, and show me this minute! For I have much to make. Much indeed!"

Mr and Mrs Redmayne watched the pair depart and then exchanged identical glances involving a single raised eyebrow, a gesture intended to signal their continuing mutual failure to comprehend the behaviour of their beloved offspring.[41] [42]

"Ah, they make me laugh, the three of them," said Rufus. "I have missed much, I fear. Too much. But still I should go, although perhaps not straightaway. Not this time."

"Father has the beginnings of a theory, dear, about something else that might be interfering in the timeline," said Mr Redmayne. "Something other than ourselves, we mean. It's a bit vague at the moment, I know. But still very serious sounding."

"Quite," replied his wife, arching a lone eyebrow once more, this time for dramatic effect. "In which case I shall fetch us all another pot of tea and you can tell me all about it."

And while she was at it, she fetched three nice homemade scones, too, each on a little plate with a healthy dollop of thick fresh cream on the side.

Given the likely seriousness of the situation, she felt it was the least she could do.

"So, let me see if I am understanding correctly what you're

---

[41] Although only a mere raised eyebrow it spoke volumes of a generational gulf, a divide impossible to cross.

[42] Okay, *two* raised eyebrows—*in total*. No one likes a smarty-pants. No one..

saying," said Mrs Redmayne, warming her fingers for a brief moment on the hot fresh pot of tea,[43] as a prelude to pouring everyone another cup. "You believe, poss*ib*ly, on the basis of what you lately witnessed in 1843, yes, that an external agency of some kind, the nature of which is still to be determined but which is *not* the TDA, has been interfering in the timeline to your advantage, on more than one if not multiple occasions throughout your life? Is that more or less *it*? Do I have that right?"

"Yes," replied Rufus, a solemn expression on his aged, intricately lined face. "That is indeed my contention, what I now believe to be true."

Mrs Redmayne looked thoughtful. She withdrew her fingers from the teapot and sat back in her chair. Mr Redmayne took up the pot in her stead and poured his wife another cup.

Then, he silently offered the same to his father who, assenting with a single nod of the head, pushed forwards his empty cup. Mr Redmayne poured, sliding the cup carefully back across the table once it had been refilled. Rufus sipped, with his little finger extended in a most unexpectedly delicate manner.

"But *why*?" asked Mrs Redmayne, after a second or so. "What *agency*? And for *what* possible reason? Are you entirely sure, Rufus, that you are not extrapolating too much from an isolated and quite very likely random incident? Is that not far more probable than the intervention of some, I do not know, mysterious third party?"

"It *is* only a theory at this point, I admit. My dear Gloriana, being so sweet you might not have noticed but I

---

[43] *Darjeeling Paragon*, of course. Yes? Ah, good, you have been paying attention. Two points to your house.

105

have been an arrogant man almost all my days. I have for some great time now thought myself better than everyone else. Everyone. Smarter, more advanced. The inventor of time-travel. What others had merely theorised about, I actually *did*. I knew better than they all did, the academy, everyone; in my mind, I *was* better. Far better. In actual fact, my arrogance only played to my vanity; I now fear it may have blinded me to the truth. How many tight spots have I somehow miraculously escaped from over the years? Too many to number. And each time I had put it down to my innate superiority. They couldn't catch me because I was better than they were. The incompetent fools. That's what I thought. Ah, the sheer arrogance!"

He took a sip from his cup, before continuing. "But now, I can but wonder: what if *none of it* were down to me? What if it were indeed all the work of this unknown party? It's a sobering and indeed quite terrifying thought. The foresight. The power. Frankly, it boggles the mind. And also, as indeed *you* ask *me*, Gloriana, yes, there is the question as to what end? *Why*? Why intercede on my behalf? I don't know. But, if what I now believe to be true *is* true, then it would be absolutely critical to understand that, would it not? Perhaps, I fear, indeed, yes, critical even to the future of humanity, to the very *future* itself."

Mr Redmayne suffered an unfortunate mis-swallowing of his tea at this point, causing him to splutter and cough an unreasonable portion of it out on to the table before him.

His wife patted his back while he regained his breath—and composure.

"My apologies," said Rufus. "I did not intend to alarm. Perhaps it is nothing but an old man's paranoia? I hope so. And, in any case, as we are all agreed, it *is* only a theory at this point. Still, the more I think about it, the more right it *feels*. Let's call it a *hunch*, shall we? Nothing more than that. Not even a theory, not yet. A hunch, only."

"Frankly, that worries me even more," said Mr Redmayne, still breathing a little too heavily. "Father, you never were one to trust in mere hunches. Empirical or measurable evidence subjected to specific principles of reasoning, that is how you taught me to proceed, with everything. Now, it would seem, *now*, at this late stage, we're to start trusting in *hunches*."

"Ah, well, maybe I'm mellowing with age?" said the old man with a chuckle. "Perhaps it was being dead for twenty years? That ought to bring a little mellowing, I should think. Don't you? Or maybe it's the effect of the very splendid cream tea—so therefore nothing but a temporary feeling, as with old Mr Scrooge's undigested bit of beef? An imbibition likely to induce visions of phantoms. Who knows? Nonetheless, the alarm bells are ringing all throughout the house and I do have a hunch I'm right. But let us leave it there for now. I'm tired."

Mr Redmayne's father got up gingerly onto his feet. He looked towards the door.

"Now, what do you both suppose those grandchildren might be up to in their rooms, do you think? Shall I investigate that? Why not? You know, all in all, I believe I would rather like to put my feet up for a few days now and let the future take care of itself, just for a little while. Rest and recuperate for a time. Relax. By the way, my dear, thank you for the tea and the scone. They were quite delicious, as ever."

Turning, he headed slow-footed towards the door.

Mr Redmayne looked at once to his wife. "*Relax?*" he mouthed incredulously, waiting for his father to exit the room before adding in a low whisper: "*Relax?* He's never *relaxed* a second in his life. Not even after—"

Mr Redmayne stopped there, but his wife appeared to know what he had intended to say. She nodded.

"Well, Chéri, perhaps it is true? Maybe he has mellowed finally? Or maybe he has new priorities now? You probably find you have a lot of time to reassess your life when you are, as it were, dead. Even if one's death is a lie. Possibly in some regards the impact is the same?"

"Possibly," said Mr Redmayne, in a tone that suggested that he really didn't quite believe it. No. Not at all. Very much no.

* * *

Unlike her somewhat more literal-minded elder brother, Felice took to the seemingly magical-like feat of engineering objects out of light as readily as one of her favourite heroes, the great French sculptor, Camille Claudel, had taken to fashioning works of art of spirit and beauty from mere lifeless clay or stone or bronze.

Initially, despite her earlier enthusiasm, it was in a mood of some scepticism that Felice first witnessed Emile's demonstration of how he'd conjured the unusual menagerie of manga monsters that was now beginning to take over his entire room, until, after some stagey séance-like concentration on his behalf, his right palm flat against the wall, the moment came when, finally—*voilà!*—another of the hideous wee monsters popped into existence, right there next to her on the bed.

As if out of nowhere, out of nothing...there it was.

A pointless, ugly thing, that was true, but there it was. Nothing, nowhere, something.

The equation made no sense, but couldn't be denied. For there it was. Right there.

Felice picked it up. The *thing*. It *felt* real. There was no denying it.

Nothing, nowhere, something. *Here.*

Her mind, quite metaphorically, was *blown.*

The demonstration her father had given in the kitchen on the previous day, chaotic as it was, had just seemed like yet another freaky incident in their highly unusual lives, not something that her little brother could master, not like something that *she* could master and use every day in her life. Nothing, something. Nothing, *some*thing. So *many* potential somethings!

Her mind, quite literally, expanded.

There was no end to what she might make!

"Let me have go at that!" she exclaimed, leaping up from the bed. The newly created manga monster thing fell from her hands, landing slap-dab in the upturned TDA bowler hat, instantly forgotten.

Emile stepped aside and let his sister have the wall. Her enthusiasm was a tiny bit intimidating.[44]

"Well, okay," he said. "Sure. You just got to put your hand flat against the wall. Yeah, anywhere would do, but, you know, right where I'm standing is good, too. I'll move, then, shall I? Okay, good, that's it. The doodah, the panel thingy, appears, yeah, like that. Can you feel that? Yup, it's kind of tingly, isn't it? And then all you got to do is picture what you want to make, in your head, I mean. Picture it in your head. Strange, isn't it? Weird. It's almost like you can feel it *inside* your head. And after a second…"

Felice opened her eyes. Before them, on the bed, had appeared a single spoon.

A silver spoon, not very long, about three inches or so.

And to Emile, it looked pretty, well, *old*, not new at all. What was the point of making something *old*?

But Felice picked up the spoon and studied it in her hand, holding it as tenderly as she might a baby bird that had suffered the horrible misfortune to fall from its nest. Judging by her expression, it required care, attention, *nursing* if it were to stand any chance of survival.

Except it was a spoon, as Emile at once pointed out.

---

[44] 'Scary' was the word Emile later used when talking about this moment. Let's call it how it is.

"It's a spoon," he said, looking on. "Isn't it?"[45]

"A mustard spoon. Yes. And it's perfect. Very perfect."

"Looks a little off to me, to be honest. The head's too small for the body, don't you think? I think so. Yeah, I do. Here, have another go."

Felice's eyes flickered at her brother much as a snake's slithery tongue might flicker seconds before the creature launched a lightning—and potentially fatal, if entirely deserved—strike.

"It's *meant* to be like that, dimwit," she whispered incredulously, before gathering herself and adding in a more normal (i.e. totally condescending) sounding voice: "It's a *mustard* spoon. And, well, it looks so old because it's supposed to look that way. Vintage. See? And *I* did all that, Emile. With my *mind*. It's amazing."

"I don't know. The body bit, that looks a bit too stretchy to me, to tell you the truth, like it's all, you know, way too long for the tiny head-part on the end? The spoony bit. *What?* I'm *just* saying. That's *how* it *looks* to me, anyway. It *does*. Look at it yourself if you don't believe me!"

Moving on (emotionally at least), Emile retrieved his latest creation from where it had fallen and placed the bowler hat back on his head. Just then, Felice spotted that one of his existing menagerie, the monster resting closest to his pillow on the bed, was sporting the exact same style of hat.

"What's that one *there* meant to be, Shrimp? You?

---

[45] That he had felt it necessary to temper his initial statement with a question spoke volumes of the unbridgeable chasm in sensibility between the pair, much like the similar gulf between the generations that we noted earlier. It's a wonder any of them got along at all. Family, eh? And if this think this is bad, you should read Book 3. Man!

Though the head is a bit small for a monster your size, if you ask me. Hardly to scale at all. But what do I know? Hey, Emile, wait, you got a little something—"

Felice pointed her finger directly at—and so close it was practically touching—his chest.

Automatically, he glanced downwards, taking the bait. At once, she flicked her finger up fast, catching the brim of his hat and knocking it straight off. He leapt back.

"Felice, you're so annoying! I'll knock—"

Quite sensibly, Felice elected to retire from her brother's room at that moment, clutching the newly created vintage silver mustard spoon tightly in her hand.

The spoon she had fashioned from the void of nothingness, with her mind.

Out of light.

It would be the first of many things. Oh yes. It would indeed. Many.

Many!

For his part, George had lost interest in the practicalities of forming objects of light; that wasn't for him.[46] No, his interest lay in the mechanics of the process, the slowing down of protons and somehow reforming them into physical matter. Now, *that* was fascinating. If he could understand that, the *theory*, the *workings* of it, well, that would be like understanding the future. He would be ahead of the curve, ahead of everyone. A modern-day Babbage.

He couldn't believe he been so blind to this possibility. All of his life he'd lived surrounded by future technology and yet he had no idea of how any of it worked. What was

---

[46] Typically, George at once lost interest in any activity at which he was demonstrably rubbish. Fact.

he thinking!

That ended now. He had access both to the technology of the future—*and* to one of its inventors. It would be a criminal waste of an opportunity entirely unique in all of history not to make the most of it. And so, he would...

Towards a Practical Quantum Mechanics of Spatial and Temporal Displacement

By RRR

His grandfather's book. George was reading it again on his bed in his room, the rather battered and consequently very old-looking volume from 2766 that he had purloined from the Library back in the house, the volume that had revealed to him the operational practicalities of the time mechanism, the surface mechanics, but he had stopped there. The theory section had been too daunting to approach, the pages upon pages of math far, far too complicated for him to understand, so he'd thought at the time, especially when he had all of time, of lived history, right there, outside the door, to distract him. And who needed to understand the theory, if you could far more easily enjoy the thing itself? But, to the truly enquiring mind...

Even so, George felt more than a little as though he were doing something he shouldn't. The book, his reading of the book, without permission, had gotten them all into a lot of trouble not that long ago—and, in fact, they were living with the consequences of that right now, were they not? All of them. Actions have consequences, after all.

So, knowing this, why had he still smuggled it into his case when they were leaving the house? They could only bring a few things each with them. Why had he picked this? Why hadn't he told anyone? At some level he knew. Knowledge. The book was knowledge. Rare knowledge. And George wanted it for himself. Even back then, he couldn't just give that up. That possibility. Knowledge made you special. Better. Better than you were. Better than everyone who didn't have it.

Better, period.

A syncopated jazz beat played in his headphones, courtesy of the single 'luxury' personal item that George had brought with him from New York,[47] his treasured portable *Magnavox* record player. Curiously, the relentless cross-beat helped him concentrate, especially when reading math. Something in the rhythm, the multiple conflicting rhythms, struck him as mathematical in itself, akin to the effect you might achieve by dividing up the bar by bigger and bigger prime numbers and playing those beats against each other. That's how he saw it.

All the same, however counterintuitive it might seem, the rapid metrical dissonance in his ears helped him focus on the pages of complicated non-linear equations before his eyes, so much so that George quite failed to notice that he was no longer alone in his room, that the tall figure of his grandfather was now standing at the foot of his bed, peering down at him.

George leapt up, as though startled to within an inch of his life. Flustered, he lost the headphones at once. The

---

[47] Although the house on 'Everywhere Street' was not technically in any *one* place, George always associated it with New York City, where he had daily gone to school after walking out of the front door. Felice, on the other hand, always thought of the house as being in Paris, for similar reasons. Emile didn't really think about it because, as he would say if asked, *Coz reasons, innit?* And then he'd add to please stop bothering him with daft questions. In short, *Like, whatever...*

ancient book from the future tumbled to the floor.

"Steady, my boy, steady, there," said the old man. "Apologies. I hadn't meant to give you such a turn. I did knock. More than once."

"I didn't hear you." By way of a flustered unnecessary explanation George nodded towards the still revolving turntable, which he then carefully brought to a stop and removed the arm from the disc. Black disc, yellow label, very obviously, to any enthusiast, a *Prestige* record, which Rufus eyed with a sideways glance.

"Ah, you've inherited your father's passion for those very same mid-twentieth century jazz *stylings* that he loves so much, I see," he said. "That's one there from his collection, I presume? Oh, I remember how he was *always* up on West 50th Street in his younger years. In *all sorts of years*, if you understand me. Couldn't keep him away, in fact, not in any era."

Surreptitiously, George attempted to nudge the illicit fallen volume a little further under his bed with his foot— without success. His grandfather, of course, had noticed.

"Sorry, what? *This*?" said George, innocently. "No, no, the record's mine. What was that about Pops? You were saying?"

"Well, only that he must surely have had the entire Prestige catalogue in the house at one point, I'm certain of that. Prestige, yes, for one, Blue Note, Aladdin, Circle, Imperial, Pacific Jazz, Liberty and no doubt many, many others. And not to mention those two perpetual interlopers— always *somewhere or other* in the house, too, the pair of them. Davis and Coltrane. Couldn't keep *them* away, either. In truth, between you and me, I rather suspect they were both very enamoured of your mother."

"What's that now?"

"Well, it wouldn't have been your father's feeble efforts on that darned flumpet of his that brought them around so very often, I shouldn't think. Do you? Hardly. Oh, they tolerated his playing, I'm sure, but did they *ever* let him record with them? No, they did not. Not once. No matter how much he begged. Draw your own conclusions, my dear boy."

"Wait! What are you saying? That the Prince of Darkness *and* Trane regularly played in the house—*our* house? And Dad—*my* Dad, *Pops*—used to *sit in* with them? On his *flumpet*? What? *No!* Get the hell out of here! No way! Tell me this is *so* not true!"

"I only wish I could. But it was, is, [48] like I say. Exactly so."

George's contorted face reflected his inner struggle to comprehend these strange new facts, as if he had somehow stepped into a bizarre alternate universe in which the natural laws not only accommodated incomprehensible and confounding phenomenon but actively encouraged it to flourish—a timeline so weird that he himself might be a completely different person in it, one whose father wasn't the most unhip person in the entire universe.

Time-travel and entire houses and cities constructed only from light George could readily accept. But the idea of his dad hanging—and *jamming*—with the greatest and coolest musicians in history was a concept too far. It did not compute with anything that he had known and experienced to date. It was, quite literally and metaphorically, far out.

Far too far. Out. *Way* out.

George's struggle continued. "But Pops is just so, I don't know, *old* and, well, dweebish... How

---

[48] 'Was / is' – on occasion Rufus had difficulty recognising the validity of the past tense. Well, you would, really, I suppose, if you were used to travelling more or less at will to any particular moment in history. You would. Take it from me.

could…this…be…?"

"Hard as it might be to accept, my lad, but perhaps he wasn't always quite so old? As for the other thing, that might be just a matter of youthful perception, might it not? Your father had a lot of interests in his youth that you might not imagine; he was up to all sorts, all the time. As you grow older, though, and you begin to feel time contract around you, your interests narrow to what's truly important, family usually. That's how it is for most people, anyway. But perhaps not myself, I admit. Being a renowned genius doesn't prevent me from also being a tremendous fool. I had to 'die' for twenty years just to realise what I was missing out on. But your father has always known what's really important, that's his genius. I could only hope to be so smart—and still do."

George blinked, once, twice, as though adjusting to the brighter light of this strange new world and its curious wonders. It would still take a good bit longer yet before he could see things properly, however, as his grandfather was indeed aware.

"You know, George, you rather remind me of him when he was your age. A good deal, in fact. And not just in terms of any physical resemblance[49] or your taste in music or anything superficial like that. No, I recognise the same intellectual hunger that your father had as a teenager. He was tremendously precocious, as are both you and Felice. But his interests were more like yours—not least, shall we say, in his choice of reading matter." An interrogative lone eyebrow was arched at this point.[50] "Unless I am very

---

[49] Although, it must be said, he had his mother's eyes. This won't be restated endlessly. Or ever again. Count on that.

[50] Yes, the arching of the single eyebrow is an established Redmayne family trait, most likely genetic. (And therefore *nothing* to do with

much mistaken, isn't that my academy dissertation that you're making something of a rather futile effort to conceal with your foot, there? I may be wrong, of course. There'll always be a first time for that, possibly."

George blushed. "No, sorry, Grandfather, you're not wrong. No. I found it in the house, in the Library, before everything that happened. I haven't told anyone that I brought it here with me, too, because, well, you know why, I reckon."

Momentarily sheepish, he bent down and retrieved the book. His grandfather took it from him and sat down at the foot of the bed. After a second, George joined him.

Rufus thumbed slowly through the pages. He seemed to welcome the feel of the old volume in his hands. Possibly it gratified him much in the same way as might a chance encounter with an old friend.

"So long ago, I don't know. It feels like several lifetimes have passed since I last laid eyes on a copy of this. Quite impossible to comprehend the passing of the years like that. Of course, I always knew your father had obtained a copy—and that he would keep it in the Library after I was gone, as it were. Indeed, I was *counting* on that fact. But, like yourself, he concealed his reading of it while I was alive. No doubt he had his reasons, which I admit I didn't much care about at the time. But, so you see, you, me, him, Felice, and no doubt Emile, too, we're birds of a feather, do you see? All of us Redmaynes, in fact. Because have all the world *and* time before us in a way that nobody else does. Once we get out of here, of course, which we will at some point. I know it. We *must*."

"I really hope so. I mean, it's very interesting here and all, seeing how everything works and stuff. Don't get me

---

any lack of variation in the depiction of gestures in my writing.)

wrong. That's one of the reasons why I was reading the book again. I was hoping there'd be something in that about how *this* house worked, the whole conversion of light into solid objects side of things. There must be some kind of supercomputer involved in it, I'm guessing? Some quantum intelligence engine or some such thing behind it all? Yes? I'm only theorising, of course. The whole field of AI really interests me but, as you know, in my time it's barely only now getting started. All of *this*, though, *wow!*"

Rufus smiled at George, with more than a hint of pride. "You're on the right track, my lad. The right track, indeed. Yes, such a volume exists, but it isn't the one you already have here in your possession. The Library back at the real house holds a copy, of course, though I should be able to retrieve another for you from my lodgings. Less risky all around. I'll do that."

"Lodgings?"

"Yes, I have a room in an old inn, a very old inn. In a very old town, I won't say where exactly. But in England. The room travels with me, in a sense, whenever it is I go, in time, that is. Actually, in point of fact I've been renting it now continuously since the fourteenth century and so my odd comings and goings do attract a little suspicion every now and then, I admit! The mysterious lodger! I do pay a very generous rate, however—very generous indeed, in fact, extravagantly so; and in consequence no one really cares too much. Money solves so many problems! You'll find this is true. Sadly."

"So, what you're saying is that you've rented the same room in an inn someplace or other in England for, like, seven hundred years? That's unreal!"

"Well, it's really a very nice room. Yes, very convenient, I must say. And, of course, I've adapted it with some of the same technology we're using here, now, except it's period specific. Everybody who enters sees what they expect to see. Makes everything less difficult. By far. But it's only programming, as you might imagine. An intelligent algorithm. We can learn about those next time I return."

Judging by the pained expression on his grandfather's face George sensed that this next trip was giving the old man some minor cause for concern; either that or George was only projecting his own anxieties. Maybe the—by this point—rather tatty X-shaped sticking plaster on the old man's forehead lent him an air of vulnerability.

But whatever the reason, George experienced a distinct sense of foreboding, which he believed that his elderly grandfather shared—an unusual intuition for him, given his teenage boy's normally narrow range of preoccupations and concerns.

Several questions formed in his mind all at the same time, however.

He turned back to his grandfather. "It must be worse than ever out there right now. Aren't you worried about the TDA, you know, that they might ever track you down sometime? In your lodgings, I mean, there at the inn? If you, well, like, always stay in the one place, doesn't that sort of make it easier for them to find you?"

"The TDA? No. I almost never worry about them, which is possibly the failing that has brought us to where we are. But, no. I take precautions. The room at the inn is secure. Very secure, as might be gauged from the fact that its defences haven't been breached at all in over seven hundred years. No, I have few concerns on that score. You see, George, I rotate the room more or less permanently on a cycle through time—and the cycle is always changing, which makes it all but impossible to track. Though there is one fixed way in and out, a failsafe, but you would need to know about it to ever find it. Hidden in plain view—in a sense, famously so, in fact."

The old man smiled to himself. George was thinking.

"So, the room, it exists in its own special bubble in time? You know, like the house does at the moment, but always in the same place?"

"Exactly, yes. Of course, the house keeps that one fixed entrance open still, the new entrance though the caves. So that one day we can all return to Everywhere Street. That's always been my intention. As I say, we must, one day, yes."

"Oh yes," said George, "through the caves. Yes, I'd forgotten all about that! We should map that out. It was pretty dark and complicated down there. I don't think any of us would find our way back. I really doubt it. Not even dad."

"Well, *he* might. But, yes, you're right. I do need to show you the route again before I go. Not for the first time, I see I've been remiss. How about we try that tomorrow? You know, I think I might have a gadget somewhere here that could help. Then, at least *you'll* always be able to find the way back home, my lad, in case of some extreme emergency or other. Best to be prepared."

"Like a boy scout," said George, smiling.

But behind George's smile, somewhere in the distant recesses of his mind, barely registered, the phrase *extreme emergency* was sounding over and over, as if a silent alarm had been triggered remotely but was yet to be noticed by anyone back at HQ.

Still, the red lights were flashing.

* * *

By the time the Redmayne family had eaten lunch on the following day the arrangements for the trip into the caves had been agreed by everyone present. A little later that afternoon, following a respectable period of digestion, Mr Redmayne and George would accompany Rufus to the distant green hills and together the three of them would enter the myriad, winding, unlit, damp, narrow passageways that seemingly ran in all directions under and through those highly porous and soft chalk hills, all of this with a view to plotting and memorising the complicated route back to the thick wooden door to the house.

When the proposal was first mooted Mrs Redmayne had declared at once that she had absolutely no intention of going spelunking on a Sunday, *any* Sunday, *ever*; and Emile was put off by the simple fact of the long walk that it would take *just to get there*—let alone the walk through the tunnels after that.

And *then*, good grief, the long walk back!

No, thank you very much. That wasn't his idea of something to do on a Sunday. Nope. Nope-indeedy. No.

Happily, Rufus had managed to locate a hand-held device of his own devising (so he claimed) in a trunk in one of the barns, where he first had stashed it long ago at some point in the future.[51] [52] To Mr Redmayne, however, it appeared suspiciously similar to the devices that he himself had developed several years previously for the purpose of tracking temporally displaced objects or people, the Quantum Displacement Monitor ('QDM') as he liked to call it, and he spent the next few minutes distractedly trying to remember whether one of them hadn't gone missing at some point. Or been taken.

Nothing would surprise him about his father.

Still, George appeared gratifyingly intrigued both by the concept and its execution in equal measure; and so, next to that quietly spectacular triumph, the matter of taking credit for it struck Mr Redmayne as both small and petty,

---

[51] Commendably, nobody around the table thought twice about the illogical nature of statements such as this anymore.

[52] Okay, if we *must*: Rufus had originally concealed the device in the trunk at some unspecified point in the future, long afterwards returning and bringing the trunk—with the device still inside—back with him into the past. Happy, now?

emotions that he had long since resolved to leave to others of a decidedly more egotistical bent, where at all possible, of course. Such as now.

Mr Redmayne was, at all times, he believed, a singularly modest man, even in his efforts at superiority. No one was more modest than him, or so he'd liked to boast (and then laugh).

"So, this device," George was saying, "tracks *tachyons*, that's what you're saying?"

His grandfather nodded. "And therefore by extension anything, object or person, that has come into contact with tachyons."

"By virtue of being displaced in time," added Mr Redmayne, "though faster than light travel enabled by the artificial curvature of spacetime."

"*Or* through association with an active tachyon field, of course," added his father.

"Well, yes," conceded Mr Redmayne, "that goes without saying."

"I thought it worth saying... And, of course, assuming you've managed to stabilize the local excitations."

"Well, obviously, yes. Without that, the field collapses into subluminal speeds."

"With the end result that decay is inevitable."

"Naturally."

"Quite."

"You know, I like to call it the Quantum Displacement Monitor or 'QDM', for short."

"Do you, now?"

"Yes, I do."

Emile rose from the table at this point and performed an extravagantly exaggerated yawn.

His mother nodded her assent to his unspoken question and he quietly left the room, largely unnoticed. She, too, rose. No one else present seemed to notice.

"But, the point *is*, surely," said George, "that in the

caves we can use this device, the, er, QDM or whatever,[53] to find the door back into the house, because the door is originally from another time? It'll find it for us and we can go home. That's right, isn't it? One day, go home, I mean. Not right now."

"Indeed. Assuming your father hasn't already lost the key I gave him. The *only* key."

"Yes, that's right, I'm sure," said Mr Redmayne, "the *only* key. I believe that."

Mrs Redmayne looked from one to the other, son to father, like to like, and then was struck by another thought entirely.

"Where's *Felice*?" she asked. "Has anyone seen her?"

"Didn't she just leave?" said George.

"No, Chéri, that was Emile. But Felice was not here to begin with, I don't think."

"What? Are you *sure*, dear?" asked Mr Redmayne, growing visibly pink-cheeked. "I could have *sworn*..."

Mr Redmayne at once realised his wife was right (as usual).

The four Redmaynes looked at each other with blank, staring faces.

In the short discussion that followed it became clear that no one around the table had set eyes on Felice since she had left the kitchen on the previous day with Emile. A brief if truly tempestuous storm of concern and guilt at once ensued for all. Squally, very. Localised heavy weather. With a chance of rain imminently.

As one, they hurried to check on her. She wasn't hard to find.

When the anxious Redmayne search-posse reached

---

[53] Mr Redmayne positively beamed at this point, on the inside at least. Yes, it's possible for a father to do that.

Felice's room they found the door ajar. Mrs Redmayne knocked, but gaining no response, pushed lightly on the door.

It swung open.

In truth, it would be fair to say that the sight that greeted their eyes would have been unexpected by all but the most perspicacious of parents.

To be even fairer, it would probably also be true to say that no one's unsuspecting eyes had beheld such a scene since the sacking of Marie-Antoinette's palace at Versailles (so *many* shoes). Such ostentatious shows of opulence can, on occasion, to those accustomed by necessity, or temperament, to an altogether somewhat, shall we say, plainer lifestyle, cause a certain befuddlement, or indeed rank confusion, that someone, anyone, could have, or need, *so much stuff*, so much finery, when they themselves got by—scraped by, actually—in comparison, on next to nothing, or in point of fact, on nothing itself.

For there, lay Felice, prone, on her bed, as if stranded on an island amid a glittering sea of *things*—a lone castaway cut off by a great, high tide of trinkets, bric-a-brac, knickknacks, gewgaws, baubles and gimcracks of every description, a veritable tsunami of random 'precious' objects that threatened to swamp the room entirely and claim Felice for its own.

All four viewers were stunned. There was simply too much to take in.

Mr and Mrs Redmayne looked at each other but neither had any words.

Presently George bent down and picked out of the countless multitude a single item, which he held up to show the others. It appeared to be, possibly, or possibly not, the base of a table lamp, of some kind? Perhaps? George wasn't sure.

Judging by their reactions, neither was anybody else.

The short metal stand was heavy for its size and had a blackened, industrial look to it.

Mr Redmayne ventured a guess. Tentatively.

"Is it a *lab* burner? Do you think? I rather think it might be. For gas…"

"Ah," said the other three in a collective sigh of recognition.

Of course, this didn't address the real mystery of why such a thing could now be found in Felice's room.

After a second, Felice spoke on this very matter.

Please note that at no point did she raise her face from the bedspread, however, presumably lacking either the strength or the will to look up. Or both.

"We have *those* at school, in le laboratoire de chimie," she said, her voice sounding muffled and strange. "Those *exact same* lab burners. Identical! Or at least we used to, I don't know anymore. Maybe we still do? See, I was thinking about what to make next and I remembered those. And then I missed them *so much* and I wanted one, and so I made it. Lovely lab burner! I can make anything I can think of. Anything! With my *mind*. I can make you one. Would you like one?"

"No, thank you, dear," said Mrs Redmayne, in a not unkind way, after a moment. "That *you* have one is probably sufficient. For all of us, I mean."

"Would you like something else? Only, could *you* think of something? I can't think of anything else to make. And I can make anything. *Every*thing! Except I'm out of ideas. What would you like me to make you? Name it and its yours."

Not that he would ever care to admit to it, but Mr Redmayne's mind did stray—just for the briefest second or so—to thoughts of the old Parker Knoll classic Oberon chair that he had in his study at home.

Lovely chair!

"No, thank you, dear. We're all fine," said Mrs Redmayne. "Really, we are. We're just a little concerned about *you*. By any chance, might you have been up all night making things with your mind? Possibly?"

While waiting for a response[54], George began to delve deeper into the seemingly unending Great Sargasso Sea of Things of His Sister's Devising.

Cutlery of all shapes and sizes abounded (why so *many* spoons?).

What else?

Several smooth stone eggs of various hues, something that resembled a brass cowbell (engraved *Genivee*), a cow broach (silver), a cat broach (gold), a large pewter soaring eagle belt buckle (*cool*) (well, you know, *-ish*), a necklace comprising three dangling pearl snowmen, a railroad lamp, a brass lizard, a cast iron Statue of Liberty, an Eiffel Tower in bronze, a miniature white Citroën car with the number '500' in a round red plaque on the hood, a quartz elephant, a porcelain dog and two bright golden giraffes (parent and young), a tiny wooden Big Ben carved into the end of a pencil, an owl in brass…

At this point George gave up, having barely scratched the surface.

He stood upright. These waters ran far, far too deep for him to contemplate.

"Felice, dear, did you hear what I said?"

"Yes, Maman, I nodded. Didn't you see? Like *this*.[55] And no, I haven't eaten anything, either.[56] And yes, *please*, I would rather like a nice cup of tea and a scone. With cream. That's what you *were* going to ask next, wasn't it?

---

[54] Which, to be fair, seemed like it might never come.

[55] Barely perceptibly, face down, Felice's head moved in an up and down motion that might indeed have been nodding.

[56] Followed by rather more vigorous shaking from side to side. No less pathetic to witness.

Thank you. That would be nice. The thing is, I can't get out. I'm unfortunately and most ironically trapped, see? By all my lovely things. So *many* lovely things. Oh, have you seen the little white polar bear yet? I made him for you, Maman, to go on your dresser at home. One day, I mean. Not right now. He's very sweet. Somewhere…"

Her hand waved in a desultory way in all directions.

Mrs Redmayne smiled in a supportive, motherly way. "That sounds very nice, dear. I know, my darling, how about we help you get out of here just now and then we'll find him later, together? What do you say?"

Another barely perceptible face-down nod of the head followed.

"Yes, please. I would like that very much. Indeed."

At that, Mr Redmayne and George began tentatively to clear a path through the debris field, to part the waters. To be frank, it was difficult to know where to put anything.

Felice's eyes peaked up above the cover of the duvet. "Careful, it's all very precious. Isn't it? *Is* it? I don't know anymore. I made *so* much. Everything I could think of. I couldn't stop. It was a God-like power. That's how it felt. Like God Herself."

George had in his hands at that moment some kind of odd, antique-looking balancing toy—a top-hatted acrobat perched on a back and forth tilting plinth. It struck him as an unusual thing for any half-decent deity to be wasting Their omnipotent powers on.

He put it to one side with a shrug.

Felice sat up on her bed. Her left, slightly reddened cheek bore the blotchy imprint of the chequered pattern of the duvet. She looked around almost as if with an air of surprise.

Ozymandias, surveying her mighty works.

In truth, she seemed more than just a teeny bit horror-struck by the sight of it all, a supposition confirmed by the fact of her then burying her face in her hands.

"I went *too* far," she said, tearfully. "Too *far*. I made *too much*. I couldn't stop until I'd made *everything*. All the precious things I'd ever wanted and could remember. And then, well, you know, *what do you, then...?*"

Tears came, the waters—rather, the storm—broke. George and Mr Redmayne sped up.

"Not to worry, dear. The rescue party is almost with you. Just hang on a bit longer."

Felice snorted, very dramatically, before regathering her wits for a moment.

A pathway to the door was all but cleared, excepting one or two minor treasures still scattered here and there. With an unexpected, doe-like sprightliness Felice sprang up from the bed and skipped down the path past her brother and father into her mother's arms, where the sobbing commenced in earnest. Storm force 12 on the Beaufort scale.[57]

Mrs Redmayne led her daughter away, to the healing balm of hot tea and warm scone. With cream. Tried and trusted.

An old Cornish recipe of Mrs Redmayne's own devising.[58]

"I think I understand *why*," Felice could be heard saying, barely, between sobs. "Why grandfather...I mean, I *know*, now, I think, *why...*"

But the rest of that sentiment—whatever it was—was lost as the pair turned the corner and passed out of sight.

Mr Redmayne looked from his father to his son, and then all three of them turned to survey the room of treasures. It took some surveying.

---

[57] Devastation.

[58] Yes, that means what it says.

"What on earth are we going to do with all of *this*?" said Mr Redmayne, in a tone that was both awestruck and perplexed.

"If I might?" said Rufus. "I've seen this before. In my time it's a less uncommon experience than you might imagine."

It was the work of but a moment to clear the room. The old man placed his palm flat against the wall and concentrated. Almost immediately, every trinket, knickknack, gewgaw, bauble and gimcrack[59] disappeared as if into thin air, which in a real sense was true.

The empty space now appeared very empty indeed—a great swathe of emptiness, in fact—especially in comparison to how extraordinarily full it had been only a few seconds earlier.

Mr Redmayne and George looked at each other in alarm.

Rufus sensed the cause of their disquiet. "Not to worry. Nothing has been lost. I've saved it all. Felice can call any of it back whenever she feels like. There's even a display mode. Objects, or groups of objects, can be recalled and displayed temporarily on a cycle, should she so desire, on a setting of her choice."

"Really? *Everything?*" said George. "Wow. That's impressive."

His grandfather seemed somewhat less taken with this facility, however.

"Perhaps, yes, in a way that *is* impressive, my lad. I suppose it is. Hmm… But, you know, the fact that the people of my time have proven that you actually can have everything *and* find somewhere to keep it all, well,

---

[59] Not to mention the assorted bric-a-brac. But, obviously, that too was gone. Obviously.

strangely, that remarkable feat doesn't seem to make them any happier. That's all I'm saying."

Rufus looked over the empty room. He made to leave, but paused. "We'd all do well to keep that in mind, I think. Don't you?"

He left. Mr Redmayne and George found themselves staring at the still surprisingly empty-looking space. *Horror vacui* writ large.

Both were nodding, however. Indeed.

CHAPTER 4

Mrs Redmayne and Felice continued their hushed conversation in the kitchen, with the latter huddled in a lovely, bright red blanket that Mr Redmayne, when looking in, couldn't recall ever seeing before. But then he remembered that they could, quite literally, conjure anything and indeed everything they wanted on command here in their Prison of Plenty,[60] their Alcatraz of Abundance,[61] which was how he was now coming to think of it.

----

[60] *They?* Well, at least one or two members of his family *could*, his good self excepted. And George, of course. While his wife didn't appear to be interested, but Mr Redmayne held not the slightest doubt that Gloriana would prove more than capable of whipping up anything she desired, if she put her mind to it.

[61] He had more of these alliterative allusions (alas), but we'll leave it there. You get the idea.

Any *material thing* they wanted, in any case.

Conjuring up their freedom and their old lives would be quite a different matter.

To that latter end, they all agreed that the trip out to the caves should go ahead as planned, despite the upset suffered by Felice. If they ever were to go home, obviously they would need to know the way. And besides, Felice was already in the best possible hands with her mother. Mr Redmayne's contributions under such circumstances often proved to be counterproductive, despite his good intentions and kind heart. As with many men, emotions made for a turbulent sea that he often found difficult to chart, especially as no hand-held device—quantum or otherwise—yet existed that might show him the way.

Alas, in this regard, as is the case for many, he was on his own.

George found the prospect of a trip out with his Grandfather from the Future to be of the utmost excitement. And with his father, too, of course, who also happened to be tagging along. Stepping out beyond the perimeter of the farm was an act of liberation in itself— and quite exhilarating, too, in the present esteemed company.[62] The distant chalk hills beckoned. It seemed almost impossible to accept that it had only been a matter of a few weeks since they had all come from there together. And beyond the hills, *inside* the hills, lay New York, Paris, London—the *world*, in fact.

And all of Time.

It quickened the step to think it.

And, for an elderly man, or indeed even for a man in the prime of youth, the legendary Rufus Redmayne, the inventor of time-travel (and as George saw it at this point,

---

[62] Again, *and* his father.

who knew what else?), set a mean walking pace with his rapid long-legged stride.

His grandson found himself hustling along to keep up.

"So, Grandfather, you don't think the TDA can have found this entrance? Otherwise they'd be here now, waiting for us?"

"How could they have found it? It's not like anybody has written the address down on a card and sent it to them as an invitation, is it? Not this time, anyway."

Mr Redmayne blushed. "Well, Father, I may have been more circumspect about the location of my time-travelling house if you'd ever bothered to tell me it topped the most-wanted list of History's very own police force. Along with the fact of your good self, of course, being Temporal Enemy No. 1, no less—*and* not to mention, the fact that I, apparently, also featured as a fugitive on that particular most-wanted list."

"Bah, fiddlesticks! No real harm done. But, George, my lad, yes, you're right. The TDA can't ever have discovered this location because they would probably have been here *before* we were, lying in wait. That's how they work. Predictable, really. I've dodged them on so many occasions."

"Perhaps they work off an algorithm?" suggested George, in what was intended as a joke.[63]

His grandfather, while appearing not to recognise the attempt at humour, nonetheless looked as if very struck by what George had just said. He seemed to be mulling it over.

"Really? You think they might be?" asked George.

"Possibly. If they operate to a set of protocols, then

---

[63] If a very geeky one. At no point in any possible future will George become a stand-up comedian.

very likely these would be AI governed, given the time period that they're from. Everything in the far future is AI governed. Everything."

"In which case, wouldn't they be smarter, the TDA? Less predictable?"

"You would think so. What I'm wondering is whether or not they've been hacked."

George performed a double-take. Who or what could hack the computers of the future? If the AI at the farmhouse was anything to go by, the operating systems must be incredibly advanced. What five or six hundred years of Moore's Law[64] would do to processing power didn't bear thinking about. Well, he'd witnessed some of the results for himself, hadn't he? But that these incredibly advanced computers might be vulnerable to hacking took him by surprise.

"What could do that?"

His grandfather shrugged. "Anything is possible, my lad. Rule nothing out. Absolutely nothing."

That didn't really help, George thought. Still, he elected not to point this out.

The green chalk hills were that bit closer now. If indeed anything were possible, he had somehow to be ready, as far as he or anyone could be under the circumstances.

For all that might be worth.

* * *

In the eyes of many, including his wife,[65] Mr Redmayne may have behaved like something of a silly if rather

---

[64] Look it up yourself. I'm busy here.

[65] *Especially* his wife.

adorable goose from time to time, but in point of fact he was also almost always the most meticulous of men. He paid very scrupulous attention to anything he considered truly important; and so, of course, he had been especially careful with the key to the thick oak door in the caves that led directly back into their old house on Everywhere Street, secreting it on the farm in a suitably safe and discreet location where, whenever required, he and his wife might readily retrieve it.[66]

Not that he believed for a moment that this was the *only* key to that particular door, despite his father's claims that this was indeed the truth of the matter. As Mr Redmayne knew far too well, his father believed himself above the truth, indeed much as had many of the great dictators throughout history. The truth was Old Rufus's plaything, or so it had often seemed, to be toyed with and dispensed howsoever he saw fit, the mouse to his cat.

And, as everybody knows, cats care little for what anyone else thinks, and least of all about the fate of the mouse.

With this complex and decidedly dodgy metaphor stalking his brain, Mr Redmayne pursued his father and son into the caves. The entrance, while taller than any of them, led into a tunnel of marginally lower height, but the ceiling appeared to descend sharply from a distance of approximately thirty metres in. Curiously, Mr Redmayne couldn't remember needing to stoop on the way out just a few days earlier. He supposed therefore that he had just been going with it at the time, relieved that he and his family had escaped the clutches of those terrible time-police fellows, the men who had wanted to 'repatriate' him

---

[66] i.e. Hanging on a hook on the back of the larder door, the *k*ey, that is, between the *j*alapenos and the *l*ima beans.

into the far future and by doing so separate him from his wife and children forever. Despicable. At least his father had saved them from that fate. Mr Redmayne would give him credit for that.

Even if he had created the problem to begin with!

"There used to be a gate," George said. "Here."

He was running his fingers along a lengthy rusty hinge on the white chalk wall beside the entrance. Another hinge of a similarly well-rusted disposition ran parallel to it further down.

"Indeed, there was, yes. Someone took it down," said the eldest Redmayne, before catching his son's eye. "Not me," he added.

Mr Redmayne shrugged as if to say that such a thought had never crossed his mind.[67]

His father went on: "At one point the caves were used by the local vintners to store wine; cool and dark, you see. But needless to say they suffered security issues and the practice was discontinued. Too many entrances and exits. Now, they're largely neglected. I don't expect we'll be disturbed. Not today."

George shone his flashlight into the gloom. "How far back do they go?"

"Far, very. Put it this way, my lad, you wouldn't want to take too many wrong turns. You'd be as old as me by the time we found you. And *so*, look, see, here, this is what we'll do."

The old man knelt down on one knee. He took something out of the pocket of his waistcoat. George couldn't make out what it was at first. Metal, he noticed. Brass. A watch.

---

[67] While simultaneously suggesting that if it had crossed his mind, well, no one could hardly blame him, could they?

"We need to bury this right here, in the entrance. See? This was your great-great-great-great-great-great-*great* grandfather's pocket watch, an antique, from the twenty-fourth century. That way we can—"

"—Find our *way back* to the entrance with the handheld device, the *QDM*, because it tracks objects displaced in time!" concluded George excitedly. "Yes, I do see! That way, we can't go wrong. But what if someone takes it? You know, comes along and digs it up. Next week, say?"

"Don't worry, George. No one does that until I do it myself, in the twenty-third century. It's here all that time. I don't leave such things to chance. I'm a Redmayne. Also, I had retrieved it from here myself so I could give it to great-grandfather Gregor as a present in the future, so that I could take it *from* him several decades later and bring it here now."

George's head spun, if only for a second or two, while he wrestled with the complex chain of causality presented by the fact of this watch from the future being here now so that it could be hidden in the ground and *then* at a much later date—in fact, some hundreds of years hence—be retrieved and stolen just so that it could be here now...

Then, with a shrug much like that of his father a few moments earlier, he gave it up.

Best if he just went with it. The watch would work as a sort of beacon, that was enough.

Mr Redmayne tutted a loud, echoey tut of disapproval, however, which his father elected to ignore, or perhaps merely regarded as no more significant than some meaningless ambient background noise and therefore of no importance whatsoever. Like elevator music. Or the chitter-chatter of everyone in the world who wasn't lucky enough to be him.

George decided to ignore it, too, seeing how easily it was done.

"This isn't where we exited the caves the other day, is it?" he said. "It looks different. The roof didn't descend so sharply, I'm sure of it. You know, I don't think it's the same place."

His grandfather smiled a broad smile. "Good lad, yes, you're right. It isn't. *That* particular point of access and egress lies east of here, about a good half-a-kilometre or so. Although it's true we're a little more distant from the farm out here, I picked this entrance today because the route through the tunnels to the door is more straightforward to follow and memorise. And also, I admit, partly because I wanted to see if you would notice and make the deduction that you just made. Not everybody would. But that's the natural scientist in you."

Mr Redmayne harrumphed at this, for some reason.

He couldn't imagine what his father thought he was trying to prove.

"Shall we move on?" he said, reaching into his pocket. "Look, here; it turns out I had this in my luggage after all. It's a handheld Quantum Displacement Monitor device of my own devising, remarkably similar to the one you produced earlier, Father. *My* QDM. I would rather imagine this is one of those instances of great minds thinking alike, wouldn't you? Either that or another example of something being borrowed from today for use in the future. Or perhaps not."

He switched it on and passed it to George, who began to examine it closely.

"Well, chaps, if we set off now," said Mr Redmayne, cheerfully, after a second, "I think we might be home in time for tea. So, George, lead the way."

Mr Redmayne's father harrumphed at this, for some reason.

Ignoring them both now as best he could, George stared down hard at the QDM device. The screen depicted a complex network of tunnels overlaid by a grid. He realised at once that the best person for this task would be

Felice. With her capacity to memorise things visually and, not to mention, *instantly*, this would be easy for her; whereas he was going to need to learn the entire route step by step. Straight ahead, left turn, left turn, right. Right, left, right. And then master the reverse coming back!

Still, for now at least he had the device to help him, whatever it was called.

"So, there are three blips together, that'll be us. I guess *I'm* displaced in time now, too. And so, then, one other blip close to us, which must be the watch. Right? Okay, and then two blips, also together, or just about, but quite far off. It'll take a while to reach them, I reckon."

"*Two* blips?" asked Mr Redmayne and his father at the same time.

"What?"

"Are you sure about that, my lad?"

Both men peered at the screen in George's hand. Two blips. He was right.

"Well, *one* of them is the door, of course," said Rufus, "but the other?"

"Perhaps one of us dropped something when we exited the other day?" said Mr Redmayne. "That's probably it."

"Yes, probably," agreed his father, with more than a hint of unease. "But we'll need to check. Lead the way, my lad. Lead the way. Let us see where this journey takes us."

Concentrating on the device George stepped ahead tentatively, remembering only at the last second that he would need to duck his head after only a matter of a few yards.

He ducked, just in time. "I think we have a couple of left turns coming up first," he said, "then a hard right. Everyone okay?"

He took the now echoey silence as an affirmative. His father and grandfather were immediately behind him. George shone his flashlight here and there, but mostly straight ahead. The cave tunnel was rough-walled, as far as he could make out, but the ground underfoot was flat. What might the mysterious second blip by the door possibly be, that's what he was thinking. A TDA trap? Or had one of them simply dropped something in tunnel a few days earlier? He guessed that did make the most sense. But he had to wonder.

So, the youngest Redmayne of the three present led on in silence. Together, they turned left, left and then right. Right, left, right. Even though it was dark all around no one stumbled. But should the flashlight fail, George speculated to himself, you really would be in trouble. In which case, it was no doubt best that didn't happen. They moved on.

After a short while, Mr Redmayne's voice echoed through the tunnels.

"Did you know, George, that in 1917 the British concealed twenty-five thousand troops from the Germans in caves such these? Right here in France. A whole underground world. Imagine that."

"Really?" said George, not quite being able to imagine it—or indeed anything else—just then. He was concentrating on the task in hand.

"Yes, in a far larger space, of course," continued Mr Redmayne, At Arras, actually. Miles and miles of interconnected caverns. They used them to launch a surprise attack on the German lines. Rather turned things their way. Helped end the First World War."

Mr Redmayne's father spoke up. "Yes, one of my better interventions, don't you think? Giving Haig the idea, I mean."

"Father, you can hardly take credit for the Allied victory in World War 1 and the end of the German, Russian, Ottoman and Austro-Hungarian empires."

"Why not? I'd seen how it turned out when the Allies didn't win and didn't much like it. And nor would've you, believe me."

Mr Redmayne's exasperation was all but tangible.

"You can't seriously be claiming to have interfered in the course of history to such a huge extent. It's unthinkable!"

"And there's the thanks I get. Typical. If I hadn't, we'd be having this conversation in German right now. Perhaps you would prefer to be living under a German autocracy? Nazis? No, I didn't think so. Listen, the day will come, my lad, when you'll happily choose to embrace your destiny as a Redmayne, when something so awful comes along that you can't live with it. That day will come, mark my words!"

The brow-beaten Mr Redmayne was about to respond when George held up his hand in the light.

He halted. "Stop. Did you hear that, you two? Listen... *That*!"

The three listened. Silence. And only that.

Mr Redmayne went to speak. But George held up his hand again.

After what felt like a long thirty seconds, he lowered it again. "Sorry, I thought I heard, I don't know, footsteps or something," he said, shining his flashlight all around. "Close-by, too. —I guess I was wrong."

"Not necessarily," said his grandfather. "Check the device. Ahead, are there still two objects marked?"

"Yes," said George, uncertainly. "But..."

He hesitated.

"What is it, George?"

"I think one of them has moved. Possibly. I can't tell for sure. Come on, it's not far now. Let's go and see."

The three of them moved on, quickly following the beam of George's flashlight. He was right: it didn't take much longer. A few more turns and they were at the door. It looked somehow different now than how he had remembered it. Secure, yes, but unremarkable. Ordinary. You would never have imagined that anything so special lay behind it. The door to all of Time.

"Well, there's *that*," said Mr Redmayne, indicating the door. "That's one of the two. But where's the other darned thing? Georgie, shine your torch on the floor so that we can look around properly."

George did as proposed. At the same time he kept an eye on the display on the QDM device. It didn't seem as though it should be far, the mystery item, whatever it was. Walking slowly, they had passed but a short way further along the dark tunnel when Mr Redmayne cried out:

"There! There! On the ground. Something flashed in the light. Didn't you see? Go back a bit. *There*, see!"

The beam of the flashlight had indeed picked out an object.

A key.

Mr Redmayne picked it up. He held it up for all three of them to look it. Momentarily, his father took it from him and examined it with great interest. A large, wrought iron key.

It was more than familiar.

"Show me yours, Eric," he said.

Mr Redmayne reached into his inside pocket and produced the key he had brought with him from the farmhouse.

The three Redmaynes examined the two keys side by side in the torchlight.

No doubt about it, even in the semi-darkness. None.

They were identical.

* * *

At the same moment as when her husband, son and father-in-law were making this unusual discovery in the dark of the caves, Mrs Redmayne was taking a turn around the orchard with Felice in the bright sunshine, the cream tea having revived the troubled girl sufficiently to allow for a short walk. Felice hadn't said very much so far—and neither, for that matter, had Mrs Redmayne. They had simply sat together in the kitchen drinking tea, the Redmayne family panacea for any difficult situation.

Nothing bonds like Brooke Bonds Tea, Mr Redmayne had once been wont to say.[68] [69] And even though he had long since switched his preferred brand, the principle remained. The healing balm of tea was an established fact in the Redmayne household, with little beyond its restorative powers. For Mrs Redmayne especially, this constituted not mere opinion but a truth universally accepted and tested throughout history, frequently by herself. No dire circumstance existed that could not be improved ever so little or large by a hot cup of tea. Fact.[70]

Also, the orchard was very pretty, which was something of a restorative in itself. The pair walked at a slow pace between the even rows of trees. The trees themselves appeared to be at the zenith of their powers, full of leaf and in bloom with what seemed to Felice as a superabundance of red apples—in truth, more than they could ever possibly pick, let alone eat. It struck her that there was an unwholesome degree of excess involved in whatever they did, the Redmaynes, of which her curious behaviour overnight was just another example. If you could have everything, what then was left? More of everything? Tons of everything? In which case, how long before you were sick of everything and wanted nothing? Still, for now, in the hot summer sun, she kept these thoughts to herself and simply walked. For now, walking with her lovely Maman through the pretty orchard in the warm sunshine was enough. For now...

---

[68] Overly wont, some would say. Anyone in earshot, in fact.

[69] Like his eldest son, Mr Redmayne will not be appearing in a stand-up venue anytime soon, or indeed ever.

[70] Try it. Go on. Thank me later.

"It *is* very pretty here," offered Felice, almost as though in its defence. "Very peaceful.

"Yes, that is true, Chérie," replied Mrs Redmayne, "if growing a little wild, don't you think? We should bring Genivee here into the orchard so that she could graze. That would help. Or perhaps we should acquire some sheep? That would be even better. About half-a-dozen would suffice, I should imagine."

"*Sheep*, Maman? Really? Are you sure? That sounds like a big commitment. We'd be, you know, *responsible* for them and everything. I mean, I'd be less than useless, and can you imagine Papa and George with sheep? It doesn't bear thinking about."

"Oh, I disagree. I think your father would make for a very good shepherd. He is very responsible. No one in the world is more so. You can always depend on him to do the right thing, or at least try his very best to do that, no matter what. George, I don't know about. Not yet. And as for you, well, sometimes making the commitment is all that is required for things to turn out fine. Very often, that is all it takes. You will see."

Mrs Redmayne halted under a tree. Reaching straight up, she plucked a bright red apple from a low hanging branch and rubbed it several times on the sleeve of her cardigan. Satisfied with its shininess, she passed it to her daughter. Felice took it from her.

"I will need all of your help soon, every single one of you," said Mrs Redmayne, moving on. "These apples, they are Delcorf apples, all of them. Early season. Already it is late-July. They must be picked, soon, or they will fall and rot. That would be very bad."

"But what will we do with them all, Maman? There's so many."

"Eat, naturally, Chérie. And store some, but of course. They are very sweet apples. Famously so. Think of all of the excellent desserts we will enjoy. Camembert and apple pie, for one. That is a favourite of your father's—

and his father's also, I believe. And many other treats, for definite. Your grandfather, he is so very clever. I'm certain it is no accident that we have this type of apple and arrive here at the perfect moment to enjoy them! *Non*, he leaves nothing to chance! I'm certain of it."

Felice looked thoughtful. She stopped and looked back towards the farmhouse. It looked so very…small. Compact. Despite the warm sun, she shivered.

"Maman, when you and Papa first met, did you know about the house and everything? Sorry, no, I don't suppose you *could* know, not at first. What I'm asking, I think, is, well, how soon did you find out about it all and how did you feel about it when you did? Did you see it, you know, as something good, a blessing? Or was it more like a curse? It must have been so strange."

"Your father *is* the blessing. I loved him long before I knew anything about his very mysterious and wonderful house that opens out its doors all over the world and in all times. He was unlike anyone else, so knowledgeable about everything, so clever, and so funny and adorable, too. So very honourable. He is the most honourable man who ever lived, your father. That is who he is. How could I not love him? And then his house. *Our* house. How could you not love that, too? We Redmaynes have opportunities unlike anybody else in all of history."

"Or at least we used to," said Felice. "You know, what I did last night, I think it was just, like, you know, *disappointment*. A lot's happened, it really has; but discovering yesterday that the village is such a, well, such a *nothing*, that's when it kind of hit me. You know?"

"What, Chérie? When what hit you, exactly?"

Felice stretched out her arms. "*This*! This, the farm, this is *all there is now*. Isn't it? Yes, we have so much, I know, but we're stuck now, trapped. Our old lives, they're gone. At the same time we can glut ourselves on whatever we want. That's a bit sickening, too. How can you stand it?"

"*Stand* it, Chérie? I don't stand it, no. I *like* it. I don't feel trapped here, no. I feel at home. Home is where my family is—that is all I need. Besides, as you know, I grew up on a farm just like this one, the unusual futuristic accoutrements aside, of course. In some ways I feel as though I *am* home again, but that is just me. I accept it. But for you, it may be different, I see that. You must find your own way, there is no doubt. Besides I do not think we will be here forever. No. Our old lives may yet be recovered. I believe that is true."

"You really think so?"

"If any family could achieve that, it is us. It may take time, I give you that. In the meantime, perhaps it is no so bad here. Is it? Vraiment?"

The pair looked down the slight slope towards the farmhouse together.

"No, I suppose not," said Felice. "Not really."

"Come. We must find the ladder. We will need that to begin the picking. Yes? But first, I think, more tea."

Felice nodded. She followed her mother towards the gate.

"Sheep, you say, Maman? Six of them? What will we call them?"

Mrs Redmayne waved her hand in the breeze, as though such a matter were none of her concern.

"Call them what you will, Chérie. A sheep is a sheep is a sheep. It is best not to get attached. You will learn this."

Felice bit her lip doubtfully. Some lessons she didn't want to learn. Not yet.

On leaving the orchard she deposited her bright red apple, still shiny and intact, on the fencepost besides the gate.

She left it there and trailed along after her mother.

"Do you really think we'll find our way back into the house someday, Maman? For real?"

"Of course, Chérie. For certain."

"I suppose if anyone can do it, it's Papa."

"Yes, if anyone can get us back inside, it is him. I am confident. Absolutely."

* * *

"We must try it in the lock," said Rufus. "If it fits, we face a bigger problem than we imagined."

"Are you sure?" said Mr Redmayne, glancing at George in the torchlight. "I'm not absolutely confident this is the right moment to be taking on the TDA, do you?"

"TDA? Who said anything about the TDA? This isn't their handiwork, I'm certain of it. No, this would be far too cunning for them to try. And as I say, there is only *one* key."

"Except there are *two*."

"So it would seem."

"Well, if this isn't a TDA plot to entice us back into the house and arrest us, then *what*?"

"That's why we need to go inside, Dad," said George, earnestly. "We need to investigate, find out what's going on. We can't just walk away. That's impossible."

Mr Redmayne realised that his son and his father were right. But he didn't like it.

"Well, okay. But I must go in first. I absolutely insist."

"Be our guest," said his father, offering him the mysterious new key. "After you."

With misgivings, Mr Redmayne put his own key back into his pocket and took custody of the new one offered by his father. It seemed to be a similar weight to the original. No discernible difference, in fact. Odd.

He approached the door. In truth, his thoughts were not with the TDA at that moment. The door to his house, to their old lives, was right *here*. Could he really just go back inside? He'd grown used to the idea that their old lives were over.

Mr Redmayne slotted the key into the lock. It fitted perfectly. So much for his father making only one! This was proof—of something—he didn't know what exactly, but *something*. Something underhand that had backfired, somehow or other. That's what he thought. They would get to the bottom of it later.

Mr Redmayne turned the key in the lock. Or tried to. It wouldn't turn. Was it the wrong key after all? He tried again.

No luck. This continued for some minutes, almost, or so it felt to all concerned, as if forever.

"Eric, my boy, what *are* you doing?" asked his father impatiently, after a time. "Can it really be so hard to open a door? Perhaps it's the key. Let me try."

"The key *fits*, Father, quite perfectly, in fact, but it won't turn, either way. For some reason, I simply can't unlock the darned door with it. Look, *see*. It's jammed."

Mr Redmayne's father pushed himself forward. "Here, let me try."

In the confined, narrow space the three of them shuffled around, or at least attempted to shuffle around, forcing an off-balance Mr Redmayne hard into the door, which creaked open—quite portentously—as a result.

They looked at each other in surprise. The door was already unlocked. That's why Mr Redmayne couldn't turn the key. It didn't need turning.

Mr Redmayne gawped extravagantly, his mouth a great wide round 'O' of astonishment.

Then, he fizzed, if only for a moment. "How is this possible?" he whispered. "What does it mean?"

"We shall see," said his father. "Once again, my son, if you will, once you're done gaping, after you."

Mr Redmayne glanced from his father to his son. There was, he realised very well indeed, no option but to proceed. With this, he found his resolve.

"Be careful, Pops," called George from the rear. "I've

got your six."

"What?" said Mr Redmayne, pausing on the threshold. "You have my *six what?* Oh, never mind. This is not the time. I'm going in. Watch my back, will you?"

He pushed on through the door, with Rufus and then George following close behind, and at once all three found themselves back in the Redmayne's basement kitchen— with everything seemingly just as they had left it and so very familiar. The cosy kitchen. Yes.

They were home.

"That's some rabbit hole," said George. "It really is."

Now it was Mr Redmayne's turn to hold up his hand and suggest they should be silent, and listening. He concentrated, leading by example. George and his grandfather waited.

Nothing.

"Anything?" whispered George.

Mr Redmayne shook his head. Impatient to proceed (as usual), Rufus strode deeper into what felt like the far too quiet kitchen, examining the scene as he went. Nothing appeared to strike him as alarming. He continued out into the short stairwell that led up to the main hallway of the house, pausing by the side-door, which, under normal circumstances, opened onto a quiet Parisian back-street.

"Father!" called Mr Redmayne in a voice that was both loud and quiet at the same time, like something of a stage whisper. "Wait! What are you doing?"

"This door," said his father, "it's no longer sealed."

"What? You mean it's no longer under the TDA's control? How can that be?"

"And the house, it's not caught in the time-loop that I'd set it in, either. At least not at this door, anyway. Not anymore. We must check the others."

"I don't understand," said Mr Redmayne. "George, stop, wait… Where are you going?"

George halted in mid-stride. "I'm going to check the

front. We might be able to see New York again. This might be over."

His grandfather shook his head. "This isn't over. And whatever you do, my lad, *don't* go outside. The TDA might actually be cleverer than I ever imagined. Hard to believe."

George nodded, and was gone.

"Father, what do you imagine might be going on? This is all very strange, isn't it?"

"For once, Eric, dear boy, I must admit, I have absolutely no idea what's going on. None."

Mr Redmayne's sense of concern at once deepened. "I'll check the rear exit. Could you *please* keep an eye on George? Gloriana would never forgive either of us if anything happened to him, I assure you. *That* would be *that*."

He made a cut-throat sign across his own neck, emphasising the fatal dimension to this with something of an impressive grimace.

Rufus frowned in response. It wasn't in his nature to babysit anybody. Experiences were formative in his view; you couldn't mollycoddle anyone through them. Ultimately it would only prove counterproductive. Therefore, he immediately decided to ignore this request on the grounds that it was, in his view:[71]

(a) wrongheaded;
(b) weak-minded; and
(c) not in the least what he wanted to do.[72]

---

[71] Which, of course, was the only view that mattered.

[72] Nb. Points (a) – (c) not necessarily listed in order of relative strength of contribution to his decision.

Instead, after watching his son depart, Rufus at once headed up towards the house Library; or, to be more precise, to the secret room within the Library, where the spatial and temporal controls for the house were concealed.

If there were any possibility of getting to the bottom of this mystery, it would be there. Yes. Indeed. He pressed on.

By this time, quite unaware of his father's decision, Mr Redmayne was already well on the way to the back-door. To his mind, the house felt familiar yet strange, as though he had been away longer than three days. And then, he realised, in a sense, he had. Or at least the house had been empty longer than three days, seeing as how, from *its* perspective, assuming it could have such a thing, they had been away for more than six weeks or so.

Or *had* they? Perhaps not. Because the house had been the means through which they had accelerated ahead in time, its duration, the volume of time passed since he was last there, was therefore the same as his own.

Perhaps it was only from the perspective of someone outside the house, someone proceeding in normal time, that they had been gone so for long? That was it.

Anyway, thinking along these lines didn't make the house feel any less strange; in fact, if anything, it accentuated the strangeness—and so he resolved to stop. In any case, he had far more pressing matters to worry about, such as the strange new key and the oddity of the side-door now being unsealed. That was more than enough to being going on with.

He passed the Library and the Music Room, his wife's Study, the Game Room and the Dining Room, thinking as he went by that each of these rooms would need to be checked for possible TDA interlopers (although what the three of them would actually do if they found any, he had not the least idea), and then continuing on at speed past the Great Dining Room (would they celebrating Christmas in there this year, he wondered?—again, no idea), the Drawing Room, the Scullery, the Middle-Parlour, the Pre-penultimate Back-Parlour, the Penultimate Back-Parlour, the Back-Parlour itself, before, finally, more than a little out of breath, Mr Redmayne arrived at the back-door. He examined it thoroughly.

The door appeared to be sealed still, as far as he could tell. That was his expert conclusion. Whatever strange thing the TDA had done to secure it was still holding. It was almost as if it had been coated in aspic, of all things, a dish that Mr Redmayne had never cared for in the least, although his father was quite partial if he remembered rightly.[73] [74] [75]

A cobweb caught his eye and held it for a moment, above the door. He's never seen a cobweb anywhere in the house before at any time, and the existence of one now added to the oddity of the situation and the sense of uncertainty and uneasiness he was feeling.

Everything was, perhaps, not as it seemed. Possibly.

Moving on, Mr Redmayne went over to a rear window and peered outside. He couldn't see a thing because there was nothing to see. The house was still looping through time, at least it was on *this* part of the tri-dimensional temporality matrix, which only made it even more strange

---

[73] George might pick at it in a half-hearted sort of way, he supposed, but Felice, almost certainly, would rather eat dirt.

[74] Emile would eat anything, dirt or aspic, with equal relish, so long as he didn't believe it to be French and it filled him up. Funny boy.

[75] Still, none of this was the point or of the least importance. And, of course, it wasn't aspic at all but some kind of futuristic sealant.

that the side-door should be unsealed and stationary. He had to report this back.

And he had to find out about the front entrance, too. Torn between hurrying to the front of the house as quickly as he could or taking his time and searching every room off the hallway thoroughly for interlopers, Mr Redmayne compromised by rushing up to each door in turn, throwing it open and glancing inside before closing it again very quietly and moving on. After all, he told himself, he had the element of surprise on his side, hadn't he? Or so he supposed. If he were stealthy enough he could take them quite unawares, whoever *they* were, these interlopers, (assuming anyone was there at all, the TDA or whoever). But, to be honest, he didn't really expect to find anybody in any of the rooms and still had no plan of action on the improbable off-chance that he might.

Hence, his astonishment when he actually did.

When he reached the Music Room Mr Redmayne flung open the door in his now customary manner—and almost jumped out of his skin to find someone standing inside.

"Great Galileo's Ghost!" he cried out. "George! What are you doing in here?"

"Nothing," said George in a tone that, despite himself, suggested he might in fact be up to the very opposite of nothing—an oddly self-conscious tone that his father couldn't help but notice.

Mr Redmayne scrutinised his son's face. Something was off.

"Really, my boy? Well, okay. Look, sorry about just now, you took me by surprise. The thing is, I wasn't expecting to see you there. That's all. I practically jumped into the middle of next week! Why *are* you in here? That's what I meant. Is the front door secured?"

"The front door's fine, Dad. No change, I mean... You know, still sealed and looping, yup, just like when we left."

"Have you told your grandfather? What did he say?"

"Er, grandfather. Nope, I haven't seen him. I checked the door and then I came in here. Isn't he with you?"

"No," said Mr Redmayne, growing suspicious. "Are you sure you're okay? You're acting very peculiarly."

"*Am* I?" said George. "Am I really? *Peculiarly*, you say? That's odd."

"Yes. You look like you've seen a ghost. What's wrong?"

Mr Redmayne stepped further into the Music Room, a concerned expression on his face. Everything in here *seemed* fine. Had the piano moved? No?

"Wrong? Nothing's wrong here," replied George, suddenly moving towards his father quickly. "Nope, everything's good, in fact. Fine. No problems. If you want to know the truth, I was just looking for something, something of *yours*, actually. A trumpet. Grandfather told me about it. I just wanted to see it."

It took Mr Redmayne a second or two for the penny to drop. "Ah, I get you, I think. You mean the one *Miles Dav—*"

"That's right, yes," said George. "*That* one. But it doesn't matter now. You're right. I shouldn't be in here, wasting time like this. Not when we've got more important things to worry about. We should go."

"But it's right over here," said Mr Redmayne. "On the shelf. It's *there*. See? We could fetch it right now. It won't take a second."

"No, no, we really must go," said George. "Right now. Because, you know, there's much more urgent things to do. Put the side-door back onto the loop, for one. That's what we *need* to do. Really, we do. Now, in fact. We don't want the TDA wandering in, do we? Or *anyone*. That's what's important. Let's go find grandfather, why don't we, and do that? Right now. He'll be wondering where we are, anyway, I bet."

"I doubt it," said Mr Redmayne. "He's probably in

the Library. I asked him to keep an eye on you as well. I should have known better. *Anything* could have happened."

"Well, nothing did," said George, with a laugh. "Absolutely nothing at all. Yup... And sorry, Dad, for giving you the fright. Just now, I mean. *Almost jumped into next week* you said, the *middle* of it. That's funny."

"Is it? Why?"

"You know, time travel and all that. We *could* jump into the middle of next week *if* we wanted to, couldn't we? If we *really had to*, you know. We *could*. Or even the middle of next *month*! The *exact middle*. The *whole house in one go*. Every door, jumping. That's even funnier. An entire house jumping in fright! Get it?"

"I suppose, yes," said Mr Redmayne, not seeing the joke.

"That's all it was," said George. "Silly, really. Not much of a joke, either."

The pair had reached the exit. As they stepped out into the hallway, George took one last long look at the empty room and pulled the door shut behind them.

"Just jump *into next month*—ha!" he said as he did. "The whole house!"

"Are you quite sure you're okay, George?" said Mr Redmayne.

"Sure, Dad. Never better, in fact."

Mr Redmayne gave him a long look. His son did seem strangely cheered up now that they were out of the room and the door was shut behind them.

"Right, let's go find grandfather, shall we?" said George, all matter-of-factly. "Come on. He'll be worried."

"He won't," said Mr Redmayne, following his son.

Mr Redmayne knew very well something was off but he couldn't put his finger on it, and then—before he could give the matter anymore thought—they were at the Library already.

The pair went inside.

At first, the Library seemed exactly as they had left it

three days earlier (or however long it had been), but almost immediately Mr Redmayne noticed that while the hands of two of the three clocks mounted on the opposite wall were spinning at a fantastic rate, the right-hand clock was proceeding normally. To an extent, this confirmed what they knew already, that that the Paris exit was no longer on the time loop. So, 2:15 p.m., Central European Time. He checked his watch. The *same* time. He wasn't sure if this was consoling or just confusing.

But not coincidence. Okay, yes, the Paris clock was synchronous with the new exit in the kitchen, but how did it get that way? Once the door came out of the time-loop, did it just revert to their present? The fixed time of the exit into the caves? Just like that? He didn't know. So much of what was going on had no obvious explanation.

With a knowing tip of his head, George directed his father's attention up towards the secret door to the concealed room, which now stood slightly ajar, presumably confirming that his grandfather was indeed inside. Together they crossed to the west spiral staircase and climbed to the upper level, with Mr Redmayne leading the way. He was hoping his father hadn't made any more strange discoveries. Everything was odd enough as it was.

The Redmaynes' two-storey Library was a grand, circular affair, with a spectacular aspect that invariably stunned the first-time visitor, not least because it was as unexpected as it was grand, hidden, in a sense, behind an ordinary door in an ordinary-seeming house. On those occasions the impression it made could be overwhelming, disorienting even, as if the new visitor had somehow stepped through a portal into one of the great circular libraries of the world, the Radcliffe Camera, or the Picton Reading Room, in this case one suffused with a wonderful, warm, welcoming golden light.

But the Library's real secret, what it actually concealed, behind a slim door built into an upper storey walled bookcase, was the small room housing the spatial and temporal controls, the mechanism that accommodated access and egress into different places in different time periods. It was from within this room that the Redmaynes controlled where and when they would end up whenever they stepped out into the world through one of the three doors of the house, when going about their everyday lives or, on occasion, unintentionally rerouted the course of history.

And, yes—also, on occasion—intentionally so.

Mr Redmayne and George found Rufus deep in thought, studying the position of the great levers in relation to each other and to the multi-dialled control panel behind. He held up his hand to them both as they appeared, as a signal for them not to speak just yet, for a mighty thought, a conclusion, was forming. They waited. It took a moment.

A prolonged moment. Mr Redmayne and his son exchanged a look.

At last, Rufus inhaled long and deeply. "That's it," he said, turning towards them.

But that was all. When he saw them waiting, he seemed almost surprised.

They waited until Mr Redmayne could stand it no longer. "Father, is there anything you would like to share with the class? Anything at all?"

"No, I don't think so. Not right now."

He started to move away from the control panel but then paused. "I *do* have a theory, yes, and that is all. My logic might be faulty. I doubt it personally but you can never be too sure. So, if you don't object I would prefer to wait until I have more evidence before I say anything. Otherwise I might make a fool of myself."

"And, *heavens*, well, no, we couldn't have that, could we?" said Mr Redmayne.

"No, indeed, quite right. That would never do. — *George*, my lad, ah, there you are. While we're here, I'm thinking we should by all means avail ourselves of the

Library, don't you agree? There's an entire shelf of books we absolutely must take back with us. They'll be most useful for your studies—and your sister's, too, should she be interested and I daresay she will once she has recovered from yesterday's minor episode. Would you please go and fetch something to carry them in? A backpack of some sort would be best, the sturdier the better. Thank you."

George hesitated. "Grandfather, sorry. Yes, I will, but… It's just, well, don't you think we should put the side-door back on the loop? Now? I really think we should. I mean, *anyone* could walk in. The TDA, anyone. We should do that straightaway, is what I'm saying. Right now, in fact."

The old man paused, very briefly, as if examining his grandson for the smallest of moments.

"What's that? The TDA, lad, you say? Ah, yes, quite right. Thank you, George. We certainly wouldn't want them in here, now, would we? No. Not at all."

The old man turned back to the controls and made several adjustments to the levers.

"There," he said, presently. "Quite secure."

George nodded. He lingered for a second or so longer, studying the position of the levers intently, almost as if he were memorising them, and then—quite abruptly—he left.

Mr Redmayne seethed with impatience.

"Father, what the *blazes* is going on?" he said, checking over his shoulder to make sure that his son was out of earshot. "Tell me this instant, I insist."

"Very well. Take out your key."

Mr Redmayne rummaged in his pockets, shortly producing the large, iron key.

His father did the same, placing the key they had found in the caves on a table beside the controls. "Put yours next to that, if you will."

Mr Redmayne did so. The two men examined them together. Quite identical.

"My son, I wasn't misleading you when I insisted that there is only one key. There is, still, only *one* key. I didn't fashion another."

"But, that *means*," said Mr Redmayne, rather slowly.

"Yes," said his father. "They are one and the same. The key we found is the *same key* you've had in your possession these last three days."

The implications of this theory were dawning on Mr Redmayne.

"And *that* means," he began, before trailing off.

His father nodded. "Yes, I'm afraid so, my lad. The villain in all of this is, most assuredly, one of our own."

* * *

Mr Redmayne and his father neglected to share this theory with George, troubling as it was. As Rufus maintained, it was at this stage nothing but a theory, and in any case he believed that whatever was going on, *was*, both now and shortly, clearly already in train and had best be left to run its course, otherwise things might take a complicated turn and not for the better—for anyone and everyone concerned. And although Mr Redmayne felt rather anxious about these developments and how they might yet work out for the worse, on balance he agreed. They would say nothing to the children about how they suspected that any one of them might be the culprit, or that there might even be a culprit; instead they would stay vigilant, and see how it went.

The mysterious second key was to remain a secret between the three of them, as agreed when George returned, along with the news of the unsealed side-door out into present day Paris, at least until they had managed to come up with a satisfactory explanation of what might be going on. No point spreading concern unduly. None. No.

They also determined between them that they should

undertake only the most cursory search of the remainder of the house, on the grounds that (a) it would take forever to do it thoroughly; and (b) if the TDA *had* infiltrated the house they would hardly be hiding *from them*, now would they? No, they wouldn't. They'd be arresting all three of them, most likely, and the fact that they hadn't done this as yet suggested their non-involvement in whatever was going on, the logic of all of which seemed incontrovertible. Best be quick about it and go, was their joint decision, before their delay here made the others suspect anything untoward might be afoot.

To Mr Redmayne's surprise, suspicion and, it must be said, considerable private disappointment, George proved more than readily agreeable to everything proposed, both willing to keep secrets and volunteering to search the upper floors himself unaided. In fact, his insistence on this latter point all but convicted him in his father's eyes. George knew something, and was keeping it to himself. But what?

And the best that he could hope for was that George's motivation in keeping his secret might be well-intentioned. Otherwise the trust that they had hoped to rebuild between them all as a family since Emile's loss and recovery would be nothing but a sham. And that would be the hardest thing of all. For certain.

All in all, therefore, they made for something of a disconsolate group when departing from the house, with Rufus locking the door behind them with the key they had found on the cave floor some few hours earlier.

Only George appeared to have something of a spring in his step as they exited the caves and set off back towards the farm across the rolling French countryside in the golden late-afternoon sunshine—and this was despite the fact that he was lugging on his young shoulders a huge canvas backpack full of some of the heaviest tomes in the Redmaynes' entire Library.[76]

And if there was a reason for this new-found spring in his step, well, quite obviously, he wasn't saying what it might be.

---

[76] The titles alone of which were heavier than many other volumes. Trust me.

CHAPTER 5

To all outward appearances the Redmayne household seemed altogether in somewhat better spirits in the weeks immediately following the trip back to the house. Felice rallied, much to her parents' great relief. Free from all of the clutter in her room she undertook not to repeat that unfortunate and disastrous exercise and instead threw herself once again into a more traditional form of artistic creation—one that she had always felt passionately about—her painting. Almost every day now she took herself off and set up her easel somewhere out in the nearby fields, spending long hours in her efforts to capture her beloved French landscape in the ever-changing morning and afternoon light, viewing herself in this regard as much like her long-time heroine, Marie Antoinette, when the unfairly maligned French queen had sought solace and respite from the cruel public eye by painting alone in the grounds of *Le Petit Trianon*, her private residence at Versailles.

Curiously, while Felice seemed determined to spend her time outside, her brother, on the other hand, more or less besieged himself in his room, studying the various weighty tomes that his grandfather had insisted they bring back with them from the house. From time to time the studious boy would appear blurry-eyed in the kitchen, and seem surprised to find that that anyone would be up at that time of the night—and then be even more surprised to find it wasn't night-time at all but the middle of the day. Not that this discovery ever slowed George down. Grabbing whatever quick-fix sustenance might be handy— and perhaps pausing only to ask if anyone had seen Felice—he soon retreated back into his room, deaf to any entreaties from his mother about taking a break or the benefits of availing himself of the comparatively old-fashioned and rather basic but, despite that, still quite effective shower facilities they were fortunate enough to enjoy here on the farm.

But no, George had no time for washing. In his newfound determination to learn everything he could about the house and the theoretical underpinnings of how it worked, George was like a man (boy) possessed. He was being driven to learn, to the exclusion of all else, and the three elder Redmaynes were quietly looking on—watching, waiting—and hoping to uncover whatever might really be going on, before any real harm was done.

Other activities were underway, too. For one, Mrs Redmayne went out one day and returned with six sheep, much to her husband's and (almost) everyone else's immense surprise, it must be said. To be precise, Mr Redmayne was quite speechless. When he first spied his wife coming along the distant, narrow, winding lane towards the farmhouse with what appeared to be half-a-dozen or so *animals* of some kind rambling on ahead of her, his first thought was that she had stumbled into them somehow on her walk and not been able to shake them off. (Maybe, he thought, she had made the mistake of feeding them and afterwards they wouldn't leave her alone, much like those cheeky, chips-pestering seagulls in

Portreath on the Cornish coast.[77] [78])

To begin with he was quite concerned, but when she drew nearer to the farm and (i) he saw that they were sheep; and (ii) it became clear that his wife appeared to be *driving* them on (again, *some*how, almost as if assisted by some invisible border collie), well, then, at this point, he grew rather very quite concerned indeed. Gloriana had acquired *sheep*. Somehow.

Mr Redmayne had absolutely no conception of how one—anyone—even went about acquiring sheep (he didn't imagine there was a shop where you might go in and say, "I'll have those six, please, with the wool" or that you might order them over the world-wide-web thingumabob that the children had told him mildly terrifying stories about), let alone what you were supposed to do with them after they had been acquired. But once his wife and her new woolly companions had departed from the little lane and turned across the fields towards the farm, he suffered the less than welcome insight that over the coming months he would in fact be finding out, in stunning detail, everything there was to know about sheep husbandry.

Mr Eric Redmayne, Esquire, former Master of Time, now Gentlemen Sheep Farmer.

Such were the vicissitudes of life.

Of course, it wasn't only Mr Redmayne who had spotted Gloriana heading across the open fields with her flock running ahead of her as if steered by some unknown

---

[77] i.e. Like all seagulls everywhere, they want your chips. Now.

[78] Mr Redmayne knew very little about animals. Nothing, in fact. He knew *of* them, yes , by reputation, much like you do, but as to the complex matters of their care & well-being, well, nope—zilch, nada and the aforementioned nothing. Fact.

form of mind control. Emile had, too, and so had Felice. The pair of them came running out of the farmhouse at the same time, paused for a second or so to confirm with a glance at each other that what they were seeing wasn't some kind of trick or mirage, before hurrying off again together towards the approaching shepherdess (who appeared to bear an uncanny resemblance to their mother).

Unfortunately, their joint and somewhat heavy-footed charge broke whatever uncanny hold it was that Mrs Redmayne held over the collective sheep-mind, scattering the herd left and right, much to her obvious displeasure. Some fun and games ensued. After a time Rufus came out to watch, it being the sort of thing you would not want to miss in this or indeed any lifetime.

There, on the grassy fields, he spied his two younger grandchildren proving themselves to be no substitute for invisible border collies, with the rounding-up process growing decidedly protracted—a situation exacerbated by the perplexing tendency of the sheep to pass at once through the loop in space-time the moment they crossed the threshold to the farm and emerge instantly on the other side, free to make off in whatever direction took their fancy.

Mr Redmayne was granted the privilege of catching a smile play across his father's face.

Mrs Redmayne came up. She was not smiling.

"Dearest, correct me if I'm wrong," began Mr Redmayne, with a hint of nervousness, "but you appear to have acquired some, well, I don't know, *livestock* on your trip out this morning. Was that entirely intentional? Just checking."

A single high-arched eyebrow from Mrs Redmayne in response informed her good husband that not only were her actions (i) singularly intentional because (ii) her actions were always singularly intentional, but that (iii) his 'checking' was therefore entirely redundant, (iv) ill-timed and (v) unwelcome.

Mr Redmayne understood. All of the above. At once.[79]

Rufus approached, his gaze still fixed on the two failing contestants in the junior sheepdog trials. With a mixture of flailing arms and cries of anguished encouragement Felice successfully stewarded one reluctant and panicky sheep across the intangible barrier of the loop in space-time, only for the poor animal to reappear at once on the far side of the farmland, some hundred or more metres away, and run off.

The combination of anguish and anger in Felice's expression betrayed a desire for vengeance worthy of Medea.

Her little brother was faring no better. At one point it appeared that two of the sheep were steering *him* towards the farm, pushing Emile on and crossing the threshold behind him, but the net result was the same—sheep, suddenly far off, free, and running.

Rufus chuckled. "At what point do you think they'll realise they must actually be *touching* the sheep for the fearful creatures to pass inside? I imagine it might take some time. Still, it's an interesting experiment, all the same, don't you think?"

Mr Redmayne looked to his wife.

"This will take forever. Can't you whistle them or something, dear?"

"The children?"

"The *sheep.*"

That Mr Redmayne apparently considered this proposal to be a serious and at all viable option brought home to Mrs Redmayne exactly how much she was likely to be on her own in the coming months in all matters of

---

[79] A single high-arched eyebrow can be extremely expressive, as we all know. On the right person, naturally.

animal husbandry.

"No, dear, I'm afraid not," she replied, as politely as she could under the circumstances. "You see, sheep respond no better to whistles than children do, *normally*... Or mice, for that matter."

"Oh," said Mr Redmayne, "I just thought that seeing how earlier you..."

But, sad to say, whatever Mr Redmayne's thought on this pressing issue might had been was never articulated,[80] for at that moment his wife had decided to intervene, striding purposefully in direction of the nearest renegade sheep.

The poor animal didn't stand a chance.

It didn't run; indeed, it didn't even move—as if realising that these choices, assuming it still had choices, would only work out all the worst for it in the fullness of time, should it exercise its doubtful right to take them.

Instead, it stood transfixed—non-literally glued to the spot, while Mrs Redmayne descended upon it and, in one swift movement, grabbed it by the thick scruff at the back of its neck, hauling the now compliant beast willingly towards the farm and over the invisible threshold.

In no time at all the new arrival was happily settled in the orchard and making free with its new bounty of fallen apples, with the air of an animal entirely contented with life and completely at home in its surroundings and *why hadn't you just said it was going to be like this?*

Rounding up the remaining five stragglers took a little longer. Well, more than a little longer.

Although Felice and Emile appeared to have grasped the point about the requirement for them to be in physical contact with the animals in order for them to cross the loop in space-time, this didn't mean they were necessarily

---

[80] Almost certainly, just as well.

that keen to try it out. *Them*selves.

Hands-on animal management. Literally. No, not at all.

Felice proved the braver. Still initially reluctant to get too close, she elected to steer from a safe distance one of the would-be lost sheep towards the barrier, only pouncing at the last possible second to push it physically inside. It worked—and soon the not so wee but very timorous woolly beastie had joined its munching companion in the orchard, in truth none the worse for its adventure.[81]

Emile followed her example, if more by accident than design.

He appeared to stumble into two sheep at once at exactly the right moment, and then to the onlookers seemed as much surprised by his success as they were.

Mr Redmayne took some pride in it all the same.

"He might have a future in this," he said. "You know, the lone shepherd, collecting strays and looking after the flock."

The two sheep ran off, and not in the direction of the orchard.

"Possibly," added Mr Redmayne. "Or not."

Mrs Redmayne sighed. A telling sigh.

"It is the present that concerns me, more than anything, Chéri, the here and now. I am tired of the future. We are ruled by the future."

"Ah, there goes another one," said Mr Redmayne, attempting to give the conversation a more positive steer. Felice had succeeded in rounding up another reluctant new arrival. "Almost there."

And then they were there. The two children rounded on the last one together. The animal crossed the threshold with two hands laid upon it, one from each junior

---

[81] Nor any wiser, it has to be said.

sheepdog-trial champion, and the result was declared a tie.[82]

And, of course, it wasn't about the winning. It was about the taking part.[83] It was about the fun they'd had together,[84] [85] and the fact that the animals now in their care had been safely put to pasture.[86]

The five Redmaynes stood at the wooden gate to the orchard, looking on together at their new charges. The sheep seemed contented enough. All of them were grazing. The morning had seemingly left them unscathed.

And there was a certain satisfaction for all present in seeing the job done.

"So, *sheep*, dear…?" ventured Mr Redmayne.

"Yes, dear, *sheep*," replied Mrs Redmayne. "Very good. Full marks."

With that, she set off back to the farmhouse. Mr Redmayne watched her walk back. His father turned to join him.

"Well, I don't know about you," he said, "but I wouldn't have missed this for worlds. Most. Fun. Ever."[87]

* * *

Mr Redmayne was sitting in his favourite Parker Knoll chair, the classic Oberon model, brown, in Dallas leather. Or, to be strictly accurate, in what was the most tremendous reproduction of his favourite Parker Knoll

---

[82] Technically, not a tie. No. Do the math.

[83] Hmm, maybe...

[84] For the record, neither Emile or Felice said anything about it being fun.

[85] Rufus, on the other hand, had enjoyed himself enormously.

[86] Let's give them that one.

[87] *See?*

brown leather chair, the original remaining in his study back in the house on Everywhere Street. This one he had made himself, in collaboration with Emile, who, much like his sister, possessed an uncanny knack for thinking visually, one that Mr Redmayne himself could at best only admire and, at worst, merely envy. Despite his many frustrations on this front he tried hard to stick with admiration, although at times it could be difficult.

Emile had proven a good and patient teacher, however, and together they had eventually fashioned the present masterpiece (the less said about Mr Redmayne's first half-a-dozen or so abortive attempts the better). Mr Redmayne himself was very pleased with it. If anything they had *improved* upon the original, as the proud owner suspected he had in fact made this one a little wider in the seat than the one to be found in his study, an amendment that subtly suited his, shall we say, steadily *maturing* form.[88] The chair was, in every way, a good fit. Literally. And it made him miss home that little bit less.[89]

Although he didn't think he could say that about everyone else. He was more than a trifle concerned about his wife, as he suspected that her sharp comments and irritated manner during the comedy episode with the sheep indicated a deeper sense of frustration. They needed to talk, and he would look for the right moment. After everything that had happened lately it would be surprising if she hadn't been affected by it all. First, losing and then finding Emile, in the distant past no less, then eviction

---

[88] You could say that.

[89] And so perhaps *this one* was his favourite chair, after all? It's just so hard to know with chairs, I find. But that's probably just me. Carry on.

from her beloved home by those darned Time-Police fellows, the TDA, and then relocating to this futuristic 'hide-out' in what was in truth nothing less than a hole in space-time, no matter how picturesque and rustic a hole, well, all of *that* would be bound to affect *anyone*. It could hardly *not*.

And now this latest business with George, whatever that was. They just didn't need anything else, not now. A quiet life with sheep, that was beginning to sound more beneficial to all the more he thought about it. A pleasant interlude, an idyll, that's what they needed. Not some madcap adventure involving duplicate cast iron keys and quite possibly time-travel, to boot. No. A comfy chair and time to sit in it, that's all he required these days. That sounded ideal. He must be getting old.[90]

Mr Redmayne shifted uncomfortably in his superiorly comfortable chair. Two keys... Why on Earth were there two keys? And why was the exit from the house into Paris unsealed—and how? And why only *that* exit? George had been very distant since the three of them had returned from the house. The lad knew something. He knew something and he was keeping it to himself. But why?

And also, why only now was George suddenly so determined to learn everything he could about the house and how it worked—and as quickly as he could. What was driving that?

Mr Redmayne had no answers. He stood up. You can only sit in a chair for so long when you suspect your world might be about to cave in around you (again). No matter how comfy.

He needed to find his father. Talk everything over with him. You could never be too sure with Rufus. The old

---

[90] Yes.

man might know more than he was letting on, or at least have a theory. In fact, it would be odd if he didn't. Very. A first, in fact. Unprecedented.

But when Mr Redmayne tracked down his father he found to his annoyance that George had beaten him to it, because the pair of them were deep in hushed conversation in Rufus's darkened room, a conspiratorial scenario that, for some reason, wasn't totally reassuring. The cracks in Mr Redmayne's ideal, comfortable world had just spread a little bit the wider. Again. Somehow.

Not wishing to appear reluctant, he joined them.

"And so," his father was saying to George, "relocating the house in time and space necessitates taking account of how many forms of motion, would you calculate, my lad? Think carefully on this, or you will certainty end up at a less than optimal destination, possibly not even on Earth at all."

George looked as though he were thinking hard. Mr Redmayne remembered having a similar lesson himself once, several lifetimes ago, or so it seemed. The correct answer was not exactly obvious, or even intuitive. Such was the arcane science of time-travel. But the boy would get there eventually.

"Motion?" said George, looking up and seeing his father standing there, his expression suggesting the extent of his surprise. "I don't know, maybe I should think about that for a while before committing myself to an answer? I wouldn't want to get it wrong."

"Well, it's the thinking about it that matters," said Mr Redmayne, "not the getting it right or wrong."

"Unless you are planning on time-travel," said Rufus. "Then you have to get it right. Every time. Getting it wrong might put you somewhere out in space, or at the Earth's core. Remember, the passage of time always involves motion. You must know how many forms of motion you're dealing with. Otherwise, *kaput*!"

"Right. A good job I'm not planning on any time-travel, then. I mean, how could I...? Ah, Pops, when did you come in? Didn't see you there, sorry. ——Oh, by the way, did you happen to spot if Felice might be in her room? I need to catch up with her on some stuff."

"I think so," said Mr Redmayne. "Unless she's out painting, of course."

George stood up. "Yeah, painting," he said, as if the very idea of his sister painting was so unlikely that he could hardly belief it were true. "I'll go check."

"For next time, read the chapter on entropy," called Rufus as George was leaving the room. "Very important to understand. I do so love entropy."[91]

"Father, only you could profess to love the concept of entropy," said Mr Redmayne, closing the door behind him so that their conversation remained private. "But, really, do you think these sessions are a good idea? Right *now*, that is. Aren't we only encouraging him in whatever he might be up to, do you think?"

"Whatever he's up to, he needs to understand what he's doing. That should be obvious. I'm only enabling his understanding. Nothing more."

Mr Redmayne looked hard into his father's face. "And what do you think he's up to, then? You must have a theory?"

"Me? I have no idea. I know no more than you do. That's the truth of it."

Mr Redmayne was disappointed. After a second, he realised he was going to receive no help here after all. He reopened the door.

"But, I'll tell you this," said the old man, as if sensing his son's uneasiness. "Whatever it is, it isn't necessarily a bad thing. Maybe it's something he needs to do, something

---

[91] Largely as he singlehandedly conquered it. Such, to him, was love.

that needs to happen? Maybe he's fixing something? You know, something important. Think about that."

Mr Redmayne nodded, at once making to leave, but then he stopped. "Do you still have the other key with you?" he asked. "The duplicate?"

"Always on my person. Yes. And yours?"

"Hanging up in the larder, as agreed. It's still there. Quite untouched."

"Good," said the old man. "Let us see what we actually catch with the bait, shall we? Yes?"

Once again Mr Redmayne nodded, if feeling rather unhappy and mistrustful of everyone and everything at that particular moment.

Then he left his father to it, whatever it was the old man thought he was doing.

George had taken himself across the farmhouse and up the far set of stairs, towards where his and Felice's bedrooms could be found. He hadn't seen much of his sister since his return from the house, partly because they had both become so preoccupied with their particular specialist interests of late, and partly because, well, he'd felt like he rather wanted to keep out of her way, for whatever reason. But time, he realised now, was pressing. Whether he was doing the right thing or not, he had no idea.

He stopped at her bedroom door, took a breath, and knocked.

Felice's voice, muffled by the door, said something or other. Was that a 'come in'? George wasn't sure. But at least she was there.

Invited or not, he opened the door.

"Hey, Sis," he began, stepping inside—and then it seemed as though he had nothing else to say.

He'd paused in the doorway. The room was altogether far more orderly than the last time he had been in here. No clutter anywhere. Very little bric-a-brac, no floor full of, well, *Felice-stuff*.

A number of canvasses leant picture-forwards in a tidy stack against the wall.

His sister was sitting on her bed, sketching on a pad, her legs out straight before her.

"Oh, it's *you*," she said, looking up at him, her sense of anti-climax obvious. "Not like you to come visiting. Usually you've got your head in one of those big books your brought back. Very important stuff, I'm sure. So, what do you want, George? Spit it out."

George came all the way in and wandered over towards the wall, a study in aimlessness.

"Want, Felice? Me? Nothing. Really. I just thought I'd come in and see you. That's all. It's been a while. I don't know why. I guess we've both been so busy. Are these your paintings?"

"Yes. Leave them alone. I'm not in the mood for making another exhibition of myself. Not today, thank you very much."

"The last time was pretty intense, you've got to admit."

"Thanks. That's helpful. I'm glad you popped in. Tell me, what do you really want, George?"

"Well," he began, but once again didn't seem to know where he was going.

But then, perhaps mercifully, his attention was distracted by the spontaneous disappearance of the three small objects—some knickknacks—that had been standing on the dresser. Within seconds, they had been replaced by three other random trinkets, which had suddenly materialised and now stood there on display, almost defiantly, as if they had every natural right to deny the laws of physics and appear wherever they wanted.

George pointed at them. "Did that, they, just…?"

"Yes, you're not going mad. Grandfather helped me set it up. All the things I made, they've been 'saved', whatever that means really. Now I can just display them on rotation, as many or as few as I want, so I at least still get to see them. All very lovely. But are they *real* or what? I don't know. Like, would they even still exist if I took them outside the farmhouse? I doubt it somehow."

"No, they would," said George. "I've seen it."

Felice was interested. "Have you? When was that?"

George thought quickly. "When we went back to the house. Both Pops and his Pops had things in their possession that had been made here. I'm sure of it."

"Really? That's weird. Don't you think? Wow, man, like, I guess the future must be really so intensely weird. Because if you can have *every*thing, what's the value of *anything*? Do you see? You know, Georgie, I actually think I *get* Grandfather better now... why he does what he does; I mean, him collecting things that are *authentic*—things from the past, rare things. Don't misunderstand me, I *like* all the lovely stuff I made the other week, on one level anyway. I do. Really. But, on another level, they just seem to me to be, I don't know, *pointless*. Do you see what I'm saying? It's only their authenticity that gives things any value. See?"

"Huh, well, yeah," said George, in a way that was intended to suggest that although these were novel ideas, now that she had pointed them out he could see they were really very true.

But in fact he was clueless. "I get you, Sis. Sure, yeah."

Felice looked sceptical. "Of course you do. So, again, tell me, why *are* you here, George? You just wanted to see me. Is that what we're going with?"

George's pained expression could actually have passed for sincere. "Felice, I really don't know why you find that so hard to believe. It's not like we're exactly spoiled for choice company-wise, is it? Okay, the farmhouse might have its compensations but in the end there's only us here, you know, us lucky, special Redmaynes. Like, you must miss all your old pals, Paris, everything, seeing how you, you know, were always so much more sociable than me. Living here must feel a bit like being in prison, I think. For *you*, I mean. Especially."

Felice bit her lip. "Not like it's going to be forever, though, I suppose, is it?"

"*Forever*, nah," said George. "Because that would be hard. So, you reckon not, then?"

"Well, yes. Of course, I do rather miss it all," she said after a moment. "Obviously. But it's not like there's anything we can do about the situation, is there? Hey, what was it like going back there that one day and then, you know, leaving right away again? *That* must have been hard. How did it all look, in the house? Everything? Just the same, I suppose?"

"Yeah, I guess," said George, vaguely.

"You know, I really wanted to hear all about it at the time but then I didn't see you. And since you all got back no one's said much about it, not even Papa. Nothing, in fact, now I think about it. You know, now that I *do* think about it, it kind of makes me wonder if there wasn't something going on. Was there? At the house? Something no one's talking about? George, if there was, you'd tell me, wouldn't you? Otherwise, why all the secrecy?"

"Going on? At the house? Like what? Secrecy? Nah, you got that wrong, Sis. —Hey listen, I got this problem I need to solve for Pop's Pops. Maybe you can help? That's why I came to see you actually. See, he says that time is movement and that I need to understand all the possible forms of movement involved if I'm going to understand time-travel, the mechanics of it. What do you think?"

Felice gave him a sceptical stare that quickly turned into more of a stabbing glare. "George, are you trying to change the subject? Tell me you're *not* trying to change the subject. That would be so lame."

George's face protested his innocence, but not that convincingly.

"No, I need to know this. Honestly."

Felice waited. When George didn't say anything more, she gasped in exasperation. "Well, rotation and revolution, ob*vious*ly. They're all forms of that. You know, rotation of the Earth, Earth re*volv*ing around the sun; solar system, solar system spinning around the black hole at the centre of the galaxy… And so, in which case…Sagittarius A has to be the focus of your galactic co-ordinates… That's generally agreed, by everyone, no?"

"What?" said George. "Hold up, so… Let me see, it's like if you want to arrive at a certain place at a certain time you need to know where it's going to be at any moment by factoring in all of that that movement, but at the same time you need to co-ordinate it relative to one unshifting galactic focal point—and that's Sagittarius A… Wow, that's brilliant."

George was smiling as though he'd solved all of physics.

"Really, George? Think you're done? There's one more. No? Really?" Felice tutted. "The *expansion* of space, dimwit. Look up the Hubble Constant and you decide if the galaxies flying away from each other is another factor you need to worry about. I recommend you think about the relative velocity rather than the expansion velocity, though—again, *obviously*. But remember, expansion isn't a force, it's a rate. So, if there's a local force that's stronger than the expansion speed, like say, well, gravity, no increase in distance. Get it?"

George looked agog. "*What?* Wait, Felice, how do you *know* all this?"

"I flicked through your big brainy books one day when you weren't in your room. There's a neat diagram that sets it all out on page… —No, wait, George, how about you tell me what *I* want to know? Then, I'll draw you the diagram, if you want. Save you trawling through all those ten thousand page books all by yourself."

George didn't say anything. Not for a moment or two. Then, it was as if all at once he caved.

"Look, Felice, don't let on I told you, I've been sworn to secrecy. But, well, it's like this, when we got to the house, one of the doors had been unsealed. Yes, I know, amazing… And it was, like, just open, in the present, you know, so if you wanted to, you could just step right outside."

For a second she looked blank, as though stunned.

"But how? Was it the TDA? It must be some kind of trap."

"We don't know how. Not even Pop's Pops knows how. But the TDA weren't there. And they could have had us easily if they'd wanted to, easy as anything. Easier."

Felice took a second. "Which door was it?"

"Paris."

Her face blanched. "Paris? Really?"

"Yeah, but don't say I said anything. The others want to keep it under wraps until they figure out what's going on, like if anything even is. Hey, maybe this means we could go home sooner than we think? Perhaps the TDA have given up? Wouldn't that be great?"

George watched his sister lay back on her bed. "I mean, think about it," he said. "Paris. Right there. We could get our lives back. Imagine. Are you okay?"

"Yeah, yeah, great, two hundred percent. Don't worry, George, I won't say anything. I'll keep the latest family secret. You're in the clear."

George stood up. "Well, yeah, thanks, Felice. I know I can always depend on you to do the right thing. Dependable Sis."

He made to go but stopped. "Hey, did you hear that? Just now? I keep hearing this odd noise all the time. You know, outside. Like, I don't know, *wildlife*, or something? But all the time and, like, close by."

Felice didn't look up. "That'll be the sheep."

"The *what* now?"

Within minutes, Felice and George had headed out to the orchard, together, so that George might witness the existence of sheep with his own two eyes, and believe.

Even then, he had his doubts. The pair leaned lightly on the top bar of the orchard fence and stood looking in. The sheep were all in the same part of the pasture, with 'safety in numbers' being hardwired into their defence strategy, not that as such strategies go it had ever proven particularly successful.[92]

Felice called out their names, to no effect. The sheep carried on with their perpetual long-lunch, heads down, seemingly oblivious to the presence of the two onlookers.

George let out a series of short sighs, gasps and even a whistle, accompanied by a profuse shaking of the head, all of which was intended to convey the extent of his incredulity.

Words, it would seem, were failing him. Sheep, *here*.

They, the Redmaynes, of London, Paris and New York City had *sheep* now. And somehow this felt like a permanent step. Which couldn't be good. Could it? No, he didn't think so.

George stood watching them eat, as did Felice. It was sort of…calming.

"Where did they even come from?" he managed eventually.

"Maman bought them in the market, you know, in the so-called 'town'. And then she herded them out here on her own—down all the endless little tiny roads, too—like some sort of ninja-goddess-shepherdess type of supernatural being, or something. A deity, finally. You should've seen it Georgie. You'd have enjoyed it. —Or at least *definitely* you would've enjoyed seeing the Grade-A-Fools that Emile and I made of ourselves trying to get them actually onto the farm at the very end. Think herding

---

[92] With a review of its fitness for purpose therefore long overdue. That's all I'm saying. It's up to them.

cats, but more woolly."

"Huh," said George, respectfully. "And you've named them?"

"I named *one* of them. Agnes. Emile, he named the rest. One of them he called 'Dragon-Slayer.' Can you believe it?"

"Yes, I can. How can you tell which one is Agnes?"

"Easy. She's the one that *is* Agnes. The rest of them aren't."

George nodded, as if slowly realising the irrefutable logic of that statement, before turning around to look at the farmhouse.

"I don't know, Sis. This is all well and good, I suppose. But maybe doesn't this feel a bit like *settling down* to you? Here, on the farm? I mean, is that the plan? The *only* plan? I was hoping this would only be a temporary solution, until we all figured something out."

Felice nodded, if in something of a non-binding / non-committal way.

"You know, I actually think Maman prefers it here. She's tired of the house and everything that comes with it. That's my impression," said Felice. "She did *lose her son*, for a time, after all. That *would* feel bad. I know she never wants to do that again."

"But we got him back! *We* did, you and me. We don't deserve to be stuck here, not when there's the house and, you know, all it can do. The opportunities…" His eyes met his sister's when he said this last part. "Surely we can't be expected to give those up forever?"

Then he didn't say anything else. He didn't want to push her too hard.

Felice stared back at the farmhouse, too. She was thinking.

"This unsealed door, George, into Paris…what do you think it means? Is it over somehow, do you think? The TDA? What's stopping us from going back there now, just to see? I mean, why can't we?"

George took a breath. "Well, we don't have the key for one thing, do we? Only Pops has that. We could go and talk to him, but you know how he is with anything to do with the TDA—and you can hardly blame him. No, I think we've just got to wait and see. Tough it out here. What other choice do we have, anyway? And until then, there's always Agnes. That's something, I guess."

"Yes, I suppose," said Felice, before adding after a second or so: "School will be starting again soon, won't it? Ever think of that?"

"Don't worry, Sis, something'll turn up," said George, with hardly a pang of conscience. "You wait and see. I'd bet money on it. It won't be like this forever. It can't be, can it?"

But Felice, despite her brother's best efforts, seemed far from reassured.

And altogether quite glum.

Mr Redmayne was feeling quite glum, also, albeit for quite different reasons than those of Felice. His wife was almost uncertainly unhappy about how everything had turned out, or was turning out, and there seemed little he could do to fix it. His father was proving unhelpful on this latter front, too, playing his cards close to his chest for his own reasons, whatever they might be. And his son, his eldest son, was keeping secrets from them all and was undoubtedly up to something. But what? On top of all of that, there they were dangling the key to the old house like so much bait on a trap for a rat. In the meantime, they were just waiting for the trap to be sprung.

No, Mr Redmayne didn't like it. Not one bit. The waiting, nor any of it for that matter. No, not at all.

And all the while he had one eye on George and the other on the key.

But he had no eyes on Felice.

The next morning, quite early, Felice got out of bed,

dressed and crept downstairs as quietly as she could, which was very quietly. She went to the larder, found the iron key to the old house hanging on a peg, between the long string sack of jalapenos and the bag of lima beans. She took it down and looked it over carefully, turning it around in her fingers so that she could take in all of the detail. Then, she held it in her hand for a moment, her eyes shut, feeling the weight.

That was all she needed.

Placing her palm flat against the wall, her concentration shifted. Within moments a duplicate key had appeared on the larder shelf. Felice picked it up, admiring the exactness of the copy. She hung the duplicate key on the peg and left with the original, concealing it inside her shoulder bag. Without any delay she went out through the front door, once again very quietly, and walked off across the farmyard and towards the open fields. She didn't look back.

From the cover of his bedroom window, George watched his sister depart. He was dressed, ready. As soon as Felice had cleared the clump of trees that marked the boundary of the farm he set off for her room, moving with a most un-George-like stealthy silence that would have surprised those members of his family more used to him thumping around the house with all the care of the proverbial teenage boy in the delicate china shop.[93] Free from detection, he went straight into his sister's room. He was curious. There was one painting in particular that he was looking for. It must be in here, he felt sure, somewhere amongst the stack leaning against the wall.

George began to flick through them, one by one. Paris scene, Paris scene, another Paris scene, Paris scene— none of the paintings were local landscape scenes, it

---

[93] Not sure that's how the proverb actually goes. Ed.

seemed. Bastille market, that covered arcade (the Passage du Grand Cerf—Felice was always going there), the statue of Pan in the Jardin de Luxembourg, one of the narrow streets of fancy little shops in Le Marais,[94] the Place des Vosges, Paris, Paris, Paris—nothing but Paris! George had a fleeting moment of insight into exactly how much his sister *missed* Paris, her life there, and he felt sorry both for her and for the way he'd deceived and tricked her—a rare moment of empathy.

But at the same time, it wasn't as though he had any choice! The die had been cast from the second he'd stepped into the Music Room on that fateful day two weeks ago. He was compelled! Que sera, sera! Literally.

Okay, this was what he really wanted, too—no denying that.

Whatever… Nope, the painting wasn't here. No matter. He'd cope without it.

George left the room. He went downstairs and slipped out of the farmhouse, exiting as quietly as his sister had managed to exit some ten minutes earlier.

He set off for the caves in the brisk mid-August morning air and, although George was in no particular rush, there was a quickening spring in his step, a bounce, as he sped towards his Fate.

What will be, will be, after all…

Especially if we decide to help it along ourselves.

---

[94] La Rue des Rosiers, in fact, where Felice loved to wander.

CHAPTER 6

Paris!

The very thought of it was enough to drive Felice on across the fields towards the caves in the hills without the slightest doubt in her mind that she was doing the right thing. Or maybe just a little doubt, but she was doing it anyway. Paris was *there*—and accessible (according to George). No one could expect her to never visit Paris again, to live all her life trapped on that little farm—with her *family* (as much as she loved them). That was unreasonable. Unacceptable.

She wouldn't—and constitutionally *couldn't*—do it. Not when Paris was right there.

Paris!

And, besides, this was only going to be a quick trip. Very short. There and back again in virtually no time at all. No one might ever know. As she strode along through the long wet grass, she could feel the weight of the heavy iron key in her bag, nagging at her conscience. Okay, there was that. Yes. The deception. And she might have felt marginally better if she'd brought the duplicate key she'd made along with her, rather than the original. In that way she wouldn't have taken something that wasn't hers to take.

But that was just sophistry, she knew that.

Still, if the duplicate hadn't worked for some reason, or if George had been wrong about light-fashioned objects maintaining their form outside of the farmhouse (or lying—she wouldn't put that past him), that would have been far too disappointing.

No, she was doing the right thing.

Or, more truthfully, she was doing the thing she felt she needed to do, the thing she *must* do, regardless of whether it was right or wrong. She felt compelled. That was all.

Felice was going to Paris!

First, she had to get there. She could find her way back to the right part of the hills just fine, but an element of uncertainty existed in her mind as to how well exactly she remembered the route through the caves to the door. One of the things she'd been sure to do when alone at last on that first night at the farmhouse was to sketch out the journey they'd taken on the way there. Of course, she'd been her usual meticulous self in mapping the passages, but could she be certain now she'd gotten it right? This was a gamble in itself. Maybe she hadn't and one day they'd find her withered, lifeless form in some dark, obscure corner of the tunnels? Maybe her ghost would haunt the caves forever? Wailing like a banshee? A French banshee, naturally. But of course.

No, none of that would happen. Her memory had never failed her yet and it wasn't going to start today. Although it may have been useful if she'd remembered to bring a flashlight. Darn.

Whatever. She'd be fine. Just fine. Absolutely. Paris. She was going.

She marched on.

After about thirty minutes, her shoes wet through from

the dewy fields, Felice took her bearings and headed for what she believed to be the section of the chalk hills where they had exited the caves those few weeks earlier. Navigating with confidence was difficult, not least as the scenery all seemed a bit of a muchness from a distance (hilly, and then, well, more hilly), but as she grew closer Felice became gradually more certain that she was heading in the right direction. Some things now seemed familiar, possibly, the long line of elm trees to the west, for one. She distinctly remembered seeing that, she thought. So, it had to be this way. It *looked* right, anyway...

And then—good—she spotted the odd upright outcrop of grey rock that she recalled running past with Emile and George on the way down the slope when they'd first arrived that day, the rock that looked like it could be a standing stone of some kind. She had wanted to check that out at the time. This *was* right. She wasn't lost.

And then, all at once—yes! The cave. There it was!

Felice changed gear and made straight for it.

Happily no one else appeared to be around (thanks to her early start, she reckoned), at least not yet, anyway. In fact, the area appeared entirely deserted as far as she could tell. Close to the opening, some random wooden crates lay scattered about and suggested there had been some sort of activity around here recently. She would need to be careful.

Moving more slowly, Felice crept closer and peered inside the cave. As expected, it was all rather dark, of course, and somewhat smaller-seeming than she'd remembered and—quite literally—forbidding, because a portcullis-like iron gate now covered the entrance and on it was a large sign in the shape of a shield that announced in large black lettering:

ATTENTION! N'ENTREZ PAS!

She hadn't remembered seeing *that* last time. But then, all of her attention had been forward-looking at the time, not behind, naïf that she was, so she surely hadn't seen it.

Discouraged, she halted. But, in fact, when she pulled on the heavy-looking gate it swung open easily, being very light on its rusty hinges, surprisingly so, and she was in.

Paris was this way, and not that far. Felice took a last long look at the map. Not that she needed it. For her, one look was enough. Always.

She went inside.

The ceiling was much higher here than had been her impression on her first visit. She recalled how it had all felt much more enclosed on the way out, although doubtless that would still prove to be the case as she passed deeper into the tunnels. Good job she wasn't afraid of the dark, unlike George! She stopped. Concentrate, Felice! Pay attention! You don't want to be wandering alone down here forever. The last vestige of light from the opening had thinned and the gloom all around her had thickened correspondingly. When she turned the first corner (ahead, left) it would likely be nothing but darkness from that point to the door. And indeed, moving on again, so it was, in front of her, anyway. Behind, there was still a faint grey light.

Concentrate. Paris! That was the prize at the end of this monochrome rainbow. Paris and her old life, just one short walk away. The prospect was dizzying. Felice pushed on. Forwards, not back. Into the darkness. Towards Paris. Although she still gripped the map tight in her hand there wasn't enough light to read it by. Luckily, the picture of the route was clear in her mind.

Left, left, right, left, left, right, right.

That was the way. She could follow it with her eyes shut (which wouldn't have been much different). Felice felt confident of the truth of that and not in the least afraid that she might go wrong. All the same, she walked slowly. The possibility of stumbling and falling, hurting herself— that was the real concern and, not to mention, if it were to happen, both stupid and counterproductive. Maybe next time she would remember to bring the flashlight? Now, *that* would be sensible. And after all, she was usually the sensible one in the family, or so she liked to think. The tunnels turned. The source of the faint breeze on her cheek had changed direction. Left.

Left, right, right. That's all that she needed to do from here.

The house was close. *Paris* was close. If she hadn't gone wrong, it was only three more turns. And if she *had* gone wrong, well, that was that.

But she wouldn't go wrong. That wasn't her. Left, right, right. Door.

Left, right, right. Door. That was all. *Left.* Ahead, ten steps. *Right.* Yes. Yes. This was it. On. *Right.*

Door. *Door! Yes!*

Felice felt the rough wood of the door under the palm of her hand. She'd made it! She was here. Home. Fumbling in her bag for the key she took it out, dropped it (*Dang!*), picked it up again and ran her hand over the right side of the door, feeling for the lock.

There! That was it. Lock. Key. Turn.

She leaned heavily on the door, which opened with a long, spooky-sounding creak. After first removing the key Felice stepped inside, closing the door behind her. She paused, taking a breath. Then, she turned and locked the door behind her.

She was in. She was *home.*

Houses may feel like they are ours, like they will always be ours, entirely familiar, ours and ours alone, always, as if you could never imagine feeling any other way. Home.

Home, now and forever.

But that can change, things happen, life moves on, and what was always the most familiar, most comfortable place in the world, the place you've known best all of your life now feels a little off. And this was how the house felt to Felice in that moment.

Stepping forward into the basement kitchen, the cosy

kitchen where she had eaten so many hurried, last-minute breakfasts before skipping out to school, everything felt at once a little different. It was a weird sensation.

Everything looked exactly the same, but it felt different somehow. Off.

Felice tried to ignore it. She *was* excited to be there, to be home, back among the things she had missed so much—and Paris was right outside the side door, which was the only reason she was here at all, to see Paris again. But as she walked up the basement steps and along the hallway, passing all the rooms where she'd always been so happy, growing up, doing this or that with George or Emile, or with Maman or Papa, it struck her what the difference was.

Empty. The house felt empty.

And more than that, as though it *should* be empty. She shouldn't be there.

She didn't belong. *Her* house. Her house was *their* house. Everyone's. Darn.

The house was the *family* home and it wouldn't feel the same without the others, especially when they didn't know she was here. It could even be said she was trespassing. Because of this, it was almost like everybody *did* know she was here, as if they could see her She could almost feel their eyes on her back in the long hallway. *Trespasser.*

That's why it felt so strange. Really she should leave. Go back. Confess. Really she should...

But, no, she wouldn't. She knew that. Not a chance.

Without the least hesitation Felice made her way straight to the Library. Now that she'd come, she thought to at least have the next few hours. That was *why* she'd come back, after all. Her conscience might ruin this for her eventually, but she wasn't going to let that happen just yet. Not before she'd even had any fun in the first place. She may as well be hung for a sheep as for a lamb. Taking the key and coming here, that was enough to get her punished. She might as well see Paris. Conscience be damned.

The Library, then, when she entered, happily seemed much as it always had, except that the hands on the three clocks on the wall opposite span continuously and at a ridiculous speed, with the turn of each hour taking but a few seconds to complete. Felice knew that this was because of the 'looping through time' effect that her grandfather had imposed on each of the three exits as a means of concealing the house from the TDA and preventing their entry. She needed to reset the clock for the Paris exit, if she could—and without attracting the attention of the TDA.

Needless to say, she had a plan, and would hardly have come all this way if she hadn't.

This is what she was going to do. Felice planned to stop the clock, but not in the present, her present, that is. No, she intended to skip a random but small number of weeks into the future, in that way no one could possibly know when she would emerge. After that, the clock could resume at a normal rate. If the door out into Paris had been unsealed, like George claimed it had, and it was part of a trap, she wasn't going to walk right into it. No way, no how. The TDA might know *where* she was, but they wouldn't know *when*. Because even *she* wouldn't know exactly when.

And Paris would still be Paris, *her* Paris, no matter when it was she was there.

Fool-proof!

Sort of, anyway—or at least that's what she hoped. Anxious to get going, Felice climbed the set of turning cast-iron steps that spiralled up to the higher level. From there, she quickly circumnavigated the balcony towards the special hinged bookcase behind which the door to the secret room was concealed. Once she was inside she would be able to adjust the controls and bring the Paris exit to a point in time that was a little ahead of the present of the caves. Not too much—she didn't want to journey into the far future (although as she thought about it, that *did* seem appealing). No, she would keep to her plan—*this* time. What she did *next* time might be another matter. (Although until that moment she hadn't anticipated that there was going to be a next time.) But, now that she'd thought of it, she could go anywhere, anytime. She could.

That was an intoxicating thought. Very. The Belle Époque...Versailles...

Right on cue Felice heard the sharp click of the concealed door as it unlocked, and the bookcase swung forwards. She was in. The world and all of time was hers.

What to do first? The secret room looked much as it always had, and of course there was no reason why it should look any different. Felice made straight for the tallest lever. She knew this one to be the 'anchor' that kept all three exits locked into the settings fixed for them by the last user. Once that had been released she would be able to adjust the exit out into Paris to the approximate time period that she required. A thought occurred to her: the new exit out into the caves and the farm, how was that controlled? There were no new levers or dials that she could see. She shrugged. No matter. It wasn't something that she need to worry about today. Today was all about keeping to her plan and seeing Paris. She loosened the tall lever.

Next her attention turned to the three shorter levers that stood together in a row. London, New York, Paris, in that order from left to right. Tentatively, Felice adjusted the right-hand lever, moving it first backwards and then—slowly—forwards. All the while her eyes were fixed on the two dials on the dashboard that she knew were relevant to Paris. One was already static, the other, although spinning wildly to begin with, slowed steadily as she manipulated the lever. Dials and levers, it was just like her grandfather to design such an antiquated set of controls. She supposed something push-button would have been out of the question. There!

The second dial, the temporal control / indicator, had

also come to a halt. That should do it. The exit was ready. *Paris!*

At once Felice turned and left the room. She didn't close the door behind her as she wasn't anticipating there would be any visitors. A glance at the three clocks on the Library wall opposite revealed that the hands of the one of the three, the clock on the right, were no longer spinning wildly, but now pointed at a little after nine, which was encouraging. Felice skipped down the spiral steps, exited the Library and hurried along the hallway back towards the basement staircase. She wasn't thinking now about how empty or strange or unwelcoming the house seemed, not now. She was only thinking about Paris. And there it was, before her, the staircase to the basement. The Paris door stood halfway down.

Felice descended the stairs—and paused. If her calculations had been correct, and she had every reason to believe they were, the Paris that she would find on the other side of that door would only be three or four weeks or so ahead of her present at the farm.

That would make it what, outside, right now? Early to mid-September?

À la rentrée. Back to school!

All of her friends, Claudia, Malou, Jeanelle, would be preparing to go back to school now that it was September. How she wished she were, too. Going to stores, buying art supplies, books, folders, pens, everything!

Right. Even if the unsealing of the door had been some kind of TDA trap, she didn't care. Not now. She was taking back her life. She was going to spend one day doing normal things, the sorts of things she should be doing— one *single* day! Was that too much to ask? No, it wasn't.

And when she was finished, she could simply skip back to the point that she'd left. Nobody would be any the wiser. They need never know.

And everything would be fine. *À la rentrée!* He favourite time of year.

193

Felice turned the handle. She opened the door.

Paris!

If the moment when Felice stepped out into the freedom of Paris had been accompanied by the sound of swelling orchestral strings it would hardly have surprised her in the least.

With a lightness of step that matched the bounce in her heart, she skipped up the short set of steps that ascended to street level. At the top the sun was shining, the sky was blue.

George, for once, had told the truth—the Paris door was unsealed!

She stood on the step, taking it all in. Birdsong! Yes. And the distant hum of traffic—*Parisian* traffic! Felice's heart luxuriated in the perfection of it all, the ordinary *wonderfulness* of everything.

In reality, the narrow street outside the Redmayne's Parisian exit was no more than a pokey back-alley, but it was the *most perfect pokey back-alley* she could ever imagine seeing, the same back-alley on which all of her schooldays had commenced, the blessed back-alley that led out onto the city that she loved. So, mere back-alley or not, she marvelled.

Home. After two long weeks away, she was back. This was actually it.

Which direction? Felice turned left towards the petit-boulangerie she so adored, with the astonishing range of pastries and elaborate, delicious-looking cream cakes (who ate them all?) (*every* day!) (and why wasn't *anyone* fat?). But immediately she doubled-back on herself and headed in the opposite direction. All at once she realised exactly where she wanted to go and what she would do when she got there. *À la rentrée*! Of course!

At this time of year Felice would always stock up on art supplies at the darling shop on the *Quai Voltaire*, before going back to school. It was a sort of family tradition (usually with *Maman* in tow) (seldom Papa). She *must* do that, today, and not just for its own sake—she couldn't go on painting with *light* forever. Authenticity came in many forms, after all.

Yes, and perhaps she could mooch around the *Musée d'Orsay* first? That would be *perfect*. Only for a little while. She didn't want to push her luck. Although *time* was on her side, if she needed more of it. That was the great advantage of being a Redmayne. Time was *yours*. Assuming she didn't get caught. By whoever. Anyone. Speeding up, Felice thought it might be an idea to keep to the backstreets for as long as she could. Just in case. Very wise. Caution. Always.

Caution, always, in theory, yes... But, alas, in truth, caution *always*? No.

For, in what was only a very short time later, after Felice had dutifully worked her way north towards the Seine through the many delightfully sunny back and side streets of the Sixth Arondissement, her sense of the need for caution and why it was in the least important had all but entirely abandoned her. Paris. She was back. That's all it took. Nothing more. Paris!

To Felice, it felt a bit like a dream—a wonderful, intoxicating dream, all of it. Saint-Sulpice, the Église de Saint-Germain-des-Prés, so much *history*. And, by the time she had reached the École nationale supérieure des Beaux-Arts and the Quai Voltaire, Felice had not only thrown all caution to the wind but was seriously beginning to doubt if she could ever return to the farm, the farm that was *literally* nowhere, *to spend the rest of her life there*—in exile, from Paris, from all of this! Non.

Non. Non. Non.

A thousand times *non*. Ten thousand times.[95]

---

[95] i.e. Non x 10^5

In actual fact, the more she thought about it, the more the idea was unthinkable (totally), absurd (ridiculously so) and, judging by her experience so far today, quite possibly *so completely* unnecessary (yes, completely). Maybe the TDA, the bogie-men from the future in bowler hats, had been disbanded? Discontinued, whatever. In which case, maybe the Redmaynes were hiding from nothing? Wasting their lives. She didn't know. How could she? She couldn't. No. But what she *did* know was that here she was, Little Felice Redmayne, the notorious Time-Criminal, quite alone, walking along the Quai Voltaire in plain sight, the warm French late-summer sun shining on her face for all the world to see, with the Seine flowing deep-blue beside her and, beyond that, over on the opposite bank, the Louvre, magnificent, as ever; and yet, despite all this, zero— absolutely *zero*—futuristic policemen were bothering her. Not a one. Yes, h*ere* she was, boys! She could hardly be in a more prominent place. Come and get her! But no one did. Because it was all fine. Normal. She had been right to make the trip.

Feeling deservedly—she felt—more relaxed now and more than a quite a bit pleased with herself, Felice passed Le Magasin Sennelier, the art shop, with a sigh, wistful but content enough in the knowledge that only a little later that very morning would she be leisurely exploring its three tall narrow storeys and the innumerable treasures to be found in the many tight nooks and crannies on every floor. Nowhere else in the world could there be such a fabulous art supplies shop. Surely not. Le Magasin Sennelier had everything, *somewhere*—and most of the fun lay in discovering it all, bit by bit. In an alcove on the second floor hung a notice board peppered with the sketches left behind by so many budding yet talented artists just like herself. Felice wondered if the tiny self-portrait drawing (4H pencil) that she'd pinned on the board last year would still be there. If it was, well, then at least some evidence of her existence remained out here on the world, regardless of her tragic fade into total farm-bound anonymity since.

But that treat was for later. First, she wanted to take a quick (well, quick*ish)* tour of the Musée d'Orsay, revisit some of *its* fabulous treasures, the Monets, the Manets, the van Goghs, the Kandinskys, refresh them all in her mind's eye. Once seen, never forgotten. In any case, who knew for sure when she would get the chance again? If ever? A moment's anxiety struck while Felice felt around in her shoulder bag for her entrance pass. Yes, it was there, of course, but so was the heavy iron key for the house. If anything, the damn thing seemed even heavier in her hand now, and she picked up speed again. The museum was only a short ways ahead. No need to think about anything else. Not just yet. Later. Whatever consequences there might be to her actions—*if any*—she would deal with at the time. For now, the sun was shining, the sky blazing a lovely, perfect, cornflower blue, and all around her Parisians were going about their normal, everyday business. Normal. Everything was normal, fine. She was going to look at some art. What consequences could there possibly be? Like, whatever (cue another, far more audible sigh). It would be fine. Quite perfectly fine. She had definitely one-hundred percent been right to make the trip. Relax. The museum-gallery was straight ahead. Deep breath. She was there.

All was normal and everything was fine. Yes. Excited, she joined the queue.

* * *

Three hours later, when Felice had finally finished wandering throughout the galleries on either side of the central nave on the middle level of the museum, all of her minor anxieties and lingering doubts had been long-forgotten. Under the great, high, arched ceiling everything seemed orderly, calm—the reduced intensity of the lighting was a factor in this, she felt, along with the consoling proximity of so many great masterworks of art. She'd seen van Gogh's supernaturally slinky *Olive Trees*, Monet's lonely *Stacks of Wheat* in the snowy sunset, Chagall's very strange, wingless old man flying *Over Vitebsk*,[96] each of which—while very different—had struck her with their common, what would she call it, vividness. That was it. Their amazing vividness. She could learn everything she really needed to know about art, she felt, just from walking around these tiny galleries and looking at everything, but *really* looking. This is what she had missed—and couldn't do without. Her life, their lives, had to change. They couldn't hide out on the farm forever. No. Something had to give.

If she were ever to become an artist, it really *had* to—somehow.

But, as inspirational as each of the great paintings were for Felice, the work of art that had most captured her attention on this floor wasn't a painting, or even a sculpture, but a desk.

Her father's desk, or, rather, more accurately, make that her *grandfather's* desk. The desk from the study in the house, with all the Art Nouveau curves. It was here. On show. Felice went as close to it as she could get without crossing onto the display. It was identical. Was it a copy?

Probably not. She knew that such Art Nouveau pieces tended to be unique. Her grandfather would be unlikely to settle for a copy when the original could be had, by whatever means. Stolen. *Collected.*

Was this one here a copy made out of light and substituted by stealth into the museum? Or might the old crook have taken the original at some point in the far future and brought it back into the house in the present, so

---

[96] Or is he falling? With a certain horizontal flair? You decide.

that this very piece of furniture currently existed in two places at once? Either of these things were possible, but she would put her money on the latter. Felice read the display's information card on the wall.

Mobilier Art Nouveau: Bureau d'Origine: 1901

Le 12 février 1901, Emile Gallé fonde L'École de Nancy en collaboration avec les artistes Louis Majorelle, Eugène Vallin, Victor Prouvé, Jacques Grüber, les frères Daum et bien d'autres.

Whether appropriate or otherwise, Felice chuckled to herself. Her family. What were they like? She looked back at the desk. Anything could be theirs. Anything at all. Was that bad? It didn't seem to be. Who was the victim in this crime, if crime it indeed was? She passed out through the end of the atrium and was about to head up the stairs to the upper level when something else unexpected caught her eye—something even more unexpected than coming across her grandfather's desk in a museum.

It was her grandfather himself.

No, not quite. To be precise, it was a portrait of her grandfather, on display in the stairwell. And to be even more precise, it was *the* portrait of her grandfather, the very same portrait in oils that hung above the desk in her father's study, in which the old man (although far younger than he seemed today, but middle-aged[97]), red-bearded, attired in nineteenth-century clothes, stared out gruffly at the viewer, while holding an enigmatically unlit cigarette in the fingers of his left hand. Felice had known this portrait all of her life. What on Earth was it doing here? It was…weird. Actually, she was beginning to feel a little weirded out. She read the information card on the wall next to the painting.

---

[97] i.e. Old.

Gentleman Traveller
Henri-Edmond Cross
1898
Huile sur toile

As it had with the desk, a set of troubling questions at once flashed through her mind. Copy? Original? Did this portrait currently exist in two places at once? And what did it mean, it being here, now, anyway? Anything? Nothing? Unfortunately Felice didn't get much time to ponder these perplexing matters, as right then—in the reflection of the glass pane covering the portrait—she caught a glimpse of the two gentlemen standing immediately behind her, both wearing bowler hats. Her heart sank. TDA. TDA. TDA. No. Yes.

Was it? The TDA? Standing right behind her? Yes, it was. It *had* to be.

What to do? Felice made the calculation in an instant. Run. That's what.

Feinting first as if to go slowly left, instead she turned quickly right, heading up the nearby stairwell rather than down. She took the stairs two at a time and didn't look back. Everything went through her mind in an instant. TDA? Was she sure? Yes, it had to be the TDA. The hats. Like Emile's. Darn. Darn. Darn.[98] They must have tracked her here. Somehow. They *were* from the future so maybe they knew what she'd do, had *always known* what she would do—and *when*. Had all of it been a trap? Had she been set up? The desk, the portrait? Whatever. Now she was in trouble. That's what mattered. Big trouble. Serious. Damn.

---

[98] For the record Felice's actual expletives were a little, shall we say, *saltier*, than the rendering given here.

Damn. Damn.[99] *Stupid!*[100] What *had* she been thinking, coming here like this? Felice reached the upper level. A lone father and his young daughter at the top of the narrow staircase scattered to get out of her way. She ran on.

Luckily, the right-hand passageway of the upper concourse was largely deserted. Felice sped across the atrium, catching glances of mild alarm on the faces of the few people who were on the upper level. Far below her stood the statue of the four figures holding up the heavenly sphere, the one she so loved from the original in the park, but now didn't have time to give it a second look. Without slowing down for an instant she sprinted on towards the huge, round, quite magnificent golden clock as it beckoned to her from the opposite end of the atrium.[101] Another set of stairs was to be found below that. Another exit. She could only hope that the TDA weren't already lying in wait for her there. The damn TDA. Damn. Damn. Never again. Damn.[102]

Only when—finally—Felice reached the cover of the stairwell under the clock at the far end did she dare pause for a moment to catch her breath and look back at the long stretch of the concourse she'd just covered at breakneck speed. A very quick look. No one appeared to

---

[99] Same.

[100] This, however, is one hundred percent accurate.

[101] Yes, even when fleeing for her life, Felice could not help but appreciate the grandeur and magnificence of the great *fin-de-siècle* clock that dominates the entire atrium. That's just who she is.

[102] Yeah, again, a far saltier oath in reality.

be pursuing her. No men in grey suits and stupid bowler hats. Odd. This was both a relief and not a relief. She knew what she had seen. She didn't linger. If they weren't chasing her right now it was probably because they were lurking somewhere close-by. In wait. For her. Felice skipped down the left-hand set of stairs (*clear*) before crossing the width of the atrium and taking the right-hand stairwell (also clear). She didn't plan to make it easy for them. The foyer, she was pleased to see when she reached the lower level, was busy now. People everywhere. But still no sign as far as she could see was there of those particular people she was desperate to avoid. Felice took a breath and launched herself into the melee. A minute of this, two, and she would be out. Some bunching-up ahead at the exit. A crowd. Nuns. Leaving. Anxiously Felice scanned left and right before joining the Sisters. She became one of their group. Still clear. The exit was freeing itself up. Now. *Now.* She went for it. She was in the queue. This was it. She was in. In. In. Push. Towards *out.* Yes!

Next breath, she *was* out. Outside, back in the world. Thank you, Sisters! Felice promised to pay attention the next time one of them led a class at school, no matter how dull.[103] Sunshine, so bright! And hot—and she was already too hot from all the running. Still a little breathless, Felice checked all around, quickly. The coast appeared clear. No one seemed poised to grab her. Not this instant, anyway. She must get back to the house. That was her only chance. Assuming that, too, wasn't part of the TDA trap. Assuming there was a TDA trap. Now that she was safely outside, Felice allowed herself the briefest moment's doubt about what she had actually seen. A reflection. That's what

---

[103] A promise, sadly, she was destined never to keep, despite her sincerity at the time.

it amounted to, didn't it? Two men in odd hats. That was all. But then, she asked herself, what about the desk and the portrait? It couldn't have been just a coincidence that she saw what she did when looking at that very portrait, could it? No, something was going on. She walked towards the river, her breathing now more or less returned to something like normal. Warily, she looked around. All clear still, both directions. Felice turned east, retracing her steps, a girl in a hurry. Everything now seemed very different.

If only she hadn't come. She knew at some level it was dangerous, even if she hadn't wanted to admit it. What had possessed her to ignore that? It was as if she'd felt compelled almost, to come here. True, it *was* something she'd really wanted to do. See Paris again, her old haunts. But it had seemed as though she'd needed to come *here* today, whenever today was exactly, for some reason. That was strange. Felice glanced back over her shoulder. No sign. High above the Seine and the Louvre on the far bank the sun still shone brightly, yet also at the same time indifferently, on Paris and everybody in it. Cold, somehow, now that she'd cooled down. Damn. She had to get home. They could be anywhere. Or everywhere, for that matter.

And then Felice knew exactly where they were. Two men in bowler hats lurking on the corner of the street ahead. Felice slowed. Had they seen her? Should she double back? She checked behind. Another bowler-hatted henchman was approaching from that direction. Felice froze. Should she run? Damn. Damn. Wait. Le Magasin Sennelier! That was just ahead. She could duck in there. Hide until the coast was clear, as improbable as that seemed. Whatever. It was all the plan she had. Felice walked fast and turned right into the store, hoping that she hadn't been spotted (but at the same time she was by now half-convinced that they probably knew everything she was going to do before she did herself). Well, they could try coming to get her in here, if they dared.

They dared. Felice paused inside the door of the store and peered out along the length of the street. The two men on the corner had started towards the shop. Damn. Damn. She darted inside. The counter was busy with customers, blocking the way through to the stairs. Felice span right, and snuck down the tight rear aisle on the far side. (Ah, alas, the lovely charcoals!) The narrow staircase was straight ahead. If she could get upstairs without being seen by anyone, she might get a chance to hide in one of the tiny alcoves up there and stay out of sight. A slim chance at best, she knew. Felice squeezed past several customers intent on nothing but browsing the stock—all of it, item by item. (Oh, how Felice loved to do that herself!) To them, she was just a momentary nuisance, passing and then gone. No one even looked at her. For once in their long history, the stairs were clear. Felice pounced.

She started up the staircase—too fast! At the first sharp turn she ran with a resounding smack straight into a descending customer, another young woman, thankfully, not a goon in a bowler hat—although it still hurt because Felice's forehead took an almighty crack, as did that of the other girl. Just her rotten luck.

For a second, dazed, recovering, both stood rubbing their heads. It took a moment.

"Fel*ice*?"

"*Claud*ia?"

Even with their identities seemingly established, genuine speech took a little longer to come online. Claudia managed it first.

"Felice, is that really *you*? Really? I can't believe my eyes. Where've you *been*? I've been looking *everywhere* for you. Since that day at your house, it's like you've just *vanished*."

"What?" Wincing through the pain Felice could hardly believe her own eyes, either. *Claudia—Now—Here*. What were the chances of that? "We've been away, that's all. In the country. *Provence*. Claudia, sorry, it's so great to see you, it really is—you have *no* idea how great. But this isn't a good time. It's sort of an emergency."

Felice glanced anxiously back around the turn in the stairs at the lower shop floor. The three men in bowler hats were now inside the shop. One had stayed by the door—the only exit. The other two were making their way through the customers cluttering the narrow aisles—or were trying to, at least. Progress, fortunately, was slow.

"What? An art supplies emergency?"

"What, *no*. Sorry, I can't explain. No time. Got to go."

Felice tried to push past her friend but Claudia held her by the arm. "Felice, wait. Just a minute. What's going on? No one sees you for long over *a year*—well, almost *two*, in fact, and now you're acting all super-mysterious and, frankly, well, *weird*. What wrong? Are you in some sort of trouble?"

"No. A *year*? *Almost two*? What? That can't be right." Felice did another double-take behind.

She hesitated. "Look, Claudia, come with me and I'll explain as much as I can. Not that you'll believe me. But we've got to go upstairs *right now!*"

Felice made to move once more. Relenting, Claudia relaxed her grip. The pair ran up the stairs, Felice in the lead. At the second floor she set off down the aisle, quickly turning left into the first of the alcoves and then left again, effectively doubling back on herself. Claudia was right behind her. A wooden door blocked their way. Felice pulled on the handle and—luckily—the door was unlocked and opened at once.

It may have been nothing more than a large store-cupboard, full of wooden easels of all sizes—a confusing mass of jutting angles, but it would do. Felice slipped inside, and after Claudia had followed her, she quietly pulled the door shut behind them. The store-cupboard darkened.

At first, neither girl said anything. Claudia was waiting.

"Are you going to tell me why we're hiding in here?" she asked after a moment, once it became clear Felice wasn't ready to volunteer an explanation. "It's a bit unusual."

"Shhh," said Felice. "Three men are after me. Here, in the shop. They're police, sort of. Not *police*. Yes, *okay*, police. In *hats*."

"Police, not police, *police*, in hats?"

"Yes, and I haven't lost my mind. I know how it sounds. Claudia I need to get out of the shop and go home, back to the house. Right now. It's my only chance. Will you help me?"

"I will if you can give me a better explanation than 'Police, not police, in hats.'"

"This isn't the time. Damn, I'm so stupid. I should never have come here. Okay, *later*. I'll tell you everything later. I promise. Just help me get away. This is serious, Claudia. I'm in real trouble. It's affects my family, everyone."

"Okay, calm down. Of course, I'll help you. My lovely VSP is parked right around the corner. Once we reach that, I'll drive you to your house, assuming you can find it—because I think it no longer exists, this very mysterious house of yours. I've searched for it *all this year and last*. Exhaustively. And it's not there. *Anywhere*. Explain *that* to me later also! Okay?"

Claudia pushed the door open by a crack. She peered through.

"Tell me, might these 'Police, not police, in hats' look a bit like *Dupond et Dupont*, at least from the rear? Because, see?"

Felice took her turn to squint with her eye jammed at the door-crack.

The two TDA policemen had wandered down towards the end of the aisle. They were not looking behind, not at that very moment, anyway.

Felice saw her chance. "Come on," she whispered,

gently opening the door. "This is it, now. We must go. Follow me."

The pair crept outside. Felice held her breath. After what felt like an age of silent tiptoeing they reached the stairs and began to descend. Claudia held Felice back and indicated with a gesture and her eyes that she should go first. Felice nodded, and her friend overtook her.

By some miracle, it did not appear that they'd been seen. Perhaps, Felice thought, her grandfather had been right to scoff about the incompetence of TDA agents. Still, they had managed to track her *here*, now. What did that say about her? How useless was she? The two girls crept on. At the turn in the stairs Felice risked a glance back at the upper level.

Her eyes met theirs. Spotted!

"Go, go! They're coming!" Ducking down, Felice urged Claudia forwards with a less than gentle push in the back. "See, another by the door. We must get past him. Hurry!"

The girls reached the lower level.

Keeping low, Felice turned left, Claudia straight on. The narrow aisles were of course just as crowded as they had been a few minutes or so earlier. With as much force as she could muster Felice struggled through the row of oblivious customers quite unceremoniously—her manners, or so her mother might comment if she could but witness the scene, were altogether quite appalling. Pushing, barging, nudging—but why was everyone in her way? In truth, she didn't know whether to be irritated or thankful that Paris was a city of artists at that particular moment. She pushed on, all the same. No time to lose.

By the time she had finally reached the end of the aisle Felice had lost sight of Claudia. Where was she? Growing desperate, Felice glanced behind. A tell-tale sinister hat—and no doubt its sinister wearer—was negotiating the crowd towards her but had stalled (a middle-aged gentlemen, possibly, it was hard to tell for certain, seemed to have objected to the repeated jostling and was berating her pursuer, holding him up). It was almost as if someone were running interference for her—or as good as, at least.

Still, she must go, now—right now—Claudia or no Claudia.

Felice forced herself to peak around the corner of the aisle, towards the door. There he stood, the TDA agent, only a matter of feet away. He seemed both displeased and distracted by the developing row in the shop behind, and was straining to see what was going on. Voices were raised. The situation was escalating.

If only he would step away from the door. Felice hung back, waiting for the opportunity to move, escape. She peaked around the corner again. No, still there. She was trapped.

What could she do? Where was Claudia?

And then, she appeared. Felice saw her friend approach the man guarding the door. What was she doing?

"Monsieur Dupond?"

He ignored her at first.

"Monsieur Dupond, is it really you? I can't believe it!"

The TDA agent was forced to look at Claudia.

"You are mistaken, Miss. I am not he."

"Then, you must be the other one, Dupont? Am I right?"

The hubbub grew more raucous in the shop. Still he didn't move, but the row had his attention. Claudia chose her moment.

"I am afraid, Monsieur Dupont, I must apprehend your hat. It is under arrest."

In one quick move she snatched the hat from his head.

He looked at her, she at him.

"I am taking it into custody," she said, retreating with the bowler hat in her hand, "for unspecified crimes against

Parisian style. Too bad."

He advanced towards her, one step, two…

Claudia held the hat out to him but, still retreating, pulling it away out of his reach as he tried to grab it— once, twice—and when, next breath, he lurched forwards towards her, she launched it deep into the store.

The bowler hat was flying. Time seemed to stop as all eyes watched it glide through the air towards the small gold clock on the far wall, which it struck and then at once fell, the spell broken.

But now the exit was clear. At last. Felice took her chance.

The door opened seemingly no wider than a sliver of light but that was enough; she was gone, in under a half-second, providing the onlooker with no more than the fleetest glimpse of a departing heel, and only then if he, she or they happened to be looking directly at her, which, happily, no one was.

Felice was out. To her relief no TDA agents appeared to be lingering on the bright, wide street outside. It was clear. Which way? Left?

She started left. At once, Claudia exited the shop, her face flushed, excited.

"This way," she called, turning right. "Felice, come on!"

They went right, racing each other all the way to the next corner. Felice fully expected their pursuers to turn up at any moment, white-hot on their tails. Turning left, away from the Seine, the two girls ran on down the street. Felice glanced behind. No sign. Could they have lost them so easily? She doubted it. Soon they turned left again, onto the narrower *Rue de Lille*. Near the end of the first row of parked vehicles, Claudia slowed to a walk and Felice, more than a little breathless, gratefully followed her friend's lead. She wondered which of the little cars might be Claudia's VSP, if any. Then, Claudia stopped. Headlights flashed. Felice stared in wonder at the tiny Citroën alongside the kerb. It was so small that it just about filled one of the more compact spaces set aside for motorcycles. It looked like a shiny red sneaker on wheels.

"*This* is your car?"

Claudia shot Felice a look. "This is my *baby*. Be careful what you say."

"No, I *love* it. It's just so, you know, *small*."

"Small, yes. But maybe you want instead I should let those horrible men in the hats take you? No? Okay, so, quick, get in. Ah, look! Quick!"

Felice followed Claudia's line of sight back in the direction they had just come from. Two—no, all three—TDA agents had rounded the corner and had clearly spotted the pair of them again. At once the three were running—and the distance they needed to make up wasn't that great.

Both girls flung open the car doors and threw themselves down into what seemed to Felice like extraordinarily low seats. Immediately Claudia locked them both in—both doors. At least now they were out of reach. Then, while Claudia fumbled with getting the key into the ignition, Felice alternated between frantically monitoring the progress of their pursuers in her wing mirror and anxiously looking back aside to Claudia for a sign that the car was about to start.

Far too rapid progress, on the one hand, versus none, zero, or so it seemed, on the other.

This was, it would be fair to say, for Felice, a very tense moment. Very tense indeed.

"Go! Drive! Now! They're *right here*. Claudia!"

All at once, the engine purred quietly into life, like a contented cat waking up by the fire.

A tabby, a tiger, a lion…

Claudia turned to Felice and arched a single eyebrow in disdain.

The car pulled away from the kerb in one smooth, rapid moment of acceleration, out into the road. Instantly, they were gone, heading away at speed down the street, the danger passed. Felice checked in her mirror. The three TDA agents had given up their chase and, in their manner, appeared reassuringly disconsolate, beaten. Felice had gotten away. For the first time in what seemed like an age she felt that she could breathe again. Now she just had to get back to the house.

And come up with a story that would satisfy Claudia.

Of these two things, the latter—at that moment— appeared by far the more difficult. What could she possibly tell her, short of the truth? What tale could she tell her friend and still sound plausible—let alone convincing? Felice didn't know where to start. Driving, that was enough for now. Just drive. Felice peered out of the window, catching her breath and her thoughts. Paris in a zippy, little car. So *French*!

They travelled the short length of the first street and Claudia took a sharp right at the next corner, turning into the very narrow Rue Allent. She was heading south, towards the approximate area of the Redmayne's house, assuming it existed, of course, which she very much doubted. Towards the end of the tiny lane, where the street broadened out suddenly on the right to accommodate a set of private garages, Claudia brought the car to an abrupt halt (loud squeak of tyres!) and reversed rapidly into that space. Her little car wouldn't be visible from the other end. Felice had the sinking feeling that it was explanation time. She had nothing.

The car stopped. Felice took a breath.

"My family are time-travellers," she blurted out, "and our house moves through time and space. That's why you can't find it. Those men are, I don't know, *Time Cops*, from the future! They want to arrest us all and we've been hiding from them, on a farm. In Provence, that bit was true, sort of. The farm's made out of light, though. I *know*, right?"

Claudia's face was expressionless. Felice had no idea

what reaction she should expect from her friend. Nothing?

"Damn," said Claudia, after a second, "Malou was *right!*"

"What?"

"Time-travellers. That was *her* theory, Malou. Everyone at school has a theory about what happened to you, all of you, your family, why you disappeared. That's what she said. Time-travellers. Damn. I said you were in the witness protection programme. Most probably. That was my theory. Except I really didn't believe it. You know why not?"

Felice shook her head. She was a bit in shock.

"Because I couldn't find your damn house. I knew where it *should* be—but it wasn't. I don't make those sorts of mistakes, so there had to be some crazy explanation. Time-travellers. Okay. I wasn't being intelligent enough, that is all."

"But," began Felice, only to be interrupted by her friend's monologue.

"And then there was that so-called *earthquake* last year, the day we were all at your house. I was *there*. I *felt* it. But it wasn't reported anywhere. Not at all. It was like it was only in your house. That made no sense, either. Madame put it down to 'local subsidence', would you believe it? I, for one, did not. No. Certainly not. A theory must be able to explain *everything* for it to be valid."

"But," tried Felice again.

"All aspects of the phenomenon must be accounted for. Otherwise, *no*. I blame myself. I should have been more logical, less conventional, in my thinking. For two whole years I have racked my brain for a theory that explained everything. I eliminated too much of the impossible, yes? And little *Malou*, of all people, she was right all along. *Malou.* Damn."

"What! For me it's only been a few months, not two damn years," said Felice, clearly perplexed. "This should be mid- September 2020, but it's not, is it?"

"No, it is September 2021. We should go."

Claudia restarted the car. The engine, once again, purred in cat-like satisfaction—or self-satisfaction, if you like. They pulled out into the lane.

Felice felt confused, but pleased. She studied the side of Claudia's face, feeling an odd mixture of recognition of something that was both familiar and yet strange, changed somehow. She couldn't quite put her finger on the difference.

"I can't believe that you just accept my story," she said, "you know, like, without question. Just like that."

Claudia shrugged. "Why should I not? Believe me, it makes sense of it all. It explains *everything*. Perfect! Now, if I drive to where I think your house should be, will we find it?"

"Yes, so long as you're with me, it'll be there. —*Oh my God!*"

Claudia looked around. "What?"

"You! You're nearly two years *older* than me now! That's it! That's what really weird!"

Felice was horrified. Her friend smiled.

"Of course. I am seventeen, almost eighteen, yes?

"And me, I won't be sixteen for another four months yet! This is terrible. Just terrible. I can't have you being this much older than me. I don't know how I went wrong! It should be September 2020! That would be bad enough. But *this—this* makes no sense."

Claudia laughed. "When we get to your house, you can tell me all about it. I want to know *everything*. —Oh no, look! Felice, *there*, on the next corner! See? They've gotten ahead of us somehow! The horrible men in hats! Your *Time-Cops!*"

It was true. The three roundly-behatted TDA agents were standing on the Rue de Saints-Père, as casually as if they were waiting for a bus. They watched with what seemed like only passing interest as the two girls sped by in the little car. Felice didn't like it. They seemed altogether too calm. Something wasn't right.

"What are they doing?" asked Claudia.

"I don't know...spectating? Not much, anyway, by the look of it. This can't be good."

"Why not? They are there, we are here... What can they do? We will be at your house very soon. Unless they have back-up. Do they have back-up?"

"I don't know. I don't know that much about them, to be honest. But they must have gone to extreme lengths to track me here, and now they're just standing around while I go by? It doesn't make sense. I don't like it."

"If they are from the future, maybe they know things we do not? That would be logical."

Felice nodded. That was her concern also. But, then, they didn't seem to have expected Claudia's intervention in the art shop. Could it be they only knew so much?

"I guess, maybe," she said. "Or perhaps meeting you has changed things? The future isn't set in stone, I know that much."

"Funny that we met like that," said Claudia. "Do you not think? Almost like it was engineered. Lucky chance, I guess."

"Yes," agreed Felice, doubtfully. "Very lucky. At least for me."

Felice studied her friend. Claudia appeared entirely unperturbed, which was reassuring, well, sort of. Weird, too.

She left it for a moment but, then, felt compelled to ask:

"Claudia, why aren't you more freaked out about this? You should be. I mean, we're talking about time-travel and crazy policemen from the future and you're like, I don't know, just going with it. What's that about?"

Claudia shrugged matter-of-factly, her eyes fixed on the road. "Well, you see, what happened to you and your family and your mysterious house, that is a puzzle that has tormented me for almost two whole years... And now—

right now—I'm solving it. Believe me, I want this more than anything. And it's *in*teresting! —Oh, look out, more trouble ahead!"

Claudia had spotted three more TDA agents on the far corner of the next junction, on the other side of the Boulevard Saint-Germain. Felice's heart sank. If there were more of them on the streets, it was going to be so much harder to get back into the house. Oh, why had she come? How could she have been so naïve? Felice studied the three new agents closely as she passed them in the car. Once again, they didn't seem particularly exercised by the fact that the two girls were—technically—escaping. Why not? What did they know that she didn't?

Felice suddenly lurched forward as if to get a closer look.

She stared, hard. It couldn't be, could it?

"What?" asked Claudia. "What is it? Felice?"

"Claudia, they're *not* three new agents. They're the *same three* we saw a few minutes ago. I recognise them. I'm sure of it."

"But how would that be possible? *Is* it possible?"

"They must be time-jumping. That's it. That must be what they're doing. It could only be that."

"Time-*jump*ing? Can *we* do that? *Please.*"

"We can't do anything until we get to the house. But once we're there we might have to, just to get away. I'm sorry, Claudia. I should never have gotten you involved. This is terrible."

"Are you kidding? No, this is *magnificent*! I regret nothing."

Despite herself, Felice laughed. It was all just so surreal. Here, she was, in a getaway car[104] [105] being driven by her

---

[104] VSP. Top speed 45mph.

one-time arch-nemesis from school, who had already helped her escape once already this morning, and who was now a practically full two years older than she was herself, and who was more gung-ho for the crazy adventure than Felice could ever have imagined.

Claudia laughed, too. "What?" she said. "What is funny?"

"I don't know—*you*! Sorry, Claudia, you're just so *not* what I expected. From school, I mean. But, listen, you *do* realise that the TDA are probably already waiting for us at the house? That's why they're not chasing us now."

"The *TDA*? The police, not police, in hats? That is who they are? TDA? Let them be waiting! —Which way now?"

"Straight, all the way to Rue de Sèvres. Then, head for Saint-Sulpice. That'll be left. Then a right on Rue des Canettes. It won't take long."

Claudia give her another arch look. She *knew* the roads.

Felice laughed again. Under other circumstances this would be a really enjoyable experience—riding with her friend in her car—and probably something that happened a lot. Every day. If her life were normal. Which it never would be. No matter what. This was a sobering thought. She peered out of the window. Paris was passing her by.

"What is it that you did, your family?" asked Claudia. "Why are these TDA trying so hard to catch you, anyway? Are you, really, you know, criminals?"

"I guess," replied Felice. "My grandfather's from the far-future—like the twenty-eighth century or some such craziness. He started all of this. And, technically, my dad is, too. They want to take them back there. And I suppose we

---

[105] *Vehicle Sans Permit.* Okay?

do take quite a lot of precious stuff from other times and bring it all back into the house. The TDA really doesn't like that. And, well, yes, we *did* destroy the timeline a few months ago. That was bad. So, yes, pretty much. Guilty as charged."

"My goodness," cried Claudia, "you and your family, you are like the *Time-Bandits*, no? From that old movie?"

Felice laughed. "Well, I don't know about that, although George does go around acting like Strutter most of the time. But maybe we are? Which one am I, I wonder?"

Claudia interrupted Felice's speculation with a forwards nod of her head, however, in the direction of Saint-Sulpice. The three agents were in sight once again, on the street corner, not chasing, but watching, ahead of the game. Something about their demeanour, the complacency, was very annoying. And quietly sinister.

Felice shivered. She needed to get herself and Claudia into the house.

Fast. Somehow.

"Well, they are just getting creepy, now," said Claudia. "If I have to pick sides, I pick yours."

"You already did," said Felice. "George, he'll be pleased. though. I'd forgotten you two had that moment at the party in the spring. I must admit I thought it was a very bad idea at the time."

"What? Oh, you mean that time during the so-called *earthquake*? That was so long ago. He will not still be thinking of me."

"I wouldn't bet on it. It hasn't been *that* long for *him*, remember? Take the right here. We've got to go left on *Rue Madame*—and pray!"

Claudia gripped the wheel. "I am ready."

"Good," said Felice. "Park wherever you can on Rue Madame and follow me. I don't exactly have a plan, but I'm not sure they'll still know where the house *is*. Last time they found it, they had an invitation, stupidly enough, to the party. Now they don't. It might not be visible to them anymore. We'll probably have that much advantage. Unless, of course, it *was* them who unsealed the door and this is all just a trap? Sorry, Claudia. I really just don't know. It's weird."

"Do not worry. I want to see this magical house suddenly appear. That's all. If you knew how much I'd searched for it, you would understand. Look, I can park here. No police in hats, unless they can be invisible, too? No? Okay."

Claudia was right. The street was very quiet. No sign of anyone, let alone their pursuers. Felice was uneasy. Exiting the little car made her feel exposed, vulnerable. If the TDA had unsealed the door, why not just grab her straightaway? Or in the house, even? Maybe they *didn't* know where the house was exactly anymore? But if not them, then who? Who else could've done that? What was she dealing with? So much uncertainty made it really hard to know what to do for the best.

She tried to stay calm (breathe, now!)—and led Claudia across the deserted street. If they were going to get through this, she needed to keep a clear head.

"Whatever happens, Claudia, thanks for helping me."

"Do not thank me, show me. I have combed this entire area so absolutely thoroughly that I think I know every single inch of it! When I came to your house for the party, it was easy to find, normal. You followed the directions and it was there. Afterwards, impossible. It has been very perplexing."

"I'm sorry. If it's any consolation, technically it *hasn't* been there. The house has been looping through time, or at least it should have been, to avoid detection. This way."

Claudia followed Felice. "*Looping through time…* To think, I had no idea you were so interesting, not until that day I came to your house. That day, you were so not what *I* expected, from school. Not at all."

"Touché," said Felice. "Probably I deserve that.

Listen, Claudia, why is it so quiet? Why would they track us—in advance—all this way, and now not be here waiting for us?"

"Maybe it isn't us that they want?"

Felice stopped dead. "You're right! It isn't me, *us*, that they want. They want the *house*. They want me to show them where the house is. Claudia, I've been such a fool. I can't go back without giving them what they want. I'm trapped out of my time. What am I going to do?"

Claudia gave her a determined look. "We are prepared, are we not? We will do what we came here to do. No future man in a silly hat is going to stop us. This is true, I know it."

"I wish I had your confidence," said Felice, but in fact she did feel a little bit better already. Claudia's determination was infectious. "Come on, this way. There's a gap between buildings that leads to an alleyway. We need to head down there."

"An alleyway? No, there is no alleyway. Not here."

"Trust me," said Felice, leading on.

The two girls continued along the street. The road narrowed ahead, with no let-up in the tall, compact buildings on either side—no spaces between them. No alleyway.

It remained very quiet, too, unusually so, without another soul in sight. Had the TDA somehow managed to reorganise everyone's lives so that at this very instant they all suddenly had a pressing reason to be somewhere else? That would be very impressive, if so. But Felice quickly dismissed this idea as extraordinarily paranoid—or so she hoped. They neared the end of the street. A municipal building stood on the right, some kind of depot on the left. But no gap either side.

"See? Nothing," said Claudia. "No alleyway."

"Wait. Give it a second. Keep walking with me."

And there it was. That's all that could be said: *there it was.*

The house.

Not overly large, at least not from the outside.

Not tall, or not especially so.

In fact, it wasn't especially *anything*—except ordinary. And inevitable. Of course, *there* it was. Why would it be anywhere else? This was where it stood. Obviously. Along this alleyway and down a short flight of stone steps on the left. As solid as, well, a house. *Any* house. You just hadn't been looking right. Somehow. Until now.

Long afterwards, Claudia would view this as *the* moment of perfect clarity in her life, when the fog cleared and looming towards her through the mist, full steam ahead, as plain as day, was the ocean liner she wanted to board, and never get off.

"Of course, this is exactly how it looked when I came here for the party. *But...*" her words trailed off for a second, "*h...how?*"

"The house recognises me. Come on. We mustn't stop. Not now."

"*Recognises* you? What does that *mean*? It is a *house*."

"Think of it as future technology. A supercomputer. It's *programmed* to allow me to see it. That's all. Let's be quick."

Despite her confusion, Claudia allowed herself to be led down the alleyway. "I still don't *see...how...?*"

She stopped. At the other end of the alleyway stood a man. In a hat. Felice saw him, too. As a reflex, the pair at once glanced behind them, back in the direction they had just travelled. The same sight. Man. Hat.

They were trapped. But where was the third? The other TDA agent?

Felice span around, a sickening lurch in the pit of her stomach. He was there, over her shoulder, close enough for her to see the yellow of his teeth. Too close. Far too close. She jumped. Terrified. Comprehension dawned on Claudia's face, her reaction trailing that of Felice by an infinitesimal lag.

In an instant she took in the situation. Man. Hat. Close. Grin. Smug. Hideous.

She struck. Making a short, swift movement, Claudia smashed the palm of her hand upright into the pleasingly squishy, flat nose of the 'police, not police man' from the future, who reeled backwards, his eyes a picture of pain and shock, his hat tumbling, his nose at once bloody—spectacularly so.

In awe, Felice looked on, the scene unfolding as if in slow motion. Then, everything speeded up. Move. The two TDA agents were running towards them from either end of the alleyway. The agent Claudia had struck—Watkins, Felice recognised him now—was recovering his wits. She grabbed Claudia, pulling her towards the steps. They had to get inside. It would be touch and go. Proceed until apprehended—that odd thought ran through her mind. *Proceed until apprehended.*

Claudia was right behind her, the steps only a metre or two ahead. Three. They would make it. They would not make it. The agents were closing. Watkins, right there. The steps. The girls. He had them.

And then the entire alleyway began to shake. Violently.

CHAPTER 7

Felice saw their chance. The sudden shaking may have felt like an impromptu earthquake but its timing was fortuitous in the extreme. She leapt down the short flight of stone steps, with Claudia following right behind her. Watkins, the TDA agent, lost his footing completely, such was the unexpected violence of the quake, and his two colleagues were helpless but to abandon their pursuit. They too were struggling to stay upright, like two awkward, cross-legged Bambis on ice.

Not wasting her chance, Felice pounced upon the door, which opened instantly at her touch. She and Claudia threw themselves inside, piling in one right after the other. The door slammed shut. They were in. Yes. But were they safe? Disturbingly, the house continued to shake, with no sign of the wild tremors ending.

"We have to move the house," shouted Felice above the uproar. "Stay here. The house should keep them out but stay here to make sure. I'll be quick. Don't let them grab you!"

For the first time Felice detected an element of doubt

in her friend's expression. "Move the house? How? And why is it shaking? Is it safe?"

"In *time*, Claudia. I have to move it *in time*, the house, so we can get away. And I actually don't know why it's doing this or if it's safe. I really don't. But moving it should fix everything, I think. Okay?"

Claudia nodded, her face now once again a model of resolve. "Fine. Do what you must. I will hold them off. No one shall pass. No hats in the house! None. Go!"

One quick nod of assent and Felice took her cue. Without looking back, she rushed up the stairs to the hallway. All of this was so strange. Everything. She had no idea why the house was shaking or why it had started at the very moment that it did. All she knew now was that she needed to get into the Library and move the Paris side exit through time—and fast. Poor Claudia. She didn't deserve any of this. But hopefully they could sort everything out once they were safe again. No time to think about how exactly how just yet. Somehow.

The Library. In a matter of seconds, she was there. Alarm bells were ringing in her head as Felice made her way with difficulty up the spiral staircase to the higher level. Fire sirens, even. All of this madness going on now was because of *her* stupid, selfish choices! Not only were the TDA at the door but Claudia—*Claudia!*—was in danger. In her panic Felice tripped, once, twice, on the narrow landing, before virtually tumbling headfirst into the secret room behind the bookcase. The violent shaking, however, was no less pronounced here. The levers. Felice scrutinised them, hard. One must have slipped. Her fault.

Wait. After their first trip together hadn't George gone on for an age about him discovering some kind of 'auto-return' setting that would take the house back to the exact moment you'd set off from? She felt sure he had. No more dangerous time-slips, he'd said. He'd fixed everything, he'd said. Smug git. But that's exactly what she needed now, if she could only find it. That would at least gain them some time. Literally. Everything could be sorted out afterwards. Fixed. Put right. As rain.

Then, she noticed something unexpected. One of the levers on the right had a tiny pale enamel plaque on the wall behind it that bore the legend 'Auto' in stark black lettering. Had that always been there? If so, why had she never noticed it before? No matter. This wasn't the time to question her normally infallible observational skills. Felice pushed the lever back to the one setting to which it would move, which wasn't very far—and immediately the terrible shaking ceased. Her relief was instantaneous and immense. No tremors now, although a kind of aftershock still lingered in her ears. The absence of the violent shaking felt almost unnatural, as though she had stepped off a particularly wild funfair ride and still felt giddy.

But at least she was okay. She took a breath. Exhale *and* relax…and

…Claudia! Felice at once exited the secret room and raced back along the narrow landing, down the spiral staircase and out of the Library. She called out her friend's name and was dismayed not to get any response. Had the TDA broken into the house? Had they taken her? Had they? She called out again. Nothing. The silence was overpowering. It hinted at disaster, foretold it, even. Felice would never forgive herself if any harm had come to Claudia—and all because of her own selfishness and stupidity. That would be impossible to bear. She rounded the corner and came to the staircase down to the side exit, her heart stilled, breath held, afraid at what she might, or might not, find. And—

Claudia was there, sitting on the floor in front of the door with her back against the wall. She looked up at Felice, two large, brown, defiant eyes.

"Is it over? Are they gone? Did we win?"

Felice nodded. "I moved the house. We're safe, for now."

As though with some effort, Claudia picked herself

up. She looked out through the pane in the door. "So, if I step outside now, it would still be Paris? Yes?"

"Yes, still Paris. But about a whole two years ago, for you at least. For me, it's my present. The party you came to here was only six weeks or so ago. ...I know, weird, isn't it?"

Claudia took a breath. "Very. I wouldn't like to live those years again. Although maybe I could go tell myself that you and your family are okay? But if I did do that, *had* done that, one, two years ago, *now*, wouldn't I know about it? And then perhaps everything would be different and I wouldn't be here. How does it work?"

"I'm not sure. I think it's something like your first timeline always happens, but it just segues into this new one that we've made and carries on, for the *you* that's out there, *now*, anyway. I don't think there's any hopping back and forth between timelines but I'm no expert. Anyway, it's George who likes to think about this stuff. The real question for me, Claudia, is how do we get you home? And the other thing, while we're at on the important stuff, is how did you *get to be such a ninja*? Tell me that! Because, girl, the way you hit that guy—he didn't see it coming!"

Claudia smiled. She shrugged. "That was nothing, easy. Training, is all. Everyone can do it. But, this, *here*, your house, I want to know all about this. This is special, unique. Yes? And you promised you would tell me everything. You will keep your promise?"

Felice saw the determined look on her friend's face. Plus, she *owed* Claudia now. It would be difficult not to meet her end of the bargain. Would that be so wrong? How could things be any worse than they were right now?

Felice helped her friend up on to her feet.

"Okay, sure, look, I'll give you the tour. But later we still need to get you home—and then I've got to figure out how to put that damn door back on a loop. The TDA could find it at any moment. That would be a disaster. All over again. I'm not sure I could take it."

"Not to worry," said Claudia, smiling, coming up the stairs. "Now you have me to help you. We are a team—and *formidable*! The future men in hats, police or not police, they have no chance. Not a hope. Now, tell me *everything*. I need to know."

Just for a second, seeing Claudia's expression, Felice hesitated, troubled once more about if she was doing the right thing. In fact, he knew almost certainly she was doing the wrong thing.

Again. But that hadn't stopped her so far. And maybe she was hesitating only because the idea of telling anyone about the house felt so strange? Maybe that was it?[106]

And a promise, after all, was a promise.

Everything, she supposed, could still turn out okay. Possibly?[107]

Whatever. She'd decided. She was doing it.

"Come with me to the Library, young lady," she said. "And prepare to be amazed."

* * *

As promised, Felice explained everything—or as much as she could think of, at least—to her eager-to-learn companion. That her crazy genius grandfather came from the far-future (as did, technically, her father, although he didn't grow up there and had been blissfully innocent of this knowledge until disturbingly recently). More, that her crazy genius grandfather was the architect of the house and so therefore the inventor of a time-machine, no less, because that's was the house was, really. A time-machine.

---

[106] Or, alternatively, maybe not.

[107] Quite possibly not, in fact.

Yes, that was right. She's grown up in a time-machine (though she, too, in her defence, had been blissfully innocent of this knowledge until disturbingly recently).

And what did he do, her crazy genius grandfather, with this incredible time-machine invention of his? To what use did he put it? Did he save the world? Cure diseases in the past? Prevent disasters from happening? End wars? Or stop them from starting? Any of that? No.

He travelled through time collecting (shall we say) precious antiquities and rare artefacts.

Yup, this whole time he's been on this ultimate antiques road-trip. That's all. And why?

Because in his time, see, in his Fake Tomorrowland, everything, every object, is nothing but a simulation made out of light, pretty good simulations, yes, most excellent simulations, in fact.

But they lack what he calls *authenticity*. They're just not real. Indistinguishable from the real thing, yes, but fake. They're *inauthentic*. And so, for this reason everything that Claudia could see here, now, everywhere in the house, was probably priceless, a true original taken from its own time. Cool, no? But, alas, for this same reason her crazy genius grandfather was also the crazy genius author of all their misfortune—for all of her family.

Because the TDA, those Men in Hats, they were hunting *him* through time—and because of *that*, they were *all* being hunted, all the Redmaynes, for *his* crimes; and, well, now as a result they were all reduced to hiding out indefinitely (in*def*initely) on a farm that existed somehow in a gap in time and space, concealed from the prying eyes of the world. Literally nowhere.

Lit-er-al-ly—No-Where!

That, worst of all, no escape, no point of return to their *normal* lives, such as they were, was in sight. And, because of this—all of this, everything, being stuck on the farm— well, she'd finally grown bored, hadn't she? Well, more than *bored*, really—sort of desperate, and come into the city today and…here they were.

While she talked, Felice led Claudia through the house towards the Library. At the door she paused. As far as she knew, no one except the Redmaynes possessed the least knowledge of what lay inside. She felt like she might be violating some kind of unspoken family bond or some such thing by taking Claudia inside. Ah, *secrets*, they had ruined their lives. She'd had enough of secrets! But, still…

"What is it?" asked Claudia.

"Nothing. It's okay. Come on."

She leaned on the door and they went inside.

Claudia gasped. The grandness of the Redmayne's Library would stun any so fortunate to be a visitor. It wasn't just the great size, or its startling *roundness*, or the reams of polished wood and gold, or the three ornate clocks all in a row, or the spiral staircase or indeed the circling shelves upon shelves of books upon books, no: it was its *unexpectedness*. How could an ordinary-seeming, domestic-looking house, at least from the outside, contain such startling grandeur? Behind an ordinary seeming door, there was *this*. How could that be? Of course, Claudia had experienced this sensation before, when entering the Music Room at the party of a few months / few years earlier.[108] Awed. She felt awed.

And yet welcome, somehow. A wonderful, warm, golden light seemed to welcome you inside and encourage you to come in for a while, sit, read, and forget about the world beyond its circular, book-filled walls. Like all the best people Claudia was of course an avid reader[109] and she felt that the pull of the room, its lure, and the sheer

---

[108] Coz, like, relative to the individual, time, innit?

[109] Like *you*, too.

attractive gravity of the books themselves, very strongly. The urge to let yourself go in there could be compelling, for anyone.

Felice could hardly not notice the impression the room was making on her friend.

"Probably some of the rarest volumes in history are contained in this room," she said, with—despite herself—no small amount of pride. "Including no doubt many that haven't been written yet, at least as far as you and me are concerned, I mean, in our time. My crazy genius grandfather, see, Claudia, this is what he does—he collects. That's it. And this is what it amounts to, in the end. *This*. And it is kind of marvellous, too, I suppose. You know, I reckon I *do* sort of understand it, now—*him*, I mean—and why he does it. To be honest, despite everything I've just said about the sly old fella, probably I wouldn't be any different, given the chance, and that's the truth. Must be in the genes."

Slowly, Claudia span around, taking everything in, as far as she could see. Her face indeed suggested she had surely stepped, stumbled, fallen, all at once, into a sort of heaven. The pale blue tint of the high domed ceiling overhead, especially when all suffused with that warm golden light, might easily be mistaken for the heavens themselves on a blue-skied, sunny day.

And if Felice had explained to her now that in fact, yes, this was the case in this mysterious future-house, that what she was seeing now was actually the sky, Claudia would not have been completely surprised.

Anything, it seemed, was possible.

"You have so *much*," she said. "At school, we could not imagine, *you*, with this, *all of this*. Everything. You seemed so, I don't know, so *ordinary*. Forgive me. That is rude."

Felice dismissed her friend's comment, and perhaps the entire contents of the great Library, the countless rare volumes collected from every era, with a careless wave of her hand.

"Ah, it's nothing. You know, I recently discovered you *can* have everything, *and* a place to keep it. It's not all that great. You know, the TDA want us to put it all back, all the objects displaced from their proper time, including Papa, my *dad*, I mean. They want to take him, sorry, you know, like, *back to the future*—and leave *us* here, right *now*—Emile and George and me. We'd be instantly dead to him, I suppose, and for us he wouldn't exist yet."

"That's horrible. They would *do* that, those horrible men in hats? Yes? Then, I am pleased I struck one in the face."

"Actually, George did that, too. He'd be impressed. But none of this is what I brought you in here to show you. There's more. Come up the stairs with me."

"What is up the stairs?"

"All of history. Come on."

Felice led on. Claudia followed her up the black steel spiral staircase and around the narrow landing towards the secret room. They went quietly, for the moment. If a Library containing many of the rarest volumes ever written wasn't the main attraction, you would feel more than a little trepidation about whatever might be coming next. Claudia could see that one of the bookcases ahead was pulled forwards on one side so that it stood at an angle to the others, much like a door ajar, which, of course, as we know, was exactly what it was.

Felice took her around into the opening. The secret room, with its many levers, switches and dials lay before them, in subdued lighting. It didn't look that extraordinary but it was.

"This," said Felice, stepping inside, "is where the magic happens."

"In truth? From here?" Claudia followed her into the room. "This is where you move through time? In here?"

"Yup, from here you can move the house to any point in history. I believe. No, actually, that might not be strictly accurate. From here, you can manipulate time and space

230

outside any one of the three exits to the point that you require. I think that is probably the more true statement. Jeez, I'm turning into Papa! Sorry. Anyway, they'd probably all kill me if they knew I was showing you this, it being top secret stuff and all. I'd be in so much trouble."

Claudia moved forwards into the room, her eyes taking in everything. "So many levers, why?"

Felice shrugged. "That's my crazy genius grandfather, I think, part of his quest for authenticity. Imagine him as a sort of *Belle Époque* gentlemen traveller—or a Victorian explorer from the future. Hence the whole retro-steampunk design vibe. No doubt the entire mechanism *could* have been rigged to run on, I don't know, *thought*, like the farmhouse is. Some kind of mind interface. Neater but less dramatic, if you know what I mean."

Claudia nodded her head, but seemed distracted. She didn't say anything. Her mind was, perhaps, as they say, blown. Felice felt the first pangs of regret, of serious misgivings. Some things, once they're switched on, can't be switched off again. Ever. She began to realise she'd maybe said too much, revealed too much.

"Well, that's the tour," she added, after a moment or two of not exactly awkward silence. Awkward-ish, at least for Felice. "I suppose what we've got to think about now is how we fix all this, you know, get you home."

"Home?" said Claudia. "But I'm not expected at home for at least a year yet, or maybe two, didn't you just say? What is the rush?"

"Claudia, we can't stay here. Not for two years! Not even for one! No, we've got to take you back to your own time and put the door back on the loop somehow. That's what we need to do. And soon. Today! Otherwise, I really will be in so *much* trouble. I'm sort of hoping no one needs to ever find out about today, you know, about what happened—okay, about what *I've* done. Not my finest hour, exactly. But I can still fix it. I just need to get you home."

Claudia's face betrayed her disappointment. She bit into her lower lip but didn't say anything. Despite herself, Felice did feel badly for her. At the same time she didn't see that there was anything else she could do.

"The thing is, Claudia," she went on, "that, well, you can't just go gadding about through time doing whatever you want whenever you want. Okay, tell that to my grandfather... But George and me, see, we learned that lesson the hard way, not so long ago—the day of the party, in fact. That day, well, to cut a long story short, that day we lost Emile in the past, or at least we all thought we'd lost him. And we didn't know *when*, either! Major drama, see? Like you could not believe! Maman, Papa, all of us, we had to go hunting though time for him. It was desperate. In the end, George and me found him in New York in 1900. But that was only after Papa had changed history by giving Shakespeare one of Maman's red pens. You wouldn't believe the amount of trouble a little thing like that caused."

"Shakespeare?" said Claudia.

"Apparently so. Not that I've met him myself. Don't get the wrong idea. The point is, it's dangerous, time-travel is. Really dangerous. And not just for you, us. Everyone. The *world*."

Claudia took a second. She drew a deep breath.

"Very well. Of course, I understand. It is your future-house after all. Forgive me. It's just, to think about, everything you could do, see, experience, all of it, it is just so, well…"

"…Tempting? Believe me, we know; George and me, I mean. We *do*. We got a little carried away with it ourselves for a while; more than a little, if I'm being honest. I guess this is why Maman and Papa hid it from us. They knew best. Because once that particular genie is out of the bottle, you can't just put it straight back in. We know this *now*, me *and* George. And I'm sorry, I should never have out you in this position, Claudia. But I'll always be grateful for your help today. You were, I don't know, spec*ta*cular. If I hadn't run into you like that, who knows where I'd be right now? What were the chances?"

Claudia nodded. "I enjoyed it. And at least now I know what happened to you and your family, George, everyone. And the vanishing house. I was not going mad. The house *does* vanish. It was difficult to accept that I could be wrong, especially about something so important. But I was *not* wrong. So, okay…"

"Okay?"

"I am ready. Take me back. If you say I must go, I will go."

"Okay, then," said Felice, a tiny bit surprised by how readily Claudia had assented. "Right. Okay. Claudia, well, yeah, it's been great seeing you. You have no idea how much I needed to see *someone*. I was going a bit stir crazy on that farm, I think. Cut off, that's how I felt. But seeing you, all this, it's been great. If mildly terrifying, under the circumstances."

"Right. I know. Listen, I have a good idea. Why don't you take me back half-an-hour before we left? That way, when you and I exit my car, I can get in and drive off. The men in hats will not be expecting that. You could be so precise with the steampunk-levers? To the half-hour? Is that possible?"

"Sure. That is more than possible. Look, see…if I do this…and this, *voilà*! That's pretty much all there is to it. Take off the 'anchor' lever, this one here, and adjust the two levers linked to it, one backwards, the other forwards, like so, and you can fine-tune the time as much as you like. It's really intuitive to use, actually. My grandfather actually *is* a genius. No doubt about it. If more than a bit crazy."

"That is great. Time-travel never looked so simple."

"Well, yeah, I guess. Of course, there's lot going on I don't understand. I don't know how to move it from one place to another. And I don't know how to put it on a loop, the door, that is. Any door. I'm going to have to find that out. There's a book, but George has it with him, I'm pretty sure. He's a freak for this stuff, especially lately."

"There is a *manual*, for this, and George, he has it?"

"Yeah, I've glanced at it but he reads this stuff compulsively. We never see him."

"That is interesting." Claudia looked around wistfully. "George, he was interesting, also. I could see he had hidden depths. So, the door, it is moved? If I exit now, it will be thirty minutes before we came in?"

"Yes, should be, give or take. But we should go now. We wouldn't want to meet ourselves on the way in. I don't know what paradoxes or whatever that would cause but the thought of it is just too weird to contemplate. Let's go."

Felice led the way. "You know, if I ever get the nerve to tell George about any of this, I *will* tell him about how you helped me and what a total ninja you were, *are*. He'll enjoy that. But from my perspective the only hidden depth George has is the extent of his ego. But, after today, what do *I* know—about anything?"

"Oh, I am sure you know much about many things. This has been very educational today."

"Huh," said Felice. "I'll take your word for it."

Silence fell. The pair had left the Library by now and were making their way along what was at this point a far more gloomy hallway than earlier, towards the side exit. Felice was racking her brains for something to say that didn't sound trite or ungrateful. Claudia *had* saved her. And Felice *was* going to miss her. To some extent, she felt like she was missing her already. They rounded the corner towards the exit—and stopped.

They stared.

"Felice," asked Claudia, after a second, "should it be night-time outside? I think, perhaps not? No?"

"Gosh, *no*. Very much no!"

Felice rushed forwards as if to confirm the obvious. Through the misty, opaque glass, only darkness was visible.

Night-time, most definitely.

She stood, confused, before the door.

"I don't understand it. I've never been this far out before. Wait here. We've no idea *when* that is out there. I don't want to lose *you* in time. I'm sorry."

Claudia nodded, a model of calm, especially given the circumstances. Felice turned away and hurried along the hallway back towards the Library. What could have gone wrong? Was this her fault? Maybe she'd missed something out, some stage in the process, but she didn't really think so. Still, she *had* overshot earlier, though, on the way out, hadn't she? By almost a year!

Maybe the mechanism was broken? But that didn't seem likely.

Felice reached the Library. No, she must have introduced an error into the calculations at some point and misadjusted the settings. Best thing she could do would be to start over. No, best thing would have been *never* to have started any of this in the first place! Damn! Another lesson learned. But failing that, the next best thing, the best thing she could do *now*, would be to start over and take it from there. That's all she could do.

Inside the secret room Felice feverishly studied the levers. They didn't *seem* wrong, but obviously they were. Somehow. Stay calm. Don't panic. Breathe. *Auto-Return*. If she used the 'Auto' setting, that would at least reset everything to the point of their last adjustment. That would undo the error she had just introduced. Wouldn't it? Then, she could take it from there. Easy!

Yes, if 'easy' meant trying to solve a fiendishly difficult algebraic maths equation while standing on the shifting quicksands of Time.

No rush. No pressure.

Felice made the adjustments. One last check. *There.*

That *looked* right. It *should* be right. That *was* right. It *had* to be. Quickly Felice exited the room. Once again she descended the spiral staircase at speed and ran out of the Library, along the hallway towards the Paris exit. The hallway was no longer gloomy. That was something. A small hope grew in Felice's heart that, against the odds, she had fixed everything, made everything right, and no one need ever know exactly how stupid she'd been today.[110]

But, at the same time, counterbalanced against this tiny, tiny hope of Felice's was the far, far greater fear that if she had gotten it wrong again—*again*—then she had literally no idea how to fix it. None.

Daylight. Felice could see that it was at least daytime again outside. Breathless, she reached the staircase down to the side-door. Claudia was there. Neither girl said anything at this point. A look passed between the pair. Daylight. This should be it. Very bright.

In fact, if anything, too bright. And cold, not warm.

Tentatively, Felice opened the door—and they could see why.

"Felice," said Claudia, staring out, "should it be winter?"

"Damn!" said Felice, closing the door sharply. "I don't understand it. I really don't! I'm doing everything right, I'm sure of it. I *know* I am, in fact! Oh, I'm *so* sorry, Claudia!"

Claudia was calm, still. "What do we do? Are we lost in time? Does this mean I can never go home? And if I went outside now, when would it be? This is interesting, no?"

Felice stared, a little confused. She thought her friend seemed altogether too sanguine about the present situation and its implications, but then Claudia wasn't responsible

---

[110] And not to mention, selfish and bad. Felice specifically asked me not to mention that. So I haven't.

for creating it. That was all on no one but herself!

"I don't know *when* it would be, Claudia, I'm sorry to say. But, no, we're not *lost*. We will fix this, I promise."

"Do not worry. I have confidence it will turn out okay in the end. Now, George, perhaps he could help us?"

Felice was loath to involve any members of her family in this debacle, if she could possibly avoid it. She hadn't reached that point yet. All at once an idea struck her—clear as any bell.

"The *book*! George *has* the *book*! I could go to the farm and bring it back. That would explain what I was doing wrong, whatever it is! No one need ever know about any of this. Claudia, you're a genius! Truly!"

"George, he will give up this book? And no questions?"

"He won't need to—in fact, he can keep it. I just need to look through it. I don't forget anything I've read. Oh, why didn't I do this earlier? Yesterday? Anytime? I'm my own worst enemy, always."

"And I will come with you to the farm? This future-farm?"

An infinity of possibilities ran at once through Felice's mind about the potential consequences of either leaving Claudia in the house alone or bringing her along to the farm, none of which seemed particularly encouraging or favourable. Bad, in fact, either way.

"I think you should come with me as far as the exit from the caves. You should be safe there and I won't be long. Ninety minutes at the most. What could go wrong in ninety minutes?"[111]

---

[111] Strictly speaking, what could go *more* wrong...

Felice attempted a brave laugh at this point. Failed.

"Caves? What are these caves? We are going spelunking now, you and I?"

"No, nothing like that. Come on, I'll explain as we go. First of all, I think I need to adjust the Paris door one last time, you know, auto-return it to where it was—sorry, *when* it was—before, you know, the sudden onset of winter just now. That way, well, I should at last have an idea where I'm starting from when we try again. I really don't understand it. I'm beginning to think something weird is going on. Possibly."

"It is, believe me," said Claudia. "This is the weirdest day ever. For me, anyway. And now we have *caves?*"

"Oh yes, well, tunnels really, I suppose." They had reached the Library again. Felice paused. "Wait here. I'll explain everything in a sec. I won't be a minute."

Felice ducked inside the Library. Once again, she ran up the spiral staircase and around the narrow landing to the secret room. Levers. Auto-return. Done. That should correct whatever error she had inadvertently introduced a few moments earlier. She hoped.

As she exited the room Felice saw that Claudia had followed her into the Library. She was examining one of the many books spread out on the long table. When she heard Felice, she looked up, book in hand. Her awed expression suggested she might be handling the Holy Grail itself, which, quite possibly, for all she knew, was lying around *somewhere*. The kitchen, perhaps. With teabags in. Maybe.

"This folio, 1603, it is *Hamlet*, yes? The *first* Hamlet. It is *signed*. Is it real?"

"Yeah, it's real enough. But, look closely, the signature, it's signed in *red biro*. Who would believe it was real, even though it's true? That's my family for you. We create calamity in exchange for dubious wonders."

Felice had descended the stairs. Claudia was gazing up and all around, almost reverentially. What *else* was in here?

"They do not seem so dubious. No." She placed the copy of Hamlet back on the table, clearly with regret. "They are genuine wonders, and yet you are so matter-of-fact. I do not understand. And what *calamity*?"

"Well, we lost Emile for one. And now, I've managed to displace *you* from your proper time as well. Calamity, see?"

Claudia shrugged. "I am not the one complaining. Home will seem very dull after all of *this*. Maybe I can stay here for a time? But, no, I can see from your face, that is not possible. Okay, then, *caves*. Yes?"

"Yes, caves," said Felice. "And we're going to need a flashlight. Two. If you get lost down there, you really *will* be lost. And that's a calamity I couldn't take. That would be the end, believe me, the absolute end. Of you *and* me, both. So, stay close. *Please*. Understand?"

Claudia nodded. But, so Felice noted, nothing about her remotely indicated that she considered the situation to be anything more than an adventure, one that, on the whole, she would rather like to prolong, if at all possible.

Displaced in time? *Oui*.

Possibly unable to get home? *Oui*.

On the run from Future-Policemen in Hats? *Oui*.

Concerned? *Non*.

And Felice was beginning to wonder—in a day of considerable weirdness—if this perhaps wasn't the weirdest thing of all.

Oui.

CHAPTER 8

In the end, following an exhaustive search of the ground floor of the house, the girls could find only the one flashlight, which would have to do. Along the way Felice explained about the additional secret exit that her grandfather had only recently (whatever *recently* meant here) installed behind the kitchen stove, which led out into the French caves. As far as she knew, that exit didn't move through time but was fixed at the one point—no, that wasn't quite right.

Not *fixed*, no… Rather it moved through time at the standard rate, contemporaneous with the farm. Or so she believed. What she was trying to say was that you couldn't manipulate it to other points in time, unlike the other exits, as far as she knew. Damn. Did she know whether that was right? A true statement? One that wouldn't leak? That was something her father would say. My God. She was turning into her father. It was just that all of the time-travel stuff was *really hard* to get right![112] You had to be precise, express it exactly *so*!

Felice took a second to clear her mind and tried again.

What *could* she be certain of? Well, the fact that no new levers associated with the kitchen exit had been built into the secret room in the Library *suggested* that you couldn't manipulate it to other points in time. That was it. That was a *true* statement. No leakage...

Although...her grandfather *was* a person of many secrets. *Many* secrets. Anything was possible. Felice paused, wavered... But, no, no, her expectation *was* that when they went out into the caves shortly it would be the same day that she'd come in on earlier that morning, advanced in time by only the few hours that she had personally experienced in that intervening period, if Claudia followed her thinking?

This last point was expressed with no small element of hope.

Claudia nodded. They were outside the Music Room at this point, having already searched the Dining Room, the Great Dining Room, the Game Room, the Scullery, the Back-Scullery and the Middle Parlour. With each new room they'd searched, Claudia reacted as though she had fallen afresh into the well of astonishment, such were the treasures on view.

Paintings, precious objects, gilt mirrors—it was bit like going around Versailles, she said, only compressed into a shorter space, and Felice had responded sceptically to this on the grounds that Versailles was so *gaudy*, didn't she think? All that gold?

Ah, the Palais de Versailles in the time of Marie Antoinette (who was, coincidentally, Claudia's long-time

---

[112] And really, *really* hard to write about... Just saying.

heroine, as well as Felice's), now *that* would be *her* destination of choice if she could have but one time-travelling adventure..[113] The splendour, the luxury, the style—no matter how gaudy—that is what she would like to see most, if only she could. But as she could not, this house made for an adequate facsimile, she felt sure.

Versailles in miniature. That is what this crazy, magnificent house was like. No?

Felice couldn't help but smile. Le Petit Trianon, the Queen's more modest private residence? Maybe, yes. But the gaudy Palais itself? *Non.* The Redmaynes were *not* like that. No. They had *taste.* Honestly. They did. Well, she couldn't speak for the men in her family. That was also true.

She was nothing like them. Of course.

Her father and grandfather dressed like stuffy mathematicians who might be able to express style in a formula or an equation but wouldn't have the first clue about what to wear to a party—or to any sort of social event for that matter.

That went for George, too, by the way. Style was not hidden anywhere in his so-called depths, regardless of whatever fanciful thing Claudia might be imagining about him.

In fact, all three probably needed a super-computer to tell them how not to dress like one!

Laughing at her own joke, Felice pushed open the door to the Music Room. In the exact centre stood the black concert grand piano, the Sauter, that she had been playing at the party when the 'earthquake' had struck. Claudia remembered this room very well from her only other visit

---

[113] Coincidence? Foreshadowing, more like. Expect to see the Austrian Queen consort of Louis XVI of France in Book 3.

to the house. It was here that she first had some inkling that there was something extraordinary, fabulous even, about the Redmaynes. This is what she said now, looking around. The walls were littered with musical instruments, cellos, oboes, and all sorts of obscure oddities, such as the trio of wall-mounted fluegelhorns and Mr Redmayne's flumpet, all of which only added to the impression that the house was occupied by a family of eccentric billionaires with an odd penchant for ethnomusicology,[114] which, in fact, may or may not have been the truth.

Either way, it wasn't *at all* what Claudia had expected, hence her bewilderment at the time.

"This room made me feel very strange last time I saw it," she said now. "I could not make the connection between the Felice from school and the Felice who lived *here*, with all of *this*. It made no sense. I felt a dislocation, like two worlds colliding. And then the earth actually shook and the next day everything was gone. Do you understand the mystery in that? Why it possessed me? I had to find the truth."

"Well, I'm sorry about all of that. I really am. But at least now you know what happened. Does that make it any better?"

"Yes."

The emphatic nature of this last response surprised even Felice, although she wasn't sure exactly why. It is perhaps always a little unsettling to find yourself the subject of someone's obsession, no matter how sound the reasons for it might be. She scanned the room.

"Not much chance of finding a flashlight in here, I don't think. We should head down. I made it here without one, so I can make it back. Just stay close. It's like pitch

---

[114] Look it up. Go on. What, no, you have? Sorry.

black night in the caves. Really. Totally. Okay, come on."

The pair wandered out into the hallway and along towards the stairs.

As they walked on, Felice tried to see things from her friend's perspective. It must have been really strange for Claudia the way everything unfolded. Her obsession probably wasn't that odd. Felice probably would have responded in exactly the same way. Her own track record with obsession was pretty strong, she knew.

"Hey Claudia, I've just realised… Every time you come here there's some kind of quake—and yet it's only ever happened twice, in my lifetime, anyway. That's a weird coincidence, don't you think?"

"Yes, but I cannot be the cause. Why does it happen? Do you know?"

Felice paused. "The first time, it was my crazy genius grandfather. He engineered the whole thing, we now think. But this time, nope, I've got no idea… Though, we were very lucky—the timing was perfect, don't you think? It saved us."

"Yes, perfect. But who would be motivated to engineer it this time? And why?"

This idea startled Felice. The quake this time had just *happened*, hadn't it? Surely the levers had slipped in some way? She mustn't have properly secured them. That had been her assumption. Her fault, but lucky all the same. Besides, nobody knew she was here, so how could anyone be engineering anything?

And yet, so much was going wrong…it *was* very strange. All of it.

Felice continued down the stairs. "Come on. We need to figure this out so we can get you home. I'm hoping what happened earlier was just down to luck, but when you think about it, what are the chances of that? It's all very strange. I'm having a very strange day."

"Me, too. Outside that door, it is Paris. But not the Paris of my time. Not quite, is that right?"

"To be honest, Claudia, I'm not certain *when* it is exactly out there right now. Not anymore. Come on, we need to fix this. And without me getting caught—or either of us arrested! Look, the book will help, I'm sure of it. Let's go try make some sense of this, huh?"

After a second Claudia nodded, a gesture that Felice at once returned. Almost solemnly, the pair were agreed. Then, Felice led them both on down into the basement kitchen.

Of course, on entering she saw that everything here was just as she'd left it when she'd arrived only a few hours earlier (although it now seemed much longer ago than that). The great range stove remained in its 'forward' position and behind it stood the new thick wooden door that gave access to the caves. It felt a bit unreal now to Felice to remember that she used to eat her breakfast in this cosy kitchen every morning with George and Emile: coffee, croissant, for her, while her two brothers had typically wolfed down the sort of full, cooked monstrosity that their father believed / insisted made for a good start to the day (fried eggs and, worse, *bacon*, first thing in the morning, *ugh*!). She'd taken all of that for granted, as though it would—naturally enough—continue forever. And now...

Somewhat less than gently Claudia nudged Felice back into the present, jolting her out of her daydream. Almost as soon as they had entered the room she had spotted the flashlight on top of one of the many tall cupboards. It took Felice a second to realise what her friend was pointing at high up there on the top. Flashlight. Good spot. Just as well one of them was still paying attention. She pulled a chair over and stood on that while she reached up for it. She switched it on to test if it still worked before stepping down. It did. They would not be totally in the dark in the caves. That was something.

"You take this," she said, handing it to Claudia. "That way you won't necessarily be lost forever if something happens and we get split up."

Claudia said nothing but switched the flashlight on and off again herself.

Felice took a last look around the kitchen. She took the heavy iron key out of her bag.

Claudia looked at it with interest.

"This thing has been weighing me down all morning," said Felice. "Unlike the other doors this one has to be locked. I think anyone can see it; although, to be honest, they would need to know where it was before they could find it. And no one does, I don't think. No."

"So, no men-in-hats waiting for us in the dark?"

"Nope, shouldn't be. Not unless they're much smarter than we've given them credit for so far, which I doubt— ser*iou*sly doubt." Felice turned towards the door. "Shall we?"

Claudia nodded again. "I will miss your future-house. I wish I had more time to explore it. It is like a Museum of Time and holds many mysteries. And it is very grand, no matter what you say. *Stylish*. You do not realise this of course because you grew up in it. Felice, you are the luckiest girl alive and you do not even know it."

"I don't know about that. No, really. I *am* currently on the run from the Future-Police and living on a two-acre farm that is literally—*literally* literally—nowhere. You know what I mean? And it's all because of *this* house. At the same time, I *do* miss it. Never mind. Look, if all goes well, we'll be back in a couple of hours. And later, after we're sorted out, back to normal, then, who knows what will happen? But come on, let's fix this first bit."

Felice unlocked the door. She removed the key and held it up to show her friend. "You know, I made an exact duplicate of this back at the farm—*with my mind!* Out of *light!* Would you believe it? It's supposed to be the only one, but you can make *anything* in the future, anything you want, *out of light…*"

Felice stepped out into the dark of the caves. Claudia

followed.

"That idea is too amazing for me to contemplate," she said, in a quiet voice. "Truly."

"Yes, you're right. It *is* amazing, really. At the same time, it's not as great as you would think. Weird."

"Why is that?"

Felice shrugged. "Not sure, exactly. Kind of takes away the *challenge*, or something. Having everything. I don't know."

"I would like to try having everything, to see."

Felice pulled the heavy door shut. Instant darkness.

Claudia switched on the flashlight. At once, the light flickered, failed. Blackness returned. Total dark.

"Shoot," said Felice. "I just need to find the lock. Wait. Stay close to me. Don't wander off. Oh, *no*! *Double-Shoot!*"[115]

The sound of something heavy hitting the floor followed.

"What was that?"

"Me, dropping the key! Sorry. It must be right here. Help me feel for it."

"Why don't we just open the door again? Then, we could see it."

A moment's silence. "Claudia, I take it all back. You *are* so much smarter than me. If you just push on the door, I'll—"

Felice froze. "Wait! Claudia! Can you hear that? Someone's coming! Someone's there! Quick, inside! *Now*, they're close."

"But, your key!"

Hesitation. Footsteps, voices—*men's* voices—echoed eerily in the caves. Getting closer every second.

---

[115] Again, not the actual oath used.

"No time! Quick, *in*!"

"Is it the Future-Men? Who?"

The door was open. Light. Ironically, now not helpful.

"I don't know. *Go* in."

Felice pushed in after Claudia, close on her friend's heels. She shut the door. With a bit of luck whoever it was out there probably wouldn't even see the door or pay it any attention if they did.

Unless, of course, they happened to be looking for it.

"Claudia, we should be prepared to hide. It could be anyone outside. *Anyone*!"

"You think *it's*—"

But Claudia didn't get to complete her sentence. To the horror of both girls it became clear that the key was being inserted into the lock. Any second now the door would open and—

A look passed between the pair. *Run.*

They ran, but only as far as the stairs. Halfway up, out of view from the door, Felice stopped. The door hadn't opened. Why not? For some reason the would-be intruders seemed to be struggling with the key in the lock. But surely it would only be a matter of seconds before they realised that the door was already unlocked?

A thud followed, as if something heavy had fallen against or banged on the door, which then creaked open. Ajar.

Felice looked on from the cover of the stairwell.

Claudia had reached the top already. She stared back down at Felice, for once looking anxious herself.

Still, no one had entered. The door opened wider and, to Felice's unspeakable pain and distress, three very familiar figures now stood in the kitchen.

That's some rabbit hole, she heard George say. *It really is.*

"*Go*," she mouthed to Claudia, and then crept silently up the stairs to join her. "We've got to hide. Now."

"Is it the Future-Men?"

"No, worse… My *family*!"

"Who, George?"

"Yes, and Papa and *his* father! Go. They mustn't find me here."

After an infinitesimal delay (option processing) Claudia turned right and half-crept / half-ran[116] along the hallway towards the rear of the house. Felice kept up. She couldn't believe the way the day was turning out. It was as if her worst nightmare had been scripted in advance and she was now being compelled to act it out scene by scene. Karma. Bad. Very. Someone—somewhere, sometime—had to pay for what she was going through today. Preferably someone other than herself, of course.

The door to the Music Room still stood open and Claudia ducked inside there. Felice followed. She took in the room in a flash. They needed to arrange things so they could hide properly.

"The piano," she said, "let's turn it so we won't be seen from the door. It'll conceal us. The *lid*. See?"

Claudia nodded. Without another word the pair went over and laid hands on opposite ends of the Sauter. Even though its four legs stood on tiny brass wheels, a piano of that size could only be turned with effort. Together, *turn*. Both girls span the piano approximately forty-five degrees to their respective left. The upright black lid now provided the maximum coverage for concealment if viewed from the door.

Then, breathless, they each took a moment to collect themselves.

Claudia looked at Felice. "Your family?" she said, very quietly. "Maybe they can help us, *me*? Maybe George, he could help?"

"Yes, I'm sure he'd love that. Prince Charming to the

---

[116] It's a thing. It *is*. Try it.

rescue. No, only as a last resort. I'm sorry. But the fallout from everything I've done today would be, I don't know, like a nuclear winter or something. Nothing would survive. And I don't want that, not *now*, anyway, not so soon after the last time. I'd be in purdah forever. Utterly untrustworthy."

Felice bit her lip. Her pangs of conscience were of no use to her now. If she could do this again, she wouldn't—this she knew.

"And if they find us anyway?" asked Claudia. "What then?"

"I don't know. Que sera, I guess. But why are they here, *again*? That's what I want to know. Not *unless*—oh no! It couldn't be, *could* it? Please, no, not *that*!

"*What*? What is it?"

"No one else was due to be coming here today. *I* wouldn't have come if they were! No, no, *no*! This must their last, first, *only* trip here, from a month ago! Somehow the kitchen door has gone back, too. I can't go home to farm now because I'm already there! Oh, Claudia, it's such a mess! I've made such a mess of everything! I'm *so* sorry!"

Claudia's reaction to this news was difficult to gauge as her expression remained steadfastly blank. Felice couldn't tell if her friend were disturbed by or indifferent to this potentially devastating turn of events. She assumed the former, because that was how *she* would feel. Or maybe Claudia just didn't understand the consequences?

"Are you okay?" Felice went on. "Claudia, listen, I'm so, *so* sorry to have done this to you, really I am. I had no idea the new door could move."

"So, now we will need your family's help? To fix it?"

"I don't know. I suppose. We *are* more lost than ever. I just don't see how all of this could happen. I'm doing everything right, I'm—"

Felice stopped. The door to the Music Room was opening. Instinctively, both girls ducked down low behind the piano. Footsteps. But whose?

Whoever it was came in further. The two girls, their faces close, eyes wide, mouthed the same questions back to each other in barely intelligible and increasingly frantic whispers. Who? What to do now? Us? Do you know? Should we?

Neither of them had any of the answers. Paralysis.

George drifted into view. His attention was focussed on the collection of brass instruments on the far wall. He was looking for something. Clearly he had no idea that his sister and her best friend were hiding less than twenty feet away, behind the piano. But all he had to do was turn around and they would be discovered.

Felice and Claudia had another silent, wide-eyed exchange.

Nothing. No clear result or decision.

Claudia stood up. "Hello, George," she said.

Such was the extent of the poor boy's extreme shock in that moment that it is almost tempting to say—if ever in all of Time such a thing might be said literally, rather than metaphorically, and still be an accurate approximation of the event itself—that George quite literally leapt out of his skin.[117]

Nothing more happened for a moment. Not only did it appear that the two main protagonists themselves were frozen, along with Felice, as sole witness, but that the moment itself had become as though so infinitely elastic, so pregnant was it with possibility and change, that the comprehension of it prolonged the instant and seemingly froze it into infinitude. Time, the perception of Time, in the minds of the beholders, again quite literally, froze.[118]

---

[117] There, I've said it, 'quite literally', when relating something metaphorical. Sue me.

[118] Again, sue me. This time I'd win.

This was, of course, the most significant moment of George's life. Afterwards, nothing would be the same or as it might or perhaps should have been. He grew up, grew down, became, unbecame, all in the same instant, severally, a man, a new man, a very different man. His Fate sealed. Time's Master, and Time's Slave. But all of that, the working though of the *detail*, was still to come. For now:

"*Wha...*?" managed Time's Master. "How? What, no? *Claud*ia? Jeez, wait a minute, no, what, Fel*ice*? Is that *you*? But...we just left you back at the house. So, *how*?"

"George, please don't freak," said Felice, throwing a quick, passing glare at her friend. "*Please*, George... Listen, it's a long story. I almost got caught by the TDA. Claudia saved me. But we're stuck here and we need your help. And I *don't* want Papa—or *Maman* for that matter—to find out. Okay, especially not Maman. Do you understand?"

George's ears may have been hearing words, but his level of actual understanding of their meaning was far from, well, shall we say, standard.[119] His eyes, on the other hand, were comprehending a much more basic truth: Claudia, here, now. Claudia, *here*, *now*.

"George, are you listening?" Felice grew impatient. "Try and snap out of it. Good grief! There isn't much time and we need your help! Papa or Grandfather might walk in any second. George!"

"I came to look for you, for all of you," interrupted Claudia, "and today at last I found Felice. Or is it tomorrow that I find her, or the year after next? I don't know."

At first George said nothing in response to this but, judging by the look on his face, you could (quite literally)

---

[119] i.e. Non-existent.

see his mind catching up with itself, with the situation.

The initial shock faded. He turned to Felice.

"She *knows*? You *told* her? *Ev*erything?"

"George, I had *no* choice. The TDA, they'd cornered me. Claudia was just *there*, she saved me. They even chased us all the way back here, right to the house. We almost didn't make it!"

Having caught up with itself, George's mind was now racing on fast-forward.

"Wait a minute, what *are* you even doing here, anyway? Oh, no—*when* are you from? What date?"

"That's just it, George, that's exactly what I'm trying to tell you. If this is your first trip back here, I'm from about a month in *your* future. Mid-August—August 15th, to be exact. But Claudia, I think she's from about two full years or so ahead of me. Isn't that right?"

"September 15th, 2021. Last time I looked, that was the date. When I left the house this morning, that *is* what it was...I am sure." She shrugged, in an exaggerated Gallic way. "Now, *who* knows?"

After a second, George managed to look away from Claudia.

"*Fel*ice?" he said.

"George, *don't*... I know. Look, I got bored on that farm. Everyone could see that. More than bored. I only wanted to come back and do some stuff, you know, *normal stuff*, in Paris. That's all. Who knew it would come to *this*?"

"But instead you brought the TDA here and got yourself *marooned* somehow. What *is* the problem, anyway? Why don't you just take Claudia back home and then reset for when you left. That shouldn't be too hard. You[120] can do that."

---

[120] i.e. "*Even* you can do that."

Felice punched her brother on the arm, hard.

"*Ow!* —What?"

"Don't patronise me! And pay attention, George, listen… There's something *wrong* with the Time Mechanism. It's not working the way it should. It's keeps misbehaving, taking us to the wrong time. I don't know why. It's almost like someone's rigged it somehow. Anyway, to begin with, to get back, we used the auto-return setting and then—"

"The *which*?"

"The lever marked 'Auto'—I used that. *You* told me about it, I'm sure. Last year, you *did*." Felice ignored her brother's equally exaggerated (if somehow non-Gallic) shrug. "Anyway, that's what we did and this is where we are, wherever this is now. Darn, it's such a mess. And I really don't want to get caught."

"What your sister says is true," added Claudia. "We have acted exactly as described. Will you help us?"

The request seemed to act like an influx of oxygen into George's brain.

"Wait, wait now one minute, that key outside, in the tunnels, the one we just found, that's the *original*. You made a copy and left that at the farm, didn't you? In its place, so no one would suspect? Felice, that's brilliant! Devious in the extreme, but brilliant. Okay, I'll help you, as far as I can. For me, this is the middle of July—July 2020, that is, of course. I'll try now and prime the Time Mechanism to Paris for mid-August 2020, that's your correct time, Felice, isn't it? August 15th. I'll try to set it up; but you can't activate it until after we've gone, other we'll lose a month when we exit. So, after we leave, move the Paris door to then. Because the farm is in France, too, the kitchen door must be linked to that, I reckon. Unless there's something else going on here that none of us understand. Anyway, that's my working theory."

George's mind was racing. He threw Claudia a quick glance. He had her full attention.

"No, wait! Felice, listen, even better," he went on, breathlessly, "I know, to be absolutely sure, move the whole house, *all the doors*—you'll need to do that. Trust me, I've been reading up on this stuff. Yeah. That'll drag the new door with it—it *must* do. Okay, yes, do *that*, right, and I'll come back with the key. Then we can look to getting Claudia here home together. Got all that? Good! Okay, phew. That should work. I think. But hey, still, Felice, tell me one thing, though. The Paris door? How's you manage to unseal it in the first place? That's even got grandfather stumped."

Felice looked confused. "George, I didn't. It was already like that. *You* told *me*, in fact. I wouldn't have come otherwise."

"Really? I can't have done that yet. Did I know how to do it? Fix the door, I mean. Was there a hypothesis? What did grandfather say about it?"

Felice glared at her brother for a second as if to warn him that this was really no time for showing off, but then—given the circumstances—she let it go.

"I don't know, George. I think I wasn't supposed to know. Oh, okay, wait, wait, wait, George, *you* could *stop all of this* from happening. You could tell me not to come here today. Then, none of this would happen. I'd be in the clear and Claudia would be safe. George, stop me! You could do that."

Neither George or Claudia seemed to like this idea very much.

"You would prevent me from having this adventure?" Claudia said at once. "I would never know what became of you all. My search would go on, and on. No, I do not see that at the better option. Not at all. Could this even be done?"

"I don't know," said George. "It might be dangerous. Claudia is already *here*, inside the house—and the house, its interior, is outside of normal time. Claudia would *still* be here, even if I go back and stop you from coming. Same goes for you, Sis, I think. This *you* would still be here, too. Then, you *never* go home. I could be wrong but I think we need to see this out, wherever that leaves us in the end. Otherwise, who knows?"

Felice appeared even more dejected than before, but a glance, almost conspiratorial, passed between George and Claudia. Call it relief. Something.

"Like I was saying," George began, clearly feeling better about all of this than his sister was, "after we go, take the Paris door ahead by—"

But this was an instruction he didn't get to complete. The door to the room flew open most dramatically and there, almost as if larger than life, stood his father.

Instantly, the two girls ducked back down behind the grand piano.

George, to all appearances, was standing alone, awkwardly, in the middle of the room. Felice—willing him to move, do something, anything—pulled Claudia into a tighter crouch. She held a finger up to her lips, just in case the staying silent part of hiding wasn't clear this time.

Mr Redmayne spoke first:

"George! Great Galileo's Ghost, lad! What are you doing *there*?"

"Nothing," replied George, hopelessly.

Felice struck her forehead. Her father went on.

"Really, my boy? Well, okay. Look, sorry about just now, you took me by surprise. The thing is, I wasn't expecting to see you there. That's all. I practically jumped into the middle of next week…"

Move, George, Felice was thinking. Don't just stand there. Idiot.

George, the idiot, just stood there. Purposelessly, begging the obvious question, which followed almost at once:

"So, why are you in *here*? That's what I meant. Is the front door secured?"

"Front door? The front's door's fine, Dad. No

change." Felice was mouthing for her brother to move—away, out, anywhere. This distracted him, although he was trying not to show it. "You know, still sealed and looping, yup, just like when we left."

"Have you told your Grandfather? What did he say?"

"Er, Grandfather. Nope, I haven't seen him. I checked the door and then I came in here. Isn't he with you?"

Felice's forehead suffered another self-inflicted blow.

"No, clearly not. Are you sure you're okay? You're acting very peculiarly."

"*Am* I? Am I really? *Peculiarly*, you say? That's odd."

"Yes, and you look like you've seen a ghost. What's wrong?"

Despairing, Felice sensed her father approaching closer. George was going to get them discovered. She began to shoo her brother away vigorously with both hands.[121] Claudia joined in, too, for good measure.

This seemed to have the desired effect, as George at once set off to intercept his father.

"Wrong? Nothing's wrong here. Nope, everything's good, in fact. Fine. No problems. If you want to know the truth, I was just looking for something, something of *yours*, actually. A trumpet. Grandfather told me about it. I just wanted to see it."

A silence. Both her brother and her father were out of view now. Felice was finding the tension unbearable. And what was George babbling on about now? A trumpet? Where was *that*, for goodness sake?

Suddenly, it all clicked. That must have been the reason why George came in here in the first place. He was

---

[121] Some would say *violently*. Especially if they could see the expression on her face. *Yup...*

looking for this stupid trumpet. Felice looked around. She could see it. There. On the wall.

And anybody who went over there to retrieve it would be able to see them.

"Ah, I understand, I think…" said her father. "You mean the one *Miles Dav*—"

The penny seemed to drop for George. Despite this, he seemed as if routed to the spot.

"That's right, yes," said George. "*That* one. But it doesn't matter now. You're right. I shouldn't be in here, wasting time like this. Not when we've got more important things to worry about. We should go."

"But it's right over there," said Mr Redmayne. "On the shelf. It's *there*. See? We could fetch it right now. It won't take a second."

Felice held her breath. Claudia, too, she saw.

"No, no, we really must go. Right now. Because, you know, there's much more urgent things to do. Put the side-door back onto the loop, for one. That's what we *need* to do. Really, we do. Now, in fact. We don't want the TDA wandering in, do we? Or *anyone*. That's what's important. Let's go find grandfather, why don't we, and do that? Right now. He'll be wondering where we are, anyway, I bet."

"I doubt it. He's probably in the Library. I asked him to keep an eye on you as well. I should have known better. *Anything* could have happened."

"Well, nothing did. Absolutely nothing at all."

Felice dared to breathe again. It sounded as though they might be going. At last. Then, it didn't. George went on.

"And sorry, Dad, for giving you the fright. Just now, I mean. *Almost jumped into next week* you said, the *middle* of it. That's funny."

"Is it? Why?"

Felice sensed them both pause, no longer leaving. *Leave.*

"You know, time-travel and all that. We *could* jump

into the middle of next week *if* we wanted to, couldn't we? If we *really had to*, you know. We *could*. Or even the middle of next *month*! The *exact middle*. The *whole house in one go*. Every door, jumping. That's even funnier. An entire house jumping in fright! Get it?"

"I suppose, yes."

George, just *leave*. Now, *go*. Were they going?

"That's all it was. Silly, really. Not much of a joke, either."

They might be going. Their voices sounded more distant.

"Just jump *into the exact middle of next month*—ha!! The whole house!"

With that, the door shut. They were gone. Silence followed.

Felice breathed again. For now.

"Remind me to punch him properly next time," she said in a quiet but determined way. "What *is* he like?"

"He was improvising. I liked it."

Felice gave her friend another odd look.

"And he was all the time giving us instructions," Claudia went on. "And in a clever way. Oh, he is not so bad. But, siblings, you cannot see it. Fortunately, I am blessed without any."

"Well, lucky you."

"Do you think he will help us? I think he will."

"Well, we'll know soon enough, I guess. Let's wait a while for them to go and then we'll see where we are and what we need to do. In the meantime, I just want to get my breath back. I thought there was no way we'd get through that undiscovered."

"But George, he did well. He kept us safe, and he will return for us. You will see."

"Yeah, and then what? I still don't know what the best thing would be for us to do—about *you*, I mean. At least now we should be safe from the TDA. But what will happen if I take you home? Oh, I've made such a mess.

I'm sorry."

"So you keep saying. But maybe none of this is your fault. Maybe it is meant to be. All of it, exactly like this? Maybe, Felice, this is how it is written?"

"I doubt that very much. We have a tendency to write the future ourselves in our family. And who would write it to turn out like this? Seriously, no, this is just a mess—*my* mess."

Claudia shrugged. For the person potentially most affected by everything that had happened she seemed disturbingly nonchalant about it all, Felice thought. Too much so. Perhaps she just couldn't appreciate the consequences? That could be it. But it was odd.

Felice stood up. Claudia followed.

"Okay, why don't we wait here for half-an-hour or so and then we can go listen by the door. After that, once we're sure they've gone, we can go see where we are—you know, what we need to do. How about that?"

Claudia nodded. "That is a good plan, yes. We can wait. Right now, I want to see this famous trumpet, the one that belonged to Miles Davis. You heard that? He is my favourite, too, a musical legend. How do you have it here? Your family?"

"I have literally no idea," said Felice, thinking this statement might apply to so much that was going on today.

And, in truth, for once, she was more right than she knew.

* * *

The girls carried out their plan. The Music Room was, unsurprisingly, rather well soundproofed. Earthquakes aside, little penetrated its calm, still interior.[122] But when

---

[122] And that was, technically, a *Time*quake. Just saying.

they opened the thick heavy oak door a short way, finally, and listened, there was nothing—not a sound stirring anywhere in the house other than themselves and the relentless, loud ticking of the great grandfather clock in the hallway, counting out time.

They were alone.

Once again the house felt especially empty. After the earlier excitement the newly restored silence hung everywhere in the air like a great heaviness all of itself. Oppressive. Very. More than ever, Felice wanted nothing more than to leave, except quite possibly, quite impossibly, now, never to have come here today in the first place. But, alas, what was done, this time, could not be undone, not even by the Redmaynes. Consequences, once again—and always—the consequences had to be faced, however unpalatable. And so it was.

Even worse, the pair were now trapped in the house. The Paris door was looping through time, and Felice's father had taken the key to the new door in the kitchen with him when he left, quite sensibly locking it behind him. He therefore had both keys, Felice none—and no means of fashioning another. No, they were trapped and had no choice but to the execute the plan they'd so rather vaguely (she felt) fashioned with George. Take the house forward a few weeks into next month and see if he came. Their saviour. The thought took root bitterly in Felice's mind. Big brother to the rescue. Darn. How could she have let this happen? Darn, indeed.

But this is what they did. Having inspected the Paris door and the kitchen, they went on to the Library. Everything looked much as it had before, except the controls—the three longer levers, in particular—now appeared to be set in a 'better' order, to be somehow more 'right' looking. Felice understood their positioning more intuitively than she had earlier. Somehow. She felt that she could now see exactly what it was she had to do.

All the same, her confidence wasn't such that she

believed she could risk taking Claudia forward to September 2021 and then returning herself to mid-August 2020 to meet George. Too risky. She had one shot to get this right. First go. Bang on the money. No second chances. This was it. Two weeks. Late July 2020 to Mid-August 2020. All controls. Easy-ish.

Or at least it should be. Felice studied the controls for a while longer. Hadn't George said he was going to prime them for this trip? What did that even mean? Whatever.

Right, okay. Let's do this. And then, she hesitated.

Claudia seemed to sense this. "What is it?"

The sign—the little black-print, enamel 'Auto' sign—it was no longer there. What had happened to that? It *had* been there. One of her family members must have taken it down? But why?

"I'm not sure," said Felice. She didn't know what this meant. "Nothing, I guess."

Slowly, taking extra care, she manipulated the smaller lever for the Paris door, on the working assumption that if this door was in sync with the kitchen, which similarly exited into France, then, finally, they might find themselves in the right place at the right time. And hallelujah to that.

Felice steadied her hand. The longer lever she didn't want to touch. That looked just right where it was. They weren't going very far, anyway, only one month into the future. One tiny little jump.

There, it was done. She stepped back.

"It is finished?" asked Claudia. "We are in your time? Out there?"

Felice nodded. "Should be. But I've been wrong before, as you know. Let's go see. If the Paris is no longer looping, that would be a good sign. We'll know that we're some*time* at least if we see that. Let's hope it's the right time."

"And then what, if it is? The right time?"

"After that, we hide, from *me*. I'm going to turn up first and start this whole ball rolling. Then, we wait, for the Boy-Wonder to show up. Our hero."

Claudia nodded now. Felice had the impression that this outcome didn't seem at all bad to her friend. This, she didn't understand.

"Come on." She led Claudia back to the Music Room, knowing her earlier self hadn't looked in there when she'd arrived, what was it, only hours, only lifetimes ago? They'd be safe from discovery in there.

But when they re-entered the Music Room, her favourite of all the rooms in the house, even that felt no longer the same to her as it once had.

Now, it felt as though violated, somehow. Ruined.

"And so, you will be both inside and outside, at the same time?" Claudia asked, all at once. "Are you not tempted to see? To meet? No, not even a little bit?"

"Then we'd be stuck with two of me. Everyone would love that. No, best avoided, I think."

"Not even a glance though the crack of the open door?"

Felice remembered how she had imagined earlier when she'd first arrived that day, that there had been eyes watching her in the house. Never had she supposed they might be her own.

"You watch," she said. "I've seen it before. I know what happens. Don't get caught. After I've gone, the other me, we have to go back and undo whatever she's done, to the controls."

A terrible thought occurred to Felice. Good grief, did she strand herself? Or was this a different future she was setting herself up for? Her other self? This sudden glimpse of the infinite number of possible futures made her shudder. It was too much. She wished—no, she didn't know what she wished. She was done with wishing.

"You look. Let me know when I'm gone. I don't want to know anymore."

* * *

Afterwards, after the other Felice had come and gone, as anticipated, like clockwork, and the controls had been universally adjusted for one final time to August 15th 2020, as they seemingly had to be, the exhausted pair waited in the kitchen for George amid what felt like an even more funereal silence throughout the entire house. Not even the great grandfather clock was audible in the basement. Silence hung everywhere in the thick air like a prelude to thunder.

On the way down the girls had checked the Paris door, peaking out. It was now off the loop, and looked as if it could be the right time—certainly it was the right season, which was something and gave Felice some hope that this time, *this* time, it had all gone well, at least for *them*.

Claudia speculated at one point about going out right then to meet *her*self and whether, if she did, about what that would do to her being here now?

Or maybe she *had* done that already—and perhaps *that* was why she *was* here today? And then she had laughed at this idea, but not in any way that made Felice feel any less uncomfortable about it.

But no doubt her friend was only messing with her head.

And so they sat around in the kitchen and they waited.

Was there anything to eat? Both girls discovered simultaneously that they were ravenous. Claudia said that her last meal (breakfast) had been over two years from now in the future, or thereabouts, and that just saying it like that had made her feel even more hungry, somehow.

And what if George was late, or didn't come, would they starve?

No. (Felice began to look though the cupboards for something for them to eat).

Did food go off in the future-house? Didn't time stop in here?

Yes, and *no.*

How about sending out for pizza? How did that work?

They didn't send out for pizza.

Not ever? Not once?

No, not once. But they ate very well, all the same.

Huh. Claudia sat at the table as if pondering a world without pizza deliveries. Time-travel, but no pizza.

Felice found some of Maman's delicious *Gâteau-aux-Noix* in a cake tin in one of the cupboards. She served them both a slice each on two small plates. Walnuts, rum—dense and yet light. How?

A physics-defying cake in the future-house? But of course! Claudia seemed very pleased with her joke. Felice began to wonder if George would ever get here.

Time, as it does, passed.

Felice was thinking. George had known about this for the last month. Every time he'd seen her, he had *known* what was going to happen, and yet he hadn't given her the slightest inkling about what he knew. Not only had he virtually lied to her every day, he might even have made sure it happened, by telling her about the unsealed door. That had made her think that coming to Paris was even a possibility. He'd *manipulated* her into making it happen, in fact.

She said all of this to Claudia.

"But, George," replied Felice's friend, "he had no choice. He explained this. It may have been dangerous for him to try and change it, seeing how, for him, it had already taken place. It might even have been harder for him, to keep this secret for a whole month. He was protecting you."

"Not just *me*," said Felice.

"Well, I think he is very brave and determined, your brother. For us, it has only been minutes; for him, many weeks. That cannot be easy. Try to think of it like that."

Felice harrumphed, evidently unpersuaded. Neither of them said anything for a while.

Out of the blue there came—at last—the tell-tale noises they had both been waiting for, the sound of the key in the door. It was still a shock. Felice's first instinct was to hide, but it was a very small and worn-out instinct at this point. She was tired of hiding. George might have played her but she had made all of her own decisions. If it were anyone else but George coming through that door, well, it was time to face the music, to own up to the mess she'd made—and get help to sort it out. Whatever. Bring it on.

It was George. His face peaked out of the darkness beyond the door, into the light of the kitchen, wearing an expression that suggested he was uncertain of what he might find—an expression that brightened when his eyes lighted on them both, or at least on one of them.

Claudia leapt up and, to his obvious surprise and delight, hugged him. Tight. Felice didn't move. Brother and sister exchanged a look, however, an exchange unseen by the hugging Claudia, but it was a significant moment.

It suggested that a line had been crossed and they both knew it.

And that things between them would never be the same again.

CHAPTER 9

In the end it took Felice several weeks to come around, and even then she didn't do so completely. But by that point Claudia had already made herself quite at home on the 'Future-Farm' with her new, adoptive family and wasn't showing much (or indeed, *any*) interest in returning to her actual home in Paris, where her actual family might or might not be actually waiting for her.[123] As with everything else to do with time-travel, the situation was complicated. Far too complicated. Fact.

When he'd turned up back at the house that day, George had been persuasive about the possibility that it could be, if nothing else, *dangerous* for Claudia to be returned back to her own time right away. The TDA knew

---

[123] Depending.

who she was now. She'd helped Felice escape from them. They could punish her for that.[124] Possibly. Or they might use her to get to *them*, the Redmaynes, even, as a bargaining chip in some way. Or other.[125] It was risky. The thing *was*, standing there, the three of them simply didn't know what might happen. Or not. Or how risky any of it might be.

And that was about the truth of it.[126]

Claudia should come back to the farm with them, so that their parents could decide what the best thing to do would be. Or they should at least be consulted. After all, this was Claudia's life they were messing with here. She should get a choice about what happened next. And, when all was said and done, it wasn't as if they couldn't return her home at the exact right time whenever they wanted, was it? And it wasn't like her parents would know any different, in any case, when they did.[127] *Was* it? No, and when you think she hadn't *asked* to be put in this difficult situation, had she? None of this was her fault.

But it *was* her life. Claudia should choose.

Claudia chose the farm. The Future-Farm, where anything your heart desired could be made out of light. This, she had to see.

And by this point Felice was so fed up with all of it,

---

[124] "Punish, *how*?" Claudia herself had asked. George didn't know. This didn't hold him back.

[125] George was extemporising. Vagueness permissible. He thought.

[126] Ah, finally. The truth.

[127] Depending, see? They either were missing her, or they weren't missing her. Or both. Depending on the point at which she were to return home. They might never know she'd been gone. Although if Claudia were to turn up and suddenly be 102 years old, that might require some explanation.

with the TDA, George, Claudia, the house, time-travel and, most of all, with herself and the mess she'd made of everything (not least, she realised now, potentially, Claudia's *life*), that she didn't put up any resistance. All she wanted to do now was to go back to the farm and lie face-down on her bed in her darkened futuristic bedroom—alone—and wait for the punishment and disgrace she was due to suffer to play out all around her, no matter how long that took.

The longer, the better, and preferably forever.

In the kitchen, George and Claudia looked on, as if waiting for the judge's verdict—expecting at the very least *some* counterargument.

But none came.

"Whatever," was all Felice could muster in response. "Let's go."

George had at least come prepared. He had brought no fewer than three flashlights and one of the handheld devices that the Redmaynes used for tracking objects displaced in time. Felice both envied and despised his preparedness but chose to keep her feelings on the subject to herself. Her brother was such a boy scout. And while that would keep him from stumbling through the dark blindly like a fool, she took solace in the knowledge that she would be able to make it back without any gadgets to help her, if she ever really needed to do that. Unlike him, or anyone else in her family for that matter. She was both better and worse than all of them at the same time. Depending.[128]

And so they set off. Once they all were outside in the

---

[128] i.e. Depending on how she felt about herself at the time. At this moment, overall, not so good.

tunnels, George locked the door to the house behind them. Claudia shone her flashlight on the lock so that he could see what he was doing. Then, as they walked along, George explained about the handheld device, or QDM as his father liked to call it, and about how he was using it to plot a route back to the entrance, back to the 'antique' watch from the future that his grandfather had buried there to act as a beacon under circumstances such as this. Felice lagged behind. Claudia clearly found all of this fascinating—along with *George*, too! She *liked* him. Good grief! Was this how it was going to be from now on? Her former nemesis and her future nemesis, to*geth*er? The prospect didn't bear thinking about. Wandering the tunnels down here in the dark forever held more appeal—even more so when she thought about the reception she was likely to face once they got home. This was not going to be good.

In truth, however, none of it turned out as badly as Felice had anticipated and feared. And, after witnessing her brother and her friend gambolling through the countryside like a pair of lovesick lambs,[129] she wanted nothing more to be back already and face the music. Compared to listening to these two, that would be heaven:

All those woods and rolling hills. Magnifique!

Where were they, did George think? Normandy? The Dordogne?

How could it be possible to walk out of a house in Paris and be here? Wherever this is. At once, right here! Incroyable!

Every single thing they said made Felice want to gag all the more. She could not get home fast enough. Despite what awaited for her there. Bring it on. Shoot her now. It

---

[129] For the record, this is only how it seemed to Felice at the time. No actual gambolling took place.

would be a mercy.

In truth, her heart relented a little when the three of them stood at the point where the invisible farm lay but a short way ahead. Claudia had no sense of what was about to happen, the stepping through into a patch of land outside of time and space, into a farm that would seemingly appear—literally—out of nowhere.

At the last moment Felice slipped her hand into Claudia's, partly to prevent her passing right through, but for other reasons, too—gratitude, regret, and other complicated feelings that she would scarcely be able to recognise, let alone articulate. Whatever.

They were home.

* * *

Mr and Mrs Redmayne seemed more relieved than anything more sinister when George and Felice rocked up at the farm that sunny morning, and not anywhere near as surprised as their children had thought they might be to see Claudia with them. To Mr Redmayne, the presence of her daughter's friend explained everything. She was the missing piece of the puzzle. With her on the board, in *play*, as it were, in a chess metaphor that he at once wished he hadn't started, even if only mentally, the endgame now made sense. Of course, as parents, they *had* known *something* was going on, ever since the business of the duplicate key, but they had concluded that it might be best to let it run its course, that to interfere might be counterproductive, or dangerous. Or even, impossible.

This last statement raised a few eyebrows, in a common sense sort of way, as it would, even in the best company, and Mr Redmayne felt obliged to explain. His theory was this: that the instant that George had (quite innocently) interacted with future Felice and Claudia when first visiting the house all these weeks ago, he had become 'quantum–entangled' with the pair of them in that moment. In effect, their present and future selves were linked, they had become bound, as it were—*entangled*—through time. Their interaction at that point stretched out across time, and their quantum states became fixed, despite the temporal dislocation. Time was only another dimension, after all, despite how our brains perceived it. And the 'binding'—once set—could not be broken, not even by time.

This explanation seemed to stun[130] the family—and Claudia—into a silent contemplation of its spooky implications.

After a moment, George grew excited.

"You mean I had no choice? Really? Wow. That's great. I don't need to feel guilty about all the creeping around and not telling anyone about what was going on? I can hardly be *blamed* for anything then, can I? Because the laws of physics were in control, not me. That's fabulous. I love it."

"It *is* only a theory, Georgie, dear," said Mrs Redmayne. "I might require more convincing before you are entirely absolved. If you want to go around believing that you're nothing more than an unthinking automaton in the grip of forces bigger than yourself, then feel free. I, for one, choose not to do that. Even so, there are likely to be consequences, for all of us. Actions have consequences. I'm not sure quite how many more times we must learn this particular lesson in this family. It is becoming something of a habit, one we can scarce afford in our present situation."

Mrs Redmayne looked pointedly at Felice as she made this latter remark. In response, Felice seemed to have found a very interesting spot on the carpet to

---

[130] Yes, let's be nice and say 'stun'. Other verbs are available.

examine in detail. Perhaps the forces of the Universe could find a way to absolve her, too, although she doubted it. Far easier for that to happen than her mother should forgive her. Usually.

But, for once, the Universe relented.

"It's not that we're trying to *blame* anyone," continued Mrs Redmayne, in a more kindly tone. "We understand how very difficult it must be for you children to be marooned here like this, on a *farm* of all places, with no clear end in sight. For youngsters of your ages, with all the world going on out there, out of reach, it must be unbearable. We realise that."

"Oh, it's not so bad," said Emile, sounding unhelpfully sincere.

Mrs Redmayne threw her younger son the most infinitesimal of glances. "But when I think of the dangers you faced, Felice, and what might have happened to you if it hadn't been for your chance encounter with Claudia here, in that art shop of all places, my goodness, I don't know, where would we be now? Tell me that."

"Exactly *here*, Mom," said George. "Our pasts and futures were entangled, remember? It *had* to be this way. Not even the Universe had a choice. Once set in motion, *this* was meant to be. I hate to say, but I really like this theory a lot."

"It's called 'timelike' entanglement," said Mr Redmayne. "Even now, here in the twenty-first century, physicists are starting to prove that the future and the past can be determined simultaneously. In a sense, a very *real* sense, the future *disturbs* the present, and vice versa…"

Mr Redmayne saw his wife's face and his voice trailed off.

"My father is a big advocate of this theory," he added quietly.

"Yes, where *is* he?" asked George.

"Travelling," said Mr Redmayne, sheepishly, as though the word was something of a euphemism, which, of course, it was.

"*Trav*elling? I see. Since when?"

"Since this morning. In fact, he left not long after you did."

"Oh." George, his face studiously blank, tried to conceal his surprise at this development—as did Felice, except that she was far better at it than her brother, but no less interested. So much that had gone on in the house had seemed odd to the point of sabotage. No one had yet explained how the Paris door had come to be unsealed in the first place.

Mrs Redmayne cleared her voice, loudly. "This is all well and good, and very *interesting*, I'm sure, to some of us, at least, but I'm sure it can't have escaped everyone's notice that we have an *actual* situation to be dealing with here, namely Mademoiselle Bouffant and how and when we help her to go home. *Safely*. You know, I'm quite sure her parents would not be thrilled if they were to discover that their charming and lovely fifteen year old daughter was now confined indefinitely to a farm concealed in a mechanical rip in time and space, now would they? No, they would not, let me assure you."

A moment's silence followed this speech. Then, Claudia spoke:

"Seventeen," she said. "Madame Redmayne, with apologies, sorry, I'm seventeen now. I'm from the future, I suppose. *Your* future. After the party, I spent an entire two years of my life searching for you all. I would *not* give up, no. But for you, here, I believe it has only been a few months. Now that I've found you, I would like to stay, for a time, anyway. I expect you can understand why that is."

Uncharacteristically, Claudia blushed a little at this point, and came to a halt. Mr and Mrs Redmayne looked on and both nodded sagely, in comic unison. George looked blank.

Because, *French*. Claudia was speaking *French*. What was *that* about? He really hadn't a clue about what she'd just said. Because, well, *French*. It was, to him, quite *littéralement*, a foreign language.

One that his Mother had strongly encouraged him to be more fluent in[131], and would be less than thrilled to discover he in fact understood less than Emile.

Or so it seemed, as George's little brother was also nodding sagely at this point.[132] This was bad.

"I, *we*, do understand, yes," said Mrs Redmayne, in *French*. "But we must all appreciate, especially you, that your parents will grow concerned if you do not return home at the expected time. Yes? We must not prevent that from happening. That would be remiss."

Mr Redmayne joined in, once again *en Français*. George looked on, bewildered.

"Well, yes, that is true, my dear, I do agree. But at the same time we must think about the TDA. From what Felice has told us, the darned TDA pursued them both most aggressively and we must assume that Claudia here now features high on their wanted list as one of our, well, accomplices. It might be *dangerous*, don't you think, to send her home without first dealing with the TDA issue? And not just for Claudia, but for all of us. What do you think, Felice?"

"I think you are both right," replied Felice, also in her preferred tongue, which George almost (but not quite) understood.

"The car is blue," said Emile, en Français.[133]

---

[131] Quite métaphoriquement, his Mother's tongue.

[132] In truth, the youngest Redmayne was merely joining in. He had no idea what was going on. Literally.

[133] This being the one of the three complete sentences in French that he could both say and understand.

This was too much. George interrupted everyone.

"Wait, wait, wait, what's going on? Why are we all speaking French now? What's that about?"

They all looked at George. Claudia seemed particularly puzzled.

"Well, *we're* speaking French because that's the language that our guest is speaking," said Mrs Redmayne in English. "But you appear set on speaking like an outraged American, which is never attractive, Georgie. Do try to join in. It's only polite."

George was literally speechless.

"I have forgotten my key," said Emile, once more in his very schoolboy rendering of the beautiful tongue. "I am very tired."[134] [135]

"But, George, your French is perfect," said Claudia (French), sensing—but not understanding—the source of the present discomfort. "I have heard you speak it many times. Only before, in the house, yes, and on the walk here. You speak French effortlessly."

George stared hopelessly at Claudia's lips as she spoke, as if the simple act of staring very hard would somehow aid his comprehension. It didn't. Not at all. Something about speaking French. Very likely that. Possibly. Was it?

"Your French, it is not perfect?" tried Claudia, in somewhat halting English. "How can that be?"

Everyone looked at George. George looked at everyone.

---

[134] These two statements constituted the remainder of Emile's entire repertoire in French.

[135] It should be remembered that Emile's formal schooling had to date taken place in England. This should explain everything.

No one said anything until Felice could stand it no longer.

"It's the *house*," she said, very pained by it all for some reason. "The *other* house, in Paris, New York, everywhere, it's translates for us, usually. Wherever, whenever. Presumably it can't do that for us here, because we're, I don't know, out of time? That's probably it. Of course, it has never been necessary to translate *French* for Maman, Papa or me—we're all fluent in French, obviously. Maman *is* French. But, George, Emile, they've never wanted to learn, because they've had no reason to learn. Apart from the beauty of the language, of course. But, well, now, I guess…"

Felice left that thought hanging, unsaid. If only for a moment.

"Well, yes, he has reason now, I see," said Mrs Redmayne.

These last exchanges had taken place in English and consequently it had been Claudia's turn to appear a little perplexed.

"George, you cannot speak French?" she asked in English. "No?"

With what appeared an incalculable degree of regret, George shook his head. For the record, so did Emile.

"Well, that is not so bad," continued Claudia, at once brightening. "I can teach you. It will give us something to do while my fate is being decided. And who knows how long that will take? Your French might be perfect, yes, by the time we have finished? I think so."

George brightened too, his face becoming a battleground between his contrary impulses to simultaneously express and conceal his delight. The former impulse won. It could hardly not. Everyone could see it.

But not everyone was thrilled to see it.

Felice went off to lie face down on her bed for a while. For as long as it took.

Forever, if need be. Whatever.

* * *

George's French was slow to progress, glacially so, it might be said, perhaps, despite his apparently increased motivation and the effort that the pair put into their lessons. In fact, it was almost as if he were getting worse rather than better, which struck Felice as especially odd, given the amount of time that that they spent together. If they weren't giggling as one over their inability to communicate, they were busy with the construction of a new room for Claudia at the farm (out of light, so no actual manual assembly required), or with activities that George had hitherto expressed not the slightest hint of interest, such as collecting apples from the orchard or feeding the sheep and Genivee. Or baking.

Watching George and Claudia bake together while seemingly struggling to make themselves understood was like a masterclass in flirtation—and Felice was sick of the sight of it.[136]

And she didn't much care for their apple pie, either, although everybody else certainly did.

For their part Mr and Mrs Redmayne didn't appear entirely displeased by the way things had turned out, although the presence of their unexpected guest give them a dilemma they hadn't anticipated. The children had needed a distraction, they could see that now. George seemed so much happier, more involved, and Felice would come around eventually, or so they believed. In the meantime, they needed to figure out exactly what had gone on in Paris and in the house. Felice's account of the goings

---

[136] Curiously, she could remember Claudia's English being perfect at school.

on there struck them both as very odd.

Why did the time mechanism malfunction so wildly for Felice and then work perfectly well once again after only a short inspection by Mr Redmayne and his father? It wasn't as if they did anything to fix it either. And exactly who had unsealed the Paris exit in the first place? That was still a mystery. Mr Redmayne maintained that most likely had been the TDA, given the way in which they had pursued the two girls, but Mrs Redmayne was unconvinced. Why would they not just occupy the house in that case? That would have a been a far simpler way to catch any of them who had gone back in. And it didn't seem as if the TDA knew where the house was anymore; they seemed to have needed Felice to lead them to it. In which case, how could they have first unsealed one of the doors? It was all very mysterious.

Mr Redmayne remarked that he wished his father had not taken this most inopportune moment to go 'travelling', so that he might talk it all through with him. Mrs Redmayne agreed, albeit for an entirely different reason, which didn't need to be said, given his previous behaviour.[137] And Mr Redmayne didn't press her on this, for reasons of his own.[138]

In any case, until all of these puzzling matters were resolved there could be no question of sending Claudia home, not to such an uncertain fate. And it wasn't as if she had to be returned 'late'. She could always go home at the expected time and never have been missed; that was in their power to do, no matter how long it took. Although, Mrs Redmayne countered, if the poor girl happened to be

---

[137] i.e. She believed him to be behind all of it—again!

[138] i.e. He didn't want to believe his father to be behind all of it—not again!

thirty-two years old by that time, it would be sure to raise a few eyebrows. And Mr Redmayne took her point.

In the meantime the children played, while Felice looked on—or tried not to look on, depending on how she was feeling at the time: George and Claudia in the orchard, feeding the sheep; George and Claudia making an unholy racket in either his or her room (trumpet) (usually); George and Claudia *and* Emile at the invisible perimeter, the three of them stepping back and forth between the world and the farm, sometimes holding hands, sometimes not (George was trying nobly to recalibrate the barrier so that it would read and accept Claudia's bioinformatic signature as well as the family's own, which his father said he could try to do so long as he didn't break it completely.) This exercise wasn't without its amusing aspects, as Claudia would frequently be flung[139]—alone—hundreds of meters across the countryside in something of a state of surprise and confusion. Fortunately, unfortunately,[140] she never failed to find the amusing side of these misadventures, collapsing in giggles *every single time* it happened, much to Felice's continued annoyance.

One day, when Felice's repression of her sense of guilt at how she was treating their guest first began to fail, an unusual thing happened. Normally, people can only stay mad at someone for so long, particularly when the reasons for feeling that way in the first place are only partly understood or obscure, and Felice was no different to everyone else in this regard. And so, once her anger had subsided, she started to feel a little bit ashamed at how she

---

[139] Well, not *flung* exactly, although Felice liked to think of it this way. Flung. Yes.

[140] Yes, *both*. Depending...

had been behaving over the past few weeks. But this was difficult to admit, even to herself. Easier by far, at least at first, was to lay face down on her bed in her room and not deal with—*anything*. So far, so normal.

But then, her imagination kicked in. Despite herself, she began to imagine how her behaviour must have appeared to Claudia—and to everybody else as well. What had Claudia done that was so wrong in the first place? Searched for Felice and her family for the best part of two years? Put herself into jeopardy against unknown (and very odd) forces without once questioning why? Acted like a ninja and saved her? Like a genuine hero, no less... All of this was true, and yet? And yet, what? Was her friend's motivation suspect? (Felice didn't know.) Did she seem too keen to insinuate herself into the Redmaynes? (What choice did the girl have at this point?) Was she stealing everyone's affection away from her? What, *no*? That was impossible. (Except maybe George's, and he didn't matter.) So, what was Felice's problem?

Oh my God... She *didn't actually have* a problem. Not really. No. If anything, it should be the other way around. Claudia should have a problem with *her*. The poor girl had given up everything, her entire *life*, possibly (tbc), to help *Felice*, and how had she been repaid? By being ignored—silences, distance—those two things that Felice did so well when she wanted to punish somebody. Good grief. Felice had behaved like such a, well, *witch*. How must she have seemed? To Claudia? To everyone? Shame flooded her. She was, quite literally, the very worst person in the world, or even to have ever lived.[141] She had no idea how she could recover from this one. She was the worst.

---

[141] Possibly not 'quite literally' so. (Tbc.)

Literally.[142]

Felice turned herself around to now lie face up on her bed. Supine, rather than prone. Always the better option.[143] Sunshine filled the room. Outside, the distant voices of her two brothers and Claudia were calling out something or other. Laughter. Probably they were messing around at the boundary again, testing the perimeter. Wait a minute... *What?* Were George and Emile shouting *in French?* How could *that* be? George, maybe, yes. But *Emile?* Felice got up at once. She went over to the window and looked outside. No sign. They must be around the other side of the farmhouse. More calling. In French. Intrigued, Felice left her room and took herself down the stairs with more urgency than at any point since returning from the house. Once outside in the farmyard she could see where they were, the three of them, over by the orchard. They appeared to be playing frisbee? Emile must have made that for them, as creating something perfectly round would be beyond George. Mr Literal.

But no, as Felice approached the group she could see that it wasn't a frisbee at all that they were tossing around. It was a hat. A bowler hat. A TDA hat. Emile's obviously, the one he had claimed as his own when the TDA had come a-calling at the house all those months ago. She would have thought Claudia might never have wanted to see one of those again. She knew she didn't. The mere thought gave *her* the shivers. But not Claudia, obviously. *Now*, Felice remonstrated with herself, *play nice.* Otherwise it's back to your room. And no supper.

---

[142] See Note 140 above.

[143] See Paradise Lost, Bk 1, line 195. Go on. Live a little. It's epic storytelling. Literally. (Thats enough 'Literally' jokes. Ed.)

"Hey, you guys," she called out as she approached, "what going on? You playing TDA-Hat frisbee? If you drop it, do you have to go back to the future? Is that the rule?"

That was exactly what Felice said, except that she said it in French,[144] knowing very well that Claudia would, of course, understand her perfectly. The surprise was that her brothers seemed to follow her without any problem, too.

"Nah, we're just throwing it around," replied George.

"But, no, like, we *really* got to *have* that rule," said Emile. "No, we *do*, because, well, George is *useless* at catching it. He'd be captive in 2775 already if we did that. A TDA drone, in a hat. It would suit him."

"Dream on, Shrimp! *You'd* be in *3775*, more like. And it's *your* hat, not mine. You're the one who wears it all the time. Maybe that's your fate, you reckon? Yeah, like maybe in the future you head up the TDA? I could see that. That would suit you. Here."

With an unexpected but (all the same) viciously effective snap of his right wrist George flicked the bowler hat in the direction of his younger brother, who caught and held it nonetheless. *His* hat, yes, and he was proud of it, no matter what stupid George said.

Emile put the hat on, as if in defiance.

The pair stared at each other for a second. No love lost.

Boys. Felice and Claudia exchanged a look. This was a conversation that Felice had heard, or something very similar to it, at least in tone, an infinite number of times. Her brothers going at each other. Always.

---

[144] "Hé, mec, qu'est-ce qui se passe? Vous jouez à TDA-Chapeau frisbee? Si vous le laissez tomber, devez-vous revenir sur le futur? Est-ce la règle?" Okay?

The only surprising aspect of the present exchange was that it was being conducted in flawless French. Given their respective linguistic skills, this was impossible. Felice smelled a rat.

A rat called George....

"Claudia, you must really be an absolute genius of a French tutor," she said, "the way my two brothers can speak it now, like natives, the pair of them. How on earth did you manage that? I mean, last week George could barely say his own name in French—and Emile couldn't even manage that! What's your secret? Brain transplants?"

"What, no? It is not me. I am not responsible." Claudia looked with admiration at Felice's elder brother. "It's George, of course. He's so clever. It is all him."

"What, he taught *himself* French, *and* Emile?"

"No, no, his French is still terrible. Very. But he fixed the translator, for the farmhouse. Now we can all understand each other. It is incredible, yes? So clever."

George had the decency to look slightly embarrassed. "It wasn't that hard, Sis, actually. The translation programme was all there; it just hadn't been activated. Once I worked it out, it was pretty easy, in fact. Much easier than learning French."

"You can say that again" agreed Emile.

For a second Felice feared George was going to make the joke of repeating himself, but mercifully he refrained from this. All the same, she couldn't help but feel more than a little disgruntled about the fact that the pair had found a way of avoiding all the hard work required in actually learning the language. The cheaters.

"And not only that," Claudia went on, still clearly delighted by everything 'George'. "*Look*! See what else he has done, your brother."

Moving off by herself, Claudia walked towards the unseen perimeter and stepped beyond it. Then, she stopped, turned, paused, before beginning to retrace her steps towards them all. All the time she wore the same (by now slightly irritating, Felice thought) expression of delight on her face. She approached, smiling, as if largely for Felice's benefit. Some secret, some great joke that everybody else knew about, was playing out. Claudia walking… Felice didn't get it.

And then she did. Claudia hadn't jumped. She'd somehow crossed the perimeter—alone—and not been flung unceremoniously like some old bowler hat to the far side of the farm. Yup. She was one of them now. Full access granted.

"Do you see what he has done, my clever George? I can come and go. By myself. I am like you. A Redmayne."

Felice saw. "Well, isn't that just dandy. Just marvellous, in fact. Fantastic. Well done, George. Good work. Tip-top."

George looked sheepish again. "Well, it's not that hard, actually. The programming's really intuitive. It is, after all, like from hundreds of years in the future—it pretty much does it for you. Reading those books I brought back from the house that time, well, they've really helped me understand the underlying programming principles, you know, the structures and sub-structures, the *architecture*, if you see what I mean, but it's like you're being guided through it by the AI itself step by step. It's seems to *know* what you want to do."

"Well, that's fascinating," said Felice. "And so well said."

"Oh, George, he is so modest. What he has done, no one else alive today could do. This is true."

"Well, I don't know about that, Claudia," said George. "There's Pops—and his Pops. They could do this in their sleep, I'm sure."

Felice was reaching the limits of her tolerance for this particular celebration of her brother's abilities. Beyond them all, the rolling, green, French countryside stretched out towards the hills. And beyond that lay everything. Everything of any importance, anyway, at least to one person present. Not to everyone, clearly.

Claudia approached. "Oh, I think there is maybe nothing you, too, could not do, once you have made up your mind."

Felice was keen to change the subject. "Well, he certainly throws a mean hat now, I can see that. You, Emile, l'il bro, let me have a turn, will you? Chuck it here, kid."

Emile appeared surprised by the request at first, but he took the hat off. "You don't 'chuck' it, Felice, you *flick* it. Like this."

He flicked the hat in his sister's direction and watched it glide elegantly through the air towards her. She caught it.

"See? Like that."

"Everyone's an expert, huh?" Felice waved the hat back and forth in her hands, as if possibly evaluating its weight. "Hey, what's the furthest any of you've ever chucked—*flicked*, sorry—the damn thing? Is there a world record, or something?"

Emile shrugged, looked to his brother. George shrugged. Judging by their expressions, both appeared a little surprised not to have thought of this somewhat obvious contest themselves.[145]

Seeing no further response was likely, Felice hurled the bowler hat off into the open spaces, towards the distant green hills. For a couple of seconds it defied gravity magnificently, before nosediving onto the grass, rolling, rolling and then coming to a halt—possibly a somewhat

---

[145] Oh, the pointlessly competitive fun these two very typical boys could have been having all these months. Which of them *could* hurl the hat furthest? They needed to know. The world needed to know. Fact.

less than magnificent grand total of fifteen metres distant from the thrower.

"Downwind," said Emile knowledgably. Expertly. Dismissively.

His brother concurred with a nod. Expertly. Dismissively.

"Okay, then," said Felice, striding off after the hat. "*Down*wind, I see. Yup. Good to know."

She stood where the hat had come to a rest, retrieved it from the ground and tossed it back towards Emile. It reached him with ease.

Upwind. Obviously.

"Okay, my go," said Emile. Taking a moment to steady himself,[146] the youngest Redmayne snapped his fledgling wrist and flicked the hat high into the air in the direction of where his sister stood facing him. The bowler hat sailed up above Felice in a great arc, but soon swooped down behind her towards the ground, a mighty eagle coming into land, in hat form, gliding smoothly along the grass until it finally came to a rest some further ten metres or so beyond Felice.

No rolling. None. Eagles don't roll.

Emile had already set off at pace to retrieve the hat.

Passing his sister, he offered as an aside the following professional (if fraternally intended) advice:

"You gotta throw up over the downwind."

"Thanks. *Over the downwind.* Right. That's *exactly* how I'll do all my throwing up in future. Promise."

Looking back, Felice saw that George and Claudia were involved in something of a tête-à- tête. She supposed it was cute, really, in a way, sort of, her brother and her

---

[146] And possibly to harness his *chi*. Just saying. He *might* have been. You don't know.

former nemesis (now BFF, sort of, in a way), being an item. Because *that*, she realised, watching them together now, they surely were. Yes. Obviously. An item.

Why did that bother her so much? She needed to let it go. Though Claudia had been *her* friend. Sort of... No, let it go. Yes.

George had the hat in his possession again, having stepped forward by some illegal number of metres to retrieve it after Emile's feeble effort to throw it back to him had fallen short (upwind fail, clearly). Under Emile's vociferous and quite specific guidance George retreated to the legal starting point.

He readied himself, the hat-projectile held in a firm and yet pliant grip, fingers spread out across the brim in a fan-like position. Possibly he was marshalling his *chi*, thought Felice.[147]

Possibly not.

Breathing deeply, George took a few steps further back and at the same time turned his hips counter-clockwise so that he now faced in the opposite direction. Damn. Was he? Yes, he was. He was actually going to spin himself around as though he was throwing the discus in the Olympic final and not in some stupid game out on the grass by the orchard. Boys.

Ready, *chi* marshalled to the max, George span around, clock-wise. He stepped forward.

He unleashed the bowler hat.

It flew. It flew high. It flew long.

They were all watching. It was still going. Quite possibly this throw *was* going to set a new world record— and then it almost certainly did.

---

[147] See, Felice thinks so, too! We can't *both* be wrong. Think about it. I'm not just making this up, you know.

Because, after a certain point, while it was airborne, or so they all agreed afterwards, the hat *was definitely* still in the air at the critical moment—the moment, that is, when it vanished.

Without trace.

Completely. In an instant.

Gone.

CHAPTER 10

The incident of the vanishing bowler hat provoked much consternation and debate within the Redmayne household during the days that immediately followed. Several theories were proposed, but none was considered satisfactory by all parties concerned. When it had first happened the four witnesses had been reluctant to believe the evidence of their own eyes—the human brain dislikes the impossible and will often allow for some more rational explanation to substitute for the reality of the matter.

So, at first George suggested that the hat hadn't simply vanished, no, but during its flight it must have been obscured by the sun for a second before dropping down behind a bush, and if they looked around for long enough they'd surely find it (no); or, a sudden upwind had caught it carried it much further and much faster than they could have expected (no). Emile proposed a theory that a passing bird had intercepted his precious hat and carried it off, back to its nest, where even now it held a clutch of eggs on the verge of hatching a new brood, batch, you know, something like that, whatever,[148] of eaglets (no, very much no).

No, none of that would do. The damn hat had been there and it had vanished, Felice had said. They had all witnessed that much with their own eyes, hadn't they? Okay, right? So, what *did* they know? The hat had been airborne when it had happened (nods of agreement). It had been about…what, twenty-five metres away when it had just, you know, disappeared (no nods of agreement). Thirty? Forty? No, *fifty*, at least, George had insisted. A *good* fifty metres, at that, and still going strong (no nods of agreement). Well, he happened to think they were all wrong and that he was right. Naturally. But in truth he didn't sound overly convinced himself.

It took Claudia to produce the first real moment of insight, the explanation that had made instant sense to everybody—the obvious truth. The hat had disappeared, she said, at the point at which it had crossed the boundary

---

[148] For the record, a *convocation*. Make a note.

with the outside world, the perimeter. This had occurred to her as she was very alert as to where this lay, this invisible perimeter, on account of her only just now gaining the capacity to cross it safely. The hat had vanished at the juncture with the real world. This was the truth and at once they all knew it. But it also gave the case of the mysteriously disappearing hat a far more sinister turn. What did it mean—for *them*?

The four returned to the scene of the incident and stood at the farm-side of the boundary, peering out as one, towards the horizon. If they stepped forward and crossed the invisible line now, would they disappear, too? And what did disappearing *mean*? George speculated that what it most *probably* meant was that the space inside the boundary had suffered a temporal disjuncture with the, you know, everyday world outside it. They were out of joint,[149] or, whatever, *sync...* A thoughtful silence followed.

"You mean you broke it?" Felice had said next.

"No, I didn't *break* it, Felice. At least, I don't think so; I don't see how I could have done, so *no*. In any case, we don't even know for sure if that's what's going on. I'm speaking theoretically. We need to test the theory."

"Test what?" Emile had asked. "What *is* going on? Where's my hat? Theo*ret*ically?"

"The theory is, Shrimp—*my* theory, anyway—is that when it crossed the perimeter the hat time-travelled an unspecified volume of time into the future, probably not very long, I wouldn't think."

"So it might just turn up any second now, you reckon?"

"Well, yes. Theoretically."

---

[149] *"Oh, cursed spite!"* Oh, look it up.

The four stared off into what had been, or still was, possibly, the hat's general direction of flight. Nothing happened.

"Tell me if it turns up," Felice said, walking away back towards the farmhouse. The others watched her go for a moment.

"So, now we must test your theory," said Claudia. "How? Should one of us step across the boundary and see what happens? That would be simple. Yes?"

For some reason, her gaze had fallen on Emile. George's eyes followed.

"No, no way," said Emile. "I've been lost in time before. We've no idea how far into the future I'd go, or even if it *is* the future. What if I couldn't get back—*again*! So, no way. No."

"He's right," said George. "It shouldn't be a person. Too risky. We need to get some objects from the farmhouse, things that weren't made here, either. Real things, from outside. We can throw them over the boundary and see what happens. If anything does, then we'll know we're on the right track."

"And if nothing happens?"

"Then, little brother, we're gonna need a new theory."

After a more prolonged deliberation than might have been anticipated by any of the three remaining participants in the proposed experiment, one object each was selected for the potential journey through time.[150] It turned out that choosing something for such a special trip, if indeed that

---

[150] Felice having retired to her room, but not—*not*—to lie face down on her bed this time: she just found the idea of standing around and throwing things to be overrated, as a rule. On this, I'm with her.

was what it would turn out to be, was much more difficult than they had imagined, it being not entirely improbable that you might never see it ever again, the chosen object; or, at best, it was uncertain *when* you might see the damn thing again, assuming you ever—someday—did.

Accordingly, George had dithered on at length about whether or not he should throw the trumpet over the perimeter, the special one they had only recently brought back from the house, but he didn't really want to do this and only entertained the idea at all as Claudia had suggested it, because (she reasoned) it was definitely from the outside, of that they could be certain.[151] In the end he picked something else, his Science High calculator, which he thought there was a good chance he might never use again. For a similar reason Claudia picked her car keys; plus she knew she had a spare set at home (or would have on her seventeenth birthday, it being not quite that time beyond the perimeter at the moment, as far as they knew still). Emile choose the cricket ball that he had accidentally given his grandfather that nasty crack on the head with just a few months earlier, on account of the fact that it was very *throw-y*, a point which everybody conceded was indisputably true.

And so, after a short break for refreshment (slices of Claudia's apple pie[152]), during which it was agreed that nothing should be said just yet to Mr and Mrs Redmayne about the experiment and the related problem they were investigating, the three young scientists returned once more to the perimeter, suitably replenished by pie and

---

[151] Though she subsequently acknowledged that its extreme specialness rendered it unsuitable for the task.

[152] And, *technically*, George's. In spirit, anyway.

ready to jettison their chosen belongings into the unknowable void of Time. Possibly. If that's what was going to happen.

Emile went first.[153] He wound back his chucking arm and threw the small, battered, red ball off in the direction of the distant hills, across the boundary. Everybody, even the thrower, at once noted the flaw in his method. The cricket ball flew high, yes, it flew far. It didn't *seem* to disappear in flight, but this outcome was impossible to verify as the ball had travelled too great a distance to be able to spot anymore in the longer grass outside of the boundary. While the ball didn't appear to have vanished, in the same way that the hat had done, George was obliged to record the result as inconclusive, because they couldn't damn-well see it, much to his—in particular—frustration.

Claudia's go was next. She stood with the others, barely a metre or so from the invisible perimeter and unceremoniously tossed the keys to her beloved, tiny Citroën onto the other side. And there they did rest, where they fell, unmoving, almost sulkily so, as if in reproach for being discarded in this wonton way.

But no disappearance, no time-travel.

George followed, throwing the large-keyed, TI-84 calculator (all the School's 'Mathletes' used the same model, naturally) only a short distance beyond the keys to Claudia's little car (the car, which, in point of fact, she didn't yet own).

Same outcome. It landed flat on the grass outside the boundary.

Clearly visible. Not vanished. *There*. Obviously.

George, Claudia, Emile studied their handiwork in silence together. The experiment had failed. The theory

---

[153] Try stopping him. Sometime.

was flawed. They were no closer to understanding what had happened to the hat. If it hadn't time-travelled, what had become of it? And why? Claudia wanted to retrieve her keys, but George had suggested there was still an element of risk involved in crossing the boundary themselves, despite the evident lack of harm to the two objects they could see on the grass just a few metres away. The hat *had* disappeared. Until they understood why, they shouldn't take any unnecessary chances—it wasn't worth it. At the same time, he was out of ideas.

There was nothing else for it. They would have to tell the parents.

Mr Redmayne was sitting—nay, ensconced—in his new, improved, luxurious Oberon chair in what now passed for his study at the farmhouse when the three excitable youngsters had burst in upon him and regaled him with the story of the mysteriously disappearing hat. At first all he could think (inner sigh) was *Whatever now? Really? Must we?* But he soon began to get the drift of their story, piecing it together from the respective breathless interjections of his two sons. They had been playing a game (Emile). George had thrown the hat (Emile), a really long way actually (George) and it had vanished, just like that (Emile) while still airborne (George) and everyone had seen it do it, even Felice (Emile) (breath, breath). Current thinking was that the hat had disappeared at the point at which it had crossed the perimeter and so they had undertaken an experiment to test that hypothesis (George) (considered pause) but the results had proven inconclusive (George, yawn). Yeah, they'd thrown things over the perimeter and watched them sit there on the grass doing nothing, that was the test (Emile). *Experi*ment, you mean (George).

Mr Redmayne thought he understood. Mrs Redmayne appeared in the doorway. She had been meditating out in the garden at the rear of the house, in the pleasant shade, when the tell-tale signs of a hullaballoo of some sort reached her ears. Even when in a deep contemplative state Mrs Redmayne, like all mothers, was attuned to the first signs of some hullaballoo or other involving her children, and so she had come at once to investigate. The look on her face, however, when she first appeared, plainly said (inner sigh): *Oh, whatever now? Really? Must we?*

Mr Redmayne took charge. The salient facts were these: the hat had disappeared in flight when crossing the boundary between the farm and the outside world; the three of them had tried to recreate this phenomenon by projecting a number of objects similarly across the boundary, but this had failed to result in the same outcome. Was that it? Nods all around, vigorously so from Emile. And the objects, they were all from outside, yes, so as to be real things like the hat, not made here from the light (this last contribution was from Claudia). Now it was Mr Redmayne's turn to nod. He saw. Yes. Quite.

"We thought it best not try to cross the boundary ourselves," added George, "not until we understood, well, the nature of the phenomenon. I thought it was probably time-travel. You know, the farm getting out of sync with the outside—a timeslip."

"We *theorised* that," said Emile.

"A good theory," said Mr Redmayne, clearly still thinking it over.

Mrs Redmayne spoke up. "But the hat belonged originally to the TDA, did it not? And they are from the future, very far in the future. It is likely the hat itself was made out of light, now that we know how things are made there, don't you agree?"

"We need to repeat the experiment with something we've made here," said George, a metaphorical light going on in his head. "It might not be a timeslip at all. Let's do that."

Emile was already off and running towards his room, which by now housed something of a vast menagerie of light-made manga-figurines that were quite literally of his own creation, some intrepid few of which were about to experience time-travel or, just as possibly, disintegration, either of which outcomes would be fine by Emile.

George and Claudia followed, squeezing past Mrs Redmayne in the doorway. Claudia, at least, had the good grace to smile apologetically on the way through.

"I'm sure Felice could spare you something," Mrs Redmayne called after them both. "After all, she manufactured an entire antique shop in her room only a few weeks ago. Ask her."

Mr and Mrs Redmayne looked at each other. They both sighed.

Time waits for no man, or so they say, and perhaps it would not be entirely unreasonable to for them to add, except when the man in question happens to be a wee small boy or similar individual caught in a technologically-generated bubble in the space-time continuum, assuming *they* could conceive of such a thing in the first place.

All the same, Emile had dashed off to his room in a manner that suggested that the window of opportunity for cool experimentation on his creations might slam shut at any moment, when in reality he quite possibly had all the time in the world at his disposal. Literally.

George and Claudia followed on at an altogether more sober pace, one which in fact belied the extent of their interest. George was very interested indeed to see the outcome of the second stage of the experiment, but was managing—to some extent, anyway—the outward manifestation of his extreme nerdiness in this regard. He wanted to find out the truth. Claudia, on the other hand, just wanted to see something disintegrate in some weird, futuristic way, if at all possible.

But in the end the outcome was rather anti-climactic and a disappointment to all parties. Emile's monster creations were not simply outlandish figures but reflected the detailed taxonomy of species that he had drawn up back at home in lengthy collaboration with his friend and fellow Linnaeus-like[154] tabulator of fanciful creatures, Steven Sparkle. The present example that he was ferrying so enthusiastically to the perimeter for experimental chucking into the great beyond was, according to their classification system, a 'wind-type', gifted with the power of flight, despite the lack of any obvious means of sustaining itself once airborne, such as wings.[155]

But luckily the creature's ability to fly was not the subject of the current test, rather whether or not it could maintain the integrity of its light-based form outside of the matrix of the farm. If it actually flew, that would, not least in the mind of its creator, be an extremely rewarding bonus.[156]

Emile had ran so far ahead of them that George was concerned that they would miss the staging of The Experiment, Part II. He thought about shouting for his brother to wait-up-*you*[157] but then he thought that shouting out like that might look uncool in Claudia's eyes and so he didn't. Fortunately, at the last moment, Emile had turned around and noticed that a substantial audience was

---

[154] Carl Linnaeus, pioneer Eighteenth Century Swedish taxonomist. Rufus found his parties a bit on the dull side. Orderly, yes, exceedingly well organised. But dull. Very. A bit like those of, Sir George Biddell Airy, the Nineteenth Century Astronomer Royal. If you've been to one of those you know exactly what Linnaeus' parties were like. Dull, very.

[155] In its universe it could fly, in our universe...meh.

[156] Don't get your hopes up.

[157] i.e. Attendez, *vous*!

forming—not only were George and Claudia coming (if very *slow*ly), but behind them, his parents, too, were now on the way—and behind them, lagged Felice, just emerging right then from the farmhouse. For a gathering of these proportions—the attention of *every*body, for once—he could wait. If only they weren't all so *slow*...

Of course, George and Claudia arrived first. Emile was waiting at the same point in the perimeter where they had conducted the first phase of the experiment. A few short yards away, although in fact it may have been some infinite distance, lay the calculator and the car keys. Reachable or unreachable? They didn't know. That's why they were here. Emile fidgeted while he waited *forever* for his parents finally to amble up into position, the home-made manga-creature in his arms ready for flight, or something. Without the slightest hint of self-consciousness or lack of cool he shouted for the two senior Redmaynes to get-a-move-on-will-you-both[158] but naturally this had no effect. Felice, well, he wasn't even going to wait any longer for *her*, man. No way. She was *miles* away. No, he was doing it now. Right *now*.

At last. With four pairs of quite interested eyes looking on at close-enough quarters Emile turned back towards the hilly horizon and launched the intrepid *Volaverunt*[159] highish—if not very farish—into the air, a lone explorer in the void, the first and last of his kind, a flyer—no, strike that, a faller, yes, definitely more faller than flyer, falling, falling, fell, crashed onto the grass; and where it fell, there too did it rest, between the car keys and the calculator, still, done, but intact.

---

[158] i.e. A*vancez-vous, les deux*!

[159] For such it was.

No disintegration.

The Redmaynes, all of them, because towards the end Felice had come running up as well, so as not to miss out, and Claudia, stood as one regarding the stricken, flightless but intact toy as it lay motionless on the ground.

For a moment no one said anything. What was there to say?

Clearly they were no further ahead in understanding what might have happened to the hat. If anything. Mr and Mrs Redmayne were entitled to think that their children—and guest—had perhaps been mistaken in what they had seen. Had *thought* they had seen, perhaps? By this point, even the witnesses themselves were suffering significant doubts. Felice, however, proved the most resolute. By far.

"It did cross the perimeter, right?" she asked, indicating the fallen toy.

Nods and an all too voluminous silence followed.

"Well, that's weird," continued Felice. "So, it can't have been the light thing, with the hat. That can't have been a factor, I mean—you know, in its disappearance."

"Are you all *quite* sure that you saw the hat disappear?" asked Mr Redmayne. "Just like that? The eyes can trick the brain into thinking its seen almost anything. It's a well-known phenomenon. In fact, it's how we make sense of the world in the first place."

"No, we did." Felice looked around for support. "Oh, come on, guys, we *did*. You all *know* we did. It was in the air and it vanished. We all *saw* it."

After a second, Claudia spoke up. "I don't know. Like your father says, Felice, maybe it is that we see what we expect to see."

"Claudia, we didn't *expect* to see the damn hat vanish into thin air, did we? Why would we expect *that*? I don't see the logic. Look, we know what we saw, don't we?"

Claudia shrugged.

Felice turned to her brother. "George?"

George shuffled uncomfortably. "Well, Sis, it's not like

we've been able to replicate the original result, is it?"

"Because there's something going on that we don't understand, that's why!"

"But what?"

Another silence. Claudia stepped forward.

"Maybe I should go and pick up my keys, yes? That would tell us everything perhaps?"

Mr Redmayne intervened. "I wouldn't do that just yet, my dear, no. Not until we're absolutely certain it's safe. I need to go and check the mechanics of the boundary first."

"They tried to get *me* to fetch them earlier," said Emile. "They both did."

"Oh, why am I not surprised!" said Felice, her temper rising.

"What is it that you mean?"

"*You*, Claudia... You've been nothing but reckless since I met you in the art shop. You've changed. It's like I don't know who you are."

"Well, if it was not for my *recklessness* you would not be here now. The future men in hats, they would have taken you away with them as easy as anything. As *that*!"

Unwisely, considerable dramatic emphasis was leant to the word 'That!' by resounding click of Claudia's fingers. George took a step back.

Mr Redmayne looked to his wife. This sort of thing really wasn't his strong suit. To his surprise, his wife didn't appear inclined to intervene.

"Well, I almost wish they had! At least then I wouldn't be obliged to watch you two simpering around each other twenty-four-seven!"

George took a step forward. "Oh, come on, Felice!"

"It's true! It's disgusting! And it's not like we can go anywhere to get away from the sight of the pair of you, is it? You know, it's almost like this is what she was after all along. There's something very weird about it all."

"I've no idea what that means," said George. "And it

isn't like we can go anywhere either, it is, Felice? Think about it. We're *all* stuck here. Together."

Felice turned away from her brother. Her temper was still high.

"Excuse me for saving you," said Claudia, before heading off in the direction of the orchard. George followed.

Felice looked to her parents. She knew she'd done wrong, a feeling confirmed by the expression on each of their faces—not anger exactly, more that, as *their* daughter, she should know better. The guilt-trip. She didn't need this right now.

Felice took herself off back towards the farmhouse. At pace.

Mr and Mrs Redmayne watched her go. George and Claudia were standing in the serious dark shade of the trees, talking. Mr Redmayne took a deep breath.

His wife turned to him.

"Chéri," she began, looking very grave, "we must find a way out of here soon, I think. Very soon. Back to Paris, New York, London—our lives. Otherwise, I fear, the longer they are cooped up here, we risk losing them all, one way or another. Life *must* be lived."

Mr Redmayne nodded his agreement, they needed to go home. Sadly at that moment he was no closer to figuring out how this might be achieved than he had been at any point since they had arrived, those few short, long months ago. As if in amber, they were stuck fast.

In short, trapped.

CHAPTER 11

The elusive hat, of course, was gone, very definitely so. Fact. An intensive multi-binocular search of the area, albeit one staged from within the safe confines of the farmland, confirmed that no trace of the damn thing was to be found anywhere in the immediate vicinity—it most definitely indeed was *not* lurking unseen behind an hitherto inconspicuous shrub or unremarked rock, nor might it be lying hidden in some sudden and obscure dip in the ground, for no such plausible place of concealment existed.

No, the land was clear, the hat was gone. That much was established.

What remained to be determined was the how and the why.

Troubled, very, Mr Redmayne contemplated this problem for what seemed like an inordinate amount of time, locking himself away in his makeshift farmhouse study for hours at a time, emerging only briefly and looking both very harried and worried whenever he did. He now accepted without dispute the children's account of what had happened, particularly as Felice had confirmed the story told by the others. She, he knew, did not forget anything she had seen. The hat had been thrown, it was in flight and then it had simply disappeared, most likely at the point at which it had crossed over the boundary into the outside world—and that was it.

The hat was no more. Troubling indeed. Very.

Naturally the first thing that Mr Redmayne had done when returning to the farmhouse on The Morning of the Mysteriously Vanishing Hat[160] was to check on the operational mechanics of the perimeter itself, run diagnostic tests, Etc., in the expectation of proving that everybody's secret pet theory was in fact true, that when recalibrating it to recognise Claudia's bioinformatic signature George had broken it somehow—that is, the *one* thing he had been asked *not* to do.

To his surprise and quiet pride, however, Mr Redmayne found that this wasn't the case. George had done a good job. The recalibration work was both elegant and thorough, the lad had a natural aptitude for it. He understood applied quantum mechanics. Nothing he had done should have caused a hat—or any object for that matter—to disappear upon transition.

The boundary wasn't broken. It just wasn't working.

Well, it wasn't working as it should work, absolutely perfectly on every occasion, which meant they were right not to attempt to cross it. Who knew what could happen? Mr Redmayne sat back in his chair and closed his eyes. Tiny black motes crisscrossed his vision against the

---

[160] A mystery narrative of which delightful title Emile was now writing, featuring an invisible hat thief of demonic origins, *Akuma-Bōshi-Dorobō*. No better theory had emerged, let's face it.

translucent pink background of the inside of his eyelids—the sun was just too bright. That busy old fool! Was there no peace to be had? At times like this he wished he could call upon the experience of that other ageless busy old fool—his father. What a time the old man had picked to go *travelling,* as if they didn't all know what *that* meant. It was just that it seemed like so much was going wrong now, so much they didn't properly understand. He needed someone's help to try and make some sense of it all.

And then there were Felice's troubles back in the house, the old house. They hadn't managed to get to the bottom of *those* yet. Everything about it strongly suggested some kind of third party interference—but from whom? That was the question.

Who else but the Redmaynes themselves would know how to control and manipulate the time-mechanism so expertly? And if it *was* one of them? Well, that would be just unthinkable.

Not even his father would do that, not again at least. Not after the first time with Emile, with the poor boy lost in time. Would he? *Would* he? Mr Redmayne swallowed uncomfortably.

He knew very well that his father was capable of *anything,* that the old man's belief that he knew better than anybody and—without exception, everybody—was the root cause of the problem. This arrogance, whether justified or not, allowed him to do things that could change lives, that could change history itself. Hadn't he admitted as much when he was in the tunnels with himself and George? So reckless. It was very worrying.

And now the old despot was off somewhere in time while they were trapped here on this damn farm, cut off from everything. They may as damn well not *ex...*!

Mr Redmayne sat bolt upright in his chair, his eyes as wide and round as Gloriana's best dinner plates.

All at once he *knew* what had happened to the hat. He knew it intuitively, and that it was the only possible explanation. It made sense of everything. His father…

A terrible thing had happened. Beyond terrible. *His* father! Oh no…

He had to find Gloriana at once and let her know. He wished he were wrong. He knew he wasn't. Alas. Alas. Indeed. Thrice alas.[161]

Felice had felt bad about how things had gone with Claudia, but only after she had finally calmed down, that is. Then, she regretted losing her temper, particularly in front of everyone. She didn't really understand why she felt so irritated by having Claudia around, by seeing her and George together. Could it be that she was jealous of them in some way? Really? *Was* she? Maybe. But was it *only* that? Some things were more than a bit off about how Claudia came to be here.

So? Did Felice truly think either of them could have set it up, or made it happen? (Other than George being so sneaky about encouraging Felice to go to the house in the first place—but even that was *her* decision, and from his perspective it was something that had already happened.) Weird. Their lives were weird. *That* was the real problem.

Anyway, here poor old Felice was again, or so she felt, all alone in her room. She hadn't seen anyone since the big blow-out except for her father, who'd appeared after a decent interval to ask about what she'd seen outside, and that conversation with him had taken place, what, days ago now? Had it? She suspected everyone of trying to avoid her, not that she blamed them. She'd avoid herself if she could. Sometimes. Wait. She sat up…

Her room was so dim. The three objects on her dresser

---

[161] Which is the permitted maximum, historically, in case you were wondering. Alas.

faded out of view—dematerialised, in fact—and were replaced by three more, as if they were part of some 3-D slide show, which in a real sense was true. She watched this happen while a thought was forming, a home-truth.

Wait. What, no…that wasn't it. *She* was avoiding everyone by hiding away in her room and now she was blaming *them* for avoiding *her*? She just had to get over herself. That was about the top and bottom of it.

This couldn't go on. Felice rose.

She went out into the upper hallway, where it was much brighter. No one seemed to be about. Given that there were so few places to go around the farm everybody sure did a good job of finding their own space. She went down the hallway towards George's room at the far end. She hadn't been down here for so long, not since before her trip back to the house. Silly, really. George's door was shut. Shut tight, most likely, to keep her out. Though probably in truth he was outside just then, picking apples for his next True Love Pie. Or something. She hoped so. It wasn't George she was hoping to find.

Another door, one that hadn't existed when they'd first arrived at the farm, now stood adjacent to the door to George's room. That one was ajar. Felice pressed on it tentatively, and as it opened she saw Claudia sitting on her bed. Claudia looked around. If she was at all surprised to see that her visitor was Felice, her face didn't show it. No show, no tell, no story. Only a blank sheet. Felice could work with that.

"Hey, girl, 'sup?" she began, as tentatively as she had pressed on the door. "This where you hang? So to speak."

Claudia straightened up. "This is the room your father created for me, out of light. It is amazing, yes? You can construct whole rooms, entire houses, everything, out of nothing but light, as you desire. The future must be an amazing place. Don't you think?"

"I guess, yeah. Suppose. My grandfather doesn't seem to like it that much though. Mostly. I think he finds it a bit artificial, life in the future, I mean. Like I said back at the house. What's the word he uses? *Inauthentic*, that's it. So it can't be all good."

"I should like to see it."

Felice nodded. Claudia's room, she couldn't help but notice, was very bare. She didn't have very much of anything. Hadn't that nitwit George showed her how to conjure up the things she needed? Didn't look like he had. George, half-boy, half-nitwit. All George. The wardrobe door was open and Felice scanned the contents, which didn't appear to be very much at all. No more than a single change of clothes, in fact—and weren't those *her* jeans? Good grief.

"Claudia, is that *all* you've got to wear? Really? Hasn't George shown you how to make more? I don't believe it. My brother!"

Now Claudia looked surprised. "What? He has been very kind. He has. Everybody has been very kind."

Almost everybody, thought Felice, shame reddening her cheeks. But still, now she had the opportunity to make it up. It was, in truth, the least she could do. She went over to the wall.

"Look, it's like this. I'm going to think of an outfit that I think would look good on you. I mean, I know everything *does*, don't get me wrong. I just want to show you how to make things for yourself. Out of light. As you desire. Watch."

Felice placed the palm of her left hand flat against the bare white wall. She concentrated.

"The trick is you need to visualise what you want, see it in your mind. That's how it works. I know, how about that neat black dress you wore to the party at the house? Short sleeves, round neckline, teardrop at the back, cotton. Vintage Chloé, I think? That was a knock-out."

"I am impressed. I did not know you took such interest in what I wear."

Concentrating hard, Felice arched a lone eyebrow in

response. Then, she muttered:

"You sort of need to visualise the texture as well. That sounds weird, I know. But you do. George is hopeless at this."

It took a moment. Nothing. Nothing. Something.

There it was, the dress. Black, as described—now resting on the one chair in the room. Nothing. Something. Just like that.

Truly astonished, Claudia reacted as though she had just witnessed the parting of the Red Sea, in her bedroom, no less. No ordinary, everyday miracle, this, and no mere trick, either. Genuine magic, live. Right before her eyes. Nothing. Nothing. Something.

She gasped, rising up from the bed quickly and at once reaching for the dress. She held it out in front of herself, more in pure wonder than anything else, examining it from top to bottom and then both front and back, as if it surely couldn't be real. Surely, no. But, obviously, yes, it was. As real as the sun in the sky—another everyday miracle. The yonge sonne, for once with something new under it for two much, much younger folks to admire, together.

Felice felt a swell of pride—and pleasure, at helping her friend.

Understandably, Claudia was more than a little dumbfounded by what her eyes had just seen. In Felice's experience it was seldom that the most prolific talker in her class was lost for words, even on those rare occasions that she chose not to use them.

On this occasion, however, she had no choice: her words failed her. Speechless.

"It…It…It…" she repeated over, which was, to Felice, cute beyond mere words, indeed beyond all telling. "It is *my* dress! I swear it. How? But?"

"Well, it's a copy, sort of. Hey, I hope the size is okay. No offence if it turns out bigger, or smaller. I guess my mind's eye sees you a certain way. No telling if it's right or wrong. But we can always, you know, send it back and, like, maybe try again?"

"No, it is perfect, I can tell. You are a genius, I am sure. Oh my god, what! *No!* It has *the label* in it, too! How is *that?*"

"Well, of course, I know what Chloé labels look like, don't I? And where they go, well, usually, I do, anyway, so I put it in. Is it right?"

"Yes, yes, it is—and this, all this, yes, you accomplished with your mind? Only with your mind? You *made it—with your mind?* Really? That is amazing. Amazing. Truly. I am amazed."

"It's not that hard. You could do it, too."

Claudia's poor face simultaneously portrayed two conflicting extremes of response: one, that this *surely could not be so*; and the opposite, that this *surely had to be so*. This magic could *not* be hers to do; this magic absolutely *must* be hers to do. Now. *Right* now.

Wonder and disbelief, mixed.

"Come on, then, over here," said Felice. "Give it a try. Come on. Look, just lay your hand flat against the wall. It's easy. Unless you're George, or Papa. That's it. Yes, right there will do. Like that, good, yes. Now, concentrate. Picture in your mind what you want to make. See it, okay?"

Claudia nodded, closing her eyes.

Felice went on: "It's a little weird, I know. How it feels, I mean. The, I don't know, in*terac*tion. You can feel it connecting, I think."

"It tingles," said Claudia. "It is strange."

She took a breath. Felice waited.

Nothing… Nothing… Something.

Something denim. Claudia's eyes sprang open. Instantly she grabbed her miraculous creation and held it up against herself. Denim, long, straps.

"Overalls," said Felice with genuine surprise. "Very *farm*."

"I know. It is the new me. The future farmgirl I was always destined to be, yes?"

"Practical but stylish. *And* ahead of your time. Hey, I *like* the flares. Nice touch."

"Flares?" Now Claudia seemed surprised. "I made *flares*? That was not my intention. Oh, my *mind*. It has betrayed me. *There*, I *like* flares. There can be no secrets!"

"Nope. The truth will out in your unconscious style choices. Want to go again? It *can* be addictive, I know. Oh, yes, believe me, I *know*."

Emphatically—*very* emphatically—Claudia nodded. She tossed her newly minted overalls over onto the bed and replaced the palm of her hand against the wall.

"What now?" she said. "Wait, I know."

She closed her eyes. Felice had a thought. It just popped into her head, but it made sense. Destiny. Choices. Same thing, in the end? Maybe we help ourselves get where we want to be? Maybe…

Nothing… Nothing… Something.

The 'something' took Felice by surprise. A hat.

But not just *any* hat. It was their *school* hat, the ridiculous blue woollen affair with the red bobble on top, the hat that made Felice feel like a partially drowned sailor whenever it rained, the hat she professed to hate but secretly loved. *Her* hat.

Claudia passed the hat to Felice, who stared at it in her hands.

There can be no secrets.

"You miss it," said Claudia, a statement, not a question.

"Every day."

"We will go home. It will happen."

Felice gave her friend a hard, scrutinising look. Something was off here—and had been all along. It was high time to find out what that was. Now.

"You sound very definite, Claudia," she said, after a second. "More than that, almost. You *know* something, don't you? I think you do. Claudia, what do you know? Like, for instance, tell me, did you know I was going to be at Magasin Sennelier that day? When the TDA tried to capture me? Was it just a coincidence that we met on that one single random day I happened to be in Paris, or did you know I was going to be there?"

Claudia shrugged. "What? How could I know?"

"I can think of a way. More than one, in fact. *Did* you know?"

The two girls stared at each other. Full on. Nothing was said, but Felice knew. Silence was not a denial, but a confession, of a sort. A confirmation. She put the hat down.

The door opened and it was George. Red-faced and breathless, as if from running. At first he seemed surprised to see the pair of them together, but quickly moved on from that. He tried to catch his breath.

"You've got to come," he said, still gasping. "The TDA, they're here!"

* * *

The TDA had indeed arrived, and so it was that—almost casually—the Great Siege began.

To begin with, George and the two girls had dashed down the stairs and out into the farmyard in a near-frenzy of disbelief and panic. Could it be true? The TDA were here? How could that be? Surely not. But, once outside, they soon discovered it was true. For over by the orchard, close to the unmarked boundary, stood Mr and Mrs Redmayne, peering off towards the green chalk hills with what seemed a grim concentration. Emile, too.

The three teenagers set off and soon came running up fast alongside. Mr Redmayne held an extra-long pair of binoculars to his eyes, and Felice, following the direction of her father's line of sight, detected a small lone figure in the sunny distance, approaching—one figure, not three, which was something. But even from this distant vantage point she could tell that he was TDA.

The long, beige raincoat (on a *sunny* day) and the all too

312

familiar hat, the damned bowler hat! Black, round—it was such a giveaway. So obvious. Someone needed to tell them to get out of their stupid uniform and blend in better. Or, on second thoughts, no, best not. No.

Still, he came, the Agent of Doom, walking in the direction of the farm, but slowly. Steadily.

"What's he doing?" asked Emile.

"He's consulting a handheld device for tracking anomalies—temporal anomalies," said Mr Redmayne.

Emile looked to George.

"For finding things that aren't in their own time," said George. "Like all of us, for instance."

"Oh," said Emile. "Can he find *us*? Is the farm a temple-normally-thingy? Will it show up on his consulting-device-PDQ-thing?"

George raised an eyebrow but said nothing.

"No, I don't think so, dear," said his mother. "Your grandfather is far too clever to build anything that would be easy for any policeman to find, even a Time-Policeman."

"Those QDM devices typically operate on a fairly short range," said Mr Redmayne. "I wonder what tipped them off to try here, and now?"

Felice threw a guilt-laden glance over at Claudia. Had they led them here? Had she, by going to Paris in the first place? What had she done?

"Where are the other two?" she said. "They always work as a team of three, we know that."

Mr Redmayne took down the binoculars. "You're right, dear. We need to scout the perimeter. This might be a pincer movement. We might already be surrounded. Darn![162] Everyone, come on. Take care to stay inside the

---

[162] For the avoidance of doubt, this was the actual word used. Mr Redmayne does not cuss in the earshot of others—ever.

boundary. We don't want to be giving them any temporary blips on their screens to be getting excited about. If we don't offer them any encouragement, they might stop what they're doing and go away."

"That might work with naughty children, dear," said Mrs Redmayne. "I'm not quite so sure about Time-Policemen. But I take your point."

Without waiting, Mr Redmayne began to skirt the perimeter, striding off with Emile behind him—Emile making crab-like pincer movements with his hands as he trotted along in tow.

"Yeah, you guys go round that way," called George. "We'll head counter-clockwise and meet you in the middle, the three of us. See you there."

Mrs Redmayne nodded. She turned and followed after her husband. Her eyes had said, *be careful*. Also, *if there is anything you're not telling me, you will be sorry*. George understood.

"Come on," he said to Claudia and Felice. "Let's go find the TDA."

It didn't, in truth, take very long.

Indeed, they had only travelled but a very short way around the boundary when they spotted the second of the TDA agents. He was much closer to the farm than the first, but approaching in the same slow fashion, head down, consulting the tracking device he held in his hands as he came methodically on towards the farm, step by step. Somehow it felt even worse to have confirmation that there was indeed more than one TDA agent closing in on the farm, on them. Feeling trapped and powerless, the three—but George, in particular—presented a common picture of anguish and frustration.

"I don't care if they find us," he said, defiantly. "I won't let them change anything. They're not splitting us all up. I'll do whatever it takes—anything—and the consequences will be on them. We just want to live our lives in peace. They should leave us alone."

"Splitting us up?" asked Claudia. "How so?"

George looked away, off, out at the slowly encroaching agent. He didn't say anything.

"The TDA's mission is to restore things, people, to their correct time," explained Felice, after a second. "They'd take *you* back to *your* present, and leave *us* two years behind you. They'd drag Papa into the far-future, seven hundred years from now, because that's when he was born, is born, *will* be born. Whatever. We'd all be instantly dead to him, anyway, because we'd have to stay here—long, *long* dead. Just like that."

"That is horrible. We must stop them."

"We will, Claudia," said George. "Oh, we *will*, believe me. I will *not* let this happen."

He kicked angrily at the ground. Felice exchanged a look with Claudia.

"Come on, let's find the third," she said. "There's always three."

They went on. None of them sighted any more TDA agents, however. About two-thirds of the way around, they were reunited with Mr and Mrs Redmayne and Emile (the latter group having made rather less swift progress in their circumnavigation because Mr Redmayne had insisted on stopping every twenty metres or so to scan the horizon with his binoculars, even though it had been plain to his wife that the coast, so to speak, was quite clear.)

All the same, Mr Redmayne was especially distressed to have the presence of the second agent confirmed, and they all went back to check on how he was getting on. Very well, as it turned out, alas, for now he was no more than thirty metres distant, head down still, eyes fixed on his device, plodding forwards in a steadfast fashion. As one, the Redmaynes and their guest froze in their tracks to see him so close.

"He can't *see* us, can he?" asked Emile, quietly.

"No, son," said Mr Redmayne, "he can't see us, no. Neither can he hear us. From his perspective nothing on this side of the boundary exists."

"But something's brought him *here*," said George. "He's tracking *something*. He *must* be. If not the farm, then what?"

Mr Redmayne shrugged. He didn't know.

"And what about when he crosses, you know, the perimeter?" asked Emile, still perturbed at the prospect. "Will he see us then?"

"I shouldn't think so, dear," said Mrs Redmayne. "He'll pass right through to the other side without being aware of anything, I should think. Remember the sheep?"

"And Claudia," said Emile, slightly encouraged.

"Yes, just like Claudia," said Mrs Redmayne. "That *was* a fun time, wasn't it?"

Claudia nodded reassuringly to Emile. "Yes, it was. And for me it was only disorienting because one second I was with you and then the next, whoosh, you were gone. Also, I was *expecting* to see the farm. I knew it was there because you had brought me inside the first time. After that, either *it* kept vanishing, or *you* did. But if I had not known it was there, I would have been not one bit the wiser. So, do not worry, little Emile. He will not see us."

"And if he does, he'll be sorry," said George.

Mrs Redmayne's eyes now said to George: *Not helping, dear.*

"Which one is he, do you think?" asked Felice. "Is he the one you punched?"

"No," said George and Claudia, together, a moment of synchronicity that evidently pleased them both (if no one else).

"No, that was Wimberley, George," said Mr Redmayne. "This fellow's Wilberforce. Which must mean you punched Watkins, Claudia. Good for you."

Really not helping, dear, said Mrs Redmayne's eyes.

"Oh, look, something's about to happen," said Emile, suddenly, and all heads turns to the approaching agent, who now stood on the threshold of the boundary.

He crossed, and instantly was gone.

"He's passed through," said Mr Redmayne. "Quick, now, everyone! To the other side!"

The four youngsters set off at once, running towards the farmhouse because that made for the fastest route straight across to the other side. Mrs Redmayne had no intention of running, TDA agent or no TDA agent, and her eyes said as much.

Mr Redmayne understood.

Still, they did walk rather briskly, the pair of them, as briskly as decorum permitted. It would be unseemly to rush for any policemen in any era, and that was a fact. Any failure in composure was something of an admission of guilt, at least in Mrs Redmayne's eyes. Excitement was understandable and therefore pardonable in the young, but as one grew older one learned the value of self-possession at all times, even when materialising a time-travelling house on old London Bridge in 1603, while dressed as Queen Elizabeth I. Time-travel did teach you the strangest life-lessons.

As they trod (briskly) across the farmyard Mr and Mrs Redmayne soon spied the children ahead, by the orchard, and beyond them the two TDA agents, one of whom was barely on the other side of the perimeter. This latter gentlemen stooped low to pick something up from the ground. Mr Redmayne could guess what that might be—one of the various components of the children's 'experiment' at the boundary earlier, the objects they had thrown over to the other side to test their theories about the disappearing hat.[163] That the TDA should find these

---

[163] More a form of observational research than an experiment *per se,* thought Mr Redmayne, but he didn't like to be pedantic if he could possibly refrain from being so. A useful lesson for us all. Yes, *you,* too.

things was unfortunate. A related thought occurred to Mr Redmayne.

"It's interesting that there's only two of them," he said to his wife, quietly, as they approached the group.

"Indeed," she said, also in a quiet voice.

The children were also talking quietly, even Emile.

"They found my calculator and Claudia's car keys," said George in a hushed voice to his parents as they came up. "They're probably what they were tracking, you know, the temporally displaced objects. And they've discarded Emile's home-made toy, no interest in that at all."

It was true. *Volaverunt* lay inert upon the grass, lifeless, unwanted.

Unloved. Unlike, it must be said, the other two objects, which were generating a good deal of most unbecoming excitement in what otherwise passed for a grown man. Both the car keys and the calculator had tested positive for belonging to another era, proof that the Redmaynes had been—or were—in the vicinity. Darn, thought Mr Redmayne. Double darn.

They *know* we're here.

The other, more distant agent, also bent to the ground. When he straightened back up, he was holding up the cricket ball as if in a gesture of triumph.

"*That's* where that went," said Emile.

"Howzat!" shouted the agent.

"Watkins," said Mr Redmayne, clearly displeased.

Tossing the cricket ball lightly to and fro in his hands as he approached his colleague, Watkins was all unpleasant smiles.

"This sporting spheroid tests from 1878," he said. "Bag it."

He threw the ball to the junior agent, who fumbled

the catch.[164] The ball fell. Watkins paid no attention. He stared, his small eyes narrowed, albeit unseeing, directly at the Redmaynes, some few short metres away, an experience that all of them found somewhat disconcerting, to say the least.

"I can almost *smell* them," he said, as he sniffed the air his nostrils flared in an exaggerated fashion.

"*He* is the one I punched?" said Claudia. "Oh, I am so glad."

"It *is* tempting," said George, "just, you know, to step forward out of the blue and, like, land one on him right on the snozzle. Imagine his stinking future-face then."

"George," said Mr Redmayne. "That's quite enough."

But it was Watkins himself who did the stepping forward, crossing the boundary and instantly passing to the far side.

Emile looked at George. They set off after him, running.

Felice looked at Claudia. They exchanged glances of resignation, before almost wearily following on. Their pace could not by any stretch of the imagination be described as brisk.

Mrs Redmayne looked at her husband. "Right. Lunch," she announced, with some determination, and turned towards the farmhouse.

"Oh, and, yes, *dear*," she called, when but a short way along, "*do* try *not* let anyone get captured, won't you? I'm preparing lunch for six, no more, no less. Do you understand?"

Mr Redmayne understood.

---

[164] And therefore of Australian ancestry, possibly? Just a suggestion. No offence.

The running back and forth from one side of the farm to the other in order to 'keep eyes' (George's phrase) on the two TDA agents soon lost its appeal, even for the two most dedicated surveillance stalwarts George and Emile, such was the frequency with which it now occurred. You can only surveil someone doing the same boring thing over and over for so long before inevitably growing bored with it yourself, no matter how critical an exercise you believe it to be.[165]

Also, all that running was pretty tiring for two boys whose lives for several months had been confined to some ten thousand square metres or so[166] [167] in what was a football pitch-sized bubble in space-time. All the same, there was something of a fascination to be found in studying somebody up close without their knowledge, especially when the somebody in question happens to be your arch-enemy. Plus, the 'intel' (George's phrase) to be gained by doing so could prove crucial to the family's survival, and so they resolved to find a better way to carry it on, one that didn't leave them (in the main) so pointlessly—and so embarrassingly—puffed out.

But all that was for after lunch.

Mrs Redmayne didn't hold back on the lunch. She went full-Redmayne for the occasion, serving up the most delicious French Omelettes au Natural (everyone but Emile), Monte Cristo Sandwich (Emile), Gratin Dauphinoise (everyone), and topped off by Almond-

---

[165] See *Surveillance for Teenagers*, Pg. 43.

[166] This may *sound* like a lot of square metres, but it isn't. No, it's *not*. Get over it.

[167] Perhaps the concept of *round* metres would be more applicable in this case? Whatever.

Apricot Macarons (everyone but Emile) or Apple Tart (Emile). When she'd called them all in for lunch, she had expressed her pleasure at the fact that no one had allowed themselves to be captured (so far); but despite this, and the obvious superiority of the fare on offer, the lunch soon palled. It would seem that having the enemy at the gate could prove something of an appetite suppressant, at least in the initial stages of the blockade, no matter how counterintuitive this appeared to the good lady herself. When the meal in front of you might be your last, you want it to be good and you should want to enjoy it. That was how Mrs Redmayne viewed the present situation— and life in general, in fact. For what tomorrow might bring…

But no. Everybody picked at their food, and the conversation peaked at nil. Mrs Redmayne, much like Nature, whom she resembled from time to time, abhorred the vacuum of silence at a social gathering. Life was for the living. Always.

This, whatever *this* was, would never do.

"So," she said, over an ample portion of Gratin Dauphinoise steadily solidifying on her plate, "if everyone has quite finished feeling sorry for themselves, what do we know?"

Nobody said anything for a moment.

"Well," ventured George, "they're here, the TDA, and they know, okay, *suspect*, we're here—and not just because they found some temporally displaced objects, which could only have come from us, but because they think there's something up with this spot, this patch of land, something odd about it that makes them keep criss-crossing it, over and over. Like they can't quite figure out what it is."

"Could just be coincidence," said Felice, "all the crossing."

George made a pained face. "Doubtful, Sis, but whatever. They haven't gone away."

"It cannot be coincidence, Felice, no," said Claudia, as though conclusively. "Because they are only interested in time things, so only a time thing would detain them for so long. Yes? They had no interest in Emile's Japanese monster toy, did they? None."

"Rude," said Emile. "The TDA, I mean. Not you."

He smiled at Claudia. Sweetly.

Felice made her 'I-give-up' face. All of her family members were beyond her help.

"It *is* possible," said Mr Redmayne, choosing carefully his moment to contribute, "that their devices are registering some kind of signal related to the farm, you know, to what must after all be a fairly significant distortion of space-time. No matter how cleverly your grandfather's managed to conceal everything here, they might be picking up *something*. If so, given that and the things they've found, it's likely they'll be motivated to stay on until the situation is resolved, one way or the other. But still, we're just guessing. We really need to know more, so we can make a plan."

"So, we need to keep a close watch on them both, all the time," said George. "Even when they're on the opposite ends of the farm. Hey, Shrimp, if I show you some diagrams do you think you could make the parts for walkie-talkies? Just an idea. That way we could keep tabs on them both and stay in touch about it, you know, in real time. Could be useful."

"I can make *anything*," said Emile. "And, you know, if I can't, Felice can."

Felice said nothing. She had something else on her mind.

"That's the ticket, boys," said Mr Redmayne. "First class idea."

Mrs Redmayne had quietly resumed her lunch.

"Why is it do you think there are only two future-policemen," asked Claudia. "*Dupond et Dupont.* Where is *Capitaine Haddock*?"

Mr Redmayne chuckled.

"Who?" said Emile.

"Thomson and Thompson," explained George, "you know, from Tintin."

This clearly meant nothing to Emile.[168]

"That's really very good," said Mr Redmayne. "*Dupond et Dupont*. Highly appropriate."

Claudia basked in the appreciation of her joke.

Mr Redmayne looked to his wife. To the accompaniment of the briefest flash of her eyes, she shook her head.

Once again, he understood her intent and let Claudia's original question drop.

"Well, *Dupond et Dupont*," he repeated.[169]

"*Who*?" said Emile.

A lull fell, and Felice seized the opportunity she'd been waiting for.

"Claudia has something else to share with us, don't you, Claudia?"

"I do? What is that?"

"Oh, come on," said Felice. "You know very well what."

"Felice?" said Mrs Redmayne.

Everyone was staring at her. Felice could keep it in no longer.

"Claudia *knew* I was going to be at Magasin Sennelier that day. She *knew*. Somehow she did. She confessed as much to me just before. Earlier."

"I did not."

---

[168] Unfortunately, the repaired French translator device converted this into *Dupond et Dupont*, leaving Emile none the wiser.

[169] Ditto.

"But you didn't deny it, either. Same thing."

"Not really," said George. "Not at all."

Now everyone stared at Claudia. A silence not filled with active denials spoke volumes.[170]

Waiting. Something had to rush in and fill the silence, preferably the truth, or something close to it.

"No, I did not *know*," said Claudia, at last. "It would not be true to say that I *knew*. I did not. But it was strange. You must remember that I had been searching for you all for two entire years, just about. The family that disappeared without a word, the house that had vanished without a trace. It was mystifying. Infuriating. Everyone at school, everyone everywhere, had forgotten you, given up, but I did not. I would not. Somehow I felt I could not. I was obsessed. It was strange."

Claudia paused. The Redmaynes were listening.

"And then, it grew stranger still. Very strange. The day before we met I received a note, through the door at home. It said if I went to Magasin Sennelier at a certain time on the next day I would meet you, Felice. It said to act surprised and go with whatever happened and all would turn out well in the end. That is what it said, and so I went. But I did not know what would happen. I did not *know* you would be there."

Another silence fell, this one consumed with unspoken questions, burning up all the oxygen in the room as they came into being.

Mrs Redmayne got in first.

"But why would you lend this note any credence, dear? Who was it from?"

"That is what was so strange," responded Claudia. "You see, it was from *myself*! From *me*! It was in *my* hand

---

[170] Well, kind of. Bit light on detail is silence.

and signed in the way that only I know, by a secret name, from my diary. It was written *by me*, this note, and yet I had not written it! You can see why I felt compelled to go, to follow its instructions. And when I was there, in Magasin Sennelier, I thought I had imagined it, the letter, that my obsession had driven me mad, finally. But then you turned up, Felice—and it was all true! And so, here I am, and here we are. Yes?"

Claudia followed up this incredible tale with the most Gallic shrug in the entire history of Gallic shrugs: one that said, effectively: *Yes, I had a letter from myself that I had not written and so here I am. Puh. So what?*

Yet another silence, this one of the generally stunned variety.

This time George was the first to speak up, a virtual explosion:

"But that's fan*tas*tic!" he declared, loudly, looking around. "What? Don't you *see*? But you must realise, all of you, what this means? No? *It'll all be okay in the end.* We get out of this, that's what it means! We *must* do. Otherwise Claudia won't write that letter to herself. And she must do that *after* we've left the farm, when we're back at the house. We get off the farm, the TDA don't catch us and we go home. It must mean that!"

Mr Redmayne was hesitant. "I'm not so sure it works that way, George. That's *one* outcome, yes. But we all have so many decisions to make, anything could change—and change everything. I don't know."

"But what was, is, will be, will it not?" suggested Claudia.

Mr Redmayne shrugged, and not in a Gallic way, more as a statement of his uncertainty. "Not always, I'm afraid, my dear."

"Oh-my-God!" said Felice, wide-eyed. "*That's* why you've been acting so strangely all along! It's why you've been so reckless. You think it's all been destined to turn out okay. Nothing can go wrong, whatever we do. That's what you *actually* believe, isn't it? Good grief! This explains everything!"

"*Que sera, sera,*" said Claudia, a phrase that required no translation.

"More *Parfois, peut-être,*[171] in reality, I'm afraid," said Mr Redmayne. "In my experience, at least. Time-travel is *very* tricky. You can't depend on things ever working out as you'd like, well, hardly ever, anyway, as we all know."

"And, my dear, it may have been useful for us to have been made aware of this strange development a little sooner than now," said Mrs Redmayne. "Certainly before the TDA had commenced their little siege operation right on our doorstep, I must say."

"But the note, it said *not* to tell you, not to tell *anyone* until I absolutely had to—and that I would know when that was."

"How very convenient!" remarked Felice.

"It is true! And I had to trust my future self, did I not?"

Claudia looked very distressed. George was beside her.

"But it is possible that there are things that even your future self might not know, that Mr Redmayne and I have kept from you, that we did not think it was safe for you to know."

"Like what?" asked George at once.

Mrs Redmayne shook her head. "I cannot say. We are not certain. But what this family does affects more people than ourselves. Think on that."

"I don't see how in good conscience you and father can still keep things from us," George continued, his sense

---

[171] *"Sometimes, perhaps."* Take my advice, write this down. Or make up a song with that as the title.

of outrage growing. "Not after last time. Remember last time?"

But Mrs Redmayne remembered last time very well, as it turned out.

"Ah, I see, George. So, it's fine when it suits you to do the same. And for Claudia here, too—*and* Felice! Yes? Now, your father and I need to talk. I would be grateful if, after your lunch, you would go back to keeping an eye on our guests at the gate. We need to know what they're thinking. That would be most helpful."

"Don't worry, I'm going now," said George.

He got up, looked at Claudia, and then left the room.

After a moment, following the faintest apologetic nod of her head to the remaining seated Redmaynes, Claudia did the same. Felice said nothing but raised her eyebrows high as her friend got up, as if such a non-verbal response were the only possible way she could summarise the impact of the past five minutes. A final hush fell over the table.

No one looked at anyone.

"Anyway, so who's this Dupond A. Dupont guy?" asked Emile, eventually.

* * *

Although in the immediate aftermath of Claudia's revelations everyone felt a lot worse about everything, in point of fact nothing much actually changed. George and Claudia kept together, with Emile tagging along until George's tolerance levels were breached. (George needed Emile for the walkie-talkie project, that was largely why he tolerated him at all.) Meanwhile, Mr and Mrs Redmayne spoke in hushed voices behind closed doors for prolonged periods of time about those matters that were— apparently, *whatever* they were—*not* for discussion in front of the children, which infuriated George and irritated Felice, more or less in equal measure.

For her part, Felice drifted about here and there at the margins of everybody else's lives, unnoticed but watching, thinking. She wasn't sure how she felt about any of it anymore—George, Claudia, the TDA. Since she had revealed Claudia's secret, i.e. her *deception*—Felice's anger had subsided away to nothing. If anything, Claudia's odd behaviour now made more sense to her. Felice *understood*. At the same time she didn't feel much like getting involved, not with George or Claudia or indeed any of them. She was working things out, paying attention.

She *observed*. Meanwhile, life went on.

The two TDA men, for instance, they had erected some kind of temporary camp a short distance over on the far side of the perimeter—one military-style tent, square with a short pointed roof, perhaps ten metres by ten, that was the most *drab* shade of *anything* Felice had ever set eyes on, a pale brown, the colour of watery mud. One morning it had just appeared—or at least one morning Felice had taken herself out to the orchard to tend to the sheep and, *voilà*, there it was, drab-looking tent. So *not* French.

But while it may have looked like nothing much on the outside but Felice wondered whether its nondescript exterior perhaps concealed all manner of hardcore futuristic technology designed specifically to track them down. Was it really some kind of TDA super-lab disguised as a second-hand army-surplus tent? Maybe it was bigger on the inside? That would be exciting. Though just from watching the two agents come and go, Felice, couldn't tell.

Whatever. One thing was clear: they weren't planning on going away any time soon.

At least George and Emile, with their far from expert attempts at covert surveillance (fancifully referred to by the pair as 'black ops'), provided some diversion from the otherwise all-consuming gloom, even when viewed from afar.

Both of them were hopeless spies. Emile still spent much of his time dashing from one side of the farm to the other every time one of the TDA agents crossed the boundary and appeared instantly one hundred metres or so distant (George having decided, for reasons unspecified, that it would the best use of his time to stay close to the enemy camp—*and* to Claudia, of course, who wasn't going to set off running every five minutes in all directions for anyone).

Unfortunately, to George's consternation, Emile's breathless reports on what he had witnessed on his many solo missions veered towards the vaguer end of the detail spectrum. He did this…he did that. Dunno. No, how should I know what he was doing? Well, okay, he looked left and right for a bit, I think, then stared at his handset for a bit. That was everything…

…*What?* It *was*.

Felice, in the main, left them to it. After a time, one thing she did reluctantly get drawn into was the making of the so-called walkie-talkies. George had found some 'very interesting' designs in one of the advanced science books he'd brought back from the Library at the house on his last visit, not for walkie-talkies *per se*, no, obviously, but for some kind of futuristic communication device, one that utilised the principles of quantum mechanics to send messages back and forth, he calculated, approximately, give or take, some ten thousand times faster than the speed of light. Needless to say, to work at all the devices needed to successfully create and maintain an *entangled* system. You couldn't achieve results like this in the ordinary *un*entangled universe. Obviously. No, no way. See, you need your particles, your photons in this case, necessarily to maintain a *mixed* state (not a *pure* state, no) (oh, no) so that the message, whatever that happens to be, flips instantly between devices irrespective of distance, no matter how vast that might be. Get me? No? Pity. It's incredible, really, the technology. You could use these devices, he reckoned, to communicate between the stars, like, you know, instantaneously. Wow.

Emile studied the complicated nature of the blueprint designs in the text book. Intricate circuitry. Thousands of tiny fine lines overlapping and connecting—in fact, some of the lines were so minute he could barely see them.

"We could just keep on shouting to each other," he suggested. "That's *pretty* instant, too. I mean, isn't it? Just saying. Because, it's not like we're an interstellar distance apart, is it? I'm only going to be, well, you know, over *there*. At most."

George eyed his brother contemptuously. His cup of pity overflowed. And then some.

"Ah, Shrimp…Shrimp, Shrimp, Shrimp. If only you had the imagination to think big. Like *BIG* big. Way big. Interstellar big. Good word, by the way. Interstellar. Yup, that's right. Always aim at the stars, my little bro, that's what I say. Always aim at the stars."

Emile had never heard George utter those words before. Obviously. Because George never had. But he went along with his BIG brother anyway because it didn't seem like he had any other choice. Which, of course, he did not. Obviously.

And so it began…

Attempt One did not go well. Emile had placed the palm of his hand flat on the wall in George's room, closed his eyes and concentrated. Something appeared. The pair of them studied this initial effort together.

Closely.

It looked *a bit* like the diagram in the textbook. Same overall shape. But it didn't take a twenty-eighth century quantum physicist to see that much of the intricate detail was lacking in the end-product.

They put it to one side.

Attempt Two went no better. Okay, a tiny bit better. But not really.

No.

Attempt Three, bad. Attempt Four, same. Attempt Five, hmmm—*bad*.

Attempt Twenty-Three. That looked entirely *mad*, to be honest. Both of them could see that. Lines and connections everywhere. *Every*where. Leading in all directions, multi-layered, but not at all like in the blueprint. Emile's mind was wandering. He couldn't recapture the detail. They both knew there was only one thing for it.

They needed Felice.[172]

First, they needed to *find* Felice. Face down in her room? No. Kitchen? (No.) Study? (No.) Barn? (No.) Farmyard? (No.) Orchard? (No.) It was a puzzler. She was nowhere to be found. Actually, now that they thought of it, neither brother could pinpoint the last time they'd laid eyes on her. Not exactly. But she'd been around, hadn't she? Had she 'only gone-and-done' another blooming bunk? (Emile's suggestion, made for some reason in an odd Cockney voice.) George, ignoring the accent, didn't think so, no, not under siege conditions. Not even their super-stubborn sister would be so stupid as to try that again, not right now, and not after she'd brought the TDA down on them here in the first place. This was *her* fault, the siege, after all.

The two boys were standing out by the orchard.

Damn their needing her like this, George had muttered aloud. So weak. Hadn't a man built the very first computer? Weren't they, him and Emile, both two very scientifically-minded men? Why couldn't they do this? What was wrong with them? Wha—

"Babbage may have designed the first computer," they heard Felice say from behind them. "But it took a woman, one Ada Lovelace, no less, the very fabulous Ada Lovelace, to program it. Without that it was useless… And, no, I haven't *only gone and done another blooming bunk,*

---

[172] For the record, Emile's 'only one thing for it' had been to give up.

thank you very much. Also I think you are very conveniently forgetting the part *you* played in setting me up to go and meet the TDA in Paris in the first place, George. Remember?"

Both boys had span around. To their surprise, no Felice... Just orchard.

"This is *not* all *my* fault," she went on. (To their ears, tuning in, her voice now sounded improbably as though it was coming from up high.) "Not *my* fault. No way."

"Are you *up* a *tree*?" asked George, stepping forward.

Emile ran towards the fence and jumped up onto it, craning his neck to peer upwards.

"Cool," he said, as if only now realising that trees could indeed be climbed. By anyone. By *him*, even. Ah, the novelty.

"What are you doing up there?" asked George.

Now that the boys had stepped forward, the three of them could all see each other. Felice looked quite comfortable, if a little strange, perched on a thick branch that was well above head height, with her back against the tree-trunk. Foliage intervened between their respective lines of sight, here and there. A camouflage effect.

He waited. "Seriously, no, I want to know. What?"

"Doing *your* job. I can see everything from up here. Everything."

"And?"

"The TDA, I've been watching them. I know what they're doing. They're working their way systematically around the perimeter and they're taking measurements. They know we're here, in this collapsed space-bubble thing, and they're trying to figure out how big it is. They must have a plan."

George looked out toward the TDA tent. One of the two agents emerged, and seem to stare straight back at George. Spooky.

After a moment George turned back towards his sister. Pride swallowed.

"We need your help," he said.

Mrs Redmayne was worried, too. Just like her children, she had been keeping a close watch on the two TDA agents and their odd doings out beyond the perimeter, but that was only part of the reason why she had become so very concerned. No, she was worried now because her husband had come up with something of a very disturbing idea recently and she was beginning to think he might be right. But if she agreed with him and they followed through on this idea of his *and* he turned out to be wrong, the Redmaynes would be finished: broken-up, separated across time forever.

On the other hand, if he were right and they did nothing, she wasn't sure that either of their consciences could bear the consequences. Either way, she felt, they would lose. The stakes were high—and the wheel was already spinning. They needed to make a decision. Now.

Not easy. Of course, not all decisions are to be taken lightly. The potential consequences were significant. Mrs Redmayne wandered around the farmhouse, doing this and that, much in the same way as ever, but in truth she was very distracted. At the present moment she was staring absent-mindedly at the alphabetically arranged contents of the walk-in larder—the larder which in every pedantic detail seemed as though it had been designed specifically for her use, as indeed it had. Her father-in-law left nothing to chance. Ever. Ruthless Rufus. No detail overlooked.

And now, if her husband's dire theory was correct, the dictatorial old man believed himself to be Fate itself.

They couldn't allow it to happen. Mrs Redmayne came out of the larder. She peered through the kitchen window towards the orchard, where she had seen the children playing something or other earlier. No sign.

For them, it would be hardest. Yes. They thought it was all something of an adventure, she felt, a game, not life and death. How would they feel if they knew what their grandfather was doing in their name? How *will* they feel? For the truth will out—and soon. The clock was ticking, always. No one was ever really the master of Time.

She came out of the kitchen and stood for a moment, listening. Voices. The children were upstairs now, in George's room. Excited voices. To be so innocent. So young. So naïve, still to realise the darkness of the human heart, the potential darkness, at least. Choices, consequences. Ruthless men could always offer up some reason to justify their terrible actions.

But nothing could justify what was happening.

If she and Eric went ahead, unilaterally, George would be angry with them. Angrier. His life, his fate, how could they decide it for him? That was what he would come to think.

And if, as a consequence of their decision, their guest—*his* guest, in truth, now—if she had to return to her own time, the Claudia he had built this special relationship with, leaving him behind, well, he would surely never forgive either of them. Never. No.

Because the Claudia of George's present would know nothing of what had happened here, or may not be interested in him, even, or might be somewhere else completely—a thousand and one things could and would be different. Paris, New York, London, who knows where they would all end up? Any of them.

If, that is, she and her husband were wrong. Because she certainly agreed with him now. They *had* to act. Conscience over consequences. The only question was when.

With this, Mrs Redmayne went directly to Mr Redmayne's study. He was inside. When she entered he looked up from his oversized chair (of which he was so beautifully proud) and she could tell at once that he understood, that just from seeing her face he knew her decision.

She agreed. The words were redundant but she said

them anyway:

"Oh, Chérie, you are right, of course. We must bring them in, yes, I fear, yes—and the sooner, the better!"

Work on the quantum-based walkie-talkies of the future had proceeded far more effectively once Felice had been co-opted to take the lead in their manufacture. All four of the interested parties had convened in George's room to see what would happen. Although everyone agreed that if anybody could pull this off it would be Felice, George had begun privately to doubt that it could be done at all. The designs were so intricate and complex, you surely needed to program some kind of advanced super-computer to spit them out—and only then via a connection to a futuristic high-tech assembly plant, the like of which most probably would not exist anywhere on Earth for another five hundred years or so.

Nope, no doubt only a bunch of idiots could hope to do this in their bedroom.

But here they were. Idiots Incorporated. CEO, George Redmayne. Go, Idiots! Yea.

Felice's method of preparation hadn't exactly boosted George's—nor anyone else's—confidence that this unlikely enterprise had any chance of working, either.[173] She scarcely looked at the designs, glancing at each page in turn for a matter of seconds before flicking over to the next. Her entire review lasted for less than a minute. Infuriatingly, she appeared *bored*, too, while she was doing it. George concealed his outrage. Actual quantum technology in a practical everyday application—the

---

[173] Emile would dispute this claim. He would be wrong. Emile's cast-iron certainty is always retrospective. He only *thinks* it isn't. He is eleven.

achievement was staggering. Yet, his sister had flicked through it as though it were nothing more exciting than knitting patterns. He would never understand some people.[174]

Felice closed the book. "Okay," she said, yawning.

It is possible the yawn was added largely for effect.

George appeared incredulous. "O*kay*? What do you mean '*okay*'? You can't be serious. No way. Each page must hold several gigabytes of data. You can't retain that much information in your head. No one could. It's not possible. Don't you want to, you know, maybe try this one page at a time? That might at least have a *chance* of working. I mean, like, Felice, come *on*."

Felice held up a hand. She spoke in a dreamy, robotic voice.

"Man, your tiny human mind cannot comprehend my inner wonder. You are ordinary. I am not. Behold."

She placed the palm of her hand flat against the wall closed her eyes.

Almost instantly a succession of component parts appeared one-by-one on George's desk, layer after layer, ready to be snapped together. Finally came the outer casing, back and front simultaneously.

At first, no one moved, as if stunned. Never had this act of seemingly spontaneous creation seemed any more like an act of pure magic than it did right then.

Bam-Bam-Bam-Bam-Bam-Bam-Bam-Bam-*Bam/Bam*.

Claudia came round first, gingerly picking up one the fragile layers by its edges. George followed. He fingered the parts with genuine wonder and tenderness.

"The detail, it is astonishing," said Claudia.

"There is no Master but the Master," said Felice, in her

---

[174] This sentence could stand to lose the 'some'. *Editor's Note.*

normal voice.

Glancing at the textbook George began to quickly assemble the device.

"This is amazing," he said, clicking the pieces together. "The tech*no*logy. Wow. I guess, you know, because the minute crystal quantum repeaters are light-based, they must interact with the transmitting photon more efficiently and so generate entanglement across enormous distances. *Interstellar* distances, I mean. To think, with this little device here we could have a conversation *in real time* across, what, I don't know, 50 megaparsecs? It's staggering. The future, I really need to go there."

"Me, too," added Emile.

Felice blinked, once, twice. "Well, this has been fascinating. Really. The Master has been pleased to help her limited human subjects but now, she's off to her room."

She made to go. Then, stopped. All faces, eyes, were on her.

"What?

"Er, Felice…we need another one. All by itself, this *one*, you know, well, it's kind of useless."

George looked embarrassed for her.

Felice laughed, realising her mistake. "That is *so* true. Well done. You have passed the test. The Master is pleased with you. Here."

Placing her palm flat against the wall once again, she repeated the exercise of a few moments earlier. This time she didn't bother even to close her eyes. Same result.

One by one the pieces appeared in rapid succession.

Once again, George took them up. Assembly commenced.

"You know, I might stick around," said Felice. "I'm intrigued to see now how this is going to work. Maybe when we eventually blow this farm-joint I could go into business rigging these quantum-talky-thingies up on an industrial scale. *What*? …George, no, I'm *jo*king.

Ob*vi*ously." [175]

George finished assembling the second device. He passed it to Emile.

"Let's go see," he said.

Outside, a short period of instruction followed, in which Emile struggled gamely to master the basic controls. On, off. Press the button, talk. Release the button, listen. That no *actual* talking or listening through the devices was attempted during the instruction and demonstration period appeared to introduce a degree of abstraction into the proceedings that Emile found confusing.

He didn't give the impression of being a boy on the threshold of interstellar communication, the first such attempt in history, even if in fact the distance involved in this maiden effort was less interstellar than inter-farmyard.

Meanwhile, George grew frustrated, a development Felice usually looked forward to and enjoyed. In truth, she had grown a little distracted, too. The four of them were set up over by the orchard once again. In the lull, the TDA agents' tent had caught her attention. It appeared to be empty, with both door-flaps wide open, blowing in the breeze, and neither of the two agents anywhere to be seen. Apparently. So it seemed. Of course, it might just be some very lame attempt at a trap, as if any one of them here would be stupid enough to leave their hideout and wander inside. Probably if you did that you would find yourself instantly transported into the far-future, into some *jail* in the far-future, no less. Probably. Cheese, trap, snap. No more mouse.

George's exasperation was growing tangible.

"Come on, Shrimp. It isn't *that* hard. Maybe we should

---

[175] i.e. Mostly.

give it to Claudia?"

"No, I got it. I got it. I *do*. Look, you make sure it's on? Yeah? Then you listen? Right? And when you want to talk, see, well, this button on the side, here, you hold *that* down? Like this? Yeah? Easy!"

"And you've got to say 'over' when you're done talking, otherwise I won't know you're through. Get it?"

"Over? How about *Over and out*?"

"Just *over*."

"Over."

"*Over*."

"Okay, I got it. Over."

"Just go," said George, with a sigh. "Go and stand over there and we'll test the damn things finally. Okay?"

"No, wait, let him stay here with me," said Felice. "I want to keep an eye on this tent. Either of you two geniuses seen either of the Agents of Doom since this morning? No? How about you, Claudia? Huh, no, okay... So, I wonder what they're up to now? Look, okay, so you and Claudia go off. Go on. I'll help young Einstein here press the right button. Chop-chop. This is *history* we're making, don't you know?"

George pulled a face. "Okay, Felice, whatever. Come on."

"And we will talk to you in a minute, through these," said Claudia.

"I get it, really I do," said Felice. "Go on. Go."

She watched them walk away. Slowly. Together. Somehow being a mouse in jail in the future was beginning to seem attractive. She turned to Emile.

"Ready to make history, Albert?"

"Albert? You're really weird sometimes, Felice, you know that?"

"Oh, *do* I *ev*er? Look, just press the damn button and say something."

"Are they far enough away, do you think?"

"Well, it's not Betelgeuse but it'll have to do."

"What? No, I think George wants to talk first, anyway. Just wait a second, will you?"

"Sorry."

Felice cupped a hand up over her eyes to shield them from the glare of the afternoon sun. George and Claudia made for two hazy figures, off in their own world. They may as well have been on Betelgeuse, the pair of them. Distance achieved.

She turned to Emile.

"Okay, Tiger. They're almost at the boundary. Try it now."

"Wait. No? What? Should I? What should I say?"

"I don't know. Anything. I know, how about, it's a cool, clear evening?"

"What? I can't say that. That's stupid."

All at once, the walkie-talkie sparked into life—George's voice, as clear as if he were standing next to them.

"What was that about the evening? Over."

Emile stared at the little device in his hand, startled. Everything George had told him about how to work it immediately departed his head.

"I didn't say *anything* about the evening," said Emile, more *at* the device than into it. Felice mimed for him to press the 'talk' button.

He pressed it, then blurted out:

"Felice *wanted* me to say something about the evening."

Emile released the button, then re-pressed it.

"Over," he added, letting go again. Silence.

"Hey, it *works*," he whispered to his sister.

Felice looked puzzled.

"What'll I say now? Oh, I *know*."

George's voice came through once more.

"*Cow*? Genivee? What do you mean? Over."

Emile was surprised. He pressed the button.

"What? *How now brown cow*—that's what I was *going* to

340

say. How now brown cow. Only I didn't."

After a second, he re-pressed the button. "Over."

A thought struck Felice. She started to laugh.

"Here, let me have a go," she said to Emile, still laughing. "I've got an idea."

With an obvious reluctance, Emile passed her the device.

"Felice, this is *not* funny," they heard George say. "Over."

This only made Felice laugh all the more. She pressed the button so she could speak, but no words would come out. She was laughing too hard.

"Over," she managed eventually, and passed it back to Emile.

Oh, her sides. It was too much. She had to sit down in the meadow.

George, again: "I *know* she is." He sounded very cross. "Over."

Emile looked perturbed. "George, Felice is acting really weird. Over."

At this, Felice, as she would herself admit, lost it. She lay back on the grass, laughing. High up above her a small white cloud shaped vaguely like a Scottie dog was being chased by a wee white bone-shaped cloud across the blue, blue sky. This, too, struck her as hilarious—and very likely possible.

"I'm sorry," she said, trying to collect herself. "But don't you see? No? Oh, tell them to come back. It's just hilarious."

She gave him back the device but, before her younger brother had chance to speak, George came through again: "Okay, we're on our way. Over."

Emile looked at Felice. He was beginning to get a sense of what might be off, not that it made any *actual* sense. Not exactly. Not yet.

He pressed the button. "Come back," he said weakly, feeling somehow that he should say it anyway. "Over."

Felice sat up, nodding. "See? Don't you see now? *They're out of sync.* It's some weird time thing. We're getting their responses *before we've even sent them our messages.* It's hilarious. Only the crazy Redmaynes could do this. I can't wait to see George's face when I tell him. He's had me make walkie-talkies with some kind of built-in temporal distortion somehow. Crazy!"

She lay back flat on the grass and laughed some more.

Crazy. Emile looked on. You said it, he thought. Yet the walkie-talkies had been a bit off in some way. Strange. Could it be? He turned over the device in his hands.

Yup, he supposed, it really could.

Given that he'd spent the early part of the summer in New York City in 1901, Emile's sense of the possible was more extensive than that of normal, non-time-travelling eleven year old boys. Didn't he now live on a farm where you could make anything you wanted out of light?

He shrugged. Yup. Anything was possible. Even this.

George and Claudia were almost back with them. Felice sat up again, resting her weight on her elbows on either side. George still looked cross.

"What?" he said. "I mean, what *now*?"

Emile nodded towards her sister. "She'll tell you," he said.

Felice tried to speak but, seeing George and Claudia's faces, relapsed into hilarity once again. No words would come. Her sides had started to hurt. She lay back down.

George looked to Emile.

"I don't know, well, not exactly," the boy began. "Something to do with being out of sync. Like, you two were getting our messages before we'd sent them. To tell you the truth, it did *seem* a bit like that. What you were saying, it wasn't right, somehow. I mean, it would have made more sense if you'd heard us first. That's all."

"But we did, didn't we?" George turned to Claudia. "We only responded to what you'd said to us. That's right, isn't it?"

Claudia nodded. Felice sat up.

"No, no, Emile's right," she said, still grinning. "The tiny ineffectual sage speaks the truth. He does. Really. Every message of yours came though before we'd sent you ours. Weird, huh?"

"It's built-in temporal distortion," said Emile. "Somehow. Of course, I'm only *theorising…*"

George stared at his younger brother as though he'd never seen him before in his life. His face suggested a new dawn of understanding was about to break over the horizon—any moment now. A strange new dawn was forming, one in which the sky was no longer blue but an odd colour no one had ever seen before. A weird shade. Off-world.

George's mind was spinning as he started to grasp the truth.

"You mean? Really? Could it be?" He examined the walkie-talking in his hand. *"This,* you mean?"

Felice was waiting for it. But George's reaction when it came wasn't what she'd been expecting. He was *pleased.*

"Really? That's amazing! You not kidding, right? This, these walkie-talkies, the ones *we* made, they, like, scramble the signal through time? Wow! That's, like, I don't know, amazing."

Claudia looked pleased, too. Which was irritating.

The fact that the experiment had failed miserably seemed to be escaping everyone's attention. Almost.

"You know, there might be a practical use for these," George went on.

"Like what?" said Felice. "If you, you know, forget someone's birthday you could send them a message before they get on your case? Something totally lame like that?"

"I don't know. But if we put our heads together we might come up with something useful. I wonder if it's the faster than light thing? I bet that's a factor. And we're probably way too close together. We probably should be some vast distance apart, after all. Megaparsecs. But it's fascinating all the same, don't you think?"

"Ah, George," said Claudia, looking at Felice, "you are always so very positive in your thinking. I admire that quality in a person. It is admirable, yes?"

"Whatever," said Felice, getting up.

"We should go show Pops," said Emile. "He might have some ideas."

"Yeah, he might," agreed George. "Good one, Shrimp. He probably will. In any case, he's sure to find it interesting. You know, it's very likely a unique scientific phenomenon. We might have done something no one else has ever done in the entire history of science."

"You reckon?" Emile seemed suddenly very impressed by his achievement. "Wow."

Felice looked on. "In the meantime," she said, nodding towards the TDA tent. No one paid her any attention. "Just saying. Don't mind me."

George glanced at his sister. "Look, we won't be long. You can hold the fort for ten minutes, can't you?"

Felice said nothing. Watching the three of them go, she held her tongue.

"Unbelievable," she said quietly to herself when they were halfway to the farmhouse. "You all go play with your toys—that *I* made for you—while I stay here and do your jobs for you, too. Why not? Go on."

She realised she'd just found a use for one of the time-warped walkie-talkies. Ironic retro-permission in advance. Something like that.

Probably wouldn't catch on.

Meanwhile, the TDA tent was still empty, door-flaps askew. You could almost see inside.

And still no sign of either underwhelming Agent of Doom. No patrol. None. Odd.

Left at her leisure, Felice climbed the fence back over into the orchard. Her branch awaited. An excellent vantage point and, besides, you knew where you were with a tree. You could depend upon a tree. It wouldn't wander off when someone—some*thing*—new and shiny chanced along. A tree was your friend for life. Lightning bolts aside, of course.

Come the storm, trees were on their own. Damn straight.

Felice lifted herself up off and the ground and into the branches. She climbed.

Reaching her former position, she settled back. From here she could see everything. The bark felt rough on her back. That was fine.

She's keep watch for everyone, whether they appreciated it or not. Be their eyes…

Now, well, all she needed was something to see.

Two hours later, George, Claudia, Emile, still hadn't returned. Felice was beyond hacked off, and bored. The two TDA agents hadn't returned either, but at least they hadn't made her any promises. She began to imagine that maybe her family had already been captured by the TDA without her knowing about it, the compound infiltrated from the opposite direction while she'd been sitting up here in her tree. Safe. Nah, that couldn't be it. George would have given her up in a heartbeat. If not him, then Claudia for sure. Or Emile, even if unintentionally. *Surely you're not going to take us and leave Felice all alone in her tree? She's in the orchard, third apple from the left.* Yup.

Or more likely they were probably all enjoying some great Redmayne family dinner while she kept watch on the enemy at the gate, or at least on their tent. Starving, that's what she was doing, while they feasted. Starving for them while they ate. *For them.*

Alternatively, Felice supposed she could climb down and go see. After all, no one had asked her to sit out here all by herself. No one was making her do it.

Except herself, of course.

But, *two* hours… Two whole *hours*. What *could* they be doing? Maybe time had stopped? That was it. George's blasted walkie-talkies had destroyed the normal operation of time somehow. Now everyone's sentences were preceding the sentence that they should have followed and people everywhere were now making even less sense than they would normally. In fact, Papa had probably spent the last two hours trying to say *Consequences-Has-Everything* the right way around in a stern voice. Possibly.

Or maybe, just maybe, she had just spent too long all by herself up a tree?

Very possibly. She felt stiff now, too, for her troubles. Maybe (and more than just maybe) it was time now to climb down, in more ways than one? Felice stretched.

Ah. Yes, it was. Definitely. Thanks, tree. Old friend. Don't be a stranger.

If you need a hug, come see me. I'll be right over there.

Just don't let me catch you with Claudia. Or George.

Gingerly, stiffly, Felice extracted herself from her secret bower, stepping down with care. Her two hours of inactivity would take a minute or two to shake off. She stretched again. And again. Looking around, it seemed as though nothing much was going on. Nothing at all, in fact.

No sign of life over at the farmhouse. Felice sighed.

It probably *was* nothing more than lunch. She actually felt quite hungry now, too, and although she knew that missing out on that had been down to her and no one else, she couldn't help but feel a bit neglected and forgotten about.

Ah well, she said to herself, I guess they've got themselves a new daughter now, meaning it, truly, in the moment, but at the same time fully aware that it was the most stupid thing she'd ever thought or said. Or imagined.[176]

---

[176] Few of us would care to repeat our teenage years.

A faint noise caught her attention. Bleeping. Was it? Yes. It was coming from—Felice span around—behind her. The TDA tent? Okay, so that was new. She went closer. Of course, the entrance to the tent was still exposed but it was difficult to see inside because of the angle and the natural gloom of the interior. But now, Felice noticed with alarm, a red light was flashing inside the tent in sync with the mechanical sound of the bleep.

Red flash, dark. Red flash, dark. That did not look good.

Could it be, she didn't know, a bomb? Is that why there'd been no sighting of the TDA agents all day? Had they set it and retreated a safe distance? Was that it? Did they plan to blow up the entire area on the assumption that the Redmaynes were concealed there somewhere? Or maybe it was nothing of the sort and she was just being melodramatic? Could be…

Felice looked back over her shoulder towards the farmhouse. No one. If she had one of those damn walkie-talkies she could pick up a message saying they were on their way over before she'd asked them to come out. She turned back to the tent. Was the bleeping getting louder? Yes. It was. Quickly, too. Zut! Felice wasn't sure what to do. But about one thing she was certain, whatever she did would need to be her decision. No time left now to wait for the others to help her. The bleeping sound was getting both louder and faster. Her call.

Taking a breath, Felice stepped out across the perimeter—into the unknown—and approached the TDA tent. Nothing untoward happened. She didn't disintegrate. No TDA agents attempted to apprehend her. Just Felice, the tent and the increasingly fortissimo noise coming from inside that, that's all there was. Good, so far. Despite now feeling self-consciously visible—and vulnerable—she walked closer. At its apex the tent stood approximately as tall as she stood herself. She peered inside. Surprisingly roomy, but (to her minor disappointment) not in any futuristic 'bigger-on-the-inside' sort of way. A good number of metre-long metal rods with ruby-like bulb attachments on one end lay scattered on the floor, and it was these that were the source of the noise and the flashing red light. Maybe a dozen of them. Otherwise, the tent had the appearance of being abandoned. More confident now that she really was alone, Felice ducked inside.

The tent gave no indication of having housed two men for a substantial period of time, except perhaps for the more than slightly musty aroma, like Emile's room on a good day[177] or the smell of long-worn socks. But there were no sleeping bags nor any other pieces of camping equipment lying around. Just the flashing metal rods. Had the TDA agents simply given up and abandoned the place? Abandoned the mission? If so, why leave these rods behind? (The noise of which was making it difficult to think.) Unless it was as she'd first feared? But the rods didn't look like any kind of bomb. She bent down and picked one of them up. At once, the bleeping sound and the flashing lights stopped. Ah, blessed relief! The silence that followed almost rang in her ears. Phew!

Felice collected her thoughts. So, what was going on here? The rod she held in her hands was surprisingly heavy. She didn't know what metal it was. Steel, for all she knew. The red gem-like bulb didn't appear to be made out of anything so ordinary as glass, however. It was denser, more crystalline. Felice turned the device around in her hands. Seven. This rod bore the number seven on one side. Huh? She bent down and picked through the others. They all had numbers. One through twelve. What were they for? And why had they been left here like this? On the

---

[177] Don't ask about the bad days.

floor. Why? Had they been abandoned? And was there anything else? She looked around in the gloom. A small jagged scar of bright light shone through a tear in the fabric of the back wall of the tent, almost as though sunlight were pouring in through the narrow slit. Weird. Camping was weird. Felice made a mental note to make sure this was the last tent she ever set foot in. No, that was it. Nothing else here that she could see.

Felice imagined how George's face would look when she told him—all of them—what she'd done, how she had crossed the perimeter (alone) (without disintegrating), *infiltrated* the TDA tent (alone) and stolen old trusty rod number seven here (alone) (had she mentioned that?). It would be, she thought happily, a special moment. A family moment. Like Christmas, or her birthday. One to remember. Felice turned to go. As she did so, something caught her attention, like a light winking in the corner of her eye. The tiny rip in the tent wall, had it *moved?* She studied it full on for a second. The picture before her, ever so marginally, *had* altered position. Her eyes never deceived her. Felice poked the tear with the red-bulb end of rod number seven. The wall gave way around it, becoming a glowing circle of bright light, expanding by the second. It was like a sheet of plastic dissolving in fire. Felice recoiled in shock. The tent wall wasn't a wall at all. It was an illusion—and behind it lay the reality.

Felice stood transfixed, staring wide-eyed at the unexpected horror before her. Some short distance away, the two TDA agents stared back. They were standing in some kind of white lab, in the midst of all manner of very technical-looking equipment. The tent wasn't even a tent. Felice reacted first. She turned, ran, glimpsing for the briefest micro-second a complex diagram sketched in detail onto a white board on the lab wall. Good grief! She had to get out, warn the others. She ran, carrying rod number seven with her, despite its weight. It was proof. And she could always bludgeon her pursuers with it if that was necessary. Hopefully not. She reached the exit.

Outside, the bright sun struck her eyes with a merciless strength. Felice didn't pause. She didn't look back. The perimeter was only a short distance away, and she knew that as soon as she crossed it she would be safe. She ran, half-expecting the rough grip of the TDA agents to haul her back. Any moment. But they didn't. At speed, she crossed the invisible boundary and carried on running until she was level with the orchard. Only then did she allow herself to stop and look back, and catch her breath. She watched as the two TDA agents emerged from their tent. Fake tent. Neither of them seemed in any particular rush. They were not exactly pursuing her, which was strange. Maybe they'd been surprised, too, and she had been too quick for them to even think about catching her? No matter. She'd gotten away. Now she had critical intelligence about their plan—and a piece of the hardware they needed to execute it. She might just have saved everyone!

Felice the hero-saviour of everyone turned and ran through the bright sunshine towards the farmhouse, carrying her trusty rod number seven like a prize. A trophy.

She could hardly wait to knock the smug look off George's face.

As it turned out, the expression on George's face was far from smug at that moment, and this became clear to Felice the moment she ran full-pelt and panting into the farmhouse kitchen with trusty rod number seven gripped tight in her hands. What else was clear was that something was up. Very much up. George was standing, for one, looking distressed, angry, as though he was point of launching into some bitter tirade against the world and everyone in it; or at least against some of the people in his immediate vicinity, namely his parents, both of whom (for two) were staring back at him with furiously irritating expressions of patience and (worse of all) knowing better than he did. The bare table did not suggest that any lunch had been partaken thereof, by anyone, hungry or otherwise.

"Felice," exclaimed George, a long-seeming moment or so after her sudden, breathless arrival, as if only belatedly registering her presence. "Do you *know* what they want to do? These two? They only want to *invite* the TDA into the farm. They want to bring them *in here*. The two agents. Can you *believe* it? And they're going to do it whether any of us agree with them or not! I won't *have* it! It'll ruin every— Wait…what's that?"

All present seemed to notice at the same time that Felice was carrying what appeared to be some kind of futuristic, high-tech glow-stick.

Still too breathless to explain, Felice held up her hand to silence all queries. Then, she went over placed her palm flat against the kitchen wall.

They all looked at her in silence. She closed her eyes. Concentrated.

Almost at once a large rectangle of white paper appeared on the table.

On it was a map. Of the farm. Set out in a perfect circle.

Mr and Mrs Redmayne, the others—almost as one— leaned in to take a closer look. Felice's breath was returning.

"I saw this in the TDA tent," she said, still puffing slightly. "Not a tent. Lab. This was on the wall. It's their plan. They've been mapping the farm somehow… (Pause for breath.) …That's what they've been doing all this time with those instruments of theirs. And, there's more. I think they're going to use these things—look—to collapse the spacetime bubble. That's what I think. See, there, all those numbers around the outside, like on a clock? They had *thirteen* of these ready to use. I stole this one. I only just got away. They're going use them to collapse the bubble, I'm sure of it."

"That would be quite disastrous," said Mr Redmayne.

He looked very grave-faced. He turned to his wife.

Nobody said anything for a moment or so. George studied the map.

He looked puzzled. "Felice, actually only *twelve* of the numbers are on the outside. One of them is in the centre. Here, see? And it's number seven as well! How is that? Why would you have…?"

"What, no? See, it was the one on of top of the pile, the first one to hand." She stared guiltily at rod number seven. No? A horrible realisation was dawning upon her at a faster than light speed. "I picked it up *because they wanted me to pick it up.* Oh-my-God! No! *No!* They *need* a rod—*this* rod—on the *inside of the bubble* for it to work. Their plan! It's *all part* of their plan. And *I* fell for it! *I* brought it inside. Like a fool. Oh, no…I'm so sorry!"

At that moment, to everyone's great alarm, rod number seven began to flash and bleep once again. Red light, bleep—Break—Red light, bleep. Panic set in.

"What's it doing?" said Emile, looking frightened. "What's going on?"

For a second, nobody moved—frozen by shock.

"We've got to get it out of here," said George. "Quick. Give it to me."

"No, there won't be time!" cried Felice. "I'll take it."

Indecision. Everyone was up on their feet now. Claudia snatched the rod from Felice. At once she darted out with it through the kitchen door.

"Claudia, run," shouted George. "*Go!*"

"It'll be the end," said Mr Redmayne, following after in a rush. "They don't know what they're doing!"

George, Emile and Mrs Redmayne, equally flustered and panic stricken, squeezed out through the kitchen door as though in a race to exit first—a competition that Mrs Redmayne somehow managed to win, despite all of George's frantic scrambling for pole position. Emile was hot on their heels.

Felice lingered behind. She knew that she had made another terrible mistake, a realisation compounded by the infinitesimal glance of reproach that her mother had made time to throw her way when rushing past. *How could you?*

How could you? Good question. *When* would she learn? Everything she did turned out wrong. That was her lesson. No matter what she did.

Wrong. Wrong, wrong, wrong, wrong, *wrong.*

Felice's eyes fell on the map on the table. She couldn't have known. She'd only had the merest of seconds to commit it to memory. An image. That's all it was. There'd been no time for her to *analyse* it. And she was in mortal danger at the time, or so she'd thought. It wasn't like she'd been supposed to see it, either. Her eidetic brain wasn't a part of their plan.

Wait. She held up the map. No. What was that? That long equation. That was *wrong.* Wasn't it? Felice liked to pretend she had no interest in math but really she was better at it than George. The equation looked wrong. They'd made a mistake, the TDA. Hadn't they?

That *meant... Did* it? —*Oh, no...*

Felice threw down the map. She ran out of the kitchen, calling for the others to wait. *Wait! They* were wrong! *I think they* were *wrong! Wait!*

But everybody was already outside, and no one was listening to her now in any case.

CHAPTER 12

Although it only took Felice a very short time to make it outside, it was clear to her at once that she was already too late. The key players were already in position. Claudia was sprinting towards the boundary with Trojan Rod Number Seven in her grasp, with George in hot pursuit. The others, especially her mother, trailed behind, well off the pace. Felice had never seen George move so fast—and Claudia was even faster—but there was too far to go. The TDA agents had been busy. Despite the brevity of the intervening period they had somehow managed to assemble the other rods upright in the ground at regular intervals around the circumference of the perimeter. The thirteen rods were flashing and bleeping synchronously at an increasingly rapid rate. Unless Claudia was possessed of Olympian javelin skills as well as lightning speed, whatever was going to happen was going to happen. Whatever that was.

The two TDA agents were standing side by side at the edge of the boundary, peering in but not seeing. Not yet. Far too smug-looking, as well, Felice thought, the pair of them, even from this distance. Tricking her like that. But had they miscalculated? Their map had the interior dimensions of the farmland significantly wrong, in that it recorded only the mass of 'natural' objects, the orchard, some original parts of the farmhouse, but not of any of those fashioned out of light—their long equation misstated the geometric vectors and the stress tensor energy that was the source of the interior gravitational field.[178] As a result, the field might not collapse in the way they'd hoped. Possibly. She couldn't know. No one could.

George was shouting as he ran. Mr Redmayne was shouting.

Felice's mother and Emile had given up the chase. They stood looking on, some twenty metres ahead of Felice. Mrs Redmayne held both hands up to her face, cupping her mouth (which presumably was wide-open with horror). It was as though she could hardly bear to see what was unfolding before her poor eyes. The flashing / bleeping of the rods had accelerated almost to the point of becoming a constant uniform beam and unfluctuating single high-pitched noise.

Claudia was not going to make it. She couldn't.

She threw the rod, javelin-style, towards the perimeter.

Everything happened all at once. Everything.

A red flash. Everywhere. A big bang. Time collapsed.

The universe expanded and with it, Felice's mind. Her immediate surroundings vanished. The sky overhead became a starry fractal-like spiral spinning in ever-decreasing concentric circles into a distant bright point of infinity. She saw it all. Her viewpoints multiplied, encompassing in an instant all she had seen and could possibly see—a continuous wave of seeing, being, feeling. She saw everything at once, and more than that—more terrible than that—multiple versions of everything at once. It was too much, far, far too much. Her mind—too much—all at once. Overload. An agony of pain ripped

---

[178] Not for nothing had she read all of her Grandfather's advanced books on general relativity and curved space-time, no matter how bloody dull and, worse, *mathematical.*

through her head. Shutdown.

She needed not to see. Not to see any more…

And then, it was gone. Time came crunching back.

Felice fell to her knees. She was back on the farmyard. Her mother and Emile were once again standing directly ahead of her, and beyond them she could see her father and George and Claudia, all exactly as they had been before *that*—whatever *that* was a second ago—had happened.

The pain had left her, thankfully. She stood up.

But something else was happening now, too. No one had moved their position but the rods—all of them, a quick glance around revealed—were gone. Then, with her own two amazed eyes, Felice witnessed the TDA tent disappear in an instant, a blink.

There, then, *not* there. Something, nothing.

The two TDA agents, they then vanished too—no, they flickered back at once—and a third figure appeared behind them. Her grandfather, out of seemingly nowhere!

From the rear the old man gripped each of the agents by the coat collar and pushed / dragged them inside the perimeter. The confused pair were taken by surprise—shocked, even—Felice could tell by their faces. But then, confusion and shock in that moment seemed universal, or almost universal.

Everything that had occurred since Felice had left the farmhouse had taken place in under two seconds. She felt dazed, as if the world were being held on pause.

And then, somehow now with the wrong button pressed, they all immediately fast-forwarded into chaos—hubbub, confusion, riot.

Once again, Mr Redmayne was shouting—something—Felice couldn't tell because George was shouting also. The two TDA agents had attempted to turn the tables and apprehend Rufus but Claudia was quickly there and had reduced one of them to his knees with a well-angled kick to the back of his legs. A bowler hat tumbled to the ground and lay there.[179]

George, screaming like a savage, then tackled the poor man with a flying shoulder charge, crushing him down flat onto the grass. Claudia turned her attention to the other agent, who in true policemen-style now held Rufus's arm and wrist tight in some kind of lock-grip. His sneering face seemed to be inviting (daring) Claudia to try something on *him*—and she looked only too willing to oblige.

"Claudia, George, no!" shouted Mr Redmayne. "Stop!"

Mrs Redmayne had now arrived on the scene also, with Emile in tow. Felice came running up. A sort of stand-off had developed.

Everybody was eyeing everyone else warily.

"Now, let's all be calm," Mr Redmayne was saying. "There's no need for any more violence. Come on. *Please, everyone.* Now, Father, I assume this is all your doing? All of this?"

The old man appeared by far the calmest of everybody present, despite being held in something of what must have been an uncomfortable grip.

"Could you be more precise?" he replied. "*Some* things, possibly, yes. One or two, I admit. Others, no. Be specific."

"You know full well what I mean."

"I may have made a timely intervention, *here*, if that's what you are alluding to, my dear boy. But other than that, I am as innocent as young Emile there, or George."

"Innocent!" scoffed the TDA agent. "None of you *Redmaynes* are innocent. By the power invested in me by the Temporal Displacement Authority, I hereby place *all of you* under arrest for multiple crimes against the timeline— against Time!"

---

[179] The first casualty of war is, inevitably, a bowler hat. Then, truth.

Rufus was smiling. "Arrest? So, that's the thanks I get for saving your life."

"E*nough*," replied the agent. "*You*, let my colleague up if you know what's good for you."

George still held the other TDA agent pinned prone to the ground, wrestling style. He made no move to alter this position, despite his antagonist's struggles.

"George, get off the man," said Mrs Redmayne, with more than hint of weariness. "That's a good lad. *Now*."

"But— " George's face reflected the extent to which he believed that this would be an act of folly—and capitulation.

Still, his reluctance obvious, he slackened his three-quarter nelson type of hold on the agent. The pair broke apart.

All at once, Rufus was no longer in the grip of the other TDA agent, either. Now, he was placed a few metres away, alongside his son.

"What?—" The agent was flummoxed. Agog. Thwarted. "How?"

"I spacetime-jumped. Obviously. Two metres and one second into the future. And *voilà*. I can make such jumps at will now. —But, as you say, enough. You must listen to me. Your lives are in danger. If I hadn't intervened at the precise moment that I did, neither of you would exist right now. You would have been written out of history."

"What are you talking about? Written out of history?"

The TDA agent appeared more than sceptical. Meanwhile, his colleague dragged himself back up onto his feet, in a slow, stiff-limbed way.

Rufus bent down and retrieved the bowler hat from the ground by his feet, but he didn't pass it back. "These last months," he began, "I've been tracking a wave through time, a wave that is doing exactly that, like I say, rewriting history. To be precise, it is rewriting the TDA out of history—our history at least… Out of this timeline, to be precise."

The two TDA agents scoffed. "This is nonsense," said one.

"No, sadly not," replied Rufus, running the rim of the black hat between his fingers while he spoke, as if straightening it out. "Believe me, I wish it were. But some unknown force is changing history. I've suspected this was the case for a long time and I've been tracking its effects. All I can tell you for sure is that it begins far, far into the future, further ahead than even I have ever dared to venture, and it is rippling backwards through time, erasing from history those unwelcome elements that it is designed to erase. And, gentlemen, one of those elements—the core target, in fact, I believe—is the TDA. That is as much as I know."

"You can't seriously be expecting us to accept this preposterous fiction," said the other TDA agent.[180] "You are an arrogant fool if you imagine this pathetic attempt at subterfuge could prevent us from completing our mission here. No, I'm afraid not."

Rufus was scathing. "You call me a fool! Watkins, look around you, man! Trust the evidence if you can't trust me. Where is all of your equipment? Tell me, where is your other colleague, the third member of your team? Where is *he*?"

Watkins and the other agent looked blank.

"Wimberley," said George. "He was with you when you came to the house last summer to arrest my father. I punched him in the face."

"I have heard this story already," said Claudia, beaming. "It is true."

News of this incident clearly meant nothing to either of them.

---

[180] Harsh.

"Sadly, yes," said Mrs Redmayne, in confirmation to the pair. "He did."

She was not beaming. Their expressions were unchanged.

Emile remembered, however, even if they didn't. "That's right. And I got his hat."

"No, we've always been a two-man team," said Watkins. "The team is kept as small as possible to prevent any unintended damage to the timeline. That's TDA policy. Unlike you vandals, our solemn duty is to preserve the timeline."

"But there were three of you Future-Policemen in Paris, no?" said Claudia. "Felice?"

Dazed still, Felice nonetheless concurred. "Always a three, yes. In fact, we'd been wondering what he might be up to, the other one... Sneaking around behind our backs someplace, we assumed."

"This is a well-rehearsed act," said Watkins. "I'll give you credit for that. Bravo. But—"

"But, nothing!" interrupted Rufus. "We speak the truth. We all remember your missing colleague because, here, on this farm, we are outside of normal space-time and protected from the ripple effect. But out there, beyond the confines of this bubble, neither you nor any of your colleagues exist. I had to time my intervention to the precise moment when you would both be close enough to pull inside. If I hadn't..."

Rufus tossed the bowler hat frisbee-like towards the open-space outside. It flew through the air as straight and swift as an arrow and, upon crossing the boundary, vanished instantly.

Something, nothing—yes, full on, sudden nothingness, very much so.

"*Akuma-Bōshi-Dorobō*," whispered Emile, in a tone of awestruck wonder.

The two agents appeared suitably impressed by this demonstration.

They turned to each other and then back to the Redmaynes. "But still," said Watkins, "you can't expect that we—"

Rufus shrugged. "No, I expect you both *not* to believe me, to tell you the truth, that you will attempt to leave the farm, either with or without us, and in that instant, be erased from history. After all, that is what you did last time."

"Last time?" Watkins blanched.

"Yes, this is not the first time that any of us have been through this moment. You wouldn't believe me then either. You wanted more evidence. So, I had you write yourself this note. If you won't believe me, believe yourself." Rufus passed Watkins a sealed envelope. "I must say your handwriting is quite appalling, by the way, a most lamentable lack of even the most basic penmanship. You should be ashamed."

Watkins stared down at the envelope in his hands, addressed by him to himself in his own recognisably lamentable hand. There was no denying it. The note was genuine.

He took it out and read its contents, before passing it to his colleague.

Presently, the pair conferred, their voices low, private.

The Redmaynes stood around, waiting.

"Father, I had assumed…" began Mr Redmayne.

"That this was all *my* doing, that I am a monster who would erase individuals from history? I know. I've had this conversation with you once before, although for you this is the first time. Still, it will be nice to hear your apology all over again."

Mr Redmayne appeared abashed. "Well, I didn't know, the evidence suggested that someone was, and who else could it have been, but…okay, I *apologise*. There. But the question remains, if not you, then who?"

"Or *what*," replied Rufus. "An unknown agency from far into the future is rewriting history, its ultimate purpose and intentions remain a mystery. And once history has been rewritten, the changes are invisible, as if they always *were*, there's the beauty of it. Only fellow time-travellers could spot it—and I've had my suspicions for some time, as you know. My son, our lives are being interfered with, and we don't know by who—or why."

Mrs Redmayne joined them. "Chéri, you were right. I should not have doubted you." She turned to her father-in-law. "He suspected this. He wanted to bring the agents inside. For a long time I did not. Those poor men—"

Her eyes fell on the two TDA agents, one of whom had now removed his belt. They watched him throw it across the perimeter. It vanished at once.

Mrs Redmayne held her hand up to her mouth. It was too awful.

"The thing is," said Mr Redmayne, "what about the missing agent, this Wimberley? Why *him*, already?"

"I've investigated that much," said Rufus. "Wimberley was born much later than the other two, and so his history was erased first. It's like a wave moving back through time and rewriting it as it goes, a change here, a change there, but always the right change. The predictive algorithm must be incredible to behold, to know which things to change. The mathematics involved, unimaginably complex, the data infinite… I don't know, in some ways, you have to admire it."

Mr Redmayne arched an eyebrow. "I still don't see how exactly it works, this interfering force. I mean, these changes, how do they even happen? What form do they take? I don't understand."

"It varies, Eric. Technology plays a huge part, I believe, but that doesn't account for everything. Think about it. Since the advent of the primitive internet, think how much data exists about every one of us. The Intelligence, that's how I think of it, far, far in the future, has access, control of, all of this data, on everything. The volume of information that must be processed, even about our lives alone, is staggering. How they came by it all is beyond me. But it's using this—and my work on time-travel—to unpick history by influencing events, often in tiny subtle ways, through technology—a delayed train, or a misplaced email, for example, these things can have a hugely significant impact. Frankly, it's terrifying. A man might be made to not exist anymore because of a missed train connection! It's unconscionably wicked."

Mr Redmayne pondered this for a moment. What Rufus said was surely right. How could such a turn of events be anything but wicked? The question was, who was behind it and why?

George came over, his excitement obvious. "Look, we've been talking. Is it true? Can't they leave? The TDA? Because if they can't, that means *we* can. Doesn't it? We're free. That's right, isn't it? We can go home. We're getting our lives back! That's right, I *know* it is."

His father nodded. "I suspect it does, yes; although under the circumstances I'm not entirely sure that it's a matter for celebration. After all, a man is missing, erased from history. That's a terrible price to pay for our freedom. Isn't it?"

"Yes, yes, I can see that." George was nodding now. "Terrible."

But when he returned to the others, he was all smiles. Excitement followed. Hugs, even some cheers. That the news was only good was apparent.

Mr and Mrs Redmayne looked on.

"They are young, Chéri," said Mrs Redmayne. "How could they understand?"

"But it's a man's life, dear. Something for us to fix, I suppose, if we can."

"Something for *you* to fix," said Rufus. "I'm tired in my bones, my lad. More tired than I've ever been. I'm going inside. Bring everyone in, including those two fools." He looked towards the TDA agents. "There is much for all of us to discuss. All of us. No one might realise it yet, but the threat is unprecedented. The fate of our world is at stake... You know, Gloriana, I rather think I'm going to need a cream tea."

"That would be a good start," said Mrs Redmayne.

She went to rally the others. Mr Redmayne and his father started towards the farmhouse.

"Try not to blame yourself, my lad," said Rufus. "For all of this."

"I wasn't. No, I was blaming you."

"Really? Ah, well, I expect you'll see it my way eventually. In time."

* * *

The Redmaynes were packing. They were going home.

Or at least the children were packing—with Emile already packed. He'd mostly wanted to bring home all the monsters he'd created out of light, but as there were far too many to fit into his case, he'd suffered agonies of indecision about which of the particular misshapen fiendish ghouls he might bring home and which he should leave behind. In the end, his grandfather had shown him how to shrink them down to a more manageable size[181] (using the same light-based apparatus with which they had been created), and so now he had a case full of these in miniature form and little else. His friend and fellow true manga-monster enthusiast, Steven Sparkle, once he'd gotten over the shock of Emile's sudden return from wherever this place was, would surely be jealous fit to die once he had seen them—and held them and played with them and all the rest of it, of course.

This, above all else, was what going home meant to

---

[181] Pocket-Monsters, if you will.

Emile.

That and not having to hang with bossy George anymore, of course.

Or bossy Felice.

Or make embarrassing old fancy chairs out of light for Pops that were too big.

All of those things he'd had enough of for a lifetime. And then some. Yup. (Although he might miss one or two of the sheep.)

George, for his part, had a small number of antique books from the future to return to the family Library, as well as 'his' precious horn (for surely the sacred instrument touched by the lips of the gods was his now by birthright?) (Technically, not, no—but he was claiming it anyway.) And the two non-synchronous walkie-talkies, he was definitely taking those (for which he held absolutely no doubt that a practical use could be found). It had to be said, he didn't have a lot of much else. Nope.

George travelled light, which, as things go for him thereinafter, was just as well.

Claudia, on the other hand, may have similarly arrived with very little but she was working with all due diligence on going back with a good deal more than that. Now that Felice had introduced her to the whole 'making-clothes-with-only-your-mind' School of Fashion Design, Claudia was pursuing the creation of her own 'label' with an admirable industry and enterprise. That the colour black featured prominently[182] in the product range of brand 'Claudia' would be noticeable even to the less discerning consumer (or her boyfriend) (eventually).

Still, the opportunity was too good to miss—a one-off—and she planned to exploit it to the full. All the same,

---

[182]Almost to the point of exclusively, in fact.

it was just as well that George didn't have too much of anything of his own to carry. His burden had grown (but his shoulders were ready) (and more than willing).

Felice was hardly packing at all, except in a desultory, half-hearted sort of way. It wasn't that long ago that she had in her possession everything that she could imagine owning, and that had proven something of a chastening experience, one that had dulled for her the lure of 'stuff' of every variety, possibly forever. Besides, she had something else on her mind, namely whatever it was that had happened earlier outside when the TDA agents had attempted to collapse the bubble in space-time. No one else had said very much about it, but her impression was that their experiences had not been anywhere as intense as her own. Not that she was exactly clear herself on what had occurred.

Something had happened. Something vast and significant. She *felt* that was true.

But the detail eluded her, almost as if it were there— right *there*—stored in the cloud but just out of reach. Storage quota exceeded, access denied. For now, anyway. That was frustrating, especially when the others seemed not to share the same sense of being on the threshold of some great insight, but instead could pass off whatever had happened with a shrug and a throwaway comment of 'Dunno' (Emile) or 'Weird' (George).

In fact, it was almost as if the entire family apart from herself couldn't remember that there was something they ought to be remembering! Maybe they didn't—or couldn't—see what she had seen? And what *had* she seen? Argh, she couldn't say. But *something*. Frustration.

And now she had to pack, as if that could be of any consequence at all.

Of all the things she had made, what would she take? Anything? Nothing?

Finally, she decided upon just one precious thing, the item she felt the greatest sentimental attachment towards, namely, the *????*[183], and packed that. The rest of it she deleted. Clutter. Her mind needed more room. That was the odd feeling she had. Distraction was a luxury. She needed clarity, to clear some space for whatever lay ahead. And something did. Something big—big to the point of immensity. She was sure of that, somehow. It was a feeling. Odd.

Then, socks. She packed those. In every crisis you needed good socks.

Crisis? Why had she thought that? Worse, she was beginning to sound like her mother. Random. Odd. Darn.[184]

Felice got on with her packing. For what it was worth.

The most curious thing was that, later, after arriving home, when it came to unpacking, Felice was surprised to find she'd brought home a good deal more than she'd intended, far more than just socks and the *????*. In truth, it would be more accurate to say that this both surprised her and didn't surprise her, because when she opened her case she remembered wishing she had packed more items to bring back and it was almost as if she had done this before leaving but then forgotten about it. Or, it was more like she felt like she'd done both things, both packed very little and a good deal more, which made no sense. Finally she put her forgetfulness down to confusion and general exhaustion. She had brought those things back with her and she was glad.

Sorted…or not?

---

[183] Guess! I know. Answer in Book 3.

[184] Yes, on this occasion she actually thought 'Darn'. Sometimes a 'darn' is all that's needed.

So, while the three Redmayne children and Claudia were preparing with varying degrees of enthusiasm to go home, Mr and Mrs Redmayne, on the other hand, were not yet packing at all. No. Not so much as an Argyle sock. Too much remained for them to sort out first, they felt. An uneasy truce had been reached with the two TDA agents, who were camped out over by the orchard, at least for now. Rufus had supplied them with a sizable tent and told the pair to make themselves feel at home. The irony in his offer of an actual tent appeared lost upon them, however. Twenty-eighth century policemen seemed no more advanced in this respect than their twenty-first century counterparts. In a grudging way they took the tent and erected it close—but not *too* close—to the perimeter, to the boundary that demarked existence and non-existence, for them at least.

It was as if they wanted to be as far away from the Redmaynes as possible but not so far that accidentally turning the wrong way out of the tent door one morning would ship them into oblivion. Because that, even they could appreciate, would be bad. Very. And not to mention ironical. Also very.

Mrs Redmayne, for one, felt very sorry for them both and took them out a cream team on a shiny silver tray. But to her astonishment the two men not only had no concept of the cream tea but were physically revulsed by the prospect. Their palates, their stomachs, they explained, could not accommodate the 'rich foods' of earlier eras, accustomed as they both were to the powdered nutrients and supplements that had formed their diet since birth. Words could not express the depth of Mrs Redmayne's pity for such lost and abject souls.

And when they later *disdained* her crusty apple pie on similar grounds, she declared the pair to be beyond all hope and understanding—in fact, beyond *everything*.

The future, she contended, must indeed be a dark and dismal place if the best meal you could hope for in fact consisted of nothing but various tasteless *powders*, and she vowed from that day forth never to set foot in any era in advance of her own, a promise, I can report now, she was tragically unable to keep, if through no fault of her own. With no small irony she came to spend more time living in the far-future than had her father-in-law throughout the entirety of his long, long and most unruly life. Still that is another story.

But back in the present, the Redmaynes' present, that is, much remained to be discussed and determined, one way or another. And so, while the children packed up their things, or not, a rather bad-tempered meeting was being staged in the farmhouse kitchen between the senior family members and the two agents, who came in from the field (literally) and acted with what Mrs Redmayne, for one, considered to be genuine ill-grace and poor manners throughout.

Such ingratitude was too much. Was it the Redmaynes' fault, she asked, that the agents' dastardly plan to incarcerate herself and her family in some futuristic prison had backfired in such a comprehensive and thoroughly ironic fashion? No, it was not.

Was it her fault that neither of them could leave the precincts of the farm without at once ceasing to exist? No. It was not.

Had the Redmaynes not only intervened to save the two agents from immediate peril but *even at that very moment* were they not continuing to preserve their two lives—their two *persecutors'* lives, no less—against persons or forces unknown, potentially at some as yet unquantifiable risk to themselves? Yes, they had, and were.

Yes, these very same Redmaynes that the TDA were so determined to imprison.

And they—the Redmaynes—did so willingly and with good manners, because surely in *any* century good manners, being the manner in which you behave in *each* and *every* social situation, must be important? Yes? *Yes?*

369

Good. In which case for goodness sake have a bloody cup of tea it won't kill you. Seriously. Yes? Tea, gentlemen? If that indeed is what they were? No?

Ah, tea must surely be an unqualified good in every age...

The two TDA agents eyed the poured cups of tea before them on the kitchen table as if the opposite of that last statement must—without the remotest doubt—be true. Tea? The primitive beverage of antiquity. Often entailing some kind of ceremony. But what could they do? This was their lives now. They hesitated, again, fatally—and Mrs Redmayne was done with the pair of them, her suspicions about the dismal nature of the far-future and its denizens confirmed irrevocably.

No, she would not be going there. Never willingly.[185] No.

And this decision she announced, with a most definitive air, before settling back into her seat and taking a sip of her own expertly poured cup. Earl Grey. Tepid. Nice.

"Perhaps, now we might," ventured Mr Redmayne, in the ensuing lull, "talk a little about the arrangements to follow? Of course, you are both welcome to stay here for as long as it takes. No question."

Watkins' stony face betrayed no hint of gratitude.

"Seeing how we have been otherwise condemned to death, Mr Redmayne, no, worse, annihilation, it would seem we are obliged to accept your offer. The convenience is entirely yours, I'm sure. Check and mate. Well played."

"Now, look here," responded Mr Redmayne, after a second, in a most aggrieved tone. "I hope you're not implying that I or any of my family had anything to do

---

[185] This bit is true.

with your current predicament, because I can assure you that isn't the case. If my father here tells you that he is not the responsible party, you can damn well take his word for it."

The most infinitesimal of glances from Mr Redmayne towards his father suggested that—perhaps unconsciously—he still harboured the faintest of doubts himself about the veracity of that last statement.

Okay, the situation may have resolved itself somewhat in their favour, after all. Completely so, in fact, which did look a little on the incriminating side, he had to admit (if only in private).

"But ask yourselves this," he said, posing the question that he had no doubt pondered over at length himself, "*why* would he go to all the trouble of erasing you both from history only to intervene and save you at the last second? Why put all of that in motion and not follow through? Answer me *that*."

Neither TDA Agent said anything.

Watkins' colleague—Wilberforce—whose eyes were remarkably close-set, cleared his throat as if to speak, but whatever embryonic thought might have been forming in his mind was silenced by a stern look from his ranking officer before he could get it out.

Everyone's eyes lingered on him for a moment, however, all the same.

He reddened, and stared down at his antique beverage.

Rufus, once again, intervened. He stood up, resting his knuckles on the kitchen table, and peered down at the two agents. "Listen to me, both of you, please. As I tried to explain outside, another force is in play, altering history. I am as convinced of this as I am of anything in all my days. These last months I have been tracking its influence throughout the key moments in my life, observing its attempts to alter, if ever so subtly, the events as they actually occurred. Friday, 13th October, 1843. Yes, gentlemen, that date is all important, I fear, as it is the date to which I first travelled back in time. But I miscalculated, I went too soon. In my defence, it was my first such trip. I was young. Yes, I altered history. We all did, for the three of you were there, you had tracked me and planned to intercept me—and *yes*, there were *three*. Somehow, I escaped, a stranger intervened. Do you recall? And Dickens got away not only with the idea for a new book but a copy of the book itself! The opportunistic rascal that he was!" The old man chuckled fondly to himself at the memory, and then resumed. "But, gentlemen, if I went back to that moment now, neither of you here before me now or your other missing colleague would be there, for none of you any longer exist out in the world. Do you see? Nothing is being left to chance. This mysterious power, this Third Force as I call it, is both merciless and relentless…"

Another look passed between the two TDA Agents. Watkins spoke.

"The Third Force. We had considered this possibility, I admit, but rejected it, on the grounds that such interventions worked out always in *your* favour. That stranger, for example, we assumed it was either you, or an accomplice, not an external party. No, the idea of a Third Force working through time to its own ends we discounted long ago, for the simple reason that its ends always coincided with your own."

Rufus slapped his hand flat on the kitchen table. Undrunk tea spilled into saucers.

"Damnation! But it is *not* me. Don't you see? We are *all* being outthought, here, myself included! That stranger, the Good Samaritan, if we were to check, I would wager that he would no longer intervene, either, for the simple reason that his intervention is not required. Not anymore. Not in this new post-TDA timeline. If so, this would make determining his identity critical, as I would then suspect him to be an agent of this Third Force of yours. Maybe even its architect. If at all possible, we must find this man.

No doubt it was he who removed your seal from the Paris exit to the house. Gentlemen, he has ensnared us all."

Mrs Redmayne coughed, just to let everyone know she was still there.

Rufus Redmayne, the Great Patriarch of Time, for once looked abashed.

"Well, of course, by 'gentlemen' I mean 'everyone'. Naturally."

His daughter-in-law arched a single eyebrow in response.

This explanation did not satisfy. She smiled a thin-lipped smile.

"Father, unlike these *gentlemen*, you may not have lived in the far-future since your youth but your manners from time to time I still find very retrograde, very retrograde indeed!"

"I take your point," said Rufus, shortly, abashed.

All of the men around the table, regardless of time zone of origin, also appeared somewhat abashed now, by gender association.

Mrs Redmayne gave them something of a final stern look.

"Very well, *gentlemen*, let us have no more loose talk as though men were the only agents of significant action throughout history, especially when we all know this is not the case. And *you*," she said, turning to the two TDA agents, "let us *please* have no more sly inferences or innuendo that *we* are somehow the cause of your downfall. That anyone around this table should have provoked the present predicament is ridiculous. Why should we have gone to all that trouble tinkering with time only to falter at the last moment? It makes no sense, as I'm sure you can agree? Yes? Yes? Good. Well, that's settled. Because, if you ask me, it would have been far simpler to have wiped you both from history, far simpler indeed, if quite beyond the Pale. But there it is."

Mrs Redmayne, her point well made, sat back in her

chair.

"We will, of course," ventured Mr Redmayne after a moment, "do everything in our power to fix this situation and restore, er, your unfortunate colleague, the missing Mr Wimberley, that is, and the timeline back as they both should be, naturally, let me assure you of that. We do, however, require something from you in return. You must tell us how to remove your seals from the remaining two exits at our house. Without that, I fear our attempts to remedy the unfortunate situation you find yourselves in here would be severely hampered. But I promise, we don't plan to leave you here to tend the sheep forever!"

Mr Redmayne attempted a laugh. No one joined in.

"*And* Genivee," added Mrs Redmayne. "Please be aware that I will expect you to provide all of the animals with the very best of care while we are gone. While you remain our guests here on the farm I will inevitably be returning from time to time to check on you and make sure that everything is in order and as it should be. And I will be very displeased—*very* displeased indeed—should I discover that any of the creatures in your care were showing the slightest sign of neglect. Do you understand me?"

Mr Watkins' face blanched. "You mean you expect us to give up our secrets *and tend to the livestock* while you're gone?"

Mrs Redmayne remained steadfast. "Well, yes, naturally. And I'm sure you will find it a very therapeutic and worthwhile activity, too. Yes?… Good. That's settled, too. Now, I'm sure we have several other important domestic matters to discuss but first, how about another pot of tea? You've let this one go quite cold. And pie? Yes? Yes. The apple trees provide for the most sumptuous pie and I'm sure eventually your anaemic twenty-eighth century palates will learn to appreciate good food. Gentlemen, I will make real men of you yet, as you will see—and that's a Redmayne promise you can count on one-hundred-percent."

The two TDA agents looked at each other. This was not going to be easy.

But the other options were all far, far worse. For certain.

It had come to this. Farmers they would be. Here in antiquity, or whenever this was.

Fate. Twisted.

Afterwards, when the gentlemen from the TDA had retired to sulk, Achilles-like, in their tent, the elder Redmaynes continued their discussion in private. Some things are best not said in company. Many concerns remained. Paramount amongst these was Rufus's fear that the house had almost certainly been infiltrated by the so-called Third Force, as recently as Felice's ill-fated trip to Paris a few months earlier. Otherwise much of what had happened there would remain unexplained. The removal of the TDA seal from the Paris door, the repeated malfunctioning of the Time-Mechanism that Felice had reported—none of this was mere chance. No, events were being manipulated, for purposes unknown. The Redmaynes were being used as pawns in a game that they hadn't known they were playing.

Mr Redmayne found this of the gravest concern.

"But how? How would they even *find* the house, this Third Force? Like the farm here, the house is programmed to only allow ourselves (and our guests from time to time) to notice it, let alone find it. I mean, it isn't perfect. There are unaccountable glitches now and then, possibly..." He gave his father a knowing look at this point. "But, for any *outsider*, it's impossible to detect, or should be."

"Yes, exactly," said Rufus. "I agree. But we may be facing an agency whose technology is far, far in advance of our own."

"I see," said Mr Redmayne. "But still, we must try, I don't know, *some*thing. We can't simply leave these poor fellows to rot here forever. When we get back to the house we must set out a plan of action."

Mr Redmayne's father held up his hand. "I'm afraid I won't be returning with you, not at first anyway. As mentioned earlier, I no longer require any kind of *vehicle*, as it were, for travel. I've internalised the mechanism, only a prototype but it appears to be functional. I can go anywhere, anytime, just by thinking about it. But it's exhausting, and I'm beyond tired. I need a rest, some time alone, and I know exactly the place. It may be an inn but it's become kind of like my real home now. Having occupied my rooms there for over seven hundred years I'm virtually part of the furniture. The house, on Everywhere Street, as you call it, well, despite my resurrection, I want you to know I hold no claim on it. It's yours, of course."

Mr Redmayne looked surprised. "I don't know what to say."

But Mrs Redmayne knew exactly the right words. "*Ours*, Father, I think you mean. *Ours*."

Mr Redmayne, realising once again that his wife always knew best, smiled.

At that moment Emile came running in, excited, red-faced.

"What are you all *doing*? We're packed. We want to go home."

The trio of elder Redmaynes acknowledged this sentiment amongst themselves with a set of wry grins and nods. Going home, that would be best. Always. In more ways than one.

And no time like the present. Home.

Despite Emile's (and the others) youthful enthusiasm for an immediate departure (at once, *now*, come on—*come on*), several important matters had to be decided first. Not least, for example, the point in time to which they should return. This was far from straightforward.

On the one hand, it would have been hugely convenient to pick up their lives at the moment at which they had departed for the farm in the first place, and that idea was attractive, at least initially, to Mrs Redmayne in particular, on the grounds that by doing so they would maintain some continuity in the children's education and they would not be obliged, as a family, to invent some elaborate story (i.e. a lie) to cover their long period of their absence.[186]

The pitfalls involved in this approach soon became clear, however. If the family did attempt to pick up their lives at the point at which they had been so rudely interrupted, they would for several months be existing in two places at once, which was never a good idea. Under this scenario Felice's trip back to the house and Paris would become fraught with the possibility of complicated entanglements and potential paradoxes. And the TDA agents, they might *now* be confined to the farm but back *then*, they were still at large and plotting to apprehend the Redmaynes, which would never do.

No, for this reason it would be extremely ill-advised, so Mr Redmayne maintained, to return to their lives at any point prior to the present of the farm, i.e. *now*.

That made sense, everyone agreed.

And then there was the problem of Claudia and what to do with her.

Claudia—the Claudia they had with them now—was from a point of time in her life that was approximately two years in advance of everyone else in the room, that is, beyond the present—the *now*—of the farm. This made for

---

[186] Such as, for example, hiding out for several months on a farm in a bubble in space-time in order to avoid capture by policemen from the future. This would at least be the truth.

several difficulties.

To return her back to her own time[187] two years hence while the Redmaynes returned to the present would in a very real sense overwrite her life of the intervening period. The Claudia who had searched so tirelessly for the missing Redmaynes since the party at the house, who hadn't given up on them in all that time, would no longer exist, as there would be no need for her to do those things, nor to be affected in that way. She would never meet Felice in *Le Magasin Sennelier* and intervene to prevent her capture by the TDA, because those events had taken place in a future which (for Felice and her family) would no longer happen.

The Claudia that the Redmaynes would know in their present would not be the same Claudia they had with them on the farm today. And naturally, this would have consequences. George and Claudia would no longer be, as it were, a *thing*.

"The chemistry of attraction is subtle," said Mr Redmayne, "for as much as it depends on unique personal qualities it also depends on timing, on events, on the sharing of particular moments together—all of that would be lost. Oh, yes, George would remember it, all of it, but the Claudia he knew in that restored timeline would not. And, moreover, *that* Claudia would not feel the same way—would not *have the opportunity* to feel the same way— about George that *this* Claudia in the room with us now so obviously does. The pair may share a bond today, but that is a bond unique to this *shared* timeline. Something similar might emerge between you both—or it might not. But, whatever happens, it would not be—could not be—the same as now. That was for certain."

"This is beginning to feel like a Maths class," said

---

[187] Okay, back to the future, there it is. Sue me.

Emile, very seriously. "Please make it stop."

"Indeed, I believe that the only way for your current relationship to be maintained as it is," Mr Redmayne postulated further, ignoring all comments, "would be if you were both to return to Claudia's true present together, otherwise, well, I'm afraid, my lad, you would never see her again, not *this* Claudia, anyway. I'm sorry."

The prospect of this strange form of separation affected them both very strongly. Claudia reacted with characteristic intensity.

"But, George, surely he could just travel forward in time to see me, no? And I would be there, yes? The me who is me *now*? Yes?"

Mr Redmayne drew a breath. "Well, no. It wouldn't work that way, unfortunately. George would be travelling forward from a point in time in which the other you would not be *you*, if that makes sense? That is, I mean, she would be the 'you' who had not embarked on any of this adventure. But the current 'you', the one talking to me right now, would be on a timeline that George could never reach, because he would have set off from a point in time in which the other 'you' was you, and not, as it were, my dear, *you*. ."

"¡*Ay, Dios, mio!*" said Emile, holding his head.

"And no one, as yet, can travel between timelines, no?" asked the bereft girl.

"I am sorry," said Mr Redmayne. "It's an uncomfortable truth, I know. But if the present state of affairs is to continue, you two must leave here together and return to the same point in time. That's inescapable, I'm afraid."

George looked defiant. "Well, that's just what we'll do. Exactly that. There's no question of me doing anything else. None. Don't even think about it. I won't."

"Georgie, I wish it were that simple, my lad, I do really. But it's a very complicated situation, one that affects all of us, not just yourself and Claudia here. Your mother and I have considered all of the options and we think—"

"I don't *care* what you think!" George was practically shouting. "If you imagine for one second that I won't do everything in my power to prevent this from happening, then you don't know me at all!"

"George!" said Mrs Redmayne sharply.

Claudia laid a restraining hand on George's arm.

Mr Redmayne resumed: "Your mother and I have considered all of the options and we think there may be a possible compromise. But, there is a condition, and that is that everyone affected would need to agree. Okay? Right. It's this: when we return to the house we shall synchronise the New York and Paris exits to the day of Claudia's entrance into the house with Felice, which we calculate to be some ten months and three days beyond the present of the farm, that is, the here and now. The London exit we will maintain at the current time. In this way Emile will only have missed a few months or so of school at worst. At his age, missing one year would be disastrous enough, but two? Unthinkable. Having said that, we are not concerned to the same extent about Felice and yourself. We know you could both make it up, given the, er, special advantages you both enjoy here. But Emile, a boy his age needs to go to school. And that's our proposal. Returning no sooner than the present should free us from the influence of the TDA, given that their existence forwards of this point has been wiped out. And, George, Claudia, returning you both to the same point in time will prevent all of those regrettable complications with the timeline that I ran though earlier. So, that's it. What does everyone say?"

Mr Redmayne looked at everyone in turn to be sure they each understood the seriousness of this decision. This was not something that could be taken lightly.

A moment's silence followed, one pregnant with possibilities.

George and Claudia, staring at each other, were suddenly elated.

"Well, yes!" exclaimed George. "Yes!"

"And you would do this? All of you?" asked Claudia, turning towards Felice. "Would you?"

All eyes turned towards Felice. Fleetingly she returned their stares.

"Whatever, okay, *yes*," she said, at last. "Let's get it over with. London is always so behind Paris, in any case. We may as well make that literal."

She smiled. More general elation followed.

"Wait a minute, wait a minute," said Emile. "*They* both get to skip what, two years of school, but *I* have to go? Where's the justice in that? Come on!"

George mussed his little brother's hair. "Shrimp, pal, buddy, no brother ever made more of a sacrifice. Hey, I promise to help you with all of your homework. I will, for real. I'm not kidding. How about that?"

"You'd better," said Emile. "Or there'll be consequences. Serious consequences. And I'm not kidding *you*, buddy."

Claudia, smiling, mussed Emile's hair a little, too. "And I will help, too. Especially with your Français, yes?" She looked around at everyone. "Oh, all of you, all of this... It is the baby Jesus in velvet shorts!"[188]

"*What?*" said George, Emile, together.

But Felice laughed, and her mother joined in.

All, for now, united.

And, thus, it began. The Great Exodus. The return to the house on Everywhere Street. Bags were packed (by all). Sheep were hugged (Felice, Emile). Trees were hugged (Felice). Final instructions and directions were given to the two TDA agents (Mr Redmayne). The pair were invited to

---

[188] *'C'est le petit Jésus en culotte de velours!'* Look it up.

move into the farmhouse after the family's departure.

Mr Redmayne explained how the food cupboards would automatically restock via a cycle of temporal and spatial dislocation (i.e. whenever supplies ran low, they would 'shift into' the cupboards from other future points in time and space). ("So, essentially, you *steal* it," Watkins had suggested, to which Mr Redmayne had responded with assurances that all, every item, was paid for in full, eventually—and in any case could, *tech*nically, a crime be said to have been committed when it was, in a strict sense, yet to take place? Really?) (Yes).

The agents declared that they would be more than content with their various nutritious powders, thank you very much, which they would be able to replicate at will out of light in the farmhouse, like any right-minded twenty-eighth century citizen would choose to do, much to Mrs Redmayne's disgust. Sad. Very.

For some reason the TDA agents elected not to witness the family's departure but instead remained stubbornly in their tent. No fond farewells would be forthcoming from that quarter, it was clear. None.

Similarly, Mr Redmayne's father had disappeared without a goodbye, as was his long-established practice (just once it might have been nice, his son had reflected afterwards, especially given their touching last conversation). But, he supposed, he should be used to it by now. That being how his father rolled (*Rolled?* Was that strictly correct usage these days, he wondered. In this context, that is?) Yes, on the whole, he rather suspected it was. Excellent. Moving on.

With regards to Claudia, something of an elaborate plan had required concoction.

She had already written the letter to herself, the one she had received the day before she had faithfully followed its instructions all those months ago and set off to meet Felice in *Le Magasin Sennelier* ("See? Everything had turned out well in the end, just as I had written to myself that it would! Yes?" [189]). The plan involved Claudia delivering the note to herself at her parents' house unseen, allowing time for her younger self's departure, and then (the older Claudia) returning home later that next day in her precious motor car (her *baby*) and resuming her life as if nothing out of the ordinary had happened, which, strictly speaking, in temporal terms, nothing had. Yet.[190]

And so, finally, all was ready.

The family gathered at the perimeter to the farm, or from another perspective, the perimeter to the world. Mrs Redmayne allowed herself a last long look back. She had enjoyed her time here, but she seemed to be in a minority of one in that regard.

Her children and their young guest, the person for whom they were adjusting the synchronicity of their lives, could hardly wait to get going. Her husband was little better, leaving with scarcely a backwards glance, although she realised this was probably because his mind was focussed on ensuring that the next stage went exactly right.

But she took it all in, the farmhouse, the orchard, the animals; she had never really felt like a prisoner here, more at home. She hoped one day they could come back and have it for themselves, perhaps just Eric and herself, when they'd had their fill of all the world and time and wanted no more of it. One day. Not yet. Alas.

And so they set off, towards the chalk hills. Neither of the TDA agents came out to see them leave, which Mrs

---

[189] Ah, alas, no. Poor naïve Claudia. If only this were the end. No. Alas.

[190] Thinking like a Redmayne comes surprisingly easily, it would seem.

Redmayne thought was once again poor form. She'd hardly expected a guard of honour but a polite goodbye and a simple wish of good luck would have reflected well on them. Perhaps they were too busy feeling bitter and plotting in their tent? Or maybe the people of the future had no sense of the value of a goodbye? That was possible. Look at the children's grandfather. He was scarcely any better. No matter. They were off. Towards whatever was coming next. Practically running, in one or two cases. *Slow down*, Mrs Redmayne heard her husband call after their two sons. *The house isn't going anywhere, you two*. Not that either of them would listen. At a certain age, only running will do. Easy to forget that.

Felice hung back after a while to walk with her mother.

"Are you okay, Chéri?" asked Mrs Redmayne. "You do not seem as happy as the others to be going home. Or is that your backpack is too heavy? Is that why you are not running ahead like George?"

"*This*?" said Felice. "This is full of clothes that Claudia has made for herself and couldn't bear to leave behind. No, I'm taking next to nothing back of my own. That's something I've learned about myself here. I can do without *things*."

"That is a good lesson to have learned at your age. Some people can never learn it, as we know."

Felice nodded thoughtfully. She was staring ahead at George and Claudia.

"I guess. But there's a lot I still don't understand. I mean, at the end there when the TDA tried to collapse the, you know, *farm*, it was like, I don't know, wow, my mind. I saw *something*, I know. Everything, maybe... I don't know. I'm still processing it all, I suppose. And then, well, there's *those* two. Sometimes when I look at them I want to scream, I'm not sure why."

Mrs Redmayne followed her daughter's gaze ahead. "Ah, Chéri, you feel left out that is all. That is natural. And, if you want to know a secret, they often make me want to scream, too. Yes, that's true. It is. But this is a happy moment. We are going home. You should be running ahead with the others, enjoying it, not allowing yourself to be left behind here."

"Ah, Maman, not to worry. They'll all have to wait for me. They will. I know the way through the tunnels. I lead, they follow! You'll see."

Felice spoke the truth. She didn't need any map to help her find her way home. Plus, this time she had a flashlight to see her way by—this made it so much easier than on the previous occasion when she had made this journey.

Everybody else, hesitant, soon fell in behind her. She led, they followed.

And it didn't take very long. It really was very surprising how much shorter it seemed when you could see where you were going.

Even Felice began to feel excited. Home. Paris. New York. London.

Everywhere!

Her father had the key—the heavy, iron key. When Mr Redmayne turned it in the lock of the rough wooden door, it seemed as though the only sound in the world was the loud, echoey click and fall of the deadbolt mechanism inside.

Then, the door was unlocked. They were home.

Mrs Redmayne went in first, quickly pursued by Emile who in turn was quickly pursued by Claudia and George. Felice lingered behind but her father ushered her inside ahead of himself.

She went on through, hearing him enter and lock the door behind them both.

As she emerged, only her mother remained in the kitchen. Mr Redmayne came forward too and greeted his wife.

"What is that smell, dear?" asked Mrs Redmayne. "Oh, this won't do. This won't do at all."

385

"Not to worry. I'm sure we'll soon have it all sorted out, dear. We've been away a long time, after all."

Felice left them to it. She headed upstairs. Home.

Mr and Mrs Redmayne followed her up.

Emile was already running along the hallway, the contents of his backpack spilled every which way across the floor. Watching him, George and Claudia were laughing—and Felice joined in. Her younger brother's enthusiasm was infectious, as always.

Her parents looked on.

"You know, Chéri," said Mrs Redmayne, "I was a little sad to be leaving the farm but now I see it is the best thing. The children, they had to get out of there. They have their all lives to live, outside in the world."

Mr Redmayne nodded. "Yes, dear. You are right as always."

But even in that very happy moment of their triumphant return he was thinking about everything that had to be done, and about what trials might lie ahead. Then, George was clapping his little brother as he ran, and Felice and Claudia soon joined in, too, cheering him on. Still, whatever it was, whatever the future brought, they would face it together, as a family.

A happy family. If they did that, how bad could it be in the end?

Time would tell.

The Return to Everywhere Street

The adventures of the Redmaynes continue in…

Book III

THE FABULOUS REDMAYNES[191]

---

[191] Title chosen by the Redmaynes, after a vote. And a recount.

The Fabulous Redmaynes

Prologue

The travellers to all are on the great high road; but it has wonderful divergences, and only Time shall show us whither each traveller is bound.
~ *Charles Dickens, Little Dorrit*

Midnight. The streets dark, and damp underfoot, slick, greasy, treacherous. A thick mist lingers in the night air, making the gas-lamps seem especially brilliant, if only in their immediate vicinity, each one its own luminous halo, lighting the way through the milky void. This is Covent Garden at night, largely deserted, the heaving daytime crowds having thinned away almost to nothing in the cold, drizzling rain. Distant singing, a joyful song for all that, rises and falls and rises again, reaching the ears of a lone, nocturnal wanderer, a small man in a tall, black hat. He stops, listens, briefly heartened, recognising the song as one he had once performed himself, a long—indeed *very* long—time ago: in another lifetime, practically; and then, turning into a wet gust of wind, at once he moves on, striding forwards into the darkness of the night, as is his habit. He has much to think on, and the walking helps. Normally. *Norm*ally, *yes*. But tonight...alas, not.

Frequently he has *too much* energy: his mind races, *teems*, in fact, as a rule; making rest impossible. The different voices, the unruly cast of characters in his head, with their endless jibes and street banter—how they cajole, insist, *demand* of him, that their stories be told—a disquieting surfeit on which—addicted—he feeds, indeed, for a time, thrives. But not tonight. No, tonight the cause of his disquiet is different, not a surfeit; instead, rather, unusually, worryingly, the very opposite: a lack, a deficit. Tonight he *needs* an idea. Inspiration. Genius. A muse. Something *new*. Something different than the relentless grind of meeting his monthly number, which even now, the damned month of October already three-quarters through, he had yet to complete, despite being in agonies of conception for almost the entire day. Mere *conceiving*. Tomorrow he must bring forth. But what? *What?* That was the nub of it. There was the rub. The very bitter rub. *What?*

Damnation! The Devil take it all! Debt, money, work! Sales of his current lackwit enterprise *were* disappointing, he couldn't deny that, certainly not enough to repay his advance. And, as much as he railed against the critics, his own dear Foster included, as the root cause of this quite unprecedented state of affairs, the weak sales were unlikely to improve now. This, he knows. It is hopeless. No, instead, he needs something *new*, some little scheme or other already that will capture the imagination of his audience in one fell swoop and, more importantly, not prove a prolonged burden to himself. But what? No answer is forthcoming. His mind is blank. His many muses have deserted him, finally. Still, on he strides, his short, strong fingers holding grimly on to secure his tall, black hat against the wind, the very picture of determination. Something will come. The night has never failed him. *On.* As he must.

Ahead—Little White Lion Street—long and narrow, like many around it. Confined. Dark. Grim. Beyond lies the more open prospect of Seven Dials, no less grim for that. He knows the area well. A terrible place, to his mind the worst in all London. Nothing but street after street of dirty, half-naked, feral children; court after court of squalid, straggling houses and their filthy tenants, brutish men and degenerate women, all. His footsteps quicken, his boots sounding with a loud clatter on the wet, greasy cobblestones. Shortly, he passes a rat-king-like knot of cold, ragged boys huddled together in the doorway of the chandler's shop. He pauses, but soon moves on. Pitiful. The times are heartless. Men are heartless. He wishes he could help them, these boys and the far too many like them, draw attention to their plight. He wishes he could change the world, change men's stone hearts. The Ragged Schools, the Workhouses—shine a light on it all, expose the endless inequity. But, at the moment, for once, he had trouble even helping himself.

He strides on—and then, first, a voice, hailing him in the mist:

Mr Dickens!

He halts, startled. No one knows he is afoot at this time of the night, let alone his likely whereabouts. Who is there? In the dark and the fog, he can't see. Anything.

Mr Dickens, it is you! In the living flesh. Astonishing!

That voice, does he know it? American? That might bode ill, if true. Nevertheless, he challenges his unknown interlocuter.

Show yourself, sir. You have me at a disadvantage. Step forward.

Out of the mist a figure emerges, almost supernaturally so in its sudden crystallisation, like a weird photograph developing before the onlooker's eyes.

A tall man, thickly bearded, if young. Familiar? Boston, at Websters, perhaps? No, he thinks not. He would remember. New York? And abroad without a topcoat and hat on such a chill night as this. Strange. Alas, it can be the lot of the famous author to be accosted by all sorts and at any time of the day or, indeed, night. Such is life in this day and age.

The underdressed Yankee interlocuter speaks, effusive, a little wild-eyed, disconcertingly so:

Mr Dickens! My sincere apologies! Forgive me, sir, I had not intended to alarm you. I mean you no harm. None at all. On the contrary, I have travelled far to make your acquaintance. Very far, indeed, believe me.

—I see. But perhaps, sir, we are acquainted already? You seem familiar. Surely we met on my recent tour of your homeland—in New York, was it? You must pardon me, if so. I meet so many people, frequently in the most unusual circumstance, as you can see.

—Not New York, no, although I do keep a house there, or will do one day. In all truth, I can categorically state that this is the first time I have the honour of your acquaintance. On reflection, however, I find I cannot assert with equal authority that the reverse is also true. No. You may indeed have met me before, if not I you. I cannot say. At this point only you yourself would know if this were the case. Not I.

A certain uneasiness insinuates itself into the proceedings at this point. All manner of madmen are abroad these dark nights. It would be regrettable to meet one under circumstances such as these—and something about the coatless gentlemen before him was indeed 'off'.

He would away.

— Well, my friend, I thank you for your greetings, but I am afraid I have much pressing business to attend to, even at this late hour. The life of a popular author is, I regret, and despite any commonly held views to the contrary, little but one of ceaseless servitude to one's readers. And so, alas, sir, on this note I fear I must bid you Good Night. Please convey my sincere regret to your most honourable countrymen at the recent misfortunate downturn in our relations—and my hope that our disagreements in this area will soon be remedied. And so, adieu…

He bows, taking care not to remove his eyes from this most unusual of footpads.

But then—his eyes spy a volume in his interlocuter's hands, one bearing his own name, but not a title he recognises. He starts at once, his curiosity piqued.

— What is that? In your hand, sir? That volume. May I see?

— Ah, yes, this—forgive me! If you but knew the great lengths I have gone to—the impossible distance I have travelled—for this seemingly trivial matter, you would assuredly think me quite mad. It

was with no small difficulty that I have tracked you to this time and location this evening. Not at all. On the contrary, in fact… But, you see, I am something of a collector of rare volumes, and I wondered if I might prevail on you to sign, yes, do take it, thank you. It would mean so much, that I can assure you. Yes, so very much indeed. Since boyhood this particular tale of yours has proven both my constant comfort and my undoubted inspiration. To secure your signature to this most special edition on this my inaugural, well, 'visit' here, or indeed anywhere, this would be felicitous in the extreme. If you would be so kind…

The famous author peruses the volume in his hand, skimming through the pages. Despite it's great age and the unfamiliarity of the contents everything about it positively sings with authenticity.

He examines the frontispiece:

A CHRISTMAS CAROL.

IN PROSE.

BEING

A GHOST STORY OF CHRISTMAS

BY

CHARLES DICKENS

WITH ILLUSTRATIONS BY JOHN LEECH.

LONDON:
CHAPMAN AND HALL, 186, STRAND

MDCCCXLIII

He finds the frontispiece to be perfect in every detail,

exactly as he would expect. Everything is right; except nothing is right. The book is ancient; but the year of its supposed release is *this* one, 1843, which already approaches its end. The illustrations, he notes as he skims through once again, are truly in the manner of Leech; but because so antique, clearly they cannot be Leech. Worse of all, the tale itself, even it's very title, *feels* to him like his own work, like it *should be his* work. The thought of it excites him, sets the most important part of his mind racing—*A Ghost Story of Christmas*. Yes. That's it. But exactly. It is so right! This could be, should be, *his*—and yet…

And yet…none of it is his. But see how it bears his name. He stands perplexed, dumbfounded. What fraud is this? The fog is closing in. He glances once more at the odd purveyor of this mysterious volume. Odd indeed. Youthful, yes. Eager, but also calculating. Perhaps those wild eyes conceal some cold-hearted disposition? Passion, yes. Greed, maybe. But genuine human feeling? No. It wasn't only the book. Everything about this scene—the individual before him—is off, wrong. He should away at once. His companion seems to sense this sudden downturn in his mood.

—*Mr Dickens, sir. You hesitate. Ah, forgive me. I have a pen. Here.*

—*Keep your pen, sir, damn you! What is your game? You accost me in the night in this friendless alleyway at Seven Dials, the most unforgiving place in all of London! And now you want me to, what, sign this absurd counterfeit? You take me for a fool, sir!*

—*Counterfeit? No, no, I assure you. Authenticity is my watchword, my life. I come from a place, a world, where nothing is real, where everything is but mere confection. Wait, no, have I miscalculated? Great Galileo's Ghost! What month is this? December, surely? Have I tracked you to the wrong time? The calculations are complex in the extreme. But, tell me no. Please.*

—*What? No! Away with you, sir! I'll stand no more of your damned nonsense. December?! Be off!*

—*But, sir, the book! I must retrieve it! It is no counterfeit. For that reason alone it should not be in your hands. The mistake is mine. I have come too soon. Please…*

—*No, I think not.*

—*Come…The book. It is not yours. Not yet!*

—*Sir, no! This volume is more mine than yours, I feel more certain of that strange fact every second!* [A newsprint cutting, still legible though greatly aged, slides askew from the book. The great author quickly peruses, grasps its contents: a state of extreme shock befalls him.] [Reads aloud, in a voice of wonder] "…THE ILLUSTRATED LONDON NEWS, 3 FEBRUARY 1844!…" *What! My God, can it be? Surely not?* [He reads on.] "…*TO CHARLES DICKENS ON HIS CHRISTMAS CAROL…*" [He pauses, for once dumbstruck, if only temporarily. Two further newspaper clippings to the same import lie behind the first, he finds, both similarly dated. His gaze returns to his mysterious interlocutor, if now more appraisingly…

—*Why, all of this is yet to come! How? … Sir, or whatever phantom of the future you may be, though indeed much of this encounter tonight may be far beyond strange, a more fantastical notion I would scarce have thought credible some five minutes past now possesses my mind and strikes me as surely true. When everything points to the impossible I therefore must accept it! Trust me, Sir, when I say to you I am long accustomed to Americans exploiting the copyright on my books for their own gain, but at least usually they have the good manners to wait for me to write them first! Now, I will tarry here in this sanity-forsaken alleyway with you no longer. Adieu!!*

—*This I cannot allow. Forgive me, I must insist! Mr Dickens, wait!*

An unseemly struggle for the ownership of the much-prized volume in question at once ensues, with the great author repeatedly fending off his more youthful assailant with all the sprightly vigour for which he was renowned. All the same it is not, from any perspective, an edifying spectacle to behold. Oaths spanning a full eight hundred years in the history of common curse-words are exchanged. With passion. But still the world-famous author holds fast to his entirely unanticipated—and indeed hitherto entirely unimagined—festive bounty.

A Christmas gift indeed come early.

Without warning, however, two other phantom figures materialise in the fog: two men, or so it becomes clear after a second, each wearing a black round-topped hat (of which the great author had never seen the like) and plain black suit. The new arrivals' stony expressions and humourless demeanour give them the unmistakable air of the constabulary, though these are clearly not policemen of the Old Bow Street variety. Their unexpected apparition and advancement on the foggy street scene for a moment distracts the young American combatant, whose grip on the object of he and his rival's mutual desire is now loosened. The great author seizes his chance, breaking away with the antique volume in his sole possession and a feeling of elation in his soul. It is always good to win any tussle, no matter how insignificant—always to the victor belong the spoils. He turns, now beyond the reach of his youthful rival.

Free.

Or not. To his immediate dismay the two stone-faced policemen, if that is indeed what they are, make as if to pursue him. Or is it the mysterious book that they wish to acquire? This thought flashes into his mind. They shan't have it! Undaunted, quick-healed, he very ably dodges the pair, twisting, turning. quite literally giving them the slip as they lose their footing on the greasy pavement. Such pandemonium on what was intended to be a quiet late night walk to soothe his disturbed senses and disquieted brain!

He will away. He will escape.

Or he will not. They have him.

No, they do *not* have him. For, in the blink of an eye, they are no longer present, vanishing as if promptly discorporated into the foggy air. Astonished, bewildered, afraid, the great author witnesses this supernatural event and finds it too much. He makes off at speed, steaming up narrow, foggy Little White Lion Street towards Seven Dials, that maze of little streets that dart in all directions. Neither man nor futuristic phantom might pursue him there with any hope of success, he thinks, hopes, prays, not on such a dark and murky night as this.

The book is his. Truly. It is done.

But, no, what!—still it is *not* done.

Another shadowy figure, phantom—no, in fact, again a man, yes—looms ahead in the fog. At first the fleeing author mistakes it for the young American, such is the similarity in outline and shape to that mysterious personage, but this is not the case. No. For, as the concealing fog withdraws, the lurking figure is revealed to be so very far advanced in years as to resemble a walking cadaver, or else some ghastly Spirit not long passed and so permitted this brief return among the living to resolve some unfinished business.

But the grisly figure only stares, an effect no less chilling for the bloody wound upon one side of its forehead, poorly dressed in a cross-like shape—did that result from the mortal blow that ended its time on Earth among men? The desperate author cares not to find out. He runs on, his own feet now slipping beneath him in his haste, his poor heart beating ever faster, while the aged Spectre does naught but point a trembling, long, bony finger at him as if in rebuke. Stop, thief!

To Dickens' great relief, that appears to be the extent of its intended intervention, seeming to possess no capacity or will for pursuit.

The Dials lie but a short distance ahead. He is safe.

The book is his. As it should be.

The next day Charles Dickens locks himself away in his study, with instructions that he is not on any account be disturbed. By anyone, not even by dear Foster should he call. In the cold light of day, the strange events of the previous night would appear to him to have all the substance of a nightmare wrought by nothing more sinister possibly than an undigested blot of mustard or a fragment of underdone potato, were it not for the fact of the antique volume in his hands, the one with entirely unfamiliar contents but which somehow bears his name.

The tale itself is a marvel. A Christmas masterpiece.

Dickens reads it straight through three times, reducing himself to copious tears and gales of laughter on each occasion. Ah, the humanity! How the story captures the wretchedness, the piteousness and yet the potential for joy in every one of us, no matter how low and mean in spirit we might be. It is perfect.

More than that, it is a godsend—literally—of this he is certain, the answer to all the difficulties that presently beset him. His undoubted deliverance.

But the, well, shall he say, *unusual provenance* of this latest work-in-progress is a circumstance of which he will never speak.

That night, late, still alone in his study, feeling quite secure from all visitations, worldly or other worldly, he writes to Professor Macvey Napier, editor of *The Edinburgh Review*, by way of accounting for his recent engagement with an alternative project than the one to which he had earlier committed.

By doing so, he provides the first evidence in writing of the existence of *A Christmas Carol*:

"I plunged headlong into a little scheme I had held in abeyance during the interval which had elapsed between my first letter and your answer…"

In the eyes of the world the book is and always would be nothing but all his own work. Obviously.

There could be no other possible explanation. None…

No. None at all.

F.M.A Dixon

ACKNOWLEDGEMENTS

All thanks go, of course, to my wife, Donna, for her steadfast belief in my writing—and, as my first reader, for challenging me to make it that bit better.

I offer thanks also to my very good pals, Ali Webster and Daiva Nacyte, for their longstanding support, and who, along with Jana Moehren, constructed a highly entertaining board game out of my first book, *The Little House on Everywhere Street* (Crowdfunder, anyone?).

Thanks are also due to the wonderful Jacqui Delbaere, bookseller extraordinaire in *The Little Green Book Shop*, whose continued support of local readers and writers has made a huge difference to the cultural life of the wee seaside town where I live.

Finally, I would like to thank Dr George Dobre, physicist and astronomer at the University of Kent, for running an expert eye over the occasionally wayward grasp of Newtonian principles held by his teenage namesake character. (Nb. Rest assured no concessions apply in this instance, George.)

ABOUT THE AUTHOR

F.M.A. Dixon can be found with surprising regularity in London, Paris and New York, assuming you know where to look. And when. Obviously.

Milton Keynes UK
Ingram Content Group UK Ltd.
UKHW020806211024
449933UK00004B/70

9 781917 224062